TORMENTED
THE GATES LEGACY, BOOK 2

Books by Lorenz Font

The Gates Legacy Series

Hunted - Book 1

Tormented - Book 2

Ascension - Book 3

Reckoning - Book 4

Redemption - Book 5 – Coming soon

Indivisible Line

Feather Light

Pieces of Broken Time

The Prodian Journey Series

Rise of Alpha

Tormented

The Gates Legacy, Book 2

By
Lorenz Font

Cover Images: © Victor Newman/shutterstock.com
Cover design: Claudia Trapp/Phantasy Graphic Design

Interior Design - Jennifer McGuire | JEMBookDesigns.com

http://www.lorenzfont.com

For Roma, Frances, and Kevin — my pride and joy.
You will forever be babies in my eyes.

Glossary

Incomis Sippanus—A disease that can be transmitted from vampire to vampire or vampire to human through feeding or sexual intercourse. Symptoms are similar to leprosy or AIDS, including painful lesions and clouded white irises. Consumption of human blood alleviates visible symptoms but also speeds the disease's progression. Harrow Gates is the first known carrier of the disease.

Vampire Council—Governing authority of the vampire world, consisting of ten purebred vampires called Elders.

Harem—Goran's mistresses, beautiful redheaded vampires who are trained in combat.

Dangeran—Metal with the strength and weight of titanium that has been infused with diamond bits, used in the construction of most vampire weapons. Vampires cut by Dangeran will disintegrate unless the wounded area is cut from their bodies.

Arnis—Three-foot-long wooden sticks used as a sparring weapon.

Kalimetal—Metal version of Arnis. Three-foot-long sticks infused with Dangeran. Animal pelt is woven to the handle to provide a safe grip.

Blanch Room—A large secured area inside the Vampire headquarters that houses humans before and during transition.

Mentha—A plant extract believed to have a calming, numbing effect on vampires.

Great Vampire Revolution—Uprising by a group of revolutionary vampires seeking freedom from Goran's rule in the 1960s.

Pure-Blooded Vampires—Elite class of vampires on the verge of extinction, they are able to reproduce and can read minds. Each possesses a unique gift, and they must feed from pureblooded vampires of the opposite sex to survive.

Tack Enterprises—A company owned and operated by Pritchard Tack that manufactures guns for the military and private companies. Profits are used to support a large group of fighters, researchers, and medical personnel who are working on finding a cure for the disease *Incomis Sippanus*.

Vampire Rebellion—A small resistance by vampires in upstate New York. Reason for the uprising is unknown.

"I'm scared," Gail cried when another deafening thud shook the underground facility.

Huddled in the I-room with the others, Allison Tack recognized the devastation of those around her. Her adopted brother, Harrow Gates, and their purebred ally, Rohnert, were conferring on the far side of the room, while Tor hovered in the background like a shadow. Tor Burns, Allison's appointed bodyguard, sent an occasional look of reassurance in her direction, but he did not speak. He must have known that there were no words that could comfort her now. Each pounding, ear-shattering strike that drilled in their ears compounded the atmosphere of regret, apprehension, and loss. A significant chapter of their lives crumbled more and more with every strike of the wrecking ball.

Finality.

Allison watched while the little girl clutched Jordan close, her young eyes reflecting a mixture of fear and confusion. When they'd been unable to locate Gail's mother, Jordan had stepped into the role, and Allison cherished the opportunity to be the adorable girl's honorary auntie. Now,

Gail's stubby fingers dug into her new mother's arms, and she buried her face in Jordan's shoulder amid the sounds of concrete and metal colliding.

"Shh. Don't be scared, baby. It's all going to be over soon." Allison reached out to pat Gail's head, stroking the length of her hair to soothe her. She felt Gail's body shudder and heard little sobs escape her lips, but they were drowned out by the relentless sound of the wrecking ball ramming the building.

At the recommendation of her godfather, General Leo Krever, she and Harrow had decided to level the building following the incident that had claimed the lives of her father and their close associates Dante and Leroy. The decision hadn't been an easy one. The building, after all, stood as testimony to her father, Pritchard's, achievements as one of the city's most successful businessmen. Seeing it broken down into nothing more than piles of debris was heartbreaking.

One of the most persuasive arguments for taking such a drastic step pertained to the security of their underground structure. How could they safeguard everyone in the facility after the office building over the underground structure had been breached by Demetrius and his band of vampires? More attacks could come, and this possibility alone was enough to justify the demolition. Without knowing whether the head of the Vampire Council had knowledge of their operation, they couldn't risk another breach. Caution was necessary, since the lives of their people took precedence over any emotional ties to the structure itself. Their continued survival would have been Pritchard's top priority if he'd still been alive, and Allison would see to it that the people and mission her father had loved continued to thrive.

There had been inquiries from all over regarding the whereabouts of her father. So far, Allison and Harrow had managed to dodge the questions with vague excuses. It would suffice for now until more specific questions came up.

Each memory of her father hit her with new pain: dread, sorrow, longing, and remorse. The what-ifs never stopped tormenting her, often leaving her guilt-ridden and filled with shame.

To his credit, her godfather had been fairly active in maintaining the facility's functions following Pritchard's demise. After all, the two men had been close army buddies, sharing horrific experiences together in the army, family holidays and the births of their children throughout the years. Although things would never be the same, Leo's presence had eased the burden of Allison's misplaced guilt. No one except Jordan would ever know that she still lay awake most nights, crying and blaming herself for everything that had gone wrong.

Jordan's amber eyes met her gaze now, conveying reassurance without speaking aloud. *It will be over soon. This is for the best.*

The stress of Allison's situation had taken its toll, and a bubble of laughter rose in her throat. When it escaped, the brittle sound, edged with fear and uncertainty, echoed through the room. All heads whipped in her direction.

Jordan took her hand and squeezed it in a firm grasp, but Allison couldn't accept the comfort her friend was offering. She wasn't entitled to such an emotion. She, who was the root cause of it all; she was the reason three people were no longer among them.

"Allison, are you okay?" Jordan's voice squeaked, contradicting her otherwise calm demeanor.

Despite her attempts to keep her emotions in check, Allison couldn't help but laugh harder, tears pouring down her cheeks. It was a crime to sacrifice innocent lives in order to protect her. Dante, Leroy, and her father would still be alive if she hadn't thrown a silly party, compromising their safety in the process. Now, they were demolishing the building that had been a prominent reminder of her father's pride and hard work. Was she even worth all the trouble her father had gone through? She tried to nod her head in response to Jordan's concern, but her body had begun to shake. Harrow shot across the room and crouched next to her, his expression laced with worry and his body taut with concern.

"Ally, what's going on?" His fingers traced her face, in order to give him the answers his eyes couldn't find. Harrow had the worst vision among all of the infected vampires. With the change in diet, his sight hadn't gotten worse, but the damage had already been done. His white irises dilated when he tried to focus on her. Allison knew him well enough to guess he wanted to gauge her state of mind.

"Harrow, this is unbelievable. All of it." She gestured with her hand, waving it above her head.

Harrow nodded in understanding before gathering her in an embrace. "I know, I know," he said.

Allison knew that he meant to calm her, but lately, each time Harrow held her, a sense of helplessness crept up her spine. The realization that she was weak and in constant need of protection chilled her.

Harrow frowned when she tried to push him away, not understanding that she needed to soothe her frayed nerves. Her friends were looking to her to rise to the occasion. If she allowed herself to succumb to the constant grief, it would forever cement her as feeble and dependent in everyone's eyes.

"I need to think. I have to get away," she said, her legs wobbling underneath her when she stood. Harrow placed a hand on her elbow to steady her.

Tor moved closer but said nothing. Lately, his words were few and far between. It seemed like he had developed the habit of keeping quiet in her presence, although she knew very well his wry sense of humor was still intact.

"Allison," Harrow said, turning her to face him. "It's fine. Go—I'll take care of things here." He turned to Tor. "Take Allison, Jordan, and Gail upstate. Stay there until I say it's safe to come back here. Clear every activity with me first."

The house upstate was one they had recently built and fortified to meet their special needs. Set in the middle of a wooded area with the Adirondack forest in their backyard, the location provided easy access to an abundance of wildlife. After careful deliberation and consultation with Leo, Harrow had bought the land and hired the best architect money could buy. Permits were secured using the General's connections, and building took less than five months. The construction crew worked night and day, and before they knew it, a two-story, ten-room home had been erected, complete with an underground section the size of football field.

"Okay," Tor grunted in reply. His eyes flickered to meet Allison's for a second before he stepped back and leaned against the wall. Yes, Tor Burns and his silences were beginning to irk the hell out of her.

"Rohnert, would you mind keeping the ladies company, too? Maybe take Drake with you so someone can run errands during the daytime."

"Not at all. How about you? Think you can handle everything here?" Rohnert asked, snapping his gaze in Jordan's direction.

There had been a widespread speculation among the fighters that Rohnert could read minds or emotions, although the vampire had yet to make that admission. "I'll stay here," Jordan said before Harrow could speak again, further supporting this belief.

Harrow's lips thinned into a tight smile. "Darling, I think it's best if you keep Gail and Ally company. I'll try to catch up with you guys when I find the time."

The admonishment in his tone was clear, and Jordan sighed but said no more. Her body language made it clear that wasn't what she'd wanted to hear but she'd give Harrow the support he needed rather than argue with him.

Harrow took a few steps in Jordan's direction and kissed her on the cheek before giving Gail a tender pat on the back. "I love you ladies—you know that, right?"

Jordan nodded, her fiery hair swaying with the movement, and tilted her head in his direction. Gail's head, still nestled in the crook of Jordan's arm, bobbed several times.

Another jaw-clenching thud shook them, and Tor sprang forward. "If you ladies are done with your goodbyes, I think it's best if we get ready leave as soon as sundown hits." He strode to the door. "Allison?"

She smiled at Harrow, placing a hand on his arm for a moment before following Tor out of the room.

Left alone, Harrow sat at the head of the table and glanced around the room. The same white walls stared back at him, a quiet witness to all that had transpired in the past months. He grabbed the remote control on the table before sinking back into the chair. The flat-screen television came to life with the click of a button, and the real-time, real-life action unfolded before his eyes. No matter how bad his eyesight, the development outside was as heartbreaking as if he had been standing in its midst, witnessing everything firsthand.

People in yellow hard hats were standing and watching; some were barking orders, others were hard at work. A crane stood next to the building while the large wrecking ball was already hard at work. Harrow pressed a button and zeroed in on Leo, who was standing with Cyrus and Lambert. The latter two men appeared somber; their pale faces, lined with stress and anxiety, showing signs of undeniable sadness. Harrow felt every single one of their emotions. Each one tore through him like a jagged knife, cutting and puncturing his tattered nerves.

Harrow leaned toward the speakerphone on the table. One punch of a button connected him to Rayce, who was now the official tech guy after Dante's untimely demise.

"Rayce." He strained to make his voice sound firm and devoid of emotion.

"Yes, Harrow?" The human's response was quick as lightning. Rayce had been recruited by Pritchard to be Dante's assistant. What he lacked in brawn, he overcompensated for with intelligence. Thin and somewhat geeky, Rayce held his own within the group of snarling vampires and smart-mouthed humans. Dante's protégé was as confident as his predecessor and just as competent. Reeking with potential, Rayce had been a fine addition to their team. Although Dante was missed, he'd left behind a lasting contribution to their team by giving Rayce all the training and knowledge he would need.

"Is it safe for me to go out there?"

There was a long silence. The speaker crackled as the pounding of a keyboard sounded in the background. "We're about to hit sunset in a few minutes, boss. I think you'll be good to go. Just wear those glasses of yours, and you'll be fine."

"Thanks, Rayce. Buzz me out through the side exit. Make sure the women and their escorts are tracked. Call me if there's anything out of the ordinary."

"Will do . . . and Boss?"

"Yeah?"

"Good luck out there. I know you made the right decision."

"Thank you." Harrow's chest tightened. "You're doing a good job, Rayce."

There was another stretch of silence while the speaker idled. It took a few seconds before Rayce answered, "Thanks, Boss."

Harrow got up. He felt for his daggers and the Glock underneath his jacket before picking up his Oakleys from the table—the same pair Pritchard had given him—and putting them on. Harrow strode out of the room and made his way down the long hallway. A few minutes later, he faced the door that would let him out into the twilight. Harrow faced another tie to Pritchard being severed. The man had not only given him and others a chance at a new beginning, but he had been a friend and savior to Harrow.

Melissa walked listlessly around her boudoir, feeling queasiness grip her like never before. It had been six months since she'd last seen or heard from her son, Demetrius. He had simply vanished.

There had been times in the past when Demetrius had found the need to take a breather from his father's relentless expectations and demands. She couldn't blame him for needing to escape Goran's unrealistic whims and summons every once in awhile. Demetrius had gone on prolonged vacations before, but this time he had left without a word. There were times when the need to scream was too great, when she wanted to pull out her hair in frustration.

Caring for Goran's redheaded pets and his children was an item on her list of assignments she was getting tired of, but she didn't have an ounce of nerve to defy him. He trusted her to do things his way, and she had come through for him, every single time. Happiness and freedom had been taken from her, but her son made those sacrifices bearable. With Demetrius missing, Melissa felt the weight of his absence like a ton of bricks bearing down on her body.

She drifted to the porch, her feet heavy, dragging with every step. She opened the french doors, which led to a vast space of nothing—a dead end of walls and concrete. This was the life she knew as the head mistress of Goran's harem: an existence underground, away from the prying eyes of humans and daylight. Although it was dank, dark, and dreary, it was the best view that could be afforded to the mistress of Vampire Council's leader.

Gathering the skirt of her gown in her hand, she swung herself onto the railing and sat down. She let her feet dangle before releasing the hem of her gown. After yet another day filled with duties and obligations, there was nothing left for her to do. The Vampire Council was settling in for its scheduled slumber, and her silent suffering began again.

She was beginning to hate the endless blur of days and nights spent watching over the needs of Goran's collection of redheaded women and their bastards. It was a big responsibility, one she would rather do without. Too bad she could no longer have children since she had been turned after giving birth to Demetrius. It was so different for the halflings, as they were often referred to by the others. Unlike their purebred counterparts, who were able to procreate at will, the created vampires no longer had that ability. Their biological clocks stopped ticking, halting the progression of life and removing the gift of childbearing. If she'd had a choice, Melissa might have wanted another child with Goran—another child to cherish and love, who could help her pass the time, but it wasn't possible anymore.

Once they were turned, life as they knew it changed. Melissa was just worth the value of the services she provided. When the glitter of her star ebbed, she'd be kicked to the curb and cast aside for another woman with a better shimmer.

Melissa sighed. For now, she remained Goran's favored female, or so Goran kept telling her. His actions so far hadn't contradicted him. If and when that time came, Melissa wouldn't know what to do with herself. Demetrius was the one constant in her life. Without him, there would just be a dull ache in her heart and countless hours of solitude.

She tried to recall any conversation she may have had with Demetrius that could lead her to his location, but she came up empty every single time. He had made no mention of leaving or of a special assignment had might take him elsewhere.

If I could only ask Goran. It was wishful thinking on her part. She sighed. He had been distracted, either by his redhead menagerie or by the Council's demand for a purebred heir. A few times she'd overheard him muttering about being betrayed by someone, but the culprit's identity was unknown to her.

The big question was where Demetrius and his band of vampires were holed up. There were about ten of them who hadn't been heard from since his disappearance. No one from the team he'd left behind had any information. Not even Hamilton, the hard-nosed and irritating vampire, could give her an answer. Melissa recalled her conversation with him a few days back. The vampire had just narrowed his eyes and had shaken his head at her question, acting suspicious of her inquiry.

"Are you baiting me to give you information you already know?" he had asked.

Melissa had felt her blood boiling. "Do you think I would ask if I knew? We're talking about my son here." The rage inside her had neared its saturation point, just like her patience. She remembered crouching and baring her fangs at the impetuous vampire.

Hamilton had sneered at her, mocking her in the manner that had made him hated among his peers, especially by her son. The lone reason she'd gone to Hamilton was the fact that Demetrius had mentioned working with him at Goran's instruction.

"Dial down your anger, woman. If I knew where the bastard went, I would have reported to Goran right away." With those words, Hamilton had strode away, leaving Melissa seething with anger and back where she started, with no leads and her hopes diminishing more with each passing day.

Desperation often led people to do stupid things, and she was afraid of reaching that point. She would give Demetrius three more months to emerge from wherever he'd been hiding, and then she would have to act upon what her instincts were already shouting for her to do.

If any unlucky fate had befallen him—*no,* she told herself, *it couldn't be.* Her son was sturdy, a fine fighter, well-trained, and fierce. He would still be out there, burrowed in somewhere on his own. When he came back, she would wring his neck—snap the life out of him for reducing her to this tangled mess of worry. She would not even think twice about taking his life for being so irresponsible and insensitive.

The drive toward the mountains had been uneventful and quiet. Everyone had retreated into their own private thoughts once they'd climbed into the car for the four-hour trip. They had taken a bulletproof limousine, a recent purchase Harrow had deemed a necessity.

Tor reclined in the front passenger seat and rested his head on the leather headrest. Dave, one of Pritchard's rescued vampires, was driving and had been silent since they had left the facility. The same burden rested on everyone's shoulders, and Tor felt it as well.

A partition glass separated the front seat from the rest of the passengers. Tor was not one to worry, especially when Rohnert was around, but given that Harrow had entrusted Allison to him, he had to make one quick check before he slept. He pushed a button, and the glass slid down.

"Everyone okay?" Tor asked. He smiled at the sight of Gail sprawled between Jordan and Allison. Her head rested on Jordan's lap, and her little shoeless feet were nestled on Allison's thighs.

Rohnert turned to face Tor and grinned. "Yes, we are. Get some sleep, my man."

Allison looked away from the window just in time to meet Tor's eyes. She gave him a blank stare, the same empty look she'd been wearing ever since her father had passed away. Tor searched her face until she offered a weak smile.

"I'm fine. Thanks," Allison said.

Only after she'd spoken did Tor nod to Rohnert and roll up the partition glass, sealing him in a semi-private world. He could imagine Allison's pain. Many times, without her knowledge, he'd heard her cry herself to sleep. Those had been the times when he waited outside her door until he was certain she was asleep before he would leave.

Yes, he took his role of guardian seriously, just like he had when Pritchard had given him his first assignment as Harrow's babysitter. Tor had parked his ass in the vampire's grill, not caring about his privacy, intent on just keeping him alive. Harrow had turned out just fine, and Tor took pride in knowing that he had been instrumental in that. They were good friends now; it was hard to believe that Tor had wanted the bastard dead in the beginning. Who would have thought that destiny would have such different plans for them?

Tor looked out the window and let his eyes rest on the looming darkness. The headlights weren't necessary for him to see what was around them. They were in the outskirts of the city now. A few more hours, and they would be in a different place, far removed from the noise and the traffic.

Tor closed his eyes, stretched his legs in front of him, and let the lulling sound of the engine soothe him. He thought about Allison, her unending tears, and the pain of losing a loved one. The sentiment was not lost on him. He'd been there, seen it, and felt every single emotion that dealt with death —terror, grief, guilt, and loss.

No, he wasn't going there. Not this time, after all these years. It had been difficult to bear then, and was even more so now. He tried to pull his thoughts back, but it was too late to prevent them sprinting down the forbidden memory lane. It was a path he dared not visit, if he could help it.

Not that he'd ever stopped thinking of her. There hadn't been a minute that he'd ever stopped thinking of his Jessie. She had become a permanent resident in his mind, occupying each day with visions and torturous memories, good and bad.

Whether it was painful or tender, she invaded all of him. Jessie had a way of reminding him of what he'd lost and what he had done that forever changed their lives.

There was no backing out now as she took hold of him again. He forced himself to relax, despite the tension building in his muscles. *Sleep, Tor, sleep,* he urged himself. He needed a respite from the nagging guilt and his inability to forgive himself.

Tor could envision that day's events as if they had happened yesterday. He had come home from work at the construction site, parking his old pickup in the designated spot of the apartment complex where he lived with Jessie, his wife. He'd turned off the engine, taken off his hat, and laid it on the passenger seat, stepping out into the afternoon heat.

Just like every other day, he couldn't wait to get home and be with Jessie. They could spend a quiet evening over dinner and maybe watch TV before heading to bed. Evenings and weekends with his wife had been the focal point of his life.

He'd attempted not to make the slightest noise so he could surprise her he'd put his key into the lock. Given his size and weight, being quiet wasn't a skill he possessed. At six-foot-three and two hundred or so pounds, he was nowhere near being light on his feet.

He'd grinned when he saw Jessie look up, a smile lighting her face. She had jumped off the couch in her robe and rushed to greet him.

"Darling, I knew it was you out there," Jessie had said, wrapping her arms around his neck and pulling his face down to meet hers. Well, dangling would have been a more accurate term, since Jessie was five-foot nothing and weighed no more than a sack of rice.

"I was trying to tiptoe, but I guess it didn't work," Tor had said and laughed against her mouth. Her sweet scent provoked his overactive libido, and he was certain of one thing alone: This kiss would guarantee a delightful frolic in bed with his wife. Her delectable mouth seizing his was more than he could handle. He was, after all, a sucker for anything Jessie.

"I missed you." Her smile was inviting.

He'd slammed the front door closed with his foot and grinned at her. Tor had closed his eyes, drinking in her scent before capturing her lips. He had cradled her in his arms like delicate china and crossed the length of the hallway to their bedroom in big strides. Even with his eyes closed, he'd known where he wanted to take her.

Jessie had broken their kiss just as they got inside the room to ask, "What about dinner? I made your favorite, Beef Strogan—"

"You're dinner for me." He kissed her again, and Jessie responded with ardent passion.

He held her after he laid her on the bed. With desire pulsating in his veins, he unknotted the tie of her robe like a ribbon on a gift, dying to see what he'd find. She whimpered with anticipation.

Tor lifted his eyelids to take a quick peek, but instead of the fair skin of her belly or the robust mounds of her breasts, Jessie's blood-soaked body greeted him. Her eyes were wide open and unmoving, and her mouth was pinched into a bizarre and painful grimace. She looked lifeless—dead!

"Jessie!" he screamed and shook her, trying to call her back to life. "Jessie!"

Tor's scream still echoed in his ears, and his eyes were filled with tears when he opened them. He struggled against Dave's hand on his shoulder, pushing the other vampire away. "Jessie," he cried out again, expecting to wake up from his nightmare.

The thing was, he was awake but seemed to be trapped in a nightmare— another one of those he wished would no longer haunt him. Tor knew, no matter what he did or how fast he'd run or how hard he tried to forget, the bitter reality would catch up with him and he could only hold the memories at bay for so long. He had to continue living with this torture, a fitting punishment for his crime.

"Tor, are you having a nightmare?"

Dave took his hand from Tor's shoulder when he growled in confusion. There was pounding on the glass partition, and Tor noticed that Dave had stopped the car.

Tor rubbed his face in shame. He hated being caught in a vulnerable state, cornered in a place he didn't want to be.

"No," he said in acknowledgment. *Welcome to my world.*

"Tor, roll down the goddamned window."

Rohnert pounded on the glass partition. Not one to curse even in the direst of situations, Rohnert was cursing now while he continued to bang on the glass.

Dave pressed the driver's side button to roll down the window as he sat and watched Tor grapple with his sanity, not daring to touch him again— not when Tor was grappling against an unseen enemy.

When the glass rolled to a stop, Rohnert poked his head through the opening and glared at Tor. "What the hell is going on with you?" he asked, his tone terse.

Silence filled the car when Tor didn't respond. He closed his eyes, not wanting to see the pity in Rohnert's eyes. At this point, he was certain the vampire knew his secret. The only sound that broke the silence was Gail's light snoring. Allison craned her neck to see past Rohnert's head to check on Tor.

He sat up straighter and rubbed his eyes, trying to push the remnants of the godforsaken images away and tear his mind away from the vision of

Jessie covered in blood. What could he do to erase the horrifying vision from his head?

"Tor, please say something."

Allison's pleading voice was like being doused with cold water. His eyes shot open, but he still saw Jessie's face, her body, and the blood-soaked bed.

"It was just a bad dream," Tor heard himself say, his voice sounding foreign even to his ears. He offered a feeble smile in Allison's direction, refusing to meet anyone's eyes.

"Let's get moving," he said at last, feeling a little semblance of his usual self creeping back in.

"Dave, let's go," Rohnert ordered when he hesitated. "Get us there as fast as you can, but be safe."

Dave glanced at Tor before shifting the car into drive. Tor grunted in response and looked straight ahead. Only when the car had eased back onto the quiet highway did he begin to relax. That had been the worst flashback he'd had so far. Not daring to close his eyes again, Tor decided to focus on the dark highway. He started to count the trees that lined the road like brooding sentinels to keep the images at bay.

It was another hour and thousands of trees later before they reached their destination. Built in a secluded area about three miles off the highway, the house was accessed by a dirt road that no one would stumble onto, even by mistake.

The brand-new house loomed before them in the darkness, guarded by black wrought iron gates and brick walls. Dave reached for the remote control inside the glove compartment, pushed the button, and waited until the gates opened wide enough to allow entry. The soft glow of the moon cast shadows around them, creating an eerie backdrop. Judging from the grand structure, there was no doubt that the interior would be lavish, in accordance to the Tack's preferences. One thing Tor was sure of—with Harrow running the show, the house would meet the demands of vampires' nature.

When the car approached the circular driveway, lights flashed from every direction. The motion sensor was an added security measure that would illuminate the entire area if triggered. The car stopped by the front door.

"I'll check the outer perimeter. You check the house," Tor said before Rohnert and Drake could get out of the car. "Drake, stay with the women."

Drake nodded and moved to the front passenger seat, his gun peeping out of his jacket. The car door locks engaged with a loud click.

Tor took the outer boundary of the property, while Rohnert walked straight to the house. It took a few minutes before they both returned and signaled for the others to follow. Drake emerged from the car first, holding the door for Allison and Jordan, who was carrying a sleeping Gail. The little girl remained dead to the world, still sucking her thumb. Rohnert walked over to Jordan while Tor took some of the duffel bags and suitcases from the trunk.

"Here, let me take her," Rohnert offered.

"It's okay. I've got her," Jordan whispered, keeping her voice low to avoid rousing the sleeping child.

When they walked across the threshold of the brand-spanking-new house, Tor couldn't help but wonder how on earth it had been built in a mere five months. And who had been behind the tasteful decorations and the state-of-the-art security system?

The dark-stained hickory floor gleamed like a winner while they all marched inside the brand new house.

"Oh my God, I had no idea it would be this beautiful," Jordan gushed when she wandered into a small sitting room just to the right of the foyer, still cradling Gail in her arms.

The house was a cube, designed with a bunch of goodies inside. Notable steel shutters were in place to block out the sun and its harmful effects on the vampires. Even with the shutters drawn tight, it was hard to miss the big picture windows lining the entire room. Jordan's footsteps echoed across the floor, her excitement palpable. Tor hung back and leaned against the wall, watching Allison press a button on a remote to roll the shutters up. A vast landscape of trees greeted them, the bare windows exposing wide acreage that stretched as far as their eyes could see.

The area was perfect for them. There were no neighbors for miles in any direction. The closest household was nothing but a faint light in the distance, like a star in the night sky: tiny, distant, and non-threatening. Building the place had taken almost no time at all; the Tack's limitless cash reserves and Leo's clout spoke volumes, and building permits had been signed faster than one could secure a marriage license in Las Vegas.

Instead of the stiff-looking decor of the old facility, the house was bathed in black and white. Other than the wood flooring, which was done in a red hue, everything was monochromatic—furniture, art prints, light fixtures, decorations, area rugs. The walls were done in a deep gray, lending a contemporary taste and a chic, macho touch to the whole room.

"You like it?" Allison seemed pleased, momentarily emerging from her cocoon of sorrow.

"Do I like it? Hell, I love it!" Jordan's face lit up as she hurried to discover more of what the first floor had to offer.

"I'm glad. Harrow and I pored over blueprints and chose styles we knew would be acceptable to everyone." Allison smiled.

Planning and designing the house with a high-caliber architect and interior designer was what had kept her sane in the months after Pritchard's death. Harrow had a lot of input geared toward safety, comfort, and optimum use of the space. Allison, on the other hand, had more influence with the aesthetics, not wanting to sacrifice comfort for beauty.

"The windows are to die for. I've never seen such big windows in all my life," Jordan said.

Allison laughed at Jordan's reaction. Funny what love could do to a person. It wasn't that Jordan had lost her edge, because the woman was still a fierce and determined vampire. Harrow seemed to have softened her. Jordan now listened before she acted, allowing her man to run the show instead of walking all over him. It went without saying that Jordan very much preferred looking after Gail, and in everyone's eyes, she was now Gail's mother.

"Too bad we can't enjoy them to the fullest, but we have nighttime to appreciate the stars and the moon. Harrow ordered a telescope so Gail can see anything she wants," Allison said.

"I can't wait to see the rest of the house," Jordan said.

Rohnert and Tor seemed to have disappeared. It was not a surprise that the men weren't as enthusiastic as the women when it came to decorations and furnishings. As far as the men were concerned, the bolts and locks might as well be the most expensive painting, since those were the details that garnered their admiration.

"Why don't we get you and Gail situated in your rooms first, and we can take a grand tour later?"

"Sure, lead the way." Jordan looked unnerved by the grandiose residence Harrow and Allison had worked to create.

Allison walked to a long hallway that had triangular sconces illuminating the path. Several closed doors were on each side; she stopped in front of one that looked very much like it would lead to a closet. Allison turned the knob, and light illuminated another hallway that led to an elevator.

"Interesting," Jordan commented as they got in the elevator.

"All the bedrooms are in lowest level, which is three floors down from where we came in. Harrow and I decided we wanted a subterranean home for protection. The next floor up is where we have our armory, the meeting room, and the audio-visual room. We're connected to the facility now that we are here. Rayce has control over the cameras, as well as the microphones. We have a well-stocked kitchen on the floor that leads up to the main floor, as well as a training room."

"This is a fortress," Jordan said, checking every detail they passed while they made their way to the last door on the left.

"You could say that. We had to make sure we'd be safe here. This will be our second home from now on. When someone feels like they want to get away, this is the place to go." Allison offered a little smile. "All the windows in the upper floor are bulletproof. Impenetrable, even with Dangeran bullets or any other weapon out there."

"A bomb?" Jordan grinned.

"Yeah, sure. Good luck with that one." Allison grinned, then pushed open a door to reveal a large bedroom with a king-sized bed. The room was sparsely decorated, which appealed to Jordan's taste.

"This is your bedroom. Harrow was clear about your preferences, so there's just a bed, a desk, and the bathroom. He said you didn't care for frills or unnecessary luxuries, so we're giving you a bare bedroom." Allison rolled her eyes.

Jordan nodded. "Harrow knows me well enough." She tested the bed before adding, "Good man."

Allison walked across the room to another door. She opened it before Jordan could ask. "This is Gail's bedroom. She has a door from the hallway, too, but Harrow wants her to feel secure knowing you guys are connected. He told me that Gail wanted to sleep in your room because she's afraid to be on her own. We hope this will solve that problem."

Gail's bedroom was decorated in dainty shades of pink, yellow, and white. Stenciled patterns of tulips graced the walls, mingling with the Aqua Pets she'd been crazy about lately. Several favorite posters hung on the wall. Hello Kitty, boy bands, and Barbie took the "hall of fame" wall closest to her bed.

Jordan surveyed the room with appreciation. Allison watched while Jordan took in every detail she had put together, right down to the tiny pillows, bedspread, and princess canopy bed on the far side of the room. Allison lifted the bedspread and folded it the foot of the bed, and then she pulled down the sheets so Jordan could put Gail down on the mattress. The little girl was still fast asleep, sucking her thumb with fervor. She had been seesawing between keeping her own sleeping schedule and that of the vampires. Although most times she ended up following their schedule, the moving vehicle had lulled her to sleep.

"There's a nightlight for her. I don't want her to be afraid when she wakes up." Allison turned the lights off and a flicker of light shone from the bedside table. Jordan followed her back into the master bedroom. "My room is right across the hall from yours. Tor will be in the one next to me, since Harrow doesn't want Tor too far away."

Jordan smiled. They both knew how bullheaded Harrow could be once he'd set his mind on an idea.

"Altogether, we have ten rooms in this house. We're at the foot of the Adirondack Mountains, so there's no limit when it comes to hunting animals."

"I can't get over how you two got this house planned and built so fast. It's amazing," Jordan said as they walked down the hallway.

"The facility can be stifling, especially since . . ." Allison stopped, not wanting to swim into the sad territory of her father's absence. The wounds were still fresh; they always would be for her.

"I know. This is perfect. For you, Harrow—and everyone." Jordan took her friend's hand.

"I hope it gives Tor a chance to settle his nerves, too," Allison said.

Jordan nodded. Before they entered the elevator, the phone on the hall table rang.

"That's gotta be Harrow," Allison said matter-of-factly. "Answer it."

Jordan grinned before picking up. "Hello?"

"Hey, I can see you guys are all settled." Harrow's voice sounded like he was close by, and Jordan looked up to find a camera pointed at them. She waved at it.

"Having fun snooping on us?" she asked.

Harrow chuckled. "Actually, yes. I forgot to tell you how lovely you look tonight."

A ping from the elevator signaled it was ready.

"I'll see you later," Allison called out, waving at Jordan after she'd stepped inside.

Jordan waved back before the elevator doors pressed together.

Allison pressed the button that would take her to the top floor. She doubted anyone was still up, since the sun would be rising in less than an hour. It was enough time to lounge on the deck for a few minutes and get her bearings.

Exiting the elevator, she zeroed in on the stocked bar. Her palate, as well as her behavior, had gone through some dramatic changes as along with her diet. The meek and mild Allison was no longer around; bits and pieces of her old self surfaced once in a while, but the new Allison was persistent and determined. God knew how much she tried to rein in her aggression. At this point, she wasn't certain if she liked the new Allison.

She strode to the bar, grabbed a glass, and was halfway into pouring a drink when a voice came from behind her. Pivoting, she sensed Tor's eyes watching her with intensity.

"Can't sleep?" Tor asked. He was standing directly behind her, holding a bottle of tequila in a death grip. Clad in his usual black leather jacket and dark jeans, Tor was a threatening piece of work. His wide shoulders were tensed, his jaw taut, and his mouth set into a grim line. She watched him push an unruly dreadlock away from his face.

"Sleep is a luxury for me these days," Allison answered while she continued to pour. Her heart had started doing the jitterbug—her bodyguard had that effect on her. She found herself drawn to him, which wasn't a development she needed at the moment.

"You need sleep. It isn't healthy to go without, even for us." Tor moved closer.

The bar was set into the far corner of the deck, where pool and poker tables sat side-by-side. An entertainment center, complete with a flat-screen television and stereo, was perched at the opposite end of the space. Designed for nighttime activity, half of the deck was covered by a roof and the rest was left open. It could be used for stargazing, reflecting, or just as a hang-out.

"You don't get much sleep yourself," Allison said.

"Sleep and I aren't friends," Tor replied gruffly. He had turned his back to her and was staring into the darkness.

Allison took his tone as a warning not to prod further. She knew something was bothering him, and the incident in the car reinforced her suspicions. What in the world could turn a confident and self-possessed man into the ball of terror she'd witnessed earlier?

This was the big question, and she intended to find the answer soon. Waiting would have worked for her before, but not anymore. Should she ask for an explanation or let him come to her when he'd decided he was good and ready? In the end, her curiosity won out over her better judgment.

Allison downed her vodka in one swig, feeling feistier by the second. She walked over to where Tor leaned against the railing; standing next to him was like cuddling up to a statue. He was so still that it appeared as though he might be incapable of breathing or movement.

"What's bothering you, Tor?" she asked.

Looking up at him, all she could see with her faulty eyesight was the outline of his face. Thanks to the Gates Syndrome, Allison had to tilt her head sideways and use her peripheral vision to get a clearer picture of Tor's expression. What little she could see of his face told her that her question wasn't a welcome one.

Tor's grip on his glass tightened. Allison waited for several minutes, the steady, soft whistles of frogs and the chirping of crickets provided a background harmony to the darkness. These were the sounds that the city didn't offer, since they were drowned out by screeching cars and human activities. These were the sounds of the purity of nature at its best.

"Would you like to talk about it?" Allison asked, inching close enough to feel when the strength of his body faltered a bit.

"Allison, I don't have anything to talk about. What makes you think I have something to say to you?" Tor asked, his voice thick with contempt.

"I know you are keeping something in there." She jabbed her finger at his chest and watched him flinch at her accusation.

Tor faced her now. She could imagine the fire in his purplish-red eyes and hear the sting in his voice. He didn't mince words. "Don't think you have the right to butt into my business just because I'm your bodyguard."

Tor seized her arms and turned her to face the door. His fingers dug into her flesh, and she winced at his sheer strength.

"You're hurting me," Allison protested, but it was a lie. His touch ignited something inside her far more stirring than any other pleasure she'd gotten in the past.

Tor drew back a little but did not loosen his grip. Marching her toward the door, he said, "I don't want to talk about myself. And don't ever ask me for any information again. You wouldn't want to be around me if you knew what I am and what I've done."

Allison pulled against his hold while he pulled her across the deck. "You can't make me do anything I don't want to do. And your words don't scare me. Now, get your hands off me and leave me be," she commanded in a tone that startled them both.

It was as if she had slapped Tor in the face. His features darkened, and he released his hold on her arms. She watched as he took a step back and appeared to deliberate for a few seconds over what he should do next. To her surprise, he spoke instead of leaving. "As much as I would love to leave you alone, I can't and I won't. Orders are orders, and I'll follow them as I was asked to do. So, let me tell you now: You're as stuck with me as I am with you."

Allison lifted her head in defiance and stared straight at him. "And I'm telling you as your employer that I don't need you watching over me night and day. You can ease up and do something else. I can take care of myself, regardless of what you or Harrow think. As far as being stuck with me, you can *un*-stick yourself any time. It's no big deal."

She shrugged and walked back to the bar, aching to get another glass; she hoped the next one would leave her numb. Grabbing the bottle from the counter, she poured another glass of Kauffman to the brim. She watched the clear liquid dance around the glass before bringing its contents to her mouth, swallowing the whole thing without missing a beat.

"Are you crazy?" Tor asked from behind her.

"What if I am? And just for the record, you need to mind *your* own business. That BS goes both ways."

Allison smirked and poured another glass. Before she could drink, Tor wrenched the glass from her hand, the liquid spilling on her and the ground.

"Stop it, Allison. Stop it. You're not in a good frame of mind. Let me take you back to your room now."

"Don't tell me what frame of mind I should be in. If you can't stand it, just leave."

At that moment, she didn't care what she said. She'd had enough of Tor telling her what to do and pushing her away when she offered a sympathetic ear, and she'd had enough of their one-sided conversations.

"As your bodyguard, I have the right to tell you when I see that your safety is being compromised. Enough of your childish tantrums," Tor said before picking her up like she weighed nothing and slinging her over his shoulder.

This made her pause, but when the heat of his body radiated to hers, Allison pounded at his back with her fist.

"Let me go!"

Tor wasn't listening. He strode to the elevator, carrying her. She kicked and pushed, but as much as she tried, she couldn't escape his hands around her waist. All she could hear was the rapid thrumming of their hearts.

"You want to act like a child, I'll treat you like one. Daylight is upon us, and I won't have you burning like bacon out there. I don't want to be the one to answer Harrow when he asks why you turned into a pile of ash." Tor grunted when he kicked her bedroom door open. He walked in and kicked the door closed with his foot. Allison continued to struggle, pounding her fists on his back.

"Put me down," she ordered when they reached her bed. Tor did what he'd been told. He held her waist and attempted to throw her down on the mattress—little did he know that she wasn't intending on going down alone.

Allison held onto his neck as tight as she could, and they both fell on the mattress, Tor landing on top of her. She didn't let go, even though the weight of his body was heavy on her small frame.

"What the hell are you doing?" Tor shouted as he pushed himself up, but Allison locked her legs around his waist, trapping him.

"Doing what I want to do," she answered and moved her mouth to his. She felt his breath catch in his throat, and a look of terror crossed his face. This reaction was not what she had hoped for, and his rejection hurt.

Tor moved his mouth away like she was offering him poison instead of herself. "You're insane." He held her shoulders with restraining fingers before he pushed her body away, despite her resistance. Her strength was no match against his, and he set her aside like a ragdoll, unwanted and rejected.

He stood, his dreadlocks falling over his shoulders. Looking at her with disgust, Tor's nostrils flared before he stalked out the door, slamming it shut. The silence that followed was deafening. Allison was left stunned and unable to move, her eyes stinging with tears of humiliation.

What had she done?

"What the hell is going on?" Zane lashed out at the television when the breaking news flashed across the screen. The building he had visited twice —once when he'd posed as a possible investor, and the next with his father, Demetrius—was being demolished.

The newscaster was saying, "The legendary architectural landmark known as the Tack Enterprises Building is being torn down as we speak. Details are still sketchy at this point. The billionaire owner is unavailable for comment and is rumored to be out of the country for an indefinite period of time. Stay tuned, and we will give you up-to-the-minute news as more updates become available."

"Damn it!" Zane pounded the arm of his chair, and his mind raced. What on earth had happened to the place? And why wasn't his old man answering his phone? It had been months since he'd last spoken to or seen his father. It had been a while since the last deposit had been made into his account, which was rapidly depleting. Not good.

Then there was the bank account his father shared with him. Zane thought about it and knew that if Demetrius didn't answer in the next week or so, he'd be forced to dip into that small fortune. He had to stay alive and maintain his goodies and his sweet ride. There was no other choice.

Something smelled rotten, and it wasn't a dead fish. Zane knew there had to be a connection between his father's theory about Pritchard Tack and the sick vampires they'd killed a few months ago. The whole thing didn't make sense. Now the building was being torn down, going up in a cloud of dust, and any answers would go down with it. Without pausing to think, Zane grabbed his cell phone and made a mad dash out of his penthouse and into the diminishing light of day.

He smirked as he ran through the busy New York City streets in the direction of the falling building. Thanks to whichever vampire gods were watching over him, he had a gift no other of his species had: the ability to go out in broad daylight. It was a glitch that he and his father celebrated. He had taken after his mother's human half; what other explanation could there be?

Zane ran down the busy street, heedless of the questioning stares and not paying attention to the people he bumped into along the way. All he had in mind was getting some information he could report to his father. He knew that Demetrius would be pleased if he could give him some valuable information regarding Tack Enterprises. The funny thing was, he had no idea where his father lived. He knew Demetrius lived somewhere in the vicinity of Rockefeller Center, but the exact location had never been divulged. Whose safety was it for, anyway? Zane had been kept a secret long enough.

That would be another project for him, then, after he found out what the hell was going down at Tack. Zane flashed across the bridge, faster than his car could have carried him.

He was approaching the site, where many uniformed soldiers were congregated. There were barricades everywhere, and checkpoints had been positioned at all corners, covering all entry points to the cordoned-off property. This only confirmed his suspicion that the government was involved in the project.

The immediate area buzzed with activity. The noise level was high, and the general mood was that of frenzied hurry. Zane heard several walkie-talkies blare while he walked by.

"General Krever is expecting this to be finished in the next day or so. Make sure you get all the other crew here by tomorrow. Copy?" The voice boomed from one walkie-talkie. Zane took note of the name and stored it in his memory. A little Googling would be necessary.

"Ten-four," answered a man in uniform, walking close by while eyeing the crowd that had gathered around the perimeter fence. Zane parked himself by the fence and tried to blend in. Acting came easy to him.

"What's going on?" he asked, trying to start a conversation with an older gentleman standing next to him.

The man glanced at him. "They're tearing down the building," he said with a hint of annoyance. "Heard from another fella that it must be a structural damage." The man shook his head. "Don't think so. The building looked fine to me."

Zane feigned interest, his fingers curled through the chain-link fence. "Yeah, it seemed fine to me, too." He tried to appear like any casual gawker while straining to listen to the conversation a soldier nearby was having via walkie-talkie.

He heard the soldier say, "If you have any questions, there's a man in a black jacket and dark sunglasses who would be able to answer your questions." Zane's eyes followed the direction the soldier's head tilted.

Man in a jacket. Zane scanned the multitude of people milling about. There were tons of them, but the only one wearing dark-colored lenses stood out. His clothes were distinctive; Zane could appreciate the fine duds the man was sporting. What made the man most noticeable was his grim expression, which exuded a deep emotional turmoil.

Zane wondered who he was and what position he held within the company. He looked young and attractive by the standards of the New York City elite. Having hobnobbed with the rich and famous for some time now, Zane had rubbed elbows with influential members of society when they were needed for a particular project his father had. He was known to them as Zane Drew, an influential businessman among the city's cream of the crop.

However, he had never seen this man before.

Zane continued to study the face hidden by the dark glasses. There was a definite difference in the man's aura, something out of the ordinary. He couldn't quite put his finger on what it was. Taking his cell phone from his jacket, Zane took a few quick shots of the gentleman in question—another addition to his growing number of research projects.

Zane continued to observe the man as he conferred with a high-ranking official, their conversation muted even to his sensitive ears. He tried to lip read, but it wasn't a skill he possessed. Too intent on his task, he was caught off guard when the strange man glanced in his direction.

Despite the dark lenses, Zane knew the man was looking directly into his eyes. For some insane reason, the hair on the back of Zane's neck rose and a prickling sensation made him uneasy. He held the man's gaze for as long as he could and tried to conceal his discomfort, even tipping his head to show empathy. It was a bizarre stare-down, without a doubt.

Harrow walked around the demolition site feeling lost. Each strike of the wrecking ball felt like it was killing him little by little. With every hit, the sense of loss tore deeper into his heart.

His conversation with Leo had confirmed the job was ahead of schedule. Two more days and the demolition phase would be over, then cleanup would start. It wouldn't end their misery, but at the very least, the noise and the constant pounding would stop. The pile of rubble would serve as a sad reminder of the place they had grown to love would no longer be there.

Inquiries about the location of the new office building bounced around like a ping-pong ball when a few reporters spotted him following his brief chat with the General. He began fielding questions as soon as he walked out into the dying sunlight. This should be a task for the lawyers. He he needed more time to assess the safety of their underground residence. At the moment, he'd rather keep to himself or be in the company of the people who understood his pain.

Mindless of the onlookers behind the fence, he was gauging the progress of the demolition when he felt eyes stabbing into him like daggers. Since the change in his diet, he'd noticed some remarkable differences in all his sensory functions. Although his central vision remained close to useless, his peripheral vision remained intact. His ears had grown sensitive to the smallest details like a scratch or an exhalation of breath. Harrow now sensed someone watching him and studying his every move. His body twitched at the prospect of danger; he'd been itching to unleash his daggers and unload some of his bottled up aggression.

Harrow sensed an inexplicable danger emanating from one bystander, and he glanced in the man's direction while he whispered to Rayce on his walkie-talkie.

"Zero in on the man in the dark jacket by the northeast section. Redhead. Do you see him?" It wasn't a surprise that he'd noticed the color of his watcher's hair; it was the same color as Jordan's.

"Got it," Rayce answered just as the man dipped his head in Harrow's direction.

He could sense the man's curiosity, and his body emitted the scent of inquisitiveness. It rolled off this stranger thicker than the rest of the onlookers.

The sun was kissing the horizon now, and the orange glow was fading, to be replaced by the promise of darkness. Still basking in the tingling sensation the diminishing sun had left on his skin, Harrow surveyed the area and focused on his two friends, who appeared to be feeling as drained and empty as he was.

Harrow walked over to Cyrus and Lambert and stood between them, putting an arm around each of their broad shoulders.

"How are you, my brothers?" Harrow asked, plastering a smile on his face.

Cyrus cast him a sideways glance before he lowered his shoulder to give Harrow a bump, and Lambert grunted.

"Is there anything else we're missing here?" Harrow asked in an attempt to draw the two trusted men into conversation.

"I think Leo's got it all figured out," Cyrus answered in a solemn voice, his eyes transfixed on the work happening in front of them. "How are you holding up?"

"Is that a trick question?" Harrow laughed. It was shallow and didn't reach his eyes.

"Well, just like you are, I'm attempting conversation here," Cyrus said without humor.

Lambert snorted.

These were Harrow's friends—men with few words but loaded with attitude. How could he not love them? He gave them a rueful smile.

"Nice weather," he commented after a few minutes.

"I'm surprised you didn't sizzle and pop, boss," Lambert remarked, his eyes glued to the demolition.

"If it's not a direct hit, there's no problem." Harrow smiled.

"I wonder about you sometimes, Harrow." Cyrus moved out from under his arm and turned to face the vampire. "Do you have a death wish? Why are you risking your hide walking out in the daylight?"

Harrow laughed. He and Jones, Leroy's successor, had tested bits and pieces of the changes to Harrow's body, and one of the first things they'd experimented with was his susceptibility to sunlight. He hadn't mentioned these attempts to the others yet. The sun at its peak still caused him to blister, so further testing had been aborted. Death from exposure was still a possibility.

In the later part of the afternoon, when the rays had toned down to a subdued glow, they only caused tingles in his skin. This was a positive change from his no-sunlight existence. However, his eyes remained sensitive to the glare.

"Tried and proven to be UV-safe at this time of the day. Besides, I need the Vitamin D," Harrow teased, and he saw honest-to-goodness smiles from Lambert and Cyrus for the first time in months.

"I think you're nuts." Cyrus slapped him on the back.

"Even a nut like me deserves a good day in the sun. The doctor said we needed it." Harrow watched the wrecking ball batter another concrete wall.

"Why don't you take a pill instead?" Cyrus glared at him, and Lambert broke into an infectious laugh, which seemed to irk Cyrus even more.

"Whatever. Don't come crying to me when you develop a mean sunburn." Cyrus shook his head in a way Harrow knew well. The human wasn't going to push it further.

"I won't. Right now, what I need is a sparring partner. Up for a little butt-kicking?" Harrow said, cocking his head in Lambert's direction. "Come to think of it, Lambert should come, too. Two-for-one sounds appealing to me right this minute."

"You're a cocky SOB, you know that?" Lambert gave him a good-natured shove.

"That's my middle name."

"Put your money where your mouth is," Lambert said. He turned to Cyrus. "Well, let's go and teach this bastard a lesson in Humility 101."

Cyrus laughed and grabbed Harrow by the neck, pushing him forward. They all laughed and started jogging toward the back of the fallen building. Before Harrow disappeared behind the structure, he took one last look in the direction of the man who had been watching him earlier.

The stranger was gone. Harrow knew he had some checking to do, like name, residence, and background. It was the basic shit he needed to establish for every questionable character that crossed his path.

"I'll see you guys in the training room in thirty," Harrow said, once inside the facility and away from the relentless noise outside the building.

"Bring it, Gates." Cyrus snickered before he and Lambert stepped into the elevator.

"You bet." Harrow waved and proceeded straight to the control room to see what information Rayce had for him.

The blasted construction noises followed him as he walked to the control room. The moment the door closed, the room's acoustics muffled the irritating sound.

"Show me what you got." Harrow positioned a roller chair next to Rayce's.

The human gave him a wry acknowledgement before pressing a button that brought several screens to life. With the flick of the mouse, the figure on the screen zoomed into focus.

"I checked him out. Name's Zane Drew. Twenty-five-years old, owns a penthouse in Manhattan, drives a Porsche GTS, bank account is almost drained. The parents' names on the birth certificate turned out to be bogus."

Rayce pushed a button, and another picture flashed on the screen. "This is the birth certificate."

Harrow was quiet while going through all the data, his nose pressed close to the screen to get a better angle. "Hmm . . . what else do you have?"

"Well, I cross-referenced his photo, and guess what I found?" Rayce pushed his glasses up his nose, looking pleased with himself. Harrow couldn't help but chuckle at his expression.

"I'm sure you're going to tell me."

"We had him here as a visitor not too long ago," Rayce said.

"Show me." Harrow felt his insides churn, and his shoulders tightened like cables. His gut screamed that this man and their unwanted visitors a few months ago were somehow linked.

Rayce quickly pulled up the segments, and several new screens opened. Harrow's heart plummeted when he saw Pritchard and Zane talking in Pritchard's office. It was the same man he'd seen outside watching him.

Who was this guy?

Harrow's mind reeled as he considered possible connections between Zane and the breach in their security that had led to the deaths of Pritchard, Dante, and Leroy. There had to be a connection; Zane was the last client Pritchard had entertained before his birthday.

Harrow strained his eyes to see as much as he could. There was Pritchard laughing and talking, and totally in his element. It sucked balls to watch him so animated and full of life, when the bitter reality was that Pritchard was no longer with them.

"Get Tor and Rohnert for me." Harrow pounded his fists on the table, exasperated at this latest development.

Rayce set up a conference call.

"Rohnert answered first. "Hello?"

And Tor chimed in, "Yeah?"

"There's something I want to discuss with you. Think you can hustle back here right away?" Harrow asked.

"Sure," Rohnert answered.

"What about the women?" Tor asked.

"I'll send Lambert, Knox, and Peyton over. They will leave in a few minutes. They should be fine with Drake and Dave around in the meantime."

"Okay." There was a tinge of hesitation in Tor's voice that Harrow didn't miss.

"Is there something wrong, my man?"

"Nothing. I'll discuss it with you when I get there," Tor said.

"Okay, then. I'll tell Lambert, Knox, and Peyton to get packin' and leave ASAP."

"Sure will. Anything else?" Cyrus asked.

"I'll see you all in the I-room in four hours. Rohnert, tell Jordan I'll call her in a few minutes."

"Will do," Rohnert answered before Rayce disconnected the call.

Harrow turned to Rayce. "I want you to keep logging any information you can on this Zane person. I want to know what he eats, when he shits, and all the dirty laundry you can rustle up. Get me an address, too."

"Right away, boss."

"And Rayce?" Harrow stood up, put on his sunglasses, and patted Rayce on the back.

"Sir?"

"Stop with the boss crap," he scolded. Rayce chuckled and nodded. "Good job."

Rayce smiled sheepishly before returning his attention to the multiple screens.

Harrow went to his room to change and give his aggression an overdue release. Walking into the bedroom he shared with Jordan, Harrow pulled out his cell phone and pressed Jordan's speed-dial number. While the phone rang, he emptied the holsters of his weapons and placed them on top of the bureau.

"Hi there." Jordan's pleasant voice greeted him, and Harrow felt a pang for her. It sucked when things weren't on the up-and-up in the facility and he had very little time to spend with her. As soon as he could, he'd make sure to get a much-needed break and take her somewhere nice.

Harrow sat on the edge of the bed and toed off his shoes. "Hey, how are you and the girls?"

"They're fine. I believe Allison's reading, and Gail is watching cartoons."

Harrow pictured Jordan rolling her eyes whenever she mentioned Gail's cartoons. God knew they had bought every available movie they could get their hands on. They needed to keep the little girl entertained enough to quit asking questions. Gail had been making a lot of inquiries about why they didn't eat as much, why they preferred to stay indoors in the morning, and why they couldn't open their mouths the whole way when they spoke. These were questions no one was willing to answer. Not yet, anyway. Maybe not ever. They had to be careful with everything they said around her if they intended to shield her from the truth of what they were.

"How are you?" Harrow asked again.

There was a brief pause at the other end of the line before Jordan answered with a sigh. "I miss you. I wish I was there with you."

"I miss you more. But I think you're needed there."

"What's wrong, Harrow?"

"Nothing. There are some developments I'm looking into. Listen, I asked Tor and Rohnert to come back here, and I'm sending Lambert, Knox, and Peyton in their place. Can you do me a favor and keep an eye on Allison while Tor's away?"

Jordan knew the reason behind Harrow's concern. They'd both agreed that Allison was somewhat teetering on the line between in-control and a possible breakdown. Since Pritchard's death, Harrow and Jordan had been watching Allison. They were particularly concerned about her well-being since she had no other close relatives other than them.

"You know I will."

"I promise we'll find some alone time soon, but sit tight for now. I'll give you the details later. Promise me you'll take care of yourself, too?"

"Yes, I will," Jordan said and added, "I love you, Harrow."

That made him smile. "I love you more."

"Take care of yourself. Don't do anything I wouldn't do."

After they hung up, Harrow changed into sweatpants and a white T-shirt. He had a date with Cyrus, and he was certain that they'd be working each other real hard during the next few hours.

"Allison?" Tor knocked on her bedroom door right after the phone call from Harrow. He wondered what had brought on the sudden decision to bring him and Rohnert home. Whatever Harrow's reason, Tor was certain it had to be important if they were to be relieved of their guard duty.

He heard footsteps approaching the door and held his breath. The kiss and the feel of Allison's soft lips were still fresh in his mind. Had he not pushed her away, he knew he would have lost control.

Allison was more potent than all the drugs he'd taken back in his human days—the same evil drugs that had fucked him up and turned his life upside down. All he could think of was her body pressed against his. Her remarkable scent never failed to make him hard and unable to think straight. He was careful to breathe through his mouth to keep her sweet aroma from assaulting his senses.

Would God ever listen to his pleas to keep him strong enough to resist her? Tor couldn't afford the torment of losing another woman he cared deeply about. The knowledge that he cared for her was a good enough reason to keep him from touching her and taking what she so willingly offered.

The door swung open, and Allison's sullen face greeted him. She neither smiled nor acknowledged his presence. She just stepped back to let him in. He noted her disheveled hair, which led him to believe that she'd had as bad a day as he had.

I'm such an ass. "Is everything all right?" he asked, stepping inside her bedroom. Allison kept her gaze averted, and Tor longed to tilt her chin so she would look up at him. Instead, he put his hands inside his pockets, where they belonged.

"Everything's fine," she replied in a clipped tone.

Jesus, he'd give anything to make her smile.

"I came by to let you know Rohnert and I will be leaving soon. Harrow called. He needs us, but I'll come back as soon as I can. Lambert and some others are on their way here to be with you and the girls."

Allison's eyes shot up. She took a step forward, but then stopped and searched his face. He saw the confusion in her eyes.

"Why do you have to leave? Is everything okay with Harrow and the rest?"

"I think so. He didn't go into details, but I figured it must be important for him to pluck us out of here."

Allison took another step forward, and Tor fought the urge to step back. It would be unfair to make her feel rejected when he was the one who should be made to suffer. He lamented in silence; one touch from Allison would guarantee his unraveling.

"You're not going out to fight, are you?" She sounded on the verge of crying.

"I don't know. It doesn't matter. I'll do what I'm expected to do," Tor answered. How in the hell would he know? Harrow had been vague during their phone conversation. Tor would rather stay and keep watch over Allison, no matter what consequences he might be up against.

"Can you tell Harrow not to send you out to fight?"

"Why would I tell him that?" Tor was incredulous. Imagine him dictating to Harrow. The woman must be out of her mind.

"Because I—I don't want anything bad to happen to you." It sounded like she was struggling to keep her words as uncommitted as possible, but she wasn't succeeding.

"I'm more than capable of taking care of myself. Don't worry about me. You, on the other hand, have to feed soon. I'll try to get back by sundown tomorrow to take you hunting. Can you wait for me?"

Allison nodded but said nothing. She looked at him before turning to her desk, where an open book laid waiting for her.

"Take care of yourself. Stay indoors until I get back," Tor said before turning to the door, his reluctant feet feeling heavier with each step.

Silence answered him.

Instead of driving the limousine, Tor and Rohnert decided to get a workout and run back to the city. When Lambert's call came in that they were en route to the upstate house, the pair set off on the long journey on foot.

The moment they walked out of the house and headed into the woods, Tor scanned the surroundings for any signs of danger in the vicinity. The sun had descended, and dusk had taken over. The air checked out clean, so he and Rohnert started their journey back to the facility.

Neither of them uttered a word when they broke into a sprint. The first half-hour of their run was spent in companionable silence, each enjoying their commune with nature.

Tor attempted to clear his mind, blocking any and every thought of Allison and her soft, inviting body. How tempted he had been to seize her and everything she had to offer. He silently reprimanded himself. *Clear your mind, asshole!*

Rohnert threw quick glances his way as though he'd heard the internal battle raging inside Tor's head. Tor bristled and increased his pace, but Rohnert matched his tempo without difficulty and remained quiet. Once he let his instincts guide him, Tor found that he was able to relax. It didn't matter where his mind led him; it was futile to try to get Allison out of his head.

The blur of green and brown energized him. Every jump and turn gave him the freewheeling sensation of being on a roller coaster. Tor loved the freedom, the smell of the pungent earth, and the unpolluted air that swirled around him. The relaxing silence and the purity of nature had been things he had missed living in the city. He'd been seeking calmness and the ever-elusive peace his mind needed.

The two vampires continued at a considerable speed while they took the back route through any connecting forest they could find, avoiding contact with civilization. Darkness was their ally, making their trip easier. An hour into their run, they caught the scent of other vampires in the area.

Rohnert signaled to Tor that they separate, and Tor nodded. With conscious effort, they kept their movements as furtive as possible. Tor took the left path, which led him closer to the highway, while Rohnert ran toward the denser area of the forest. Before Rohnert disappeared from view, he flashed four fingers, indicating the number of vampires in their midst.

Tor removed his axe and dagger from their holsters but kept them inside his jacket. He heard the rustling of leaves as the wandering vampires' footsteps drew closer. It was inevitable that their paths would cross. Tor braced himself before the foursome cleared the brush.

"Evening, gentlemen." Tor greeted them, flashing his fangs to establish his identity right away. He kept his hands underneath his jacket.

Startled to find unexpected company, the foursome stopped dead in their tracks and glanced at each other. Tor halted just a few feet away and watched while each of them moved their hands closer to their weapon.

Out of the corner of his eye, Tor saw Rohnert streak by in the background, and he drew a deep breath. If it went down and dirty right away, he knew that he'd be swarmed no matter how fast he could launch his weapons.

"Who are you, and what are you doing here?" the vampire in the middle asked.

"Just passing through, my man. Last I checked, this was a free country, right?" Tor said, tracking each subtle movement. Their stances were rigid while they sized him up.

"I don't like smartass vampires," the same vampire said, eyeing Tor's hands, which were still concealed in his jacket. Tor saw the sideways glance the vampire threw at his companion. "I have to let you know this place is off-limits to vampires. It was decreed so by the Council after the rebellion."

"Is that a fact?" Tor took a step to the right, assessing his position and trying to get a read on which of the four was prone to jump first. The one next to the leader twitched at his movement. "No laws govern me, and I'm not a part of any rebellion."

At the very least, Tor had been able to establish the leader of the group. He took another step, and the one closest to him reacted a little, taking a step forward. Not good—there were two twitchy suckers who were going to react as soon as he made his move.

"You're a vampire; therefore, you are a subject to the Vampire Council. And I'm telling you now, take your hands off your weapon, or else we'll be forced to kill you."

"I'm not subject to anyone's rule. And I will defend myself as I see fit," Tor said, meeting the man's threat with defiance.

"Seize him," the leader said, nodding to the two vampires. They glanced at each other before taking off faster than Tor had anticipated, crisscrossing to throw him off while opening their jackets to reveal their weapons.

Tor figured it was better to get them before they got him. His body tensed for a millisecond before he sprang into action. He unleashed his axe and dagger simultaneously, attacking each vampire faster than eyes could follow. He got one in the chest with the dagger, while the other one got hit in the head with his axe.

The duo convulsed before they even knew they'd been hit. They landed on the ground, and the disintegration process began. The remaining two wielded their weapons, snarling at Tor with rage in their crimson eyes. The leader acted fast, launching a throwing star in Tor's direction and narrowly missing his head. Rohnert jumped in from behind, severing the head of the other vampire. The unexpected turn of events stunned the leader.

"You'll regret this attack on the Council's soldiers," the vampire hissed and pulled two daggers from his holster. For someone who was surrounded and outnumbered two-to-one, the leader showed a shitload of courage and an incredible amount of stupidity. Applause-worthy, but still very dumb.

Tor retrieved his axe from the pile of vampire ashes while Rohnert and the leader faced off.

"Gentry, don't make me kill you," Rohnert said, his Kalimetal poised for attack.

The leader's face contorted into a confused expression before recognition flashed in his eyes.

"Your grace." He dropped his weapons, fell to one knee, and bowed his head in reverence.

"Get up, soldier," Rohnert commanded before glancing at Tor. "I got this."

Confused, Tor couldn't figure out what had just happened. One moment, he had been enjoying the liberating experience of the kill, and the next thing he knew, their attacker was acting like a total moron.

The vampire stood up, but his weapons remained on the ground. He kept his head low. "Your Grace, we have been searching for you."

"I'm no longer part of the Council. The title is not necessary, Gentry." Rohnert's voice sounded less severe than it had.

"Why did you spare my life, Your Hi— Rohnert?"

"I don't kill for sport, Gentry. You know that."

Gentry nodded and glanced in Tor's direction.

"He's with me. You're free to go. Tell Goran that there are some of us who refuse to be subjected to a tyrannical ruler. Most of us wish to live in peace, and we won't follow laws that are meant to serve his selfish purpose."

"He will have me killed with those words, Rohnert." Gentry maintained his submissive stance, his head bowed in deference.

"Go to Iden and serve him. He is a fair and level-headed Elder. I'm sure he'll take you in. With the size of Goran's army, he won't even notice you're missing."

Tor listened to the conversation in amazement. Sure, he'd heard about Rohnert's past connection with the Vampire Council, but he hadn't realized that his friend was some type of royalty. None of it made sense. He'd be happy once they went on their merry way and Rohnert enlightened him.

"Thank you. Maybe it's about time you returned to us." Gentry looked up, his eyes almost beseeching. "It was never the same after you left."

"There is no room for me in the Council. Not with Goran's oppressive leadership in power. I shall call on you when the time is right. Go now," Rohnert ordered.

"I shall be available should you call on me." Gentry bowed again and murmured words in a foreign tongue Tor had never heard. Gentry then picked up his weapons and bolted away, the darkness swallowing his figure in mere seconds.

"What the hell was that about?" Tor demanded. He checked the ashes of three *very* dead vampires, which were being blown away by the wind.

"Let's get going," Rohnert said, sheathing the Kalimetal on his back, his mouth set in a grim line.

"Not until you tell me what just happened here." Tor holstered his axe and picked up his dagger from another heap of ashes. He blew away the residue before placing the weapon back in his chest holster.

"You're not going to let it slide, are you?" Rohnert began jogging away.

Tor followed, falling into step with him before he answered. "No."

Rohnert seemed to consider Tor's response for a few moments. "Fine. You might have heard that I used to be connected with the Council."

"Who hasn't been?"

Rohnert ignore his jibe. "Well, I was their operations expert. I trained all their soldiers. I was a teacher, so to speak."

Tor's eyebrow arched while he let the info settle in, and yet, he found that he was more confused than ever. "Why on earth did that vampire call you 'Your Grace'?" Tor couldn't help but add a hint of malice to the question.

"Damn it, Tor. What's with the Q-and-A?"

"Answer the question, buddy. Didn't your momma teach you to answer when asked?"

"Better make good on your words, Tor. I will be asking you my own questions soon, and you'd better give me some straight answers." Rohnert sounded too smug for his own good.

The bastard knew something, but Tor dismissed his taunt. "Yeah, yeah."

By this time, they were running at full speed again, covering miles in mere minutes. They had wasted precious time, but they weren't far from the city now. Skyscrapers loomed ahead, their lights serving as beacons. They were early for their meeting with Harrow, but Tor knew that Rohnert would be hard to avoid after this. He was more and more certain that the other vampire could read minds or, at the very least, emotions.

"I'm one of the few full-blooded vampires left in existence."

Rohnert sounded more embarrassed than proud. Tor couldn't fathom why that would be, and his eyebrows shot up.

"Whoa, isn't that special?" he teased. "So that makes you royalty?"

"Hell, no. That makes me an important commodity. Long story short, they want me to provide stud service. To breed babies."

"Are you shitting me?"

Rohnert shook his head. "But that's not the reason I broke away from the Council. It's more personal in nature, so I hope you don't mind if I'm not too ecstatic about airing my dirty laundry."

"We all have dirty secrets. You're entitled to keep yours."

"Yes, we do, but you gave me your word. Out with it," Rohnert said.

"I have a feeling you know my shit already, but let's talk about it another time."

"You are quite transparent, my friend." Rohnert chuckled while they walked around the pile of rubble that had once been the Tack Enterprises Building. Demolition crews were hard at work, and several gawkers still lingered around the area.

"You're creepy, Rohnert." Tor slapped the vampire on the back, and they made their way into the tunnel that led to the facility's secret entrance.

Harrow's legs were propped comfortably on the I-room's table when Tor and Rohnert walked in. He looked up and nodded at them. Tor checked the time on the wall clock, and snorted; Harrow was beginning to act like a drill sergeant, always on time.

Judging from the bags under his eyes, Harrow looked like he could use some time off or maybe a healthy dose of Zs. He logged more time running the business and the facility than everyone else on their team combined.

"You're early," Tor commented when he settled at the far end of the table. He swung his feet up and made himself comfortable.

Rohnert took the chair on Harrow's left.

"I have nothing better to do." Harrow grimaced. He sniffed once, and then sniffed again. "Have you guys been playing around?"

"Huh?" Tor asked, throwing Rohnert a knowing look.

There had been some gossip circulating in the facility that all of the infected who had changed their diets had experienced remarkable enhanced sensory perception. Harrow was exhibiting one of the more noticeable side effects: a superior sense of smell.

"Do we offend?" Tor asked, lifting his jacket to his nose.

Rohnert pretended to sniff around before smelling his own clothes. Tor laughed and raised an eyebrow at Harrow.

"Don't play dumb with me, fools. I smelled it the minute you stepped foot inside the facility." Harrow jerked his legs down and leaned forward, his elbows on the table. "Tell me what you've been up to."

Tor looked at Rohnert again, asking for permission to divulge everything that transpired on their trip. Rohnert swept his hand in response.

"Well, on our way here, we ran into some VC soldiers."

Harrow shot them a questioning look. "What about them?"

"Well, we got rid of the twitchy ones right away, before they could make their move. Rohnert let the leader go. I guess they'd had some sort of *affiliation* in the past," Tor answered.

Harrow turned to Rohnert and removed his sunglasses. His irises were almost frosty white. "I'm sure you had a good reason for letting one go, and I trust your judgment. I just want to make sure there'll be no surprise repercussions."

"Don't worry about the one that I let live. He was a trusted student and a faithful soldier," Rohnert answered without blinking. It was apparent that Harrow's trust in his decision meant a lot to Rohnert.

Harrow shook his head. "Trusted? What does that mean for us? Not that I'm worried at all. It seems to me that you guys had some action already. So maybe you want to sit this one out?"

The door burst open, and Cyrus walked in, looking bedraggled. He kicked the door shut before flopping down in a chair.

"Sorry, I overslept. Damn alarm clock forgot to do its job," he muttered, smoothing his palm over his hair.

"Hey, Sleeping Beauty. No worries, man." Tor chuckled.

Cyrus was one heck of a guy. He'd gone to hell and back after getting stabbed months ago, and the human could still kick some serious butt. Loyal to the cause and one of the most trusted men in the organization, Cyrus was everyone's friend. It would have been a shame if he hadn't survived the knife wounds he'd sustained during an altercation with a Council soldier.

"I think I ought to get you a new alarm clock," Harrow said, teasing. "You're not late. We're just early."

Cyrus laughed and relaxed against the chair. "What did I miss?" he asked.

"Well, for starters, seems like our boys here saw a little action on their way home." Harrow nodded his head toward Tor and Rohnert. "They had a little fun with some soldiers from the VC."

"Huh." Cyrus stopped to think before a small grin formed on his lips. "And we weren't there to join the fun. Bastards!"

"That's what I was thinking," Harrow seconded.

"Well, two for two would have been much better odds, but our boy Rohn here decided to let one go," Tor said. "And guess what?"

Rohnert shot him a glare, but Harrow and Cyrus's interest was already aroused. Tor had no choice but to blurt out his newly unearthed information.

"What?" Cyrus asked.

"Our Rohnert here is royalty," Tor said in a conspiratorial way.

Harrow turned to Rohnert, intrigued. "Really? How royal?"

"Tor is an idiot." Rohnert rolled his eyes and shook his head.

"Tor isn't." Tor pounded a fist on the table. "And here's another deet about our boy. He is also pegged to be a stud muffin, a baby-making machine."

"What does that mean?" Cyrus shot up from his seat. "You're making little Rohnerts?"

"I think it's about time I clamp Tor's mouth shut," Rohnert threatened, flashing his fangs at Tor.

Whether Rohnert was joking or not, Tor was pumped for more action. It seemed like fighting, whether sparring or picking fights, was what kept him sane these days. He exposed his fangs and snickered. "Stand down, my friend. It's not every day we meet such a valuable species. We're deeply honored." He bowed his head in mock respect.

Rohnert snorted, turning his attention to Harrow and switching to a safer topic. "You were saying?

Harrow slapped Rohnert good-naturedly on the back before he addressed the group. He looked at Cyrus first, his expression turning somber. It was the sort of look that almost always accompanied bad news. Harrow pressed a button on a remote control, and the lights in the room dimmed. Another click turned on the flat screen on the wall.

"Watch this."

The four men fixed their gaze on the monitor, which showed Pritchard and a redheaded man talking in his office. Tor didn't have to turn his head to know that Cyrus and the others were affected by the scene unfolding on the screen.

Seeing Pritchard alive, talking and smiling, was painful for all of them. The man had been more than just a friend. He was the symbol of hope, freedom, camaraderie, and equality. Anyone who had spent time with him, no matter how meager, knew this. Pritchard Tack had left an indelible mark on every person who met him, which made him impossible to forget. Missing the man whose life had ended so abruptly felt like a jagged pill shoved down their throats.

"The man right there," Harrow pointed at the screen, "was the last client Pritchard entertained before the unfortunate breach of our office building. He was the big client Pritchard mentioned. The one he'd thought would be his last big account, and the beginning of his prolonged vacation." Harrow voice was low and filled with despair.

"What are you trying to tell us?" Cyrus voice cracked.

"The very same man talking to Pritchard was here today, at the demolition site."

Tor whipped his head around to look at Harrow, his jaw clenching in disbelief. "What the hell?"

"He was watching me out there. I had Rayce track him down and find out who he is. And sure enough, Rayce dug up some information I think is quite suspicious." Harrow paused and pressed another button, and another scene flashed on the screen. "Watch him."

Again, they examined the man standing behind the chain link fence, watching the proceedings. Several shots showed him looking at Harrow with the utmost interest. Fists pounded on the table as each person registered the link Harrow had established for them.

"You think he knew the vampires who infiltrated the office building?" Cyrus asked with an unmistakable hint of anger.

"I believe so. Just look at the similarity."

Harrow played a video of the vicious attack months before, when Demetrius and his team had infiltrated the office building. Harrow stopped the video, focused, and zoomed in on Demetrius's face. A side-by-side showed the striking resemblance between the two men.

"Looks like blood relation," Rohnert muttered.

"His name is Zane Drew, twenty-five years old, maintains a residence in Manhattan, drives an expensive car, and is known as an eligible bachelor in the city. His bank account is dwindling, but prior transactions show that he was getting a fat monthly paycheck from an unknown and untraceable source. I—"

Cyrus cut Harrow off. "Are you telling us that you see a connection between him and Demetrius?"

"Call it a gut feeling. The bank deposits stopped around the time Demetrius died. Connect the dots. It's hard to think otherwise."

"I see your point. Now, how do we prove it?" Tor asked.

"That's why I called you here. I think it's about time we widened the scope of our purpose here. Not only should we keep saving infected vampires, but we also have to find their link to Pritchard's death. I don't know about you guys, but I don't think I'll ever find peace until I get my hands on the people responsible for our friends' deaths." Harrow stood and began pacing the room, waiting for the rest to absorb the new information and voice their opinions.

"What are you suggesting?" Cyrus also stood, walking to the wall with the monitor. His shoulder muscles were taut, straining against his cotton shirt. He pushed a button, and the revolving bar emerged. "Drinks, anyone?"

"A glass of tequila with lime, please," Tor said.

Harrow shook his head while Rohnert deliberated for a second. "I'll take an XO, no ice."

"I'm thinking we should at least scout the place he lives tonight and maybe get someone to follow him around after that. It's a gut feeling, man.

I'm inclined to trust it." Harrow locked eyes with Cyrus, as if begging him to agree with the idea.

"I'm good with that," Rohnert replied.

Cyrus came back, juggling three drinks. He handed one to Rohnert and walked to the other end of the table to give Tor his drink.

"To Pritchard." Tor raised his glass and, without waiting for the others, downed his drink like it was orange juice.

"I don't have a problem with it. I dig the plan," Cyrus said. He took a sip of his cognac and smacked his lips. "My one concern is who Zane is to Demetrius. I want that established."

"No problem," Harrow said, satisfied with the support from the group. "Now, why don't we go out and see what this Zane character is up to?"

"Are you telling me that you're planning to stalk the poor guy right away?" Tor grinned, his red eyes flashing with excitement.

"I don't know about you guys, but I'm digging some action tonight." Harrow stood, turned off the TV, and brought the lights back up.

All of them blinked in the sudden brightness.

"Let's not get ahead of ourselves. Right now, all we have is speculation. Let's wait until there's enough evidence to prove the connection, and then we'll make our move. Understood?" Harrow picked up his Kalimetal from the floor.

"Yep," Tor said, as Cyrus and Rohnert nodded.

"Why don't we drive this time?" Cyrus suggested.

Harrow looked at Cyrus, knowing the human couldn't keep up with them when it came to running, even if he was physically fit. Vampires, unlike humans, could withstand extreme physical exertion for a prolonged period of time.

"Your car—we ride," Harrow answered, and Rohnert chuckled.

"Give me the address, and I'll meet you there," Tor said.

Harrow's brows lifted. "What's going on?"

Tor shrugged. "I need some fresh air." He turned to leave.

"Rayce will give you the info. See you there," Harrow called out just before he got to the door.

"Want some company?" Rohnert followed Tor as the group walked into the hallway.

"No, thanks. One more night with you and everyone will think you have the hots for me." Tor chuckled, knowing the other vampire wouldn't be offended. He wanted to be alone so he could think without the stress of knowing someone was reading his mind. Rohnert smirked, and Tor knew he understood.

"Goran, do you have a minute?" Melissa asked, hesitating in the doorway.

"Certainly. What's on your mind?"

Goran looked up from the pile of books he was reading, giving Melissa his undivided attention, just the way she liked it.

She closed the door behind her and walked across the room. Goran was happy to see her. Although they hadn't been together in months, he knew she would service him without hesitation the minute he asked. But he was tired, so damn tired. Having a harem had its pros and cons.

That was the power he had over them as their creator. One call, a mere whistle, would bring them all scrambling to his feet to give whatever was asked. Just thinking of his women filled him with lust, pure and potent.

Melissa had been the fairest of them all, but in recent days her luster had ebbed. The once-eager vampire had been wilting like a neglected flower, looking torn and lifeless.

She stopped in front of his desk and fingered the bust of his father's father, a bronze replica of one of the more famous vampires in the Council.

She traced her hand along the sculpture absentmindedly. Goran already had an idea what she wanted, but he waited for her to voice it.

"Darling, would you care to sit down?" Goran asked after a few moments of silence.

Melissa looked up and nodded. He patted his lap, and a hint of smile graced her face. She walked around the desk and dutifully sat across his thighs. Turning her body to face him, she put an arm around his neck. Her scent wafted around him, and his lust began to rise.

"Tell me what's on your mind," he ordered, keeping his voice low, yet retaining the authoritative tone everyone understood.

"I have been wondering if you've heard from Demetrius," she began, and he felt her body shudder with sadness. The once-vivacious female was now an empty piece of shell, just because their son had been irresponsible enough to leave without a word.

"As a matter of fact, I haven't. I tried calling his mobile, but there was no answer." Goran kept his voice even. He held her tight, and his shaft responded with a jerk, ready to accommodate his healthy appetite.

"He's been missing for six months. Aren't you in the least bit worried?"

Melissa's mouth quivered. It was a weakness he loved among his women, but a weakness nonetheless. He reached out and touched her mouth, willing her to stop. Melissa bit her lip, her fangs digging into her lower lip. That did it for him. He felt himself spring to life underneath the zipper of his pants.

"This is not the first time our son has left without a word. Of course, I worry about him. But he is a grown vampire, able to take care of himself. You shouldn't worry so much. He'll resurface soon," Goran said as he rubbed her back to soothe her.

"Shouldn't we be looking for him? Even a master would look for his missing dog." Melissa's voice broke, and she looked at Goran, beseeching him to understand.

The comparison was absurd, but he kept his expression light. He studied her face for a moment. She was right—he should send out a team to look for their son, even if the bastard had refused to give them the benefit of a "Hey, Dad, sorry I'm caught up in some shit, but I'll be home soon" phone call.

How could he not grant her little wish? The woman had served him well throughout the years. "All right. I will send some people to look for him," he said, granting her wish.

"Will it offend you if I look for him myself?"

Goran frowned. His hand stopped in midrub while he considered her request. "No . . . but I want you to take a few people with you. Arm yourselves, and make sure you're back well before daylight."

"Thank you." Melissa's face lit up, and she flashed a gracious smile. "Your consideration knows no bounds."

"I will hold you responsible for the people you take with you," Goran said, a warning tone in his voice.

"You have my word, my dear Goran." Her voice tinkled with excitement.

In the blink of an eye, Melissa's demeanor changed. She pressed her body against him, and her mouth came down to seize his. She sought entrance with her hard kiss, and he opened his mouth in welcome.

Melissa turned to face him and straddled his waist, and he inched forward to give her luscious limbs enough room to move. Her mouth stayed on his, tongue twisting and inviting. Goran's hands ran along the curve of her back and made their way to the coil of her glorious mane. With one twist, he removed the elastic that held up her red hair. It fell across her shoulders, framing her face like she was aflame.

"You are a beautiful creature, Melissa." Goran's voice grew husky, a sign that she got his attention. To him, nothing could beat a woman with flaming red hair.

She tossed her head and let her hair brush his face, the scent arousing him even further. Without waiting for further invitation, he slipped his arm around her back and lifted her without effort. Goran walked to his bed and laid her on the soft, satin sheets. He jumped onto the mattress with the lithe movement of a panther ready to devour its prey. This was a going to be a feast fit for a king. He smiled, and his fangs elongated. He could feel every fragment of his body reacting to her magnificent offering.

He straddled her body, and Melissa gathered her hair in one hand. She arched her neck, encouraging him to drink from her. Not needing more provocation, Goran sunk his fangs into her jugular, releasing his zipper at the same time.

He let her velvet blood coat his mouth before swallowing. Feeling the rush of his arousal flooding his senses when her blood began to fill him, he continued to take long pulls from her vein. One hundred percent pure bliss enveloped him as he rubbed his body against hers.

Goran could do this forever. Melissa, Milla, Annie, and the rest of his harem would bring him infinite satisfaction.

"Ally, I want to play outside." Gail looked up from the educational show they'd insisted she watch instead of the cartoons she preferred.

Allison gave the little girl a questioning look in response. "Bored already?"

"I've been watching TV since we got here. Daddy said I could go outside and play here because there are no cars," she said, whining.

Daddy, as everyone knew, was Harrow. Gail had developed an intense affection toward Harrow. One thing about the little girl, Allison recognized, was her flair for manipulation. The little imp could get away with anything just by using her puppy eyes and batting her long eyelashes.

"Let me see if Uncle Lambert is up to it."

Yeah, she was just like everyone else. Ready to give Gail anything she asked for. What was it about this little girl that made it difficult for them to deny her?

Allison took the elevator one floor down and found Lambert and Drake in a sparring match. Their grunts filled the room while they kicked, smacked, and punched. Their bare feet swished against the rubber mat as they circled each other, sizing each other up and planning their next moves. The protective vests and headgear made them look like overgrown kindergartners in their first sparring class. Allison swore under her breath, not sure if she was amused or irritated.

She had asked several months ago to be trained and armed just like the rest of them, but it seemed that her request had been pushed to the bottom of the pile and forgotten. Either they were too busy or they were ignoring her. Allison suspected it was the latter. No one wanted her fighting. Harrow had expressed his displeasure many times with her desire to fight. He, along with Cyrus and Tor, would rather she remained the porcelain doll they thought she was. Funny—she knew she had what it took to fight, if one of them would just take the damn time to teach her.

She coughed loudly and impatiently enough to make her presence known. Both men stopped and swung their heads to look at her.

Allison chuckled at their surprised expressions, as well as their unspoken question.

"Gail wants to play outside." Allison stated her business with a rather forced smile.

Lambert rolled his eyes, and Drake laughed.

"I guess we're back in the babysitting business," Drake said. The human was tall and lanky, in his late twenties, smart, and always eager to help. He was another of her father's trusted recruits.

"Yep, sun's too bright. I don't think I'd last three minutes out there," Allison said and turned to leave. "Get her out of here before she drives us all nuts. I'll have her ready in ten minutes."

"Allison," Lambert called after her. She turned to him, and he walked across the room, removing his sweaty helmet to reveal a disheveled flat top haircut.

"Yes?"

He took her by the elbow and escorted her out of the room, out of Drake's earshot. Lambert looked behind him, and his face glistened with the sweat still pouring thick from his forehead.

Allison twitched her nose when the powerful scent of his sweat swam around her.

"I just wanted to ask if you're okay," Lambert whispered. His voice was deep, and his brown eyes searched her face. Sure, he had the right to ask and worry. After all, he was like an uncle to her; she had known him before she transitioned to what she was now.

She didn't meet his gaze, afraid he'd see right through her. "I'm fine. Why do you ask?"

"Well, for one, you have been acting a little strange lately. Two, you're never abrupt. I'm just wondering if there was anything you wanted to talk about." Lambert, no matter the circumstances, had always been straightforward.

Allison had always found him easy to talk to, and yet today, she couldn't. "Define strange."

Lambert drew a long breath and blinked. Twice. He focused on her face and tilted her chin up to him. "You seem angry, sad, confused, and most of all, lost. I can sense you want something."

Newsflash, I feel all of the above, Allison wanted to scream. Instead, she shook her head. "I'm fine." Lambert narrowed his eyes, so she added, "Really."

"I'll pretend to believe you this time. But I want you to know that you can talk to me anytime. I'm sturdy, and I promise not to squeal." He grinned.

"Believe me, I'm fine. I just feel like I need to get away. But everywhere I go, I have people following me, trailing me, keeping vigil as if I'm going to suffer a breakdown all the time!" Allison threw up her hands in indignation.

"We're here not to crowd your space, Ally. We're just here for protection. You're very precious to us, if you didn't know it yet."

Touched by his words, she felt like crawling into the nearest hole for the way she acted. Lambert deserved better. After all, he just wanted to help, and here she was, biting his head off for offering.

"I'm sorry. I didn't mean to yell. Thanks for your offer, Lambert. I'll keep you in mind if I need a shoulder to cry on." She turned and walked away.

Allison returned to the top floor and found Jordan tugging the zipper of Gail's sweater. The steel shutters were tightly drawn, but a glint of sunlight still managed to slip through the tiny slits. The room was dark except for the glow from the television, where four different-colored, bloated-looking aliens and sporting televisions on their tummies were dancing around. Despite her crushing mood, she let out a brittle laugh at the absurdity of the characters.

Jordan's head whipped in her direction. "What's so funny?"

"They are," Allison said, not even sure what about them was funny anymore. She was about to unravel and had to get away fast. But where would she go?

"Duh, Ally. They're the Teletubbies." Gail rolled her eyes, sounding like she was ready to share a wealth of information about these funny-looking humanoids. "They're cute. I like them a lot."

"I know, honey," Jordan said.

Lambert and Drake appeared at the top of the stairs, still dressed in their sparring outfits of black T-shirts and nylon sweatpants. They both wore jackets to conceal the weapons they carried.

"Ready, princess?" Lambert asked and smiled when Gail rushed to his side and wrapped her arms around his thigh.

"Yes, Uncle Lambert." She jumped. "Can I bring my bike?"

"Sure. Bring your kneepads and helmet, too."

Gail jumped again and rushed out the door. "Daddy said my stuff's inside the garage," she said, squealing.

Lambert shook his head and Drake chuckled as they followed Gail out the door. The sound of little girl's rambling echoed long after they had left.

Allison went into the kitchen, opened the stainless steel refrigerator, and surveyed the well-stocked interior. There was nothing she wanted to eat. What she craved was outdoors, and she wouldn't be able to help herself until Tor returned.

She slammed the door shut and stomped to the entertainment room. Jordan watched her with mild concern.

"Are you okay, Ally?"

She tapped the control and loud music blared. "If anyone asks me again if I'm okay, I swear I will scream!" she yelled.

Tor reached the upscale part of the city in a fraction of the time it would take the rest to arrive by car. The chance to be alone and clear his mind of all the muddled thoughts of Jessie and Allison was invaluable.

He surveyed the area and stood across the street from the impressive rows of buildings, which housed the city's finest condos, co-ops, and penthouses. In the dead of night, a handful of people, mostly couples, strolled by. They avoided him, going the other way when they saw him looming in the shadows, menacing and edgy.

Although humans had no idea what kind of beings walked among them, they had an inherent sense of self-preservation. Tor knew that a quick glance told them he was dangerous, and he was all right with that. It didn't bother him one bit when people pretended he didn't exist.

Leaning against a lamppost, he watched the humans trip over their own feet to avoid him. Men tightened their grips on the waists of their women and glared. Tor chuckled under his breath. Why were they so threatened by him? Did they have an idea of what he was? Or were they judging him on his appearance?

And there he was, thinking how great he looked in his tight jeans and leather jacket. Well, whatever. He glanced at his reflection in the window of a parked car. God, he looked like he'd been in a train wreck. His hair was downright filthy. The dreads he'd been sporting were in bad shape and in need of a detangler. Part of his face was concealed by the grimy, unkempt strands. He was sure his appearance was the primary reason people were avoiding him. He looked like a cross between a gangster and a washed-out musician—someone you wouldn't ever dream of bringing home to your mother.

It made him wonder what Allison had been thinking when she offered herself to him without reservation. Didn't she possess a functioning intellect to alert her that he was bad news with a capital B? Couldn't she sense the danger? No matter how much he pushed her away, she seemed to come back harder and more persistent. Allison had better clear out of his way, because there would come a time when his threadbare self-control would snap, and heaven help them if that happened.

There was no doubt in Tor's mind that Harrow wouldn't see him as a good boyfriend candidate for his adopted sister. Harrow had seen his massive tattoos back when they were roomies. Tor had been careless about hiding his body art, and Harrow had done a double take in spite of his bad eyesight. Despite his stares, Harrow had kept his questions to himself, sticking to his favorite policy: Mind your own business.

It worked for Tor. He kept his ink hidden, so there were no questions from others and he didn't have to tell any lies. At one point, he had told Harrow about his incarceration, but they'd left it at that. That conversation had never been revisited.

Several more minutes passed, and more hand-in-hand couples paraded past him, bringing back the old feelings of regret. Could he be more fucked up? He'd had the best life he could have imagined for himself, but he'd thrown it all away because he had been too weak to say no. If he could turn back time and change his life, he'd gladly do it. He would do anything to have Jessie back in his arms. But no, she was gone. Dead. Because of him.

Burns focus! He swore at himself.

He heard the hum of an engine and turned to see the guys pulling up to the curb. It looked like they had been laughing at him as he stood motionless while staring into space. Rohnert was the only one who did not look amused. Tor guessed the royal vampire was well aware of the thoughts screwing with his mind. He shuddered, knowing he'd have to explain to everyone some day, beginning with Harrow. Just as soon as Tor could muster the courage to drag his deepest, darkest secret into the open.

"Traffic was a bitch," Cyrus complained when they joined him in the shadows. Each had their preferred weapons tucked inside their jackets.

"Is there anything going on?" Harrow asked.

Tor shook his head. "Negative. Just couples strolling by. No one who fits the bill."

At that moment, a kick-ass Porsche pulled up in the front of the building, and Zane stepped out. He wore a sleek, black suit, his red hair was pulled back in a ponytail. Handing the keys to a waiting parking attendant, he walked around the car to open the door for a lovely woman in a floor-length white dress. Zane looked around before leading her into the building, where they disappeared from view.

Tor let out a growl. "Fucker's gonna score tonight, no doubt."

"Abso. Guess we'll park our asses here and wait," Harrow quipped before heading back to the car to begin the stakeout. The rest followed.

Tor groaned at the prospect. His body twitched for some action. "Boss, you mind if I bail?"

Harrow looked up and considered the question for a minute. "I'll go with you," he said, not giving Tor a chance to refuse. "Cy, you guys don't mind?"

Cyrus shook his head. "Not at all. Have fun."

Tor wanted to scream. He didn't want company, but refusing would raise more questions, so he tilted his head. "Ready?"

Melissa left Goran's chambers on feet that were light and buoyant. The simple fact that Goran had consented to let her leave Council grounds was a cause for celebration. Normally, as soon as his women were acquired, they stayed closeted in their own quarters until he summoned them. They were his puppets, and their existence was based on servicing his insatiable needs and whims.

She first went to Graciela's door and instructed the vampire to get ready. The harem was Melissa's pet project, despite the fact that they all belonged to Goran. She was their leader, and they followed every command she gave them.

Melissa went to Milla's quarters next. She could hear Milla's half-human baby girl crying when she was about to pound on the door. Although she and Milla had forged a close relationship, the younger vampire was still competition. One call from Goran would wipe out any bond between the two women. Deciding against pulling Milla away from her maternal duties, Melissa threaded down the hall to Annie's room.

Annie was their newest member and, by far, the most beautiful. A vibrant redhead, her timid smile, waiflike figure, and unassuming personality could melt anyone's heart. Despite being Goran's flavor of the month, Annie had been a reluctant vampire. She was often tearful and restless, crying for the daughter she had left behind.

Melissa had no idea where Goran found his women or what his criteria were for selecting them. The one glaring similarity between them all was the color of their hair. He hadn't discussed any other considerations with her, and so their real purpose remained undisclosed. Aside from being sexual partners, they were his trophies. They were also lethal due to the countless hours of training.

Melissa had realized the women were an army he could call on when needed, such as when he used them to settle the vampire rebellion. She smiled at the memory of the carnage they had left in their wake. Unsuspecting vampires had been put to the test when they faced an army of beautiful women. Beguiled and almost in a trance, the rebels hadn't been prepared for the slaughter that followed. They were stupid creatures besotted with lust, which had led to their downfall. Goran had been right—the rebellion had been quashed without much effort.

She knocked on Annie's door and heard the rustle of footsteps inside.

"Yes?" Annie opened the door and stuck her head out. Her mouth twitched into a small smile upon seeing Melissa.

"Want to get some fresh air?" Melissa asked.

The door opened wider, allowing her a glimpse of Annie's sparse, haphazard domicile. Books littered the table, their spines showing wear. Boxes of designer clothes lay untouched on the floor by her bed. Unlike Melissa, who dressed to please Goran, Annie wore what pleased her. She had yet to learn to adhere to their lover's preferences, but it hadn't ticked off Goran, who adored Annie with animated perversion.

Dressed in boot-cut jeans and a white cotton T-shirt, her feet were bare. "I don't know if we're allowed to," Annie answered in a plaintive voice.

Melissa stepped into the room, and Annie closed the door. The scent of her sadness hung heavy in the air. Taking this female with her might just be a good idea.

"Goran is allowing me to go out and take a few females with me. I thought you could use some time out of this place."

Overwhelmed by her invitation, Annie hesitated before she accepted, acting as though the offer had been for a lifetime of freedom, rather than a few hours of unmonitored abandon.

"Bring weapons and dress in comfortable clothing. I'll come for you in ten minutes." Melissa turned to leave, but then remembered an important detail. "Annie, let me just remind you that this is a few hours of liberty, nothing more. When I say it's time to go, I mean it."

Annie nodded.

Melissa had no idea where to look for Demetrius first. Where to start in such a massive city? She went out so seldom that this adventure was both exhilarating and terrifying. The last time she had been out was when she'd led the harem to squash the rebellion upstate. Goran had been pleased with the outcome of her mission.

Ten minutes later, Melissa and her companions stepped out into the balmy summer weather. With the two women flanking her, she walked with purpose despite not knowing where to begin. Graciela looked confident and very much at ease, and Melissa sensed the vampire's eagerness by the spring in her step and the rapid pumping of her heart. Annie, on the other hand, was quiet, tentative, and scared-looking. They were all dressed similarly: comfortable slacks, dark sweaters, and their hair pulled away from their faces in elegant buns.

"Where to?" Graciela asked, her eyes darting left and right. They were in the heart of Rockefeller Center, where throngs of tourists milled about the concourse.

"Let's walk around and see where it leads us," Melissa said, and she led the way out of the tangle of revelers and into the bigger and denser jungle of Fifth Avenue.

"What is the purpose of this outing?" Graciela had always been the outspoken one. Svelte and beautiful, she was a chatterbox but a likeable female among the group. Graciela kept her hands in her pockets while she and Annie matched Melissa's graceful strides.

"I just wanted to get a breath of fresh air," Melissa answered, ushering the women across the street, where cars fought for every inch of space.

From the way Graciela snorted, Melissa knew she hadn't bought the explanation, but she didn't feel any pressure to divulge her true reason. Maneuvering through the madness around them, they made their way deeper into the heart of the city.

What had Demetrius done when he was out on his run around the city each night? He frequented establishments where he sought infected vampires. This had been Goran's focus—to rid his city and its neighbors of the diseased ones.

With no plan or lead to follow, Melissa decided to start with a benign-looking club, but the line at the entrance snaked around to the alley. Waiting for admission to a grungy club was the last thing on her agenda, and Melissa knew nothing of patience. She walked to the front of the line, with Graciela close on her heels and Annie trailing behind.

The doorman glanced at them. Melissa knew how to charm stupid vampire males, and humans were even easier. She pasted on her brightest smile. Her fangs contracted until they were almost nothing but prominent canines. The bouncer gave her body a quick once-over, stripping off her clothes with his eyes. Melissa swayed closer and whispered in his ear, "Let us in, darling."

The man sighed, no doubt mesmerized by her proximity, and removed the velvet cordon to let them in. Groans of disapproval trickled from the long line, and Graciela flashed the waiting patrons a cheery smile and a shrug before walking into the standing-room-only club.

Hardcore rap music pounded from the speakers. A mass of bodies jumped and jerked to the beat, and the sharp scent of sweat mingled with the distinctive scent of vampires, making Melissa draw in a sharp breath.

"Let's separate and mingle," she said.

"What for?" Annie asked, recoiling at the notion of being alone.

"What are we aiming to accomplish here, exactly?" Graciela narrowed her eyes.

"I'm looking for Demetrius," Melissa answered, feeling her heart constrict with pain at the mere mention of her son's name.

"Who is Demetrius?" Annie asked. "And I . . . don't know what he looks like."

"Don't worry. Between Graciela and me, if he's here, we'll find him." Melissa felt sorry for Annie, but she wasn't here to babysit. The other woman would have to learn to fend for herself. "Why don't you order us some drinks?"

Annie looked aghast. She hadn't known life outside the Council chambers after her transition and had no idea what they were capable of as vampires. "Drinks?" she asked as if the very thought would cut off her air supply.

"Yes, we drink. Just like before. I'll have a Cadillac Margarita. Graciela?"

"Um . . ." She paused to think. "Get me a strawberry daiquiri."

"Okay." Annie left, dragging her feet and looking like she off to face a firing squad rather than the simple task of buying drinks.

"Jesus." Melissa exhaled and began walking around. Anyone in her way moved aside like the parting of the Red Sea. She had no way of knowing if these humans sensed her otherworldliness, but the awe showed on their faces.

Vampires and humans gawked at her like they were seeing god for the first time. A mix of amazement and curiosity showed in both the briefest glances and the most prolonged stare. Melissa enjoyed the attention and smiled but reminded herself of her mission. She straightened her shoulders and made her way slowly forward through the maze of bodies on the dance floor.

She was intent on finding her son.

Tor sat idly at the bar, Harrow next to him talking on the phone. The moment they'd secured a seat, Harrow's phone had rung, and he'd been deep in conversation with Jones ever since. It sounded important, but that was beside the point. They were out to have a good time. Tor wanted to drink until he slipped into oblivion.

Might as well be alone, he thought, feeling glum.

As heavy rap music pounded in the background, Tor looked around the room, relying on the strobe lights bouncing around to provide entertainment. The mix of vampires and humans was thick in the club, making it more than interesting. He and Harrow were on a break, but Tor still found himself on the lookout for any danger that might be waiting to happen.

"What will it be for you?" a tall, slender bartender with her arms covered in tattoos asked, eyeing Tor with more interest than necessary.

"I'll have two shots of Patron silver, and he will have . . ." Tor nudged Harrow and hissed, "Drink order?"

Harrow covered the receiver with his palm and thought for a second. "I'll have what he's having." And then he returned to his phone conversation.

The bartender nodded and went to fix their drinks. Tor studied her ink. The tattoos were showcased across her arms and the back of her neck. Tor noticed the phoenix and tribal tattoos blended well, despite the disparity between the mythical and savage styles. For lack of anything better to do, Tor kept his gaze glued on the intricate work on her flesh. The bartender returned and caught him staring. She handed him his order and placed Harrow's shots in front of him.

"Like what you see?" she asked, her voice taking a quick dive into husky.

Instead of answering her, Tor picked up a glass, not bothering with the salt or the lime, and downed the shot. He went for the next glass and did the same thing. The woman's brow shot up.

"Want another?" she asked.

"Just give me the damn bottle."

The woman smirked. "I'll get you a fresh one then." She held out her palm and rubbed her thumb and forefinger together. Tor pulled out his wallet and slipped two hundred-dollar bills into her hand.

The bartender smiled. She came back with a bottle and change, which Tor pushed back to her. "Keep the change and bring me some more shot glasses, will ya?"

"I'll bring you that and more." She leaned forward, took the bills from the bar, and slid them into her cleavage while licking her lips. The smile she gave him would have given him a huge hard-on in the past, but his focus at the moment was on getting blessedly drunk.

When he did nothing but stare at the robust enticements that were inviting him to take a bite, she blew him a kiss, handed him some shot glasses, and left him alone.

"What the hell, Harrow?"

"Jones, I gotta go. Tell me more about it later," Harrow barked into the phone before hanging up. He turned, looked at Tor, and chuckled. "I think someone needs a hug. Stop pouting, my dear child." Harrow lifted a glass in salute before slugging it back. "So what do you want to talk about? I'm all ears, darling," he said with mock sweetness.

"Shit, Harrow, don't even attempt to annoy me," Tor said, pushing the bottle in Harrow's direction. "Shut your mouth, will you?"

"Payback's a bitch, isn't it?" Harrow laughed.

Truly it was. The tables had turned, and it was Tor's time in the hot seat. The barbs and teasing he'd showered on Harrow one too many times in the past were now raining down on him.

Harrow's laughter stopped in an instant. He turned and looked around before closing his eyes.

"What's going on?" Tor asked, feeling for his weapon and standing up. Harrow pushed him back down into his seat.

"Hold it, Rambo. I just caught the scent of some infected ones we might want to see later. Go on and get drunk. I'll see to it that we get you home in one piece, sweetheart."

"What will it take to shut you up?" Tor scowled.

"Tell me what's bugging you. Been having a lot of dreams about the boogeyman?" It was not a question—they all knew Harrow monitored everyone. He said it was for their safety.

Safety, my foot! It was a clear invasion of privacy. Tor snorted and drank some more. Mr. Patron would love him for supplying him with so much business in just one week. They'd be best friends soon at the rate Tor was going.

"You know I don't like people snooping in my business. If you want to know something, all you gotta do is ask."

Harrow seemed to consider this. "Well then, tell me what's bothering you." He maintained a steady gaze behind his glasses, which were a safety precaution in a place like this. After all, his hunted status hadn't changed, even if his disease hadn't made a return appearance.

Ah, finally—the question. There was nobody he would tell his deepest and darkest secret to but Harrow. Tor would be insane not to trust the vampire. They had been through a lot of shit together. At the very least, Harrow would listen before he booted Tor out of the operation.

"I'm not as pure as they come," Tor started.

Harrow raised an eyebrow, and Tor felt like an idiot for his choice of opening line. He poured another shot and took a quick swig. *How long before this goddamn alcohol floored him?*

"Tell me something I don't know."

"That's what I'm trying to do here, if you'd give me a moment and stop with the smartass comments."

Harrow laughed and gestured, zipping his mouth after flashing his fangs for a quick second.

Tor was about to speak when a face on the far end of the bar caught his attention. "Lord, have mercy," he muttered.

What the hell is wrong with the world? Was God asking for payback? He felt his loosened muscles tense back up. There, at the far end of the bar, stood a woman looking lost and out of place. She was a dead ringer for Jessie.

"What's wrong, Tor?" When he didn't answer, Harrow followed his line of sight. "Who the hell is she?"

Tor couldn't answer. He wanted to know the same thing. He felt all wound up and unable to breathe. How in the world had he ended up sitting here on his drunken ass and staring at the spitting image of his dead wife? Well, except the hair. Jessie had brown hair, and this woman's was fiery red.

Harrow nudged him now. "Tor, you're acting crazy, man. Who is she?"

"How the hell would I know?" He got up, but Harrow blocked his way. "If I were you, I would leave me alone."

"Well, go ahead. Make an ass of yourself. Be my guest." Harrow stepped aside.

Tor didn't even hear his parting words. All that mattered to him was to get to know this woman and find out why the hell she was tormenting him.

He walked the length of the bar, shoving people aside, his gaze transfixed on the woman. The music wrapped around him, but the only sound he heard was the beating of his heart, which was doing the electric slide inside his chest. Tor stood behind her while she paid for her drinks, his tongue tied into a nice ribbon inside his mouth.

She turned around, trying to juggle three drinks, and almost ran him over. When he didn't move to let her pass, she paused.

"Excuse me," she said.

"I need a name," he croaked, which was the last thing he'd intended to do. He mentally kicked himself for sounding like a pussy.

"Pardon me?" the redhead asked, looking as puzzled as he was by the situation he'd found himself in.

"Your name. I want it," he choked out. Damn it. It looked like his voice box had gone MIA on him.

"That is the funniest pick-up line I've ever heard." She laughed, but it was a shaky one that told Tor that she wasn't very comfortable in her own skin.

"What are you?"

"What kind of question is that?" Her earlier uneasiness was replaced by annoyance.

"I . . . err . . . I just want to get your name. I'm sorry. I'm Tor. Would you care to sit with me? I have a seat over there." He gestured to where Harrow was sitting and watching them.

The woman hesitated, but then slowly nodded. "Let me get these drinks to my friends, and I will join you in a bit."

When Tor heard her response, he almost skipped aside to let her through. What had gotten into him? He returned to his seat, still in a daze.

"What the hell was that all about?" Harrow asked as soon as Tor had parked his butt on the swivel stool and picked up another shot.

"She looks like my dead wife," Tor stated without pretense, and he watched as Harrow's face went through an array of emotions in several seconds. He had to laugh at Harrow's shock over his announcement.

"Are you kidding me? You had a wife?"

"Surprise!" Tor pumped his fist in mock jubilation.

"Why on earth are you just telling me this now?"

"What good would it have done? Can't bring her back," he murmured.

"You're right, but I could still say I'm sorry." Harrow stopped when Tor threw him a warning glance. "How long ago was this?"

"Not long enough to forget. And now that woman shows up looking like —you know. I don't know what to do with myself." Tor turned to check on the woman and saw her making her way over to them. She was even around Jessie's height.

"Just to let you know, in case your radar missed it, she isn't human. She's one of us," Harrow whispered just before she came within earshot.

Was this another one of Harrow's tricks? How on earth had he known she was close by without even looking? The vampire was seriously scaring him now.

Tor dismissed Harrow's comment and turned to face the woman when she reached them. "Hello," he said, getting up to offer his seat.

Harrow beat him to it. "Take my chair. I need to stretch my legs." He gave her a small smile, which she returned with hesitation.

"Thank you." She sat on the barstool, looked down, and tinkered with her drink.

"Your name," Tor said as soon as Harrow had left.

"Annie Butler," she said after moment.

"Why does that name ring a bell?" he asked.

"It's a common name, I guess."

The room was bustling with energy, brought on by free-flowing alcohol and drugs. This was the type of place where drug dealers were in abundance.

Tapping his foot to the music, Tor tried to think of things to say. "What are you doing in a place like this alone?" What kind of a dumb question was that? He wanted to kick himself. At the rate he was going, he'd be kicking himself to death over the collection of idiotic things he'd be blurting out.

"What makes you think I'm here without company?" Annie asked.

He noticed the cute little freckles dusting her face. How old could she be? She could be an infant compared to his sixty years.

"Well, let's see . . . men don't let their women grab their own drinks."

Annie laughed. It was shaky at first, but the last tinkle sounded more real, more relaxed.

"You're right. We're just hanging out. That's all." Annie sipped the last of her drink.

"Can I buy you a drink?" Tor asked, wishing she'd say yes so they could spend more time together. Yeah, he wanted to talk to her a bit longer so he could tell himself that he was a loser, using the woman to drink to the memory of his dead wife.

"Shirley Temple, please."

Tor laughed. "What is a beautiful woman doing in a rap club filled with questionable types and drinking a virgin drink?"

"Are you one of the questionable people, Tor?" Annie asked, genuinely interested in his response.

"Most definitely. But don't worry about me. I'm reformed now. I wouldn't hurt a fly." He gestured for the bartender. "Shirley Temple for the lady."

Annie laughed and Tor grinned. "Do you come here often?" she asked.

"This is my third time here, but who's counting? Is this your first?"

"Yeah."

"Annie!" A voice called from across the room. It was loud enough for vampires to hear no matter what the situation but inaudible to human ears given the loud music that drowned out all other noise with its powerful bass beat.

Annie's head whipped around at the call, and Tor looked across the room to find another knock-out waving at her. *What the—? Another redhead?*

"Listen, I gotta go. It was nice meeting you, Tor, even though you are questionable. I'm sorry about the drink." She fumbled in her pocket. "Let me pay for it."

"Forget it. I think it's time for me to try Shirley."

The joke elicited another delightful laugh from Annie. "You're a funny one, Tor."

"Meet me here again?"

"Why?"

"No reason. Just want to get to know you. Nothing heavy, just new acquaintances hanging out. Sound innocent enough?"

Annie paused and thought about his invitation. "Sure. How about same day, same time next week?"

"Sounds good." Tor reached out his hand. "It was a pleasure meeting you, Annie Butler."

Annie placed her hand in his calloused one and shook it. She was lovely, and her hand was oh-so-soft, just like Jessie. He would love to see her familiar face again and punish himself further. Yeah, he was a glutton for punishment. It was masochism in its truest sense.

"I'm sorry for screaming," Allison said after her short tirade.

It seemed like a monumental task to control herself these days. Her anger and aggression, and even her raging hormones, were off the chart. The latter was most problematic, since Tor had been reluctant to indulge her —not that she'd ever confess she was interested. Although the abruptness with which their kiss ended should have given him a hint.

Jones had better give them some straight answers soon, or she'd go nuts. This whole dormant disease thing was like winning the lottery, but the side effects were something she hadn't signed up for. Harrow had passed the test with flying colors since Jordan threw caution to the wind and decided she'd be with him no matter what.

It was much different for Allison because she was unmated, single, and alone. It would have been easier to deal with life's curve balls life if she had someone, like Harrow had Jordan.

"It's okay. I think I understand what you're going through." Jordan glanced at her.

The two women were lounging on the deck. The sun had disappeared, and another night beckoned them to leave the protection of the shutters.

"You think? What do you mean by that?" Allison propped her chin on her arm and leaned in Jordan's direction.

"You know, Harrow can be a pain in the ass, too. He's had moments of volatility. He's cold one moment and exploding the next, biting my head off." Jordan laughed. "We're like an old married couple; we bicker all the time but our . . . *you know*," she said, batting, "is *amazing*." Jordan flushed, and their laughter bounced off the walls.

"TMI!" Allison covered her ears. "I'm so happy for you, Jordan." She smiled and leaned back in her lounge chair, but the smile dulled a moment later. "I wish I could say the same," she admitted. "My one claim to fame from our diet of animal blood is that I act like a menopausal maniac."

Jordan gave her a half-smile, not denying her claim. "It's not too bad. I wish you could have who you want."

Allison's face fell. "Who do you think I want?"

Jordan rolled her eyes. "Tor. I've seen the way you look at him. The way your body responds to him, whether he's being stupid or not."

"That bad, huh? I wonder what everyone else thinks." Allison groaned. It was no use. Tor wasn't interested, period. The way he'd pushed her away confirmed what she had already suspected. He was just doing his job, and she was his assignment. She stared into the darkness.

"Not at all. I thought you weren't interested in what other people think."

"That's true. Well . . ." She smiled.

Ever since her diet change, some aspects of her personality had gone through some subtle changes. A few were more noticeable than the others. One of those was her inability to keep her opinions to herself and the increase in her sex drive. The latter was more problematic, considering her single status, not to mention being a carrier of a communicable disease.

"I say you should go after him."

"I did, and he turned me away." Allison gazed up at the sky and sighed. "It wasn't pretty at all."

"Oh, I'm sorry to hear that." Jordan turned thoughtful. "I suspect Tor is going through something. You know how men are. They don't talk about their feelings or what's bothering them. It's that whole 'grin and bear it' attitude."

"They're idiots." Allison sighed again.

"You're not giving up, are you?"

"I don't think so. At least not yet. I want him to open up. If we can't be anything more, then we can be friends. Except—there's the Gates Syndrome. That is not going to be easy to ignore."

Jordan nodded. It did pose a problem for anyone infected because there was a risk of spreading it to his or her mate. Some might be lucky like Harrow and Jordan, but the disease seemed fickle. It bounced around, with different side effects in different people. No two cases were ever alike. The only things that were constant were the white irises and the distinct scent the lesions produced. Once a vampire had changed their diet, then their reaction would vary. In Harrow's case, he had experienced halo around images, improved hearing, and an odd way of sensing what others were thinking. It had nothing to do with mind reading, but he likened it to sonar —someone could make a sound, and he understood what they meant. It was something that he had discussed with Jordan and Allison in passing, but he'd been unable to elaborate further because he lacked solid proof. Furthermore, Jones was merely scratching the surface on his research, since Harrow had experienced many more changes than he'd detailed to them so far.

Jones had been hard at work, and eventually the resident surgeon, Dr. Shelly Anderson, had joined to lend a hand. Since the facility's operation had been trimmed back to a minimum and the appearance of infected vampires had dwindled, Shelly had tried to find more time to help Jones researching the cure.

"I'm sure there'll be a way for you and Tor to be together," Jordan said after a long silence.

"Not sure about that. Remember, he pushed me away. I don't know why I even bother sometimes. Before I turned, I was doing pretty well with the opposite sex. It's not like I ever lacked male companionship, know what I mean?"

Jordan nodded.

"On the contrary. I was a normal college student who was enjoying life." Allison couldn't help the deluge of memories that hit her. There would be no taking back what the years had done to her and her family. She had found herself alone, and heaven knew what she would be willing to give to have her parents back, to feel the sun on her face, and to be able to lead a normal life again.

Allison couldn't get those things back for all the billions she had in the bank. She'd rather live like a pauper than lead a lavish life in the darkness, always afraid and ever-vigilant. Not normal. Fate's only design was to screw her up.

"Don't fret, Ally. Everything will turn out okay in due time. I have faith in what we're doing here and all of the good people surrounding us." Jordan reached out and squeezed her friend's hand. "Who would have thought I'd feel this way after what I went through?"

Allison squeezed back. "I hope you're right. I really hope you are."

Cyrus and Rohnert spent the better part of the evening cooped up in Cyrus's car waiting.

"I say, let's bail. The bastard is probably defiling that poor lovely lady again and again," Cyrus said.

"Didn't Harrow say he wanted coverage here?" Rohnert asked, although it was obvious the vampire was getting antsy.

"True." Cyrus pulled out his cell phone. "Lemme call Holt. He's a good at stake out jobs. I'll have him park his ass here so we can take a little stroll."

After Holt had agreed to relieve them, Cyrus and Rohnert made their way home through the city. It was a good night to be on a stakeout. Cyrus popped in a CD and Aerosmith began playing. Rohnert sat in silence, trying to ignore Cyrus while he sang with Steven Tyler for the entire song.

"What do you feel like doing?" Cyrus asked.

"Whatever you want, I'm good with it." Rohnert shifted his legs in the cramped car.

"How about we scout out a local bar? It's been a while since I've been out. I wonder where all the infected ones are hiding?"

"That is the million dollar question. We have to give Jones and Shelly something to do," Rohnert remarked.

Cyrus snorted. "So have you seen the good doctor lately?"

Rohnert glared at Cyrus. "What for? I'm not sick."

Cyrus snorted again and laughed. "Nothing. Just asking. With Harrow working them so hard, we ought to give them a chance to take a break. You know how Harrow is. The vampire can get anal about the smallest detail. He's worse than Pritchard."

"Do I hear a complaint?" Rohnert laughed.

Cyrus shot him a quick glance. "Hell, no. The guy is doing a freaking good job. I betcha Pritchard had been pretty damn smug over his decision to get Harrow up in there and leading our group." Cyrus returned his attention to his driving, although their location hadn't improved all that much. They were still stuck somewhere in the vicinity of Times Square.

"I think so, too. But that vampire needs a break or he'll snap."

"I agree. Maybe we can kick him out once the whole demolition thing is over and done with." Cyrus looked thoughtful, stroking his chin.

Rohnert leaned back and tried to block the thoughts that were on a rollercoaster ride in the human's mind. It wasn't impossible to do; he just needed to tune out and channel his attention to other things. He closed his eyes and began scrubbing Cyrus's internal chatter out of his mind.

But then thoughts of Shelly crept in, just like they had so often in the recent past. She happened to be the most effective block for the cacophony of thoughts that swirled around him.

Yeah, the good, smart-mouthed doctor could distract him for minutes at a time, but he shouldn't go there. It was impossible. Humans and vampires didn't mix that way, not with the Vampire Council's edict that he should procreate like a damn stallion. He'd rather be alone than force himself to be with someone he didn't care about.

Complicated shit wasn't his style, not since he'd let go of his feelings for Jordan. He'd hopped onto a solo saddle, and he preferred to stay that way.

The car made a sudden turn, and Rohnert lifted his eyelids to check what was going on. Cyrus stopped the car in a loading zone, shifted into park, and rushed out of the car, leaving the engine running and the keys in the ignition.

"Where the hell are you going?" Rohnert's question came a little too late, since Cyrus had already bolted out of earshot.

Rohnert pulled the key from the ignition and ran after Cyrus, who had disappeared into the alley next to a cigar shop. He caught up with the human in no time. "What are you doing?"

Cyrus signaled for him to keep his voice down and pointed ahead. Once they reached the dead-end alley, Rohnert understood what Cyrus was up to. A woman screamed for help before the sound was muffled.

A human woman was trapped by two male vampires, and one of them was about to take her vein. Cyrus acted swiftly and threw a dagger at the vampire's head. The second vampire pulled out a gun and aimed at Cyrus, but Rohnert pulled out his Kalimetal and deflected the bullet before flipping in the air. The first vampire fell to the ground, releasing the woman, who began to scream again, and the sizzling sound of the disintegration process began.

"Be quiet!" The other vampire ordered the terrorized woman while he yanked her backward to use as a shield.

The vampire was fast and rained bullets in the air while Rohnert flipped to evade the shots. This gave Cyrus the chance to drive a dagger straight into the vampire's heart. The ensuing crackling sound joined that of their first kill.

"Thanks." Cyrus nodded at Rohnert and rushed to the woman to quiet her down.

"No thanks necessary," Rohnert said, kicking the ashes with his boots and scattering the powder in the air.

"Stop screaming. We don't want cops involved here. Go!" Cyrus told the woman, whose eyes were wide with fear.

"But they disappeared. What is going on?" she asked, her legs unable to support her sagging weight.

"Speak of it to no one. You'll be better off. Do you need a ride?" Cyrus was a gentle man, despite his appearance, and his expression now was filled with compassion.

"I don't . . . know," the woman cried, and her body shook violently from the shock of being attacked.

Rohnert knelt next to Cyrus and tilted her chin up to look at him. When she met his gaze, he said, "You're not going to talk about this experience. It never happened. We'll get you a cab to take you home, and everything will be all right."

The woman drew her head back as if mesmerized. "Yes."

"Good," Rohnert said and helped her to her feet. Instead of letting her walk on her own, he held her arms and led her out of the alley. Cyrus followed them, scratching his head in amazement.

"Gotta bounce," Tor said into the walkie-talkie before he strode out of his room.

The intermittent sounds of the wrecking ball still rang through the structure.

Many of the facility's inhabitants were either cloistered inside their quarters or out for the night. Harrow had made it a point to have most of the active members of their team patrol each night, looking for more infected vampires to rescue.

Their first and foremost goal remained in place: to save the unfortunate vampires caught in the massive dragnet of the Vampire Council, which continued to eliminate each and every vampire they considered a stain upon their name.

"Where are you headed?" Harrow's voice crackled on the radio.

"I told Allison I'd take her out hunting tonight."

"Why can't Knox or Peyton take her? You've barely had a chance to rest after all that drink you guzzled last night."

Tor was getting sick of Harrow's mother hen act. "Because I told her I'd take her. And besides, I don't trust those vampires."

"You don't trust them? Why?"

"Damn, Harrow—what's with the questions?"

"Tor, I'm not one to tell you what to do—"

Tor pressed the button and spoke into the mouthpiece. "Then don't. I'm outta here." He threw the walkie-talkie on the hallway table before going up the stairs to the parking garage.

Looking around the huge parking lot filled with cars of different size, make and model, he weighed his options. Negotiating the busy city streets in a car would slow him down. Running was out of the question, since he was tired to the bone. Even so, his muscles were wound tight and his mood was edgy. The last thing he needed was to sit in traffic and risk a lethal case of road rage.

Tor continued searching for a suitable mode of transportation until he spotted a Ducati sitting in the corner of the lot. The sight made him smile. He walked to the brand-new machine and caressed the shiny body. Borrowing it wouldn't be too difficult—the key was in the ignition, and a helmet hung invitingly on the gleaming handle.

He hopped on the motorcycle and smirked at the camera on the wall. Tor waved at the device and drove away, the gate opening in response to the sensor on the bike. He sped out of the facility, using the underground tunnel.

The temperature had been fickle that evening. With the thermometer dipping into the low thirties, the frigid wind slapped his face while he wove in and out of traffic until he eased the motorcycle onto the freeway. He left the headlights off and stealthily zoomed by each car like a thief in the night, alert and very much enjoying himself.

Three hours later, he reached the compound with a smile still plastered on his face. The ride had been exhilarating, and it had given him the period of solace he had sought. After parking the motorcycle in the garage next to the bulletproof car, he closed his eyes and tried to get the feel of his environment. He could hear several muted voices chattering and the television belching a SpongeBob song. No doubt Gail was having one of her cartoon marathons again.

Pulling off the helmet, Tor smoothed his dreads as best as he could, but it was no use. The bastards had minds of their own. Giving up, he hung the helmet on the handlebar and strode to the door leading to the house.

When he entered, Jordan looked up from the sofa where she sat with Gail and smiled. He gave her a quick nod and proceeded to the bottom floor, taking a deep breath as he stopped in front of Allison's door.

Tor could sense her, which was all good, but it was perverted at the same time. He'd done this too many times in the past six months: absorbed her emotions and watched her every move. Was it stalkerish? Pervy? He wanted her safe and happy, and most of all, he wanted her.

Tor, you bastard! Stop swimming in stupid thoughts. You're nothing to her. Nothing! He scolded himself before knocking on the door. The sound echoed in the empty hallway.

When Allison opened the door, instead of the smiling face he had grown accustomed to, her expression was empty. She looked at him with impassive eyes when she pulled the door wider to let him in.

"Ready?" he asked. He remained by the threshold, not wanting a repeat of the incident two nights ago. The memory was still fresh in his mind, and it was a constant struggle to erase the visions.

"Yes, but don't you want to rest first?" Allison asked. Even her voice sounded dull.

"I'm good. After you." He gestured to the door, and Allison walked past him, pulling the hood of her sweatshirt over her head.

They walked the hallway in silence. Tor had no idea how to break the ice. He was not one for smart conversations. If the subject wasn't about action flicks or the elation of a kill, he drew a blank, so he decided to keep his mouth shut.

"Jordan, we're going out hunting. Let Lambert know if he asks, will you?" Tor said.

She nodded in acknowledgement before Tor and Allison walked out of the house by way of the garage.

"Where do you want to go?" he asked once they had reached the small creek not too far from the house.

Without giving him a response, Allison planted her heels into the muddy ground and sprinted away, leaving him in a blink of an eye.

"Damn woman," Tor said under his breath and bolted after her.

Allison might have been a female, but she was fast. It took Tor several heartbeats to catch up with her. Running beside her, oblivious to the direction in which they were headed, Tor snuck a glance at Allison's face. She was intent on her undertaking, but her expression showed a side of her at which Tor often marveled. The mischievous part of her personality only surfaced during their hunting expeditions.

Watching Allison hunt and feed was a sort of a paroxysmal experience for him. There was something sensual about the way she prowled, stalked, and caressed the animal before latching her fangs onto its vein.

That wasn't to say that he was keen on taking down an animal for his own consumption. He preferred the red juice above anything else. He would rather rot and shrivel up instead of taking in animal blood. No matter how hard Jordan and Harrow tried to persuade him about its benefits, he couldn't imagine himself tugging at a four-legged creature's veins. No sir. He wanted his meal in a crystal goblet in the comfort of his room, with his fingers wrapped around the remote control. The comfort of the facility was his heaven, and a reprieve Pritchard had shared with him and the others.

"Earth to Tor, earth to Tor," Allison teased.

He hadn't even noticed she had stopped running. He eyed his surroundings first and then settled on Allison, who seemed to get a kick out of seeing him all zoned out. True, he had been having a lot of "duh" moments lately. He shook his head and brought himself back to earth.

"Sorry," he grunted before his ears pricked up at the faint sound of hooves moving nearby.

Allison's head whipped in the direction of the dim noise, and she brought her finger to her lips, signaling for silence.

Tor crossed his arms over his chest, letting Allison find her groove in time to pounce on a stray elk. He watched her elegant movement as she lifted up onto the tips of her toes before she jumped up like a crazed monkey and landed on the animal's back.

The sight was magnetic, and he allowed his eyes to feast on Allison's amazing form when she began to devour her meal. Each pull and tug mesmerized him, reminding him of a James Bond movie when 007 grabbed a girl and kissed her until she almost passed out. He walked to a tree and leaned against it, observing Allison's every move. From this vantage point, he had the best seat in the house. Even under the cloud of darkness, he had no trouble seeing everything, and every sound was like a loud whisper. Tor let the harsh cold embrace him while he continued enjoying the sight before him. Allison's fluid motion was graceful, and she was beautiful. He was struck with a sudden urge to hold her, but he restrained himself, keeping the errant emotion at bay.

Allison looked up at him, her eyes wild.

"What's wrong?" he asked, taking several steps in her direction.

She didn't answer right away. Her steady gaze seemed like she were searching his face for something. Uncomfortable, Tor shifted on his feet several times, looking down at her with his tongue tied in knots.

"Do me a favor and bury the carcass for me. I want to hunt for another one." She sprung to her feet, her eyes fiery and energized.

"No problem. Stay close where I can hear you," he muttered.

Allison gave a half-smile, the corner of her mouth dripping with blood. She wiped away the remnants of her meal with the sleeve of her sweatshirt before turning toward the sounds of creatures that moved not far away. Like a breeze, Allison was gone, leaving her scent for him to enjoy.

Tor got to work. He ignored the tautness of his body and the discomfort from his hardened shaft. The damned thing was hard enough to use as a weapon. Cursing under his breath, he picked up the drained animal, surveyed the area, and spotted an area with soft enough earth where he could dig. With his bare hands, he dug away the dirt, working like a maniac and ignoring the throbbing between his legs.

Within a few minutes, he had excavated enough soil, and he threw the carcass in the grave, smoothing the dirt back on top of it. He smirked at his handiwork, content with the half-assed funeral he'd performed, and wiped his grimy hands on his jeans. The thought of adding "gravedigger" to his resume made him laugh out loud. It was funny how everything had turned out for him. One day, he'd been nothing but a vampire without purpose, and in the blink of an eye, everything had turned upside down. Well, at least it was in a good way.

He turned on his heels and followed the cry of an animal being slaughtered. What had begun as a loud and ear-splitting howl soon eased into a whimper, and he followed his nose to where he knew he'd find Allison. Just when he turned into a dense formation of trees, he caught the scent of outsiders unexpectedly close to where Allison was. Tor sprinted to her location. He spotted two men approaching Allison, who at the moment was rather preoccupied with her kill and oblivious to the danger looming behind her. Tor pushed himself faster, hurling his axe in the direction of one of the vampires.

No can do. No one dares touch her, not while I'm alive.

The element of surprise was in his favor. Before the other vampire knew what happened to his buddy, Tor was already pulling out his T-dagger. He flung it through the air and straight into the chest of the unsuspecting vampire.

The fizzling fireworks followed, and what used to be two vampires ready to pounce became nothing more than a heap of ash on the ground. He glanced at the metal Vampire Council badges on the ground and the weapons, which were the only survivors of the disintegration process.

Had he acted on impulse without asking what the deal was first? Hell yeah, and he'd be happy do it again.

Allison looked up from her feast with dazed eyes. Her face registered confusion before the details clicked into place. She bolted upright, dropping the lifeless animal and running to Tor, who closed his arms around her. He tilted her face up and searched it, just to confirm she was unscathed for his own benefit more than hers. He felt her body quiver under his touch, and he held her even tighter.

"From now on, I go where you go." His voice brooked no argument.

The short trip back to the house was spent in uncomfortable silence. Tor jolted at every little sound, and his fingers dug possessively into Allison's arm. She could see the veins in his neck straining underneath his skin, and his mouth was set into a grim line. Everything about him screamed "Livewire! Beware!" There was nothing she could do to help the situation, so she decided to keep her mouth shut.

When they reached the house, Tor moved so fast he blurred while he checked all the doors and windows, making sure they were tightly shut. Afterwards, he called the rest of the men and Jordan together for an emergency meeting in the kitchen.

Lambert gave Allison a sympathetic look when he passed her on his way to the meeting. She sat on the sofa and closed her eyes. What had started as a simple outing had turned into a potential disaster, all because she'd gotten a bit too excited and had left without Tor. It shouldn't have mattered. She had to be able to go out wherever and whenever she damned well pleased.

She sighed and strained to hear the conversation in the kitchen. The hushed exchange was hard to catch, even with her extraordinary hearing. She knew the only ones missing from that meeting were her and Gail.

Something about the whole situation was wrong. It wasn't that she was out of Tor's visual range or even out of his control, but that everyone in that room was talking about, well, *her*. For crying out loud, every damn person in that house was on her payroll. They could, at the very least, give her the courtesy of an invite, fighter or no fighter.

That was the sticking point in this whole scenario. Allison would always be different, just because she was the precious daughter of their fallen leader. She would always be the damsel in distress, the one who'd always needed protection, and the weakest of them all. They treated her like they would Gail: a child unable to protect herself.

Thinking about it made her angry, and not knowing what the others were discussing made her angrier. It wasn't in her nature to throw a tantrum, but at that moment, she was aching to let loose. Instead, she stomped out of the room and down the spiral staircase rather than taking the elevator. She burst into her room and slammed the door shut. *Sure, Ally, no tantrums, right?*

Allison slumped onto the bed and curled into a tight ball. She wasn't tired. On the contrary, she should be feeling invigorated. However, her body seemed to be shutting down. There had to be some changes in the system, a way to make Harrow listen and give her a chance. She should be able to protect herself like the others could defend themselves.

They were all equal, according to her father. Harrow believed the same thing. A little sliver of hope made her push her body up, despite its unwillingness to uncoil, and she grabbed her cell phone on the nightstand.

Selecting Harrow's number, Allison was connected to Rayce even before the first ring had ended.

"Where's Harrow?" she asked, not bothering with pleasantries.

"He's sleeping. That's why his call routed to me," Rayce said.

"Please get him for me. Ring me back when he's on the line," she instructed before hanging up.

She blew a frustrated breath, moved further under her sheets, and closed her eyes. Within a few minutes, her phone rang.

"Allison, you wanted to talk to me?" His voice was thick, an obvious sign he'd been asleep.

Allison felt bad for taking such precious rest from him, but this couldn't wait any longer. She dove right down to business. "Yes. Harrow, remember I told you I wanted to learn how to fight?"

There was an immediate silence at the other end of the line, and she knew Harrow well enough to guess he was deliberating his answer.

"What's going on?"

Allison let her lids drop and whispered into the phone. "I'm sick and tired of being the odd one out. I have to be able to do something more productive with my life. Something I can be proud of."

"Ally, c'mon. I'm sure you don't think of yourself that way. You're very important; that is why everyone will fight to keep you alive."

Although she wanted to believe him, there was the pressing issue of what she wanted for herself. "I don't doubt what anyone would do for me, for my father's sake if not for mine. I want this for myself, Harrow. Surely, you of all people know how it feels to be singled out and treated like a rare species."

It wasn't fair to bring up Harrow's past torments, but she needed to prove her point. What would give him more understanding than the memory of his own experiences?

"I don't know . . .," Harrow paused. "Hold on. I have a call on the other line."

With a click, he was gone. She waited and listened to the silence, fixing her eyes on the ceiling. Dusk was arriving and soon they'd be prisoners of the sunlight again. The limitation was terrible and unfair, but there was no one to blame for their predicament.

After another minute of waiting, Harrow came back on the line, and his tone made her flinch. "Allison, why didn't you tell me that you were almost attacked in the forest tonight?"

That was unexpected. Who could have told him? Tor? Lambert, maybe? Nevertheless, she still wanted to get her message across. "That is precisely why I'm asking to be trained. I want to be able to help out with patrolling and protect myself at the same time."

"Damn it!" Anger was something Harrow had never directed at her before, although she had heard him raise his voice to others in the past. "I don't want you going out to feed until I know for sure whether the area is safe. We have tons of preserved blood in every refrigerator. That's what you and the rest will have to use until the situation is assessed."

"What about my training?" Allison cried.

She heard an exasperated sigh, as if Harrow were trying his best to sound calm and collected. When he spoke again, it sounded like he was talking to a child.

"Ally, listen to me. I don't want you fighting. I don't want you out there for the same reason your father didn't want me to go. I was too important to risk, in case you've forgotten. I was the key to the cure."

"But . . . but we found a semi-cure, didn't we? It's not like I'm the one we have to experiment on." Tears trekked down her cheeks. Her suffering was nothing compared to the nightmare Harrow had endured during the experimentation period. She shuddered at the memory of his gaunt appearance during the purging days, when he had to rid his system of human blood in preparation for ingesting animal blood. The hunger in his eyes still haunted her.

"Good Lord, Ally, don't make this hard on me. Can't you understand? You're the one surviving piece of Pritchard, and we want to keep you with us. You're a symbol of hope for all of us. Your existence is what's keeping us from slinking back into the dark ages and going back to where we started."

"That's not fair," she said, sobbing. The floodgates were now open, and tears streamed down in a mad rush.

"Nothing in this life is fair, Ally. If I were you, I'd stay put and let the others keep me safe," Harrow said, his voice turning softer.

"Harrow, please!"

"Sister, I'm doing this for your own good. I have to go now—"

Allison didn't hear the rest. She hung up the phone without letting him finish. She was upset that Harrow wasn't more sensitive to her plight. Throwing the phone across the room in a rare display of anger, she buried her face in a pillow. The down feathers muffled the sound of her sobs. It felt like the walls were closing in on her—she was trapped by the very people she loved. This was the life she'd be leading, and acceptance was the only answer to her woes.

A soft knock on the door drew her out of the pillows. "Go away!" she yelled.

"It's Tor. Allison, let me in."

Let you in? Damn you to high heaven. How about you *let* me *in?*

She had the energy neither explain nor to drive him away. Knowing Tor, the vampire would set up camp outside her bedroom door until he saw her with his own eyes. How could he have let Harrow talk him into this bodyguard business?

"Open the damn door, Allison, or I swear to god, I will break it down!"

"I don't care about the damn door!"

"You're acting like a spoiled child," Tor muttered, his voice muffled by the thick wood dividing them.

"A spoiled child?" Her anger skyrocketed, and before she knew it, she was on her feet and opening the door with so much force that the hinges rattled. "What do you want?"

Tor appeared startled when he saw her tear-stained face. He walked inside, a few steps toward her and looked her over, as if to reassure himself that she was all right, before he spoke. "I wanted to see if you were okay."

"Do I look okay to you?" Allison wiped away her tears and glared at him.

"You're angry."

"Anything else you want to point out?" She slammed the door shut and faced him.

"I admit I called Harrow and told him what happened."

"You couldn't wait to blab." Her whole body was shaking with rage.

"I had to. I don't think you have any idea what kind of danger you were in back there," Tor said in a low voice laced with edginess. "Those were Vampire Council soldiers. They will kill any vampire who is infected. Once they had realized what you are, they wouldn't have hesitated."

Allison was taken aback by Tor's revelation. She knew of the dangers in the city, but who would have thought she'd be in any danger here in their isolated new home? "I had no idea."

"That's why I had to tell Harrow. These are the things we worry about. That's why one of us has to be watching you every single time you are out there," Tor said as he gestured in frustration. His eyes never left her face, as if there was more he wanted to tell her.

"But it doesn't change the fact that I can't protect myself in any given situation!" She picked up a crystal vase and hurled it at the wall.

"I'm always with you. Why would you need to learn to fight?" he asked, eyeing the pieces of broken glass on the floor.

"Have you ever felt vulnerable in your life, Tor? Like your hands were tied and you couldn't do anything?" She turned to him in frustration.

Tor didn't answer. He slid his hands into his pockets and looked at her.

Frustrated, Allison started pacing again, unable to rein in the raging frustration building inside her. Her tears just made her angrier. How was she supposed to make the others see that she was capable of fighting alongside the best of them if she kept crying like this?

"Fine. Don't give me an answer. But that's how I feel. If someone jumps me, am I supposed to just smile and look pretty? Don't you see that I need to be able to do something if I'm ever in that type of situation again?"

She stopped pacing and faced him. Tor walked toward her, his eyes darkening and his expression intent.

"Ally," he whispered.

She jerked when he used her nickname. Tor had always been formal around her, so the last thing she expected was this show of tenderness. It sounded almost like a term of endearment, which only made her tears flow faster.

"Damn these tears!" Allison complained.

"There's no shame in crying. Your feelings mean that you're alive."

This was a side of Tor she'd never seen before. Allison was certain she saw concern . . . and maybe something more. She'd give anything to get inside his mind, but she doubted he'd tell her what he was thinking even if she asked.

"Crying means I'm weak, too," she whispered.

By this time, her body was drained of energy, and her sobs had become unstoppable. Allison went to her bed and laid down, facing the wall in an attempt to hide her face, even though she was too tired to care if Tor stood there and watched her. She was tired of it all.

"Do you want me to keep you company while you sleep?" he asked.

She thought about it. No matter how much her mind told her to say no, she nodded her head. "I want you . . . to hold me." *There it was, out in the open.* Allison closed her eyes and waited.

She expected Tor to argue or, at the very least, to stomp out of the room. What he did was more than she had dared hope for. There was the dull thud of shoes being toed off, and then the bed dipped under his weight when he lowered himself beside her. Tor folded one arm around her shoulder and slid another under her waist. "Sleep, and I'll be right here with you," he whispered in her ear.

Allison took a deep breath and closed her eyes, unable to speak for fear of ruining the moment.

The first day of each new lunar phase meant a meeting of the Vampire Council would commence. Goran left his study and went to the assembly hall. All of the members were expected to be seated and waiting for him.

He had a list of agenda items he wanted to discuss, among them the disturbing disappearances of soldiers over the past week. One team hadn't returned from its scheduled patrol. A two-vampire team had disappeared from their rotation and hadn't been heard from since. There were two possible explanations he could think of. One, the soldiers had been killed, but this was unlikely since they had been trained to fight and were lethal. Besides, killing Council soldiers warranted a punishment of death. Goran was well aware that no one wanted to tangle with them.

Another scenario was that the soldiers had defected or had left the force, which might be a likelier possibility. He'd be damned if he'd allow such betrayal to happen. Being a soldier for the Council was an honor and a privilege not afforded to many. It would be an insult for soldiers to leave such a coveted position without notice. If this were the case, then he would have no other choice but to add them to the list of the Council's enemies. They would be hunted down and marked for death, once found.

Goran reached the assembly hall, and the doors were opened by two Council guards, who bowed their heads low in veneration. "At ease," he said as he passed them.

All the seats in the chamber were already occupied. Five vampires sat on one side, and four on the other. Every Council member dipped their heads in a customary show of respect for their leader. Goran climbed the five steps to the chair that faced the council elders and sat down. He acknowledged each member, bowing his head to them in turn.

"Greetings, my fellow elders. We have much to discuss. Who will address their concerns first?"

All the members looked at each other, each reluctant to speak. When a few seconds had elapsed without anyone speaking up, Goran turned to August, who was the eldest vampire and in charge of the Council's finances. Money always perked people up; it was a favored topic, whatever the time or the circumstances.

"August, would you like to make your monthly report?"

The vampire nodded and spread papers on a heavy wooden desk in front of him, shuffling through them. Goran hid his impatience. After all, by human standards August was approaching his 583rd birthday. This made him a very old man, but the vampire still sported the gait of a fifty-year-old human.

"Our business dealings are all in good standing. Every investment is bringing in solid returns." August motioned for a Council aide to distribute the reports. Once each Council member had a copy and had begun looking through the reports, August spoke again.

"As you can see, most of our holdings show profit, and the margin for returns is positive. I am well pleased with our investments."

"As I am," Goran said after he'd leafed through the stack of papers on his lap. He looked up at August with a satisfied expression. "Anything else, my old friend?"

August's smile faded a fraction, and he shifted in his chair in apparent discomfort. "Goran, I'm afraid I found questionable spending in your son's account," August admitted.

"Tell me." Goran felt the heat rising up to his cheeks.

"There were several transfers made from his account to another." August paused, his expression that of someone who'd rather be anywhere else. "My apologies for not speaking to you about this sooner. It must have escaped my notice." The aged vampire turned pale under his wafer-thin skin.

Goran stared down each of the Council members, daring them to speak. None uttered a word, although a few shifted in their seats, hungry for more information.

"How long has this been going on?" Goran asked, feeling his fangs piercing his lower lip, despite his intention to keep his composure. No one, and that included his son, should keep vital transactions from him. Demetrius had pushed him to the limit. There would be consequences for his actions.

August remained quiet, and Goran knew the reason. This had gone unnoticed far too long. He would have to have a serious talk with the vampire after the meeting.

"Long enough, Goran," August said, sounding abashed.

Goran nodded in understanding. "We shall talk more about it after this meeting. I'm sure we have more important matters to address right now."

Marania raised her hand, and Goran shifted his attention to her. "Marania, my dear. What do you have for us?"

The keeper of old records and tallies of purebred vampire names, Marania stood up in all her glory, her black velvet robe sweeping behind her luscious figure. Her regal features reminded Goran of a French queen he'd met in the last century.

Marania looked at Randolph as if requiring a backup before she spoke, her crimson eyes sparkling. "Goran, you have been in power for three centuries now." She paused to gather unseen strength. "And I might add, doing a phenomenal job."

"You flatter me, Marania." He laughed without mirth and gestured for her to continue.

"It's our law, if I could humbly remind you, that as a leader of our race and a pureblooded vampire, it's time for you to produce an heir. The time is upon us." Her voice trailed off after she'd confronted him with such a significant demand.

While Marania shrunk in her skin, Goran stood up and walked down the steps. He stopped in front of her, his manner cold and calculating, and he smiled. It was a smile that showed how pissed off he was at being placed in a compromising position.

"I have not forgotten our law, and by my blood, an heir will be produced. I don't require a reminder that it needs to be done," he said through gritted teeth.

To her credit, Marania didn't ease off like others did under Goran's evident anger. Instead, she continued to further establish her point. "You are two centuries away from stepping down from your seat. By our sacred law, you must have an heir before the end of the fourth century for your bloodline to continue ruling. If this does not happen, we will be forced to appoint another bloodline to rule."

Goran glared at her.

Randolph stood up and spoke. "Goran, the aristocrats have been soliciting information about you and your plans. I'm aware that you are familiar with the integration of bloodlines. Many are interested in providing you with a suitable mate who may be of help in continuing your line."

In short, they had rich and influential whores willing to sleep with him in exchange for a shot at the seat he would soon vacate by law. How could he not be interested in women of his own class? The sticking point had always been clear. None of these women were redheaded, and so not one of them appealed to him, not one.

How in the name of all that was holy and sacred was there no vampire redhead with pure blood? The peculiarity of their inherent makeup baffled him more than ever. Getting around the law would be tricky, but he wouldn't stop until he found an acceptable solution to alleviate the concerns of the Council members.

"I will call on you, Randolph, if I need your help," Goran said, growling, unsuccessful at masking the antagonism raging within him.

"And you will have it any time it is needed," Randolph said before he retook his seat. He was a straightlaced vampire from an impeccable bloodline, not a vampire Goran would cross lightly. The man was, without a doubt, a competent character, and he wouldn't have second thoughts about leading the council if he were ever promoted to the position.

Such a shame the next family in line wasn't his.

Goran walked the dark carpet that bore the Council's seal. "Anyone else have an important topic they want to address?" After reaching the outermost edge, he paced back to the front, where he turned to face those he ruled.

Iden, a newly inducted member of the Council, looked at him but didn't say a word. It had been less than fifty years since he had taken the seat vacated by his father. Goran tried to read Iden's mind to discover any unspoken discontent, but they all possessed the same gift and could change the direction of their thoughts. It was a trick halflings had no idea the pure bloods possessed.

Goran leveled a steady gaze at the other Council elders. Alphonsus shook his head, while Wendell and Icarus looked straight ahead without comment. Bretania and Serena both smiled but remained silent.

"Very well. I have a concern I want to address." Goran went back to his seat and lowered himself into it. "We have several soldiers missing. Six are unaccounted for."

"By missing, do you mean they are dead?" asked Bretania, their weapons and tactical expert. A female of great standing, she was fair and beautiful, but not to be mistaken as weak. She had taken Rohnert's place when the vampire had vanished without a trace. From Demetrius's last report, Rohnert might be responsible for the recent sightings of vampires adept in a martial art form that was his unique specialty.

"That could very well be, but they also could have abandoned their positions," Goran said, clarifying his statement. "Either way, we must get to the bottom of this soon."

At last, Iden spoke. "Then we should send out your army to gather that information for us." It was general knowledge in the Council that Goran kept an army of female soldiers for his own use. No one had ever found the nerve to question his motives.

Goran met the vampire's gaze and tried take in the general tenor of his emotions, but he drew blank again. Iden was just as canny as he was, never lowering his mind shield even for a millisecond to allow others to catch a glimpse of his thoughts.

"I might just do that," he answered. "If I discover that any of our soldiers have abandoned their positions, I will order immediate execution. I don't believe in second chances; that would lead to our downfall."

Everyone nodded in agreement before moving on to discuss other routine matters that required less of Goran's concentration. He half-listened to whatever Randolph was explaining, already caught up in his plans.

He needed to find a pureblooded mate soon—a redhead if he was expected to get aroused enough to sire offspring. Where in the hell would he find such a woman?

"Got time for a quick sparring match?" Harrow said. Pritchard had left him with a tremendous amount of responsibility, and all of it was weighing down on him. Hard.

"Sure thing. Meet you in the training room in a few," Rohnert replied before the line went dead.

Harrow took a quick inventory of his clean clothes and grabbed an old pair of sweatpants and shirt. He'd had to let go of some staff, and that, of course, meant they had to do much of the menial work themselves. He wasn't complaining; he didn't mind doing the work at all. Heck, a change of clothes hadn't even been an option before he met Pritchard. A bed that got made every single day and a closet full of clothes, courtesy of their personal shopper, was more than he would have hoped for. But that was all gone now, for safety's sake. The fewer innocent lives associated with them, the better.

Christ, he was bone tired. As much as he wanted to be there for everyone, he felt like a wound-up cable, ready to spring.

Harrow decided against wearing his sunglasses. Sparring with Rohnert would only get them broken, and he'd been going through Oakleys like they were disposable razors. He did a quick glance in the mirror and didn't like the man staring back at him. His irises were almost white; even the retinas were turning dull now. Although his disease had been kept in check, its effects were enough to let anyone know that he was a carrier.

There was no reverting back to normal. Jones had suggested Harrow wear colored contacts, but with his bad eyesight they would slow him down even more.

As of late, he found it helpful to depend more on his other senses. His sonar-like hearing had much improved after his diet alteration, a remarkable change. If he kept his eyes closed during practice or actual fighting, he seemed to perform much better. This had led to the discovery of his greater advantage when fighting in close quarters: Somehow, the echoes of sounds created by others could be used against them. The echolocation Jones mentioned had sounded freaky at first, but it made sense once Harrow experienced it firsthand. Saying that he was blind as a bat couldn't have been more accurate. He was able to use the pulses from the small sounds his opponents made to get a mental picture of their movements and location.

After slipping on his running shoes, Harrow left his room and into the hallway. His earlier conversation with Allison drifted back while he made his way into the training room. Oh, man, how he wished he could grant her request.

Rohnert was already warming up on the mat and gave him a good once-over before resuming his warm up.

"You look like shit," he said.

"Thanks. Good morning to you, too, sunshine!"

Rohnert snorted and gave him a longer look. "Spit it out, man, before you burst."

"Before I do that, tell me something, and please don't lie to me. Do you know what I'm thinking at the moment?" Harrow sat on the mat next to Rohnert. He spread his legs and started stretching.

Rohnert stopped mid-stretch and released a lungful of air. Instead of meeting Harrow's eye, he fixed his stare on the deep blue mat in front of him.

"Yes. It's an advantage we full-bred vampires have over others."

Others, meaning the created vampire population, Harrow thought. "So you know exactly what's in my mind?"

"I won't call it spot-on."

Liar! Harrow decided to push.

"I'm anything but that." Rohnert smirked. "It's more like perceiving, getting a glimpse. It's hard to explain, so I guess, to put it in simpler terms, yes, I have an idea of what you're thinking." Rohnert looked uncomfortable with the admission.

"There's no shame in that, my friend. Besides, you're keeping whatever you know to yourself, right?"

Rohnert nodded.

"So it's all good. I can imagine it must be tough on you."

"You have no idea."

"I'm sure some of thoughts are downright stupid, maybe even comical."

"I learned the art of fine-tuning. I try to respect everyone and give them privacy. If their body language tells me that I may be able to help, that's when I'll turn the dial and give a damn." Rohnert grinned and continued stretching.

"I knew you were fucked up when I first met you," Harrow said.

"You didn't answer my question earlier. Spit it out. I know something's bothering you."

"Well, what's the point in saying it if you've got the whole picture already?"

"Stop. It's about Allison, isn't it?"

Harrow stopped stretching and looked at Rohnert in the eyes, despite the haze. "She wants to learn how to fight," he stated plainly.

"What's the big deal? She wants to learn, then by all means, let her."

Rohnert was missing the point.

"I don't want her fighting. I can't imagine her out there. She has us. We can protect her," Harrow said, insistent.

"Don't pull that crap on Allison you tried with Jordan. She's a tough girl, although she doesn't know it yet. Yes, we're here, but she needs the confidence of knowing she can take care of herself, too. You, of all people, should understand that."

"Funny, she said the same thing." Sighing, Harrow tried to picture Allison in the rotation. "I don't know, Rohnert. Tor is able and willing to watch her."

"Sure, but the man has his own demons to contend with. He's capable, but that's beside the point. Don't take anything away from Allison. She has the right to defend herself from any threat."

Rohnert's explanation made sense, and Harrow took his time to digest everything the vampire had said.

"Damn it, Rohnert. I would almost think Allison put you up to this." Harrow narrowed his eyes and studied the other vampire.

Rohnert did not respond.

"What about Tor and his demons?"

"Not my story to tell," Rohnert answered, pressing his lips together.

"What about those vampires Tor killed in the forest? They were from the Vampire Council. What were they doing there?"

"I don't have the slightest clue. I have been out of the loop for a long time now, but I will call the soldier whose life I spared and ask what business they had in the area."

Harrow voiced the nagging thought he'd had since Tor's call. "It gives me the creeps to think our family is out there where the Vampire Council can get to them at any time."

"I'll get to it right away. In the meantime, what will you do with Allison?"

"I think you're right; she has to learn how to defend herself. And you, my friend, will teach her all the shit you taught me." Harrow finished his last stretching exercise and got to his feet. "What are you waiting for? Let's get this show on the road."

Rohnert sprang to his feet and moved away. With a snicker, he flashed his fangs at Harrow and crouched into a fighting stance, drawing his Kalimetal from its sheath on his back.

Allison woke up and glanced at the red digital numbers on her nightstand. It was one o'clock in the afternoon. Feeling disoriented, she was about to get up when she felt an arm tighten around her waist, preventing her from moving. Everything came back to her. Tor had offered to stay with her until she fell asleep, but he had fallen asleep, too, his massive body wrapped around her like a shield.

Feeling grateful, she smiled to herself and snuggled against him. If this was a dream, she'd be waking up soon, so she had to enjoy the embrace while she could. She'd take whatever she could get. After all, Tor was likely to run away as soon as he realized that he was holding her this close.

Allison pressed her body to his, enjoying their position. He was spooning her smaller frame, just how she'd pictured couples lying together on a lazy Sunday afternoon. Of course, Tor didn't know what he was doing, but she didn't care. She listened to his even breathing and inhaled his masculine scent. The musk of earth and plants still lingered on his clothes. Allison closed her eyes at the feel of his hard cock against her butt. She could lie like this forever, unmoving within his firm embrace.

The steady beating of his heart provided the background music to her daydreams. Each even inhalation and every exhale were music to her ears, making her wish this moment would never end.

Tor twitched in his sleep, and his hands began to quiver. After a few minutes, he jerked again, and his arms loosened their hold. This gave Allison a chance to turn and face him. His eyes were firmly shut, his eyes rolling underneath the lids. Sweat beads began to form on his forehead. Another minute lapsed, and Tor started to turn. There was nothing Allison could do, and she debated whether she should wake him up. For a time, she watched him, feeling helpless.

When he started mumbling, she knew he was having a full-blown nightmare and that she had to do something. Although his words were nothing but gibberish and Allison knew she should wake him up, her curiosity got the better of her. She leaned closer, trying to make sense of what he was saying. Tor's body began to toss. He was drenched with sweat, and Allison removed the flimsy sheet that covered them. It didn't help.

Violent hand thrusting and kicking followed, and his words became clearer. "I didn't mean it. No! I'm sorry, Jessie. I love you, baby. No . . . no . . . come back to me."

Who was Jessie? He loved her? The realization that he had somebody else hit Allison hard. No wonder he kept denying her. He was taken. Not wanting to hear any more, she decided to rouse him. She stored his words in her memory for later.

"Tor . . . Tor." Allison shook him gently, and Tor gave another hard kick, hitting nothing but air. She got up and straddled his body. Turning his face, she gave his cheek a little slap to wake him. "Tor. Tor, wake up. You're having a nightmare."

It took another minute of calling his name and shaking him before Tor's eyes popped open. His immediate reaction was to jump, sending them both tumbling onto the floor. He unsheathed his axe from its holster and aimed.

"Tor! You're having a nightmare. It's okay. It's just you and me here." Allison pulled her body off the floor where she'd landed a few feet from him.

Tor looked around in confusion before her words registered, and he lowered his weapon.

"Christ, did I hurt you?"

She shook her head and crawled over to him. "Everything's okay. I'm fine. You're fine."

Tor flinched. "No." He pushed himself off the floor and held out hand out to her. She let him pull her to her feet. "I will teach you how to fight. You have to learn how to defend yourself. You need it against . . ."

Allison touched his face. "Against what, Tor?"

Tor shook his head with a pained expression. "We start now," he said, not bothering to answer her question. He raised her hand to his face and kissed her palm. "Before I change my mind."

Although she wanted to ask about Jessie, Tor's expression restrained her. This wasn't the right time. He pulled her to his chest and crushed her in a quick, fierce embrace.

"Is there anything I can do for you?" Allison asked once he'd released her.

"Yeah. Learn well and fast," he said before he shuffled her to the door.

"Harrow?" Rayce's voice came over the loudspeaker just as Rohnert landed an axe kick to Harrow's face that sent him staggering back to land ass first.

Good call on not wearing the Oakleys. Anyway, no one in the facility seemed to mind looking into the eyes of the *Omega Man* anymore, so it was all good.

"Are you okay?" Rohnert asked before Harrow raced to the desk to pick up the phone.

He placed a hand on his jaw, feeling for any damage, and nodded his head. "Rayce, what's up?"

"Just got a call from our team on patrol tonight. Harding is injured, and they're bringing him home." Rayce's voice held a trace of nervousness. After all, he'd been in the position for just six months. This was his first experience with situations of this nature.

"Damn." Harrow raked his fingers through his hair. "Alert Dr. Anderson and tell her to be ready. I'll meet the group at the clinic." Harding was one of their newest recruits, a human Cyrus had found during one of their night patrols. He was a resilient young man with a knack for learning martial arts.

After they'd hung up, Harrow looked up at Rohnert and shook his head. "Is this ever going to end?"

"Not yet," Rohnert said.

Whatever Rohnert meant, Harrow didn't have time to ask. He slipped on his shoes and ran out of the training room as fast as he could. Rohnert trailed behind.

Music was already blaring through the clinic by the time they arrived. Their doctor, Shelly, was a real gem. She moved fast for a human and possessed a strong stomach. Not only could she handle the blood and gore, but she also took the slew of vampires, who came to the facility for rehab, in stride.

One would think that a woman of her caliber, intelligent and in demand, wouldn't be caught dead in a place like this. Shelly could have landed a job in a much more desirable work atmosphere, but she insisted that she preferred serving the less fortunate members of vampire society, as well as their legion of human supporters.

Shelly's efforts and hard work were well compensated, although money and accolades seemed unimportant to her. Whatever her reasons were for staying, no one dared question it any more. Harrow was thankful for her mere presence and willingness to share her expertise.

"Smoke on the Water" pounded out of the speakers, and the doctor was scrubbing in when Harrow and Rohnert walked into the room. Several nurses were getting some apparatuses in place, while others were prepping the instruments likely to be used. Shelly glanced up when they entered. If Harrow hadn't been paying close attention, he would have missed the falter in her scrubbing rhythm as she set eyes on Rohnert.

Hmm . . . her body language gives her away. The doctor has a thing for our royal stud. Interesting!

"Don't even go there," Rohnert warned, speaking low so no one else would hear.

Ignoring him, Harrow parked his ass in the corner of the room where he wouldn't impede traffic, and Rohnert did likewise. "Hey, doc, are you ready?"

"As ready as I'll ever be," she answered in a chipper tone.

"Hello, Shelly" Rohnert said

"Rohnert," she said without sparing a glance in his direction.

Bingo! Harrow smirked. Something was going on between these two. He just couldn't quite put his finger on it yet. Rohnert's reserved demeanor combined with Shelly's gung-ho attitude was a match he'd loved to see. Shelly was in her corner with her guns blazing away, only to be met with Rohnert's little trickling water gun. It was quite a contrast.

Just as the music changed to another Deep Purple song, a commotion came from the hallway. The door burst open, and three men rushed in carrying the injured man. It was like a scene out of *House*, but instead of paramedics wheeling in the patient, one human and two vampires carried in their unconscious comrade.

They placed Harding on the bed and shuffled away, backing into a corner opposite Harrow and Rohnert. Grateful for their efforts, Harrow dipped his head in their direction, and the three returned his salute with grim expressions.

At that point, Harrow wasn't sure if he should be thanking some human god or a vampire entity for singling out a human to be injured this time. It wasn't that he wanted *any* of his men to get hurt, by any means. But if a vampire was injured, it would be by a Dangeran weapon, and they would be left with nothing but a pile of ashes. There wouldn't even be a body to bury. However, a human might still have a fighting chance at survival, no matter how great or slim. Thank God humans weren't susceptible to the Dangeran weapon. Injuries from a Dangeran blade would not kill unless the wounds themselves were fatal. It didn't have the same devastating effect on humans that it had on vampires.

They watched in silence while Shelly worked on Harding. Endless minutes ticked by before Shelly let out a loud whoop, deftly extracting the lead from Harding's abdomen. A blood transfusion was already in progress when she sewed him back together.

"He'll make it," she proclaimed once she'd removed her mask and the bloodstained gloves. She tossed them in the biohazard bin and washed her hands.

The three fighters, who had been quiet until now, pumped their fists and hollered in jubilation when they heard the prognosis. It was all good. Once again, Shelly had come through for them.

Harrow walked over to the sink and patted the doctor on the shoulder. "Good job as usual. Thank you," he whispered.

"Don't mention it," she answered. Harrow spied a little smile tugging at the corner of her mouth.

As the three fighters left the clinic, he followed them for some questions, although he noticed Rohnert stayed behind.

"Wait up," Harrow called after the others.

The men stopped and looked over their shoulders. Their wide smiles remained while they waited for him to catch up.

"So tell me what happened, beginning to end," Harrow demanded.

The three looked at each other, as if deciding who would be the official spokesman. Deuce, an infected vampire, drew in a sharp breath before he spoke. He was around Harrow's age, and judging from the brownish tint of his eyes, he hadn't been dealing with the disease long enough for the harsher side effects to develop before he got some help.

"Well, we were in a pool hall in the East Bronx when some goofy character started harassing me about my sunglasses. We had a heated exchange, and before we knew it, it escalated into an all-out brawl. Harding stepped in right when one of the idiots fired a shot. Everything happened so fast. People ran in every direction, and we just slipped out the back exit and brought him back here. The cops were already in the vicinity, but we got out before they locked it down."

"Sounds like you guys got lucky." Harrow studied each of his men, gauging their well-being before he spoke again. "Next time, avoid exchanges with anyone even if they're taunting you hard."

Deuce gritted his teeth but nodded. So did Mark, a human, and Firman, another vampire. "We will," Deuce agreed.

"Good. I know it can be difficult to pry yourselves away from such situations, but please practice more restraint. You may not be so lucky next time."

Once Harrow felt he had gotten his message across, he sent the three back to their quarters to rest and get ready for a debriefing with Cyrus in a few hours. He could still sense their edginess lingering minutes after they were gone.

Since he had nothing scheduled for the afternoon, Harrow went back to the bedroom he shared with Jordan to catch up with some family business. A call to Leo was in order to get a full report on the demolition. He hadn't dared step out into the open since the sighting of Zane Drew. A call to Holt would be the next on his agenda. The human was assigned to keep tabs on Zane's activities, and Harrow would love to hear the report.

Third call would be to Allison. Harrow needed to let her know how stupid he'd been for not listening. He was being overly protective, and he'd neglected to consider her feelings. The fact was, he had too much on his plate, and no matter how he tried to move faster, there were endless things that needed his attention.

He wondered how Pritchard had managed to keep his head above water and still maintain a smile on his face.

"Where are you taking me?" Allison asked, flinching away from Tor's fingers, which were digging into her arm.

"I'm going to teach you how to fight," Tor said, his voice sounding strained.

Jordan stepped out of her bedroom door and blocked their way. "What's going on?"

Allison wished Jordan would look at her instead of facing off with Tor. This wasn't a good time. Tor seemed like he was going to burst at any moment, and his eyes blazed.

"I'm going to teach her how to fight," he repeated, giving her the same explanation he'd given Allison.

Jordan's eyes shifted to Allison, and then down to Tor's death grip on her friend. She bared her fangs. "Tor, I suggest you take your hands off her," she demanded.

Tor turned and faced Jordan, but his hand remained on Allison's arm. Allison spoke up before anything ugly happened. "It's okay, Jordan. This is what I want."

"That may be so, but I don't like him handling you that way." Jordan stepped closer.

"How am I handling her, Jordan?" Tor's tone held contempt and something else Allison couldn't pinpoint. Tor might not be a gentle guy, but he wasn't known to have a mean streak either.

"Tor, ease off her a little bit," Jordan ordered.

Allison had tried to hide her discomfort, but Jordan knew her too well. Still, she didn't want Tor agitated any further. He looked like he was about to snap.

Jordan motioned toward where his fingers gripped Allison, and Tor released her at once.

"I—I didn't realize what I was doing," he stammered.

"It's all right, Tor."

Allison placed her hand on his shoulder, but his muscles remained tense.

"Let's go." Allison tugged at his hand, pulling him in the direction of the training room.

Jordan stood and watched them leave. Allison had no doubt Jordan's next call would be to Harrow. There must be something they could do to help him out. Maybe Harrow would be able to get through to Tor.

The vampire needed some time off. By the look of things, he was a walking time bomb. Whatever was bothering him had to be addressed soon before the inevitable explosion.

"Do you mind telling me what that was all about?" Melissa had asked when they left the club.

"Nothing. The vampire just wanted to talk. He seemed as bored as I was," Annie had offered.

Melissa had considered the fib with narrowed eyes. Good thing she couldn't read minds, Annie thought. She wanted nothing to thwart her next planned outing.

Annie glanced at the carved wood table clock on top of her dresser. She had one hour to get ready for training. Shifting lazily in bed, she kicked at the satin sheets to allow her legs some freedom.

Thing was, she wasn't supposed to leave her chambers at any time without Goran or Melissa's express permission. The only time the women could be out of their rooms was during their workouts and training with Bretania.

The reason for their training was lost on her. Melissa had been tight-lipped on the whys behind their grueling daily routine. She'd cited no reason or purpose. Annie marched out of her room at exactly three o'clock every afternoon for scheduled weapons and combat training.

It was strange how she and the other vampire females didn't refuse or possess any unwillingness. They all seemed to be at Goran's disposal, displaying nothing but eagerness to fulfill his wishes and remain in his good graces.

Melissa, their reluctant but loyal warden, was different. Her position often required her to exhibit a ruthless and aggressive attitude. She was diligent in fulfilling her responsibilities and followed Goran's orders with without question.

It wasn't a big secret they were all Goran's whores. Melissa preferred to call them redheaded mistresses. Annie smirked at the embellished title. No matter how you looked at it, it meant the same thing. One whistle from Goran, and they all ran to heed his call. Their label didn't change a thing. Everything about the situation was wrong and immoral. But then, who would dare question Goran? When he said bow, they bowed lower. When he wanted good sex, they performed like sex kittens. And when he wanted them to dress up, they'd be wrapped in the finest gowns.

Why she'd ended in his harem was not a big secret. Her carrot-colored tresses were the culprit. She should've dyed her hair like she'd planned weeks before she was abducted. New life and new hair color. Yeah, lame-ass attempt to forget that the best years of her life were gone—gone with Daniel when he passed away.

Life hadn't been easy with just her and Gail. She'd missed Daniel so much. Her pining and questions about her father made Annie want to shrivel up and die. They had been a trio, a happy family. Things couldn't have been any better. But then her world had made a sharp U-turn when Daniel's death bulldozed their quiet lives. Now, she was a doxy to a vampire and a vampire herself, leaving her little girl alone, lost, and maybe even dead.

Anguish seeped back again, reminding her of the fateful day of their separation. Before she had a chance to stop herself, she wept at the unlikelihood of ever seeing her daughter again.

Daniel was dead, but she still held hope for Gail. Annie hugged her pillow tighter.

Goran had no patience for her tears, and she had been repeatedly told to keep her sorrows to herself in her solitude. Even though she appeared to be his favored girl at the moment, Goran showed no sympathy. Her longing and inconsolable grief must be kept hidden. They had become her constant companion, her shadow.

Angry at herself for allowing the bitter memories to overcome her again, Annie wiped her tears away and focused on the original painting on her wall. Only the finest for Goran's girl. The autumn scene painting was signed by Leonid Pasternak. How Goran had rounded up this original artwork, in addition to the others splattered across the Council walls, was something that spiked her curiosity.

The man had taste. Not just in the arts, but also in the women he picked. She couldn't deny that all of them, if judged by beauty on the scale of one to ten, would push eleven.

Annie sighed and decided that staying in bed longer would not accomplish anything. But then, without the liberty to come and go as she pleased, she was a mere mote of dust spinning in the air without a purpose. This thought led her to ponder a new dilemma. How on earth would she be able to slip out of the headquarters unnoticed?

What had begun as a scary evening searching for Demetrius had ended rather well. She'd capped the night by making a friend and setting a date to meet him again. What was his name? Tor? It wasn't a date, anyway—just two acquaintances meeting to talk and hang out. She wasn't holding her breath for anything more than that.

This would test her skill at lying, which was nonexistent to begin with. Annie needed help, but who could she turn to? No one in the harem came close to being her friend except Melissa and Graciela. Melissa was not a solid choice, for she was often summoned by Goran. Graciela, on the other hand, was on the "seldom used" list. Perhaps she could approach the vampire for help.

Annie had two days left to plan before her meeting with Tor. Energized, she jumped out of bed and hurried into the shower.

"Harrow, General Krever is here to see you." Rayce's voice buzzed through the intercom moments after Harrow had hung up the phone with Jordan. She had raised some concerns regarding Tor's behavior and general well-being. Another pebble lodged in his shoe, so to speak.

Harrow pressed the intercom button. "Send him to the I-room."

Taking his sunglasses from the desk, Harrow slipped them on. A minute later, he was walking out of his room. Christ, if he ever got out of through demolition process without killing himself, he'd thank his lucky stars. There were too many decisions to make. Although Allison was half of the decision-making team, she pretty much had given him the power to make every judgment call regarding the business and running the facility.

Then there was Tor . . . Harrow knew something was up, but he hadn't gotten the chance to corral the vampire into giving him the 411. Rohnert did mention in passing that Tor had his own demons to fight. Maybe it was time to the get the vampire off rotation, as well as assigning a substitute bodyguard for Allison. It wasn't fair for Tor to be working such long hours. Harrow knew how much time the vampire had logged. Tor hadn't complained, but it'd be wise to give him a break to catch some sleep and regroup.

The I-room was empty when Harrow got there. Within minutes, Cyrus walked in with Leo. The General, as usual, looked spiffy in his starched uniform, complete with all the military patches of rank and designation.

Leo broke into a big smile as he spotted Harrow, who was already seated, a bottle of scotch and other items littering the surface in front of him.

"General." Harrow rose to his feet and reached out a hand to the older gentleman. Leo shook it firmly, the dimples deepening in his leathery face.

Harrow smiled in return before gesturing for him to have a seat. Cyrus walked to the bar and retrieved a couple of glasses, setting them on the table before he sat at the opposite end.

"You shouldn't have wasted your precious time coming here. I should be the one coming to you," Harrow said.

The General was a very busy man, but as a favor to Harrow and Allison, he'd taken some time off from his busy schedule to lead the demolition project. With Leo's connections, contracts were processed and signed in the shortest time possible. Any questions were directed to him and answered by him. Most importantly, all records pertaining to the demolition were sealed.

"Nonsense." Leo raised an eyebrow. "You and Allison are my top priority."

"Thank you." Harrow smiled. "Would you care for a drink?"

"Pour me a tall one of whatever you're having, will you?" The General eyed the bottle on the table and relaxed in the chair. He looked around the room while Harrow poured his drink.

Handing the drink to the General, Harrow got down to business. "So what are we looking at?"

"Demolition's done, and the cleanup begins tonight. It'll take . . . oh, let's say about a week or so. That is, twenty four hours, nonstop, so you're looking at maybe ten more days before there's peace and quiet around here." Leo took the glass and chugged half of the scotch like he was drinking water.

Tough guy, Harrow thought while he let the information sink in. "Ten more days . . . I think I can live with that. Now, I wanted to run this piece of info by you before I make a decision."

"Go ahead." Leo's eyes watered, and his face flushed—no doubt from the amount of alcohol he'd just swallowed. Harrow laughed, and Cyrus chuckled from his seat. Even the toughest ones out there would go crazy with the Armagnac.

"I found a building for sale in mid-Manhattan. It's not as good looking as our boy here was, but I think location-wise, it's solid. What drew my attention was the underground entrance. Should there be a need for me to be there during the daytime, it wouldn't be a problem. All our business vehicles have been fitted with impenetrable steel against sunlight and bullets. We call them our new-and-improved armored vehicles." Harrow grinned, and Cyrus nodded with pride.

"Do you want me to have my guys check out the place first?" Leo's deep green eyes searched Harrow's face. "For security measures and maybe accessibility, too?"

"Yeah, that's exactly what I wanted to ask you. Then, I'll bring Rayce in afterward to do his own thing."

"No problem. Give me the address, and I'll have it looked at first thing in the morning."

While Harrow scribbled the information on a piece of paper, Leo chugged the remaining contents of his glass. When Cyrus leaned forward to pour another, Leo shook his head. "I think that's all I should be drinking. I'm technically on the job," he said, laughing.

"Here you go." Harrow handed him paper. He wasn't even sure his handwriting was legible. Using prescription glasses made the words jumble over each other, but employing a magnifying glass was too embarrassing. "Can you decipher my handwriting?"

"Clear enough," Leo said after he'd scrutinized the scribbled address.

"How long will the process take? I'm afraid the sellers wanted a quick turn around."

"Give my men two days, and I'll tell you what they think." Leo got up and fixed the beret on his head. "I have another meeting to attend, but I will call you as soon as I get their full report."

Harrow nodded and stood up to escort the General out. Leo turned around just before he reached the door. "How is Allison?"

"She's fine. Well . . . She asked me if she could have some fighting instruction. I initially refused, but after thinking things over, I think she should learn."

"That's my girl. I thought she'd never ask." He patted Harrow on the back. "Good call. There's no point in making her sit around and do nothing. It'll help her heal faster." The General gave a brief wave before disappearing down the hallway, Cyrus walking with him. Leo had been devoted to Pritchard and Allison, and there was nothing he wouldn't do for his late friend's family. He was a good guy to have on their team.

Harrow sunk back in his chair, feeling dead tired. He had been working like a dog for never-ending, countless days. Man, he would give anything to get a day of quiet—just twenty-four hours for him to recharge without interruption. Yeah, right, that would be the day. Until Allison decided to be an active participant in running the business, R & R remained a distant hope. With a sigh, he poured another generous portion of Armagnac. At least, he could numb himself until he passed out.

He was about to make himself comfortable when his phone rang. Suppressing a scream of frustration, he clenched his jaw and reached into the pocket of his jeans, glancing at the caller ID before taking the call.

"What's up, Rohn?"

"I just had a talk with Gentry, the soldier I was going to ask about the deluge of VC soldiers upstate."

"What did he say?" Harrow sat upright.

"They've been concentrating in that particular area ever since the rebellion not too long ago. According to him, they didn't get as far as where we are. They concentrated in the general vicinity of the forest where Tor and I found them."

"How do you know he's telling the truth?" Again, there was the hint of distrust that bled into his tone, but Harrow couldn't help it. He was protecting a lot of people—his family. Since Rohnert was one of them, he should understand Harrow's concern, at the very least.

"He was one of my most trusted men before I left. Gentry's reliable. I would trust him with my own life."

Harrow tried to take consolation in Rohnert's guarantee, although there was still the nagging feeling about their proximity. It was just too damn close for comfort. "What do you suggest we do?" he asked, too tired to think.

"Sit tight. Stay indoors if necessary. Go out in groups. The soldiers won't disturb a home. They keep to themselves. At least that's how I instructed them in the past."

Rohnert's recommendations were sound, and Harrow had no reason not to heed them.

"Thanks. I'll pass it on to Lambert."

Tor let Allison drag him into the training room, their positions having switched during the journey. She released his arm as soon as the heavy door shut behind them but said nothing, leaving him to swim in a sea of guilt that made it difficult for him to breathe.

He had handled her with excess roughness and, for that, he was sorry. They both knew he had no right to treat Allison in such manner. Still, he wished his voice hadn't chosen this moment to take a leave of absence.

The training room they were using was much smaller in size than the main facility, but the contents remained the same. Rows of mats lined the center of the room, with two adjoining rooms dedicated as a firing range for different weapons.

Instead of asking her how she was doing like he should, he walked over to Allison and scowled at her, unable to control the emotions raging within him. God, he needed a vacation. A long one. The last thing he wanted to do was to hurt anybody, least of all, Allison.

"Are you ready?" he struggled to speak.

She looked up at him with no hint of what she was thinking. "I'm ready." Her eyes flickered to the rows of weapons displayed in a locked cabinet.

Tor followed her gaze and considered where they should start. Perhaps, it would be best if they started with basic self-defense. He had no formal training, unlike the rest of the fighters in their group, apart from a few classes taught by Cyrus and Rohnert. Other than that, he'd learned most of what he knew from his years of experience fighting, both as a human and a vampire.

Flashbacks of his imprisonment began racing through his mind. The fights, the physical abuse from other inmates, and the revenge that almost ended his life came back with crippling clarity. He had been a marked man from the moment he'd stepped into the jail, where mental torture from the other inmates was an integral part of the program.

Tor shook his head, trying to dispel the painful memories. This was neither the time nor the place. He yanked himself out of the trip down memory lane and focused on what he should teach Allison.

"Would you walk to the mat, please?"

Allison did as he'd requested. Tor watched the confidence in her walk. Her movements belonged on a modeling runway, not in a life-or-death battle.

Tor shook his head and followed her into the middle of the room. "Okay, first things first. Remove your shoes, and lose the jacket and jewelry," he commanded, doing the same. He pulled an elastic band from his pocket and tied back his dreads in a bulky ponytail.

Allison propped her glossy, pointy-toed boots on the edge of the mat and removed her dangling earrings and bracelets. Satisfied, Tor motioned for her to meet him in the middle of the mat. She hadn't spoken much, he noticed, but her actions were compliant, so he left her alone in her thoughts. After his display of temper and the way he'd manhandled her, he wouldn't be surprised if she were considering taking him off bodyguard duty. He wouldn't blame her if she kicked him out for good.

"The first thing you have to learn is how to recognize danger and how to react to an attacker holding a weapon."

Allison nodded and wrapped her arms around herself, as if realizing for the first time that this wasn't going to be as easy as she'd thought. Tor watched her and wished he could protect her from the rude awakening she was in for. It was all good, though. She'd be better for it.

"If the attacker has a knife or gun, he'll likely use it. So here are the scenarios I can teach you. It's different for humans because they don't move as fast as we do. And the weapons we're armed with are very deadly. Please remember that."

"O . . . kay," she answered, looking a little rattled.

"Are you anxious to learn?" He walked to the steel cabinet, retrieved a little dagger, and walked back to the mat.

"Yes."

"Because it won't be easy. I won't go easy on you. We possess strength and agility you're not aware of, and those are only a few of our gifts."

Allison nodded again.

"What I'm using is not made of Dangeran. If by chance either you or I get stabbed accidentally, we will live. So don't worry." Without any warning, he stepped closer to her in a threatening manner, his weapon aimed in her direction.

Allison looked at him, her expression blank, lost, and scared in the face of his sudden assault.

"I want you to react!" he roared. "You have to react." He repeated his attack.

Instinct soon kicked in, and Allison's next move surprised him. Instead of cringing or stepping back, she threw a front kick, straight up into his chin. The kick itself wasn't hard enough to disable him, but she'd nailed him. Allison was off to a great start.

Tor rubbed his jaw where the kick had connected and smiled. "Not bad. Not bad at all. Are you sure you didn't take any lessons in the past?"

"No, never." She gave him a half smile, looking pleased with her first attempt.

"Where on earth did you learn that?"

She smiled again, wider and more at ease this time. "I don't spend all my time reading, you know. Daddy and I enjoyed watching *The Ultimate Fighter* together," she said with utmost pride. It was the most she'd said about herself since he'd been assigned to her.

Tor laughed at the vision of Pritchard and his daughter watching the same series he'd followed in the past.

"You're off to a good start, but I have to remind you that our *fights* are much different from what you see on TV. Out there, you don't have time to think. Often times, you have to rely on your instincts and act quickly. It's kill or be killed. Remember, our opponents won't show mercy, and neither should you."

Tor stepped back, shaking his arms to loosen his tight muscles. "Now, I will teach you some hand-to-hand techniques, as well as avoiding, evading, and blocking. This might take time, since you need to get comfortable and familiar with each of the strikes and blocks."

"I'm ready."

Tor sensed her confidence, which was good. She would need it.

"Stand in front of me," he instructed and sheathed the dagger in his waist holster. "For now, you'll be the attacker. Punch me, and I will show you the foot movements and how to block the strike."

Allison did what she was told. When her hand punched forward, Tor sidestepped to avoid the strike. At the same time, he blocked the punch with an open, relaxed hand. "See what I'm saying?"

Allison bobbed her head eagerly.

"Did you follow my movement?"

"Some of it. Can we do it again?"

"Of course. Now strike a—"

Tor hadn't finished talking when Allison struck again. This time, she delivered a harder and more confident punch, which Tor blocked.

"Good job. How about we switch? Think you can handle it?"

When Allison nodded, Tor didn't waste time and threw a quick punch. Allison responded by executing a flawless sidestep to block his strike.

Tor let out a whistle, impressed with Allison's concentration and fast reaction time. "Perfect."

He stepped back and demonstrated another move, taking into consideration her faulty sight. Tor wanted her to be able see the techniques, but also he needed a little space to breathe. Her proximity was creating havoc in his head. Their closeness and her scent were already playing tricks with his mind. The last thing he wanted was to sport a hard-on that would embarrass them both.

"These types of moves happen fast. You have to be able to respond to your opponent's movements as fast as possible. None of them would stop at one strike. It's imperative that if they strike again, you're ready to block and do some damage. Remember, no mercy."

"No mercy," Allison repeated.

For the rest of the afternoon, they went through different blocks and foot positions, as well as striking techniques. Allison was an eager student and absorbed all of his instructions like a sponge.

The afternoon drew to a close when they heard the shutters roll down for the night. They were sweating beyond belief by the time Tor called it quits.

"Can we do this again sometime soon?" Allison asked when they stopped in front of her bedroom door. She clutched her shoes, excitement written across her face.

"Anytime you want. Just let me know." Tor grinned and turned to leave but abruptly stopped when he remembered something he should have said earlier. He pivoted to face her just as she was closing the door. "Hey, listen. I'm sorry if I hurt you earlier."

Allison glanced up and licked her lips. He stared back into her pale eyes and waited.

"You didn't hurt me. But Tor . . ." She paused as though unsure whether she should go on.

"What?"

"I'm worried about you."

His face hardened, and the mask was right back in its place. "Don't."

She didn't answer right away, but he could see her hand tightening on the doorknob. When she spoke again, her tone was soft. "If you want to talk about it . . . if you ever do, I'm here. I'm always willing to listen."

Before he could tell her that if he wanted a shrink, he'd go to Shelly or Jones, Allison had closed the door, effectively barring any snide remark he could've thrown her way.

Once he reached his room, Tor peeled off his sweaty clothes. Wearing just his boxers, he walked straight to the refrigerator and pulled a bag of much-needed nourishment, setting the bag on top of the little fridge and pulling out a glass from the overhead cabinet. Not bothering to look for scissors, he bit on the bag and let the contents drip into the glass.

The aroma of the blood drifted around him, and he felt his muscles twitch in anticipation. He had been lusting for blood, and this was the quickest and safest way to get it. With the influx of infected vampires around, there was no guarantee his next bite wouldn't be from someone who was harboring the disease. It wasn't like he'd stop and flash a badge, demanding full disclosure. Nope, this was the better alternative, even if the rush of sucking and tugging was absent.

Tor took the glass to the sofa and sat down. Damn he was tired. He hadn't slept well in ages. Every time he slept, he woke up feeling more tired than refreshed, and guilty to boot.

"Damn it!" he muttered and chugged half of his drink. This was going to be another long night. He was on guard duty, and since sleep wasn't in the schedule, he needed to stay awake. Reaching for the remote control on the coffee table, he thought of calling Harrow. It was a good time to come clean.

Pressing the power button, Tor started channel surfing. Food Channel, no sir! Discovery Channel was talking about apes—not in the mood for that at the moment. There was nothing interesting that could hold his attention, so he flicked the television off. Tor heaved his body off the sofa, and with weariness sucking his leftover energy, he picked up his pants off the floor. He pulled out his cell phone and decided to do what his head had been telling him for the last several days.

He pushed the code for Harrow's number and waited.

"Hey," Harrow said.

"Is there any way we could talk? You know, face-to-face."

"Um, lemme see. I have to meet with our broker tonight. I can swing by tomorrow evening. Is it something urgent?" Worry crept into Harrow's voice, a tone Tor knew too well. Anything and everything could set Harrow into a worried frenzy these days, and he could only sympathize with his friend.

"No, tomorrow evening's fine," he said before hanging up, quelling the urge to blurt out what was on his mind.

Tomorrow's fine, so long as I don't sleep.

Zane slipped a finger between the draperies, parting them a fraction to get a glimpse at the man down the street who was staking out his penthouse.

It had been several days since he'd first noticed he was being followed. This time it was a black sedan, and it had been the same man for the last two days. Zane smirked. There were a lot of ways he could have lost them as they trailed him, but he wanted them to see his activities for now. He'd go underground soon, and they wouldn't have any idea where he had gone. But for now, he was sitting tight. There was a lot of stuff that needed his attention—things necessary to maintain his lifestyle, just like his father had planned.

He walked back to his desk and waited for the Mac to power up, pulling his robe tighter against the blast from the air conditioner. Damn. If his father didn't surface soon, he wouldn't be able to afford the electric bill. Without Demetrius and his generous monthly allowance, Zane could see the end of happy days ahead. It had been more than six months since he'd last heard from his father, and his absence was becoming worrisome.

Demetrius was more than competent when it came to fighting and survival. The last thing Zane could imagine was his father getting jacked into an early exit. But then why hadn't Demetrius contacted him? Why would he leave without a word? And there was the more pressing question: How would he survive without his father's generous funding?

Desperate times called for desperate measures, and if you needed something, you had to go out and get it. He logged into his bank account and wasn't surprised to see how low his balance had dipped. "Shit," he muttered. Pointing the mouse to the last transaction, seven months ago, Zane clicked on the linked account. Feeling like a criminal, he transferred an exorbitant amount that should last until he figured out what to do. It wouldn't have been necessary if he wasn't already in deep shit. Demetrius's account had been linked to Zane's for a reason, he rationalized in an effort to make himself feel better.

Feeling relief sweep over him, he closed the laptop and leaned back in his chair. What else could he do? Then he remembered the picture of the man he'd taken at the demolition site. Maybe it was time for him to do a little investigating. After all, his father had shown a great deal of pride in and appreciation for all the work Zane had done for him in the past. All his research and long hours spent poring over clues had paid off.

He took out his cell phone and downloaded the pictures onto his laptop. When the desired image came up, he began looking at the man's face. He was average looking, tall, and somewhat on the thin side. Zane dug deeper into his memory to see if the image would strike a chord.

Nope, not someone he had seen before. He tried to recall any telltale sign from the demolition site, anything that would give him some information, but there was none. There were so many questions, but one thing was certain—the guy wasn't human.

Zane stood up, closed the lid of the Mac, and grabbed his helmet. It was a good night to go for a ride. After a weeklong pounding heat wave, there was a slight breeze, a sign a freak storm was probably headed their way.

He knew just where to go.

Annie rushed out to the empty hallway. She moved with trepidation, hoping that no one would see her out and about. Goran's number one rule was "stay in your room at all times unless summoned." So, here she was, breaking a sacred rule.

There was nothing much Goran could do with her if she continued to please him just the way he wanted. As his current favorite, she held power over him. She'd heard whispers about Goran being lenient when it came to his favored ones.

Five doors down, Graciela's room was quiet, but Annie knew the female would still be awake. She had to be—she was deep into a love affair with romance novels.

Annie tapped at the door and heard quick footsteps approaching. "Grace, it's me," she whispered.

The door opened, and a pair of hands yanked her inside. "What are you doing here?" Graciela asked, hissing under her breath. Her hair was pulled into a ponytail, which gave her an almost innocent look. Make no mistake, Graciela might look docile, but the vampire packed plenty of viciousness inside.

"I wanted to ask you something," Annie whispered conspiratorially and sat on the edge of Graciela's bed. She looked around while the other vampire settled next to her. Romance books were piled on both bedside tables.

"What do you want? You know that if we're caught together, we're looking at a severe punishment," Graciela said as a warning, but there was no sign of fear in her expression. Instead, she looked genuinely curious.

"I know. Don't worry, I'll leave right away. I just want to ask you a favor." Annie held her breath, not knowing if Grace would even want to hear it. She blurted it out before she could be attacked by cold feet. "I'm planning on going out tomorrow night. I'm just wondering if you can cover for me."

Graciela's face registered surprise, but then she laughed.

Startled, Annie jumped to cover the other woman's mouth with her hand. "Shut up! Do you want to get us in trouble?"

Graciela kept laughing but somehow managed to keep the noise down. Annie left her hand clamped over her mouth like duct tape, muffling Graciela's laughter in case she hollered again.

"What's so funny?"

"No one has attempted the unthinkable yet. Once you're in, you never go out. Hasn't anyone told you that?" Graciela's laughter was beginning to irk Annie. Although she was telling the truth, it was a buzzkill on so many levels.

"I know, but I can't stand this place any longer. All we do is to wait for his call or lie in his bed. Do what he wants us to do. 'Spread your legs, Annie. Pull your hair up. Dress in a white gown tomorrow'," she said, mimicking Goran.

Once more, Graciela howled with laughter while Annie gritted her teeth in frustration.

"You're courageous, I'll give you that," Graciela enunciated every word. "And incredibly stupid, too."

"Does that mean you won't help me?" Annie's face fell. She'd hoped Graciela could help her figure out how to slip in and out of headquarters unnoticed.

"I didn't say that. Just make sure he is worth it. If Goran finds out, you're gone for good." Graciela made a slashing motion across her neck.

Annie grimaced. "What made you think it's a male?"

Graciela's eyebrow shot up. "I've never been wrong. I just don't understand why you would gamble with your life. You have it good in here. You're Goran's favorite—"

"For now," Annie said, cutting in. "I need to go out before I go crazy. A little change of atmosphere. And I'm coming back."

"You better make sure you do, because I'll deny any involvement at your insanity hearing."

Annie nodded, letting her plan firm itself in her head. It wouldn't be easy. Force of habit made her cross her fingers. She hoped she could pull it off. "I plan to leave when Goran retreats to his chambers after the last meal of the day." That was, after he had his way with her.

There was lingering doubt in the other vampire's face when she spoke. "Fine, but make sure you keep your mind clear around Goran."

Annie looked at Graciela in confusion.

"One thing I'm sure of—our keeper knows what we're thinking."

"What do you mean?"

"He's always ahead of the game, often answering me even before I ask the question. He's reading my mind, I know it. It's disconcerting just thinking about it. One suggestion—keep your thoughts clean, and don't even think about your plans until after you're outta here."

The intensity with which Graciela had spoken her suspicion made Annie's skin break out in goose bumps. "You're scaring me."

"I'd better be. I like you, and last thing I want is to find out that you went buh-bye." Graciela waved her hand to underscore her words. "I'm not kidding."

"Thanks for the fair warning. And please don't say a word to anyone."

"Do I have a sign on my forehead that says *stupid*?"

Annie shook her head. On the contrary, Graciela was very smart. During their simulation testing and combat exercises, the woman almost always came up with the most logical answer or the highest score.

"I will take you to the side exit. After that, you're on your own," Graciela whispered when footsteps sounded outside her bedroom.

After the sound faded, Annie took Graciela's hand in hers. "Thank you. I know you won't believe me, but the man I met was very nice. I want to ask him for help in finding my daughter."

Grace face softened. "Then make sure you come back here right away, before anyone notices that you're missing. And don't make a habit of it."

Annie squeezed Graciela's hand before she stood up. "I will be back right away."

With those words, Annie floated to the door, excited by the prospect of being free again, even for a few hours. Opening the door as quietly as possible, she looked toward each end of the hallway. Since the coast was clear, she pulled the door behind her and walked as fast as she could. She was a mere shadow in the darkened hallway, but the smile she wore was dazzling.

Harrow and Rohnert hurriedly left the facility after their meeting with the broker. The offer for the building had been drawn up and would be submitted the next day. There was nothing left to do but to wait and see if their bid was high enough.

Deciding against going on foot, they took one of the vehicles with Deuce, a reliable vampire, at the helm. Cyrus had agreed to stay behind to make sure rotations were carried out and every fighter was accounted for at the break of dawn.

Lazily stretching his legs in the spacious cab of the Suburban, Harrow closed his eyes, hoping for some much-needed quiet time, if not a quick snooze. The drive would afford him an opportunity to think things through. Things around him were moving on fast forward: the demolition, their injured comrade, the task of finding another base . . . and then there was Tor, his biggest concern.

Tor was too much of a he-man to accept that he needed help. Harrow had no idea what the vampire was going through because he clammed up every time anyone asked. Whatever it was, they would help him as best they could.

"There's nothing we can do if he doesn't open up," Rohnert muttered out of the blue from his spot riding shotgun next to Deuce.

Harrow opened his eyes. "You can really read my fuckin' mind?" he asked, still unable to grasp the idea. He wondered how many times Rohnert had been laughing his ass off while listening to him silently.

"There weren't too many times." Rohnert looked over his shoulder and grinned at him.

"Man, you're creepy. You're a mind stalker!" Harrow shook his head.

"Hey, I like that—mind stalker. Just like Freddy Krueger." Rohnert laughed.

"Anything else I need to know about you? Do you eat lizards? Move things with your mind?"

"I'm a pure bloodsucker." Rohnert laughed, causing Deuce to shoot a sideway glance his way before letting out a hearty laugh.

"Cyrus told me you did some X-Men shit on a woman in the alley," Harrow said, referring to the hypnotism job Rohnert had performed on the hysterical woman after they'd obliterated the vampires about to make a meal out of her.

Rohnert grunted and thought for a while, not relishing the idea of talking about himself. He fiddled with the handle of his Kalimetal, which was propped against the dashboard, before he spoke. "I don't talk about this much . . . but all purebred vampires have specific gifts. All of us have the ability to take in the general mood or emotion of those around us. I call it the gift of discernment. But it seems like most people want to call it mind reading. So be it."

He shrugged, still toying with the leather handle of his weapon. The light coming from the dash illuminated his profile, and his eyes were fixed on the road. "And then we each have a talent that is uniquely ours. Goran, for instance, can manipulate the minds of those around him who are weak."

Rohnert started thinking about Goran's special ability: the gift to summon the ones he had created. As strange as it sounded, all he had to do was to use his mind to call on them when he wanted. No one had been impervious to his power except one and, to this day, Rohnert had no idea how Jordan had remained free. The animal diet theory was a good one, but he still had his doubts.

Harrow's eyes flew open. The mention of Goran's name sent his blood to its boiling point. He knew about Goran and Jordan's campaign to kill her creator.

"What do you mean by that?" he asked, leaning forward, his body wedged between the two front seats and his arms resting on the center console.

Rohnert wasn't sure how to describe the whole situation to Harrow, but once that can of worms had been opened, he knew there was some explaining to be done. He turned sideways and leaned against the window. "Well, he created Jordan, right?"

Harrow nodded.

"So in a way, he has a power over her and everyone else he's created along the way. Goran's power is known as The Call. I knew all along that, when he decided to call on her, she would go. But somehow, something in the process went haywire. I don't know why, but Jordan for some unique reason is not responding to him."

Harrow thought about it for a moment. One distinct difference came to mind. *Animal diet?*

Rohnert nodded in agreement. "Might well be the reason why she isn't reacting to his summons at all."

"I'll be damned if I would stand around and let him take her." Harrow's expression grew intense, and Rohnert could tell by the tone of his voice that he wouldn't take this new information lightly.

"I'm with you, my friend."

The rest of the drive was spent in silence. Harrow fumed inwardly at the idea of Goran's potential hold on Jordan. The idea disturbed him quite a bit.

After a few minutes, Deuce began tinkering with the radio dial. When he didn't find suitable music to drown out the pregnant silence, he popped a CD in the player. Rap music filled the cab for the rest of their drive upstate.

Tor dragged himself out of bed, feeling like his legs were made of lead. He hadn't slept a wink. Thoughts of Allison occupied his head, and she was there to stay, no matter how hard he tried to keep her out. He had sat there in the dark, staring at the ceiling and praying for sleep, even if he abhorred the nightmares that would inevitably follow.

He had no idea where he would find himself next. For sure, he would be back on the streets soon if he didn't get his act together. Hopefully, Allison would find it in her heart to let the last incident slide.

Tor would talk Harrow into giving him a leave of absence as soon as they could spare him from the rotation. As much as he hated having somebody else watch Allison, it'd be for her own good if he took some time off to clear his head and get his shit together.

Allison was turning him all soft and gooey inside, despite his failed attempts to stay detached. It was impossible when he was around her. The last thing he wanted was for her to hate him, but all his recent actions had her poised to head in that direction. He was dumb as hell and couldn't do anything about it.

Then there was Jessie. She was still haunting him. Once again, he was powerless to stop the barrage of memories. Everything came back in a rush, tugging his emotions into upheaval and rendering him irrational and thoroughly mad.

Tor walked to the bathroom, flicked on the light, and took a look at his reflection. He stared at the man in the mirror and hated him. His hair was more than a mess—the tangled strands were horrendous looking, and nothing could make it any better.

Acting on impulse, he yanked open the bathroom drawer. He rummaged through its contents like a madman. Tor grabbed a pair of scissors and looked at himself one more time. He snarled at his reflection and, without further ado, grabbed a handful of his dreadlocks and started snipping away. Bit by bit, he cut each bulked up strand, tugging each one until it fell onto the tile floor.

Tor didn't even give himself a chance to feel regret. He knew that if he stopped to think, even just for a second, he'd feel like an ass for reacting this way. Despite all the years it had taken him to grow his dreads, they were now lying at his feet, the brown strands littering the floor.

When the last crumpled tangle fell to the bathroom floor, he checked his appearance in the mirror. Half an inch of jagged and uneven hair was all that was left. Sure, his head felt light for the first time in three years, but why did he end up feeling shittier than ever? He stared at himself, but the sense of triumph or relief he was hoping to get from his impetuous act didn't come.

At that moment, he knew his childish antics would garner stares and jabs from his friends. And whose fault was it? His, the dumbass who couldn't decide what was right or wrong anymore.

Tor knew that he needed to get away. With disgust, he punched the mirror. A loud crack sounded, and the mirror shattered. Cracks snaked out in different directions from the point of impact. He pounded his fist against the mirror until he could no longer see himself and his knuckles were nothing but a mass of broken and bleeding skin.

Pain? What pain? He kept beating the mirror until the whole thing shattered and fell to the bathroom counter. Tor howled with an intense fury he could no longer hold in and turned on the shower.

Red, warm, sticky blood dripped from his knuckles down to the floor. Stripping off his boxers, he stepped into the warm shower and let out the cry he had kept inside for a long, long time. The primal sound bounced off the walls, while the running water drowned out everything else.

Under the hot spray, Tor attempted to wash off the blood that continued to pour in torrents. It stung when he pulled out the shards of glass embedded in his skin. Hundreds of shards later, he stopped to brace himself on the tiles with his hands and let the running water pound his head while he stood unmoving.

What had he become? He'd thought he had buried all the memories, but it seemed like all he had done was sweep them under the rug, and even that had been pulled out from underneath him. Fresh waves of guilt and sorrow had resurfaced with a vengeance.

If there were anything he could do to atone for his sins, he would do it without a second thought. However, there was no going back in time. What he had done had forever destined him to a life of hell—the same hell to which he'd condemned Jessie.

He'd robbed her of life, and the payback was his jacked-up existence. The torment he was now living in was impossible to forget. It was too painful to move forward, and so he would be forever haunted.

When Harrow, Rohnert, and Deuce entered the quiet house, they heard a resounding crash from one of the downstairs bedrooms. Each man palmed a weapon and ran across the wooden floor and into the stairwell that led to the lower level.

Several doors flew open, and Cyrus, Jordan, Knox, and Peyton bolted out of their respective rooms with weapons drawn. Harrow eyeballed them and did a quick headcount. Allison was missing, and so was Tor.

"What's going on?" Lambert asked, running barefoot across the hallway to meet up with Harrow.

Before he could answer, another loud crash sounded. The sound came from Tor's room and was followed by cursing. They all looked at each other before moving toward the door.

Harrow pressed an ear against the door to listen, and his face darkened with each noise that resonated from the room.

"I think it's our buddy rearranging the bathroom mirror," he said. Although it was meant to lighten up the situation, no one laughed. It was clear that everyone present was as worried as Harrow. "Go back to sleep or whatever it is you were doing. I'll go talk to him." He dismissed everyone and gave a quick apologetic look to Jordan.

"Baby, I'll see you after I talk to him, okay?" From the expression on Jordan's face, he knew she understood. She waved at him and closed the door behind her. The crowd dispersed, but Rohnert hung around.

"You want me to talk to him?" Rohnert asked.

"I got this," Harrow said.

Rohnert turned and headed to his room. Once the hallway grew quiet, Harrow took a deep breath, sheathed his Kalimetal, and knocked on the door. He wondered where Allison was during all this commotion. Maybe she was asleep. With the noise Tor had made, he doubted anyone in the goddamn house could have remained asleep.

"Tor, buddy, let me in," he called.

When there was no answer, he pressed his ear on the door to listen and heard the shower running. He crossed the hallway and leaned against the wall to wait. He allowed ten minutes to pass before he pounded on the door again. It took several more knocks before it opened. Tor held the door for him, and he walked in. Unable to put his surprise into words right away, he just stared at Tor.

"Didn't your parents teach you that it's rude to stare?" Tor slammed the door, rattling the frame.

"What the hell have you done to your hair?" Harrow asked when he found his voice. He was still unable to take his eyes off Tor's half-assed shaved head.

"I got bored with it. I wanted a new look," he answered wryly, not seeming at all interested with what Harrow thought of it.

Harrow's eyes narrowed, and he lifted his nose. Inhaling, he caught the scent of blood. His eyes slid down to Tor's hand, which was covered by a blood-stained towel.

Even though Harrow couldn't see very well, the poor camouflaging didn't fool him. "What's wrong with your hand?"

"Nothing."

Undeterred, Harrow moved forward and yanked the towel off. Blood still oozed from his friend's knuckles, and Tor flinched in pain. Harrow knew what had happened as soon as he walked into the mess in the bathroom. There was hair all over the floor, mixed with blood and broken glass.

"Talk," he said, turning to Tor with a frown.

"Do you mind if I get dressed first?"

"Go ahead."

"You wanna watch?" Tor snarled and, without waiting for an answer, let the towel covering his lower half slide to the floor.

Harrow shook his head in disgust and walked to the door. "Meet me outside the house in five minutes," he said before closing the door behind him.

Tor took his sweet time, pulling faded jeans from a hanger and a black Led Zeppelin T-shirt from the drawer. With a little flinch, he put on his pants and shirt while trying not to stain his clothes with the blood that still oozed from his hand.

Once his boots were laced up, he took another towel from the bathroom and wrapped his hand with it. What a joke. Some cuts might even require stitches. Great, just brilliant. Shelly wasn't around to sew him back up.

Tor didn't even check himself in the mirror, knowing whatever he saw there would only disgust him. With difficulty, he managed to get his holster of weapons strapped around his waist before heading out the door. He wasn't sure he still wanted to talk to Harrow after what the vampire had seen in his bedroom.

He took quick stock of the happenings in the hallway—it was remarkably quiet—before he took the stairs two at a time to get to the upper level. The aroma of homemade chili cooking in the kitchen made his stomach lurch. He found Harrow in quiet conversation with Lambert when he walked into the kitchen. Both men glanced up, but neither said a word. Lambert nodded his head in Tor's direction before returning his attention to the pot on the stove.

Harrow pointed to the door, his expression unreadable, and Tor followed him outside. The darkness greeted them. There was a distinct rumbling noise in the background, and occasional streaks of quiet lightning meant that a storm was headed their way.

They strolled into the chilly evening. Harrow walked ahead, and Tor maintained a steady pace behind him. "Say it," he said when they were well into the forest.

"What's bothering you, Tor?" Harrow stopped, turning to face Tor.

Tor drew a long breath and kept walking. He was feeling rather edgy, and the stinging of his hand added to the raw anger building inside him. Harrow followed this time, but he didn't push for an answer.

When Tor found a small clearing, he stopped. In the stark darkness, all sounds were amplified—every chirp of the birds, every rustle of the leaves, and even the mild howl of the wind. He pivoted to face Harrow, still cradling his injured hand in the towel.

"I . . . killed my . . . wife."

He stated it as plainly as he could, and then watched Harrow's face go through an assortment of expressions. Tor waited for an all-out tongue lashing from his friend, but none came.

After a period of awkward silence, he spoke. "Aren't you going to tell me I'm a son of a bitch?"

Stretching the silence even further, Harrow just kept staring at him, but he had began fiddling with the dagger handle at his waistband.

"Look, you wanted to know what's going with me. Explain the nightmares and all. This is what I have to tell you. C'mon, I'm sure you have a lot to say. Say it."

Harrow gave his head one good shake, then drew several deep breaths. Tor knew his little piece of information had come as a big shock, but Harrow had yet to utter a curse or any kind of reproach.

After the deep breathing stopped, Harrow found his voice. "Why?" he whispered.

Much better.—at least he'd gotten one word out. It was Tor's turn to heave a painful breath. Where to start? It was a long story, but an abbreviated version was in order, right this minute, since there was a big chance he might not live to see the next day.

"I killed my wife because I was an substance junkie."

Harrow remained silent, which made Tor feel the need to explain further.

"We were newly married, not even a year in, when I was stupid enough to try crack cocaine. At first, I thought I was better than the crack heads; that I could have a few smokes, and I'd be okay. But I underestimated the power it had. It had an intense high and short-lived effect, so I went back for more.

"One thing led to another, and before I knew it, my wife . . . Jessie . . ." He whispered her name with reverence, and remorse seeped from every pore of his body. "She couldn't handle our situation anymore. Our funds had dwindled, my temper flared whenever I wasn't high, and I began spiraling out of control." He paused to gather another breath.

Harrow didn't move a muscle. A drawn-out hush descended on them, and Harrow stepped forward. Putting a hand on Tor's shoulder, he squeezed. "You killed her while you were under the influence?"

Tor shrugged his hand away, not wanting sympathy or any excuses made for his horrendous crime. He'd killed his wife, plain and simple. And for that, he deserved hell and more.

"I killed her because she loved me enough to stay. She hoped I'd reform. I killed her because I was a loser who couldn't distinguish the one good thing in his life from the one thing that could break it apart. I killed her because I was weak." With one powerful swipe of his arm against his face, he angrily wiped the tears away.

"Tor . . . I'm not trying to make excuses for you, but this was a crime committed when you were not in your right mind. I'm very sorry you had to go through the ordeal of losing her."

Harrow had no idea what he'd said that set off Tor. Because next thing he knew, Tor's hands were clamped tight around his neck, and his back was plastered against a red spruce.

Tor's eyes radiated more than hatred—they spewed fury, but Harrow realized it wasn't directed at him. He was just an outlet for Tor's anger, and he needed to figure a way out of the grip that was cutting off his oxygen supply.

"Jessie should still be alive, and I should have died in jail."

Harrow tried prying Tor's hand off his neck, but there was no messing with an angry vampire. "Tor—bud—let—me—go." He choked, barely able to form the words. Just as his eyes began rolling to the back of his skull, Tor's grip eased a fraction.

"Damn it!" Tor cursed before letting go of Harrow's neck.

Harrow felt the air slam into his lungs, and he crumpled to the ground, his legs refusing to support his weight. He sputtered and coughed.

It took a long time before he found enough strength to talk. He ended up leaning against the tree, and soon Tor slid down next to him, sobbing like a broken man.

"I'm so sorry. I thought I had gotten everything under control, but the nightmares haven't stopped. It's worse than ever. I think I need to get away for awhile. That is, if you're not kicking me out." Tor sounded drained.

Harrow scooted closer, using the wide tree trunk to brace his still-weakened body. "Tor, go. Find whatever peace you can and come back to us. We're not here to judge you, my friend. We all make mistakes."

With the blood-soaked towel covering his face, Tor's voice came out muffled. "Thank you. Please tell Allison I'll be back."

Hard-core grief struck Tor as he left Harrow in the forest. There was no use in subjecting his friend to more of his personal drama. The sooner he got out of everyone's hair, the better.

The last thing he needed was a sympathetic pat on the back when all he deserved was the same fate he'd handed to Jessie.

As he headed to the city on foot, the rumbling of thunder continued, and bolts of lightning slithered across the dark sky. It was as if nature were making its anger known. Tor zigzagged across the forest floor, taking short reprieves under tree branches when the sky began to open up. What had started as a light drizzle turned into a raging downpour within minutes. Tor kept running as fast as his feet could take him.

Halfway through his sloshing trip through the rain, he heard voices not too far from him. Any other time, he would have avoided the encounter, not wanting to be outnumbered. But now, he was jonesing for a fight. Any way to release his pent-up aggression was good for him, as long as he didn't hurt people he cared about this time around.

The two unsuspecting vampires were on the verge of crossing his path. Instead of slowing his run, he whizzed faster along the muddy ground. A big blur to human eyes, and an even bigger surprise for the unprepared fighters, he came at them. Tor knew their scents, recognized the swagger in their steps, and most especially, noted the seal of the Vampire Council on their breasts. It was the ultimate prize, and he zeroed in.

Without warning, Tor released his axe and throwing star, aiming straight at the centers of their chests in one quick movement. There was no time to lose—he had few weapons to spare, and the element of surprise was his best ally.

His weapons reached their targets in one fluid stroke. The vampires didn't even have a second to recognize his presence. The rain had muted his footfalls, which worked to his advantage. With snap, sizzle, and popping sound, the two vampires disappeared under the heavy downpour like ghosts of Christmas past.

Their ashes dissolved in the rain just like sugar in coffee. Tor sneered in satisfaction when he emerged from the thick shadows of the trees. He walked over to retrieve his weapons, wiping the blades on his soaked jeans before putting them back in the holster.

All was well in his universe again. For the time being.

Continuing his long-ass run, Tor reached the heart of the city and headed to the club to meet with Annie. The doorman holding a massive umbrella took one good look at his wet and wild appearance and shook his head. Tor felt his muscles twitch, a snarl almost rumbling out of his mouth, but he restrained himself.

Getting on the doorman's bad side was not on his agenda tonight. Deciding against introducing the human to his fangs, Tor walked close enough for him to sense the threat of danger swirling all around him.

The man released the rope and let Tor in without another glance his way.

Tor made his way to the bar, where he spotted Annie seated in the corner. Just as he stopped behind her, she looked over her shoulder, and their gaze met for a split second before she looked past him and scanned the crowd.

Damn, she didn't recognize him without his usual mop. Tor wasn't sure how to take it, so he stepped aside and let her get an eyeful of the other people in the room. He took a deep breath while her eyes ran over every male before returning her attention to the drink in front of her.

A Shirley Temple. He had no idea what to make of that, either. Tor was having fun just watching her. The same tattoo-covered bartender looked up from the counter, and her surprise was obvious when her eyes searched for the hair that no longer crowned his head.

"What the hell did you do to your hair?" she yelled above the blaring music. "I love it now!"

"I needed to give Brad Pitt a run for his money." Tor chuckled. "I'll have the usual. Keep it coming, please." He leaned forward between two patrons and slipped a fifty on the counter.

The bartender laughed, drawing Annie's attention to the source of her amusement. This time, she tilted her head, as if questioning whether she knew him. Then she smiled.

Tor chuckled when recognition flashed on her face, and he moved closer to her spot by the bar. "How are you, Annie?" he asked, eyeing her red hair, which was out of its severe bun. This time it lay gracefully on her shoulders, making her look younger. She reminded him of Gail. He scratched his head at the sudden thought but dismissed the idea right away.

He turned to the guy sitting next to Annie. The human had the good sense to make a beeline for the dance floor, and Tor claimed his seat.

"I'm fine. And yourself?" She stared at the haphazard haircut he sported. Her face scrunched in a thoughtful yet comical expression while she considered his new hairstyle.

"I've seen better days, thank you," he grunted.

Annie stared at his wet clothing. "Have you been playing in the rain?"

"As I matter of fact, I just finished a photo shoot. I'll be Mr. December in the new Vampire Council calendar," he joked. When Annie's face dropped, he knew he'd struck a chord. "What's wrong?"

"I don't know you too well, Tor, but I feel like I can talk to you," Annie said before swirling her drink around in the glass, a sign of nervousness.

Tor waited.

"I'm not a free vampire," she whispered and looked around to check if there was a slightest chance that anyone had overheard her confession.

Tor heard what she said but couldn't quite comprehend what she meant. Not free? Who in the hell wasn't free these days? Especially their kind?

"What exactly do you mean by 'not free'?"

The bartender came over with two shots of Patron. Tor took one right away and handed her back the glass. The bartender gave Annie a quick once-over before turning away.

"Keep 'em coming," Tor called after her.

Annie waited until the bartender was out of earshot before she replied. "I belong to Goran. You know—the head of the Council. I'm one of his creations," she said in an unhappy tone.

"I know who the bastard is." He felt his insides begin to churn in anger. Habit made him raise his hand to his shoulder to push the hair that was no longer there.

Annie's eyes watched him, and her expression became worried. "Tor, what happened to your hand?"

"Nothing." His answer came out clipped, shutting down any more questions she might have had. Annie shifted in her seat, and Tor felt like a douchebag for speaking in such a manner. "Tell me what you plan to do about your captivity."

The word sounded odd, but what other term could he use? Annie sounded like a pet. What sort of task had she been created to perform?

"I don't know. The only other vampires I know are in the same dilemma."

There was undeniable sadness and hopelessness in the way she answered, and it tugged at Tor's heart. Hell, their group shouldn't cater only to infected vampires. He knew Harrow wouldn't turn the others away. If Jordan had been able to escape Goran's clutches, then Annie's future prospects didn't look too bleak.

"If you want out, then I have a proposition for you," he said.

"More Silver for you?" The bartender returned with another glass. She wiped the counter while giving Annie another glare.

"Yeah, bring me another shot right away and leave us be." He popped another fifty on the counter, which the girl snatched with a nasty smirk.

"You were saying something about a proposition?" Annie asked, hopeful.

Tor watched the bartender with narrowed eyes until she was caught by another patron clamoring for drinks.

"Yes, but don't think it's anything but just a friend helping a friend. I want to make that clear from the get-go."

Something in Annie's demeanor gave him the idea that she was in the same boat, which was a good thing. As it was, he was way in over his head with his own emotional baggage. He had a past that kept creeping up on him, no matter how hard he tried to reconcile his mistakes with his redeeming qualities. And then there was Allison. The woman had no idea what kind of emotions she stirred within him.

He was a screwup who had been lucky enough to be adopted into a loving, mismatched family of humans and vampires. For that, he should consider himself blessed.

"Tor?" Annie nudged him.

"Yeah?"

"Didn't you hear what I said? I have no expectation. An *out* is all I want."

Somehow, he believed her. Maybe he'd been watching too many action movies that featured crazy love stories, too. Tor shook his head to dispel thoughts about his own concerns. "I live in a place where we take care of down-and-out vampires." He chose to withhold the word *infected*, unsure if that was something he wanted her to know right away.

"Is that what I am?" she asked, a half-smile playing at the corner of her mouth.

"I didn't mean to sound like I think you're desperate. I—"

"But I am, so please tell me more."

"Well, we're a bunch of misfits," he said. "But we have a purpose, which I will explain further if you feel we're a good fit for you. My only concern is that we have humans working with us, and last thing we need is to have to shoot down a vampire because they decide they want to make a meal out of our human friends."

Tor saw the hesitation in her eyes.

"How do you do it?"

"We're well fed in our facility. We don't even have to hunt for our next meal. A promise not to kill humans is a part of the conditions of acceptance into the facility." Tor watched her reaction to this information.

"What if there are accidents?"

"It is the decision of the injured party or newly created vampire to decide whether or not the vampire who turned them will be allowed to live. All our humans are aware of the dangers, but we haven't taken down anyone since I joined."

"Well fed, you said?" she asked.

"Well fed."

Annie seemed to consider her options. In Tor's opinion, she was better off leaving the fiend she served to join them. It sounded like Tor's associates believed that freedom was to be taken as seriously as life itself. She smiled, the tips of her fangs showing. "I'd be happy to join your misfit gang of humans and vampires."

Tor grinned, feeling lighter than he had in all the years since he'd become a creature of darkness. This was how Harrow felt, he thought.

It sounded like his plan had changed. "Let's go then." He stood up and showed Annie to the door.

Allison realized when she woke up that taking three sleeping pills had been a very bad idea. She felt disoriented rather than rejuvenated, as she'd hoped to be.

Rolling onto her stomach and glancing at the clock, she saw she had been sleeping for ten straight hours. Her body ached like it'd been through a grinder.

Of course, there was a very good reason for the soreness. She had talked Rohnert and Lambert into giving her fighting lessons. She'd needed to work off the rage after she'd learned that Tor had left. He hadn't even said goodbye. Her heart ached at the thought, but the pain in her body was hard to ignore. The lessons were not as easy as she'd thought they would be.

Lambert had said, "You'll wish you were home knitting instead of going out there night after night. It ain't pretty, and it isn't a walk in the park, either." That had been an understatement.

They had flipped and tossed her without mercy. No consideration had been given to her newbie status, and no pity had registered in their faces when she landed on the mat, twisted like a ragdoll. Without the pain, she wouldn't learn anything. So she had kept pushing herself up, even when the rest of her body screamed for her to stay down. She had kept coming back for more, thirsty and anxious to learn everything they were willing to teach her.

The pain was a temporary thing, a by-product of fear. It was all in the mind. It was how you handled it that would show what you were made of.

Rohnert had first given her several codes to live by before he had unleashed his own brand of terror on her. "Heroes are hard to come by. And I don't want heroes. I want fighters who want to win at any cost. Once fear takes you, you're as good as gone. You try to fight clean, but protect yourself at all times. Don't think too much, and react fast. Kill or get killed. There is no other way to survive in this world."

Rohnert had punched, and she had blocked and dished out her own version of a strike. They went at it regardless of how she responded. All he asked for was some kind of reaction to every hit and kick.

"If you really want to learn, you'll learn it the hard way," Rohnert had said. When she'd looked at him with confusion, he had added, "But it will also be the right way."

Allison's muscles were good as dead by the time the three-hour session ended. She could neither lift her arms to get out of her sweaty clothes nor pick up a glass to drink. Though the exercise had left her winded and bruised, the promise of more lessons excited her.

For the first time in a long time, she felt she had a purpose. No longer an outsider in the cause her father had championed, she could now say she belonged there.

Allison stretched her legs under the sheets. While her muscles flexed, pain radiated from her calves. Flinching, she tucked in her legs and massaged her calves until the knots relaxed. Yep, she'd asked for this, and there was no doubt in her mind that she'd keep asking for more.

She let her legs go and turned to her side, testing whether she had the strength to heave herself up. Some maneuvering was necessary before she could sit up, her aching back supporting the rest of her body. Smiling, she recognized the clothes she had worn for training were the same ones she'd worn to bed.

With a grimace, Allison planted her socked feet on the floor and used her knuckles to push herself up. It took several minutes for her to walk into the bathroom. One look in the mirror told her that the meat grinder she'd been subjected to had at least spared her face. No black and blue marks were visible.

Damn those men. No one had even bothered to ask her how she felt when she'd walked out of the training room feeling like her legs had turned to jelly. They wanted tough? Then by all means, she'd give them tough.

If they were checking to see if she'd change her mind, then they were destined for disappointment. Although she seemed like the fragile, girly girl type, they'd be surprised to discover she was not a quitter. She wasn't her father's daughter for nothing. If there was anything Allison had inherited from Pritchard, it was his bullheadedness and persistence.

She twisted the shower handle to start the water and winced at the small movement. While she waited, her legs wobbled, forcing her to brace her body against the tiled wall. When the water was hot enough, she began the difficult task of removing her clothes.

Allison stepped into the shower, glad to feel the hot spray on her skin. She knew the aches and all the trouble she'd gone through were worth it. Tomorrow, she and her body would be ready for the next round.

Tor and Annie sat side-by-side in the cab he'd hailed to take them upstate. They had been quiet during the first few minutes of their trip, the only sounds the steady hum of the engine and Spanish news on the radio. Tor wasn't complaining since it had taken them some time–and a wad of hundred dollar bills–to find a cabbie willing to drive them that far.

After some quiet deliberation, Tor cleared his throat. He needed to make an effort to safeguard their location in case Annie decided against joining their group.

"Annie," he whispered, casting a cautious glance at the driver.

She turned her gaze away from the window and fixed her eyes on him. "Yeah?"

"I have to blindfold you now until we get to our place. It's to protect us in case you choose not to stick around." He remembered how it had been when Pritchard had taken him and Harrow from the subway station a year ago.

If Annie was startled by the request, she didn't show it. "And if I opt to stay?"

"Then by all means, you'll be free to come and go as you want."

She looked at him, and her expression made it clear that she was vacillating between trusting him and bolting. After a few moments, she spoke. "I guess it has to be done."

Tor pulled out a black cloth napkin he'd stashed in his back pocket. He unfolded it and tied it around her head. After he secured the blindfold, they again lapsed into silence for the rest of the journey. The cabbie drove like he was vying for a spot in NASCAR, and in a little more than three hours, they arrived in the house's general vicinity. Tor asked the cabbie to stop so they could go the rest of the way on foot.

After the driver had sped away, Tor scanned the surrounding area, inhaling deep for any signs of trouble. He found none.

He led Annie through the thick vegetation, zigzagging through the maze of trees. Guiding her with a hand on her elbow, Tor walked with rhythmic strides and they were able to cover the three-mile trek in fifteen minutes.

The steady sounds of chirping crickets, hooting owls, and their own footsteps against the damp earth kept them company. Neither one spoke. It was a clear night. The wind lightly brushed their skin, and the sound of the swaying branches complimented the serenity of their surroundings.

"I'd say we have about one hundred more meters to go before we get there."

"This blindfold is nice. I've never experienced learning about my surroundings just by listening before," Annie said with contentment.

When they approached the house, the lights surrounding the property began prickling through the gaps in the trees like raindrops. Tor decided it was safe to remove her blindfold.

He halted his steps, bringing Annie to a stop with a tug on her arm.

"Are we there yet?" she asked, turning to follow his scent.

"Yes, and I'm going to remove your blindfold."

After releasing the knot, Tor returned the cloth to his pocket and pointed in the direction of the house. "Let me remind you: We have humans. No sudden movements, and do not show aggression. No one will think twice about gutting you down if they feel threatened in any way."

"I haven't forgotten." Her eyes blinked several times to adjust to the light.

"Follow me," Tor said and walked a few steps in front of her. When they reached the foot of the circular driveway, floodlights illuminated the entire property. Annie's expression became startled, and her feet faltered.

Tor looked over his shoulder at her. "What's wrong?"

She breathed deep. "Nothing. The lights surprised me."

"Don't worry, I'll make sure that everyone is on their best behavior," Tor said with a grin. He reached out and took her hand, encouraging her to move forward.

They climbed the brick steps and approached the massive double doors. With quick movements, Tor punched the combination on the keypad and a beep sounded before the one of the doors opened.

They could hear voices and peals of laughter before they even crossed the threshold. Tor smiled at the sound of the familiar voices.

Harrow and Jordan were cuddling on a loveseat, while Rohnert, Lambert, and Allison sat together talking. The rest of the group was congregated in the nearby dining room. When Tor and Annie entered the room, Gail, who had been lying on the floor twirling her legs in the air, looked up, and her expression transformed to complete and utter surprise. She bolted up from the floor as if her bottom were on fire and ran toward them. Annie's face turned pale, and with a shriek, she ran to meet Gail. As quick as lightning, everyone in the room intercepted them, and weapons of every description were drawn and aimed at Annie. Jordan held Gail back while the little girl tried to break free.

"What the hell? Didn't I tell you not to make any sudden movements?" Tor shouted, ready to launch his dagger.

Annie was too focused on Gail to pay attention to the threat that surrounded her.

The little girl continued to struggle against Jordan's protective embrace. "Mommy!" she cried, and at once, the whole room fell silent.

"Mommy!" Gail cried again, reaching for Annie, who was surrounded by tense and jumpy fighters.

It took Tor a second to realize how fucked up the whole situation was. How could he have missed the name? Now they had a situation.

Tor moved fast, like a bolt of lightning, and wedged himself between the weapons and Annie. Harrow snarled at him.

Peyton, Knox, and Gabe, three soldiers from the facility, were on their feet, waiting. Just pull the pin, and wham! An instant brawl, guaranteed to break out. Lambert signaled for them to stand down.

Rohnert lowered his weapon first, while Harrow and Tor continued to scowl at each other, neither backing down.

"Stop this," Jordan said, leaning forward to yank Harrow out of the way. He didn't budge but he threw her a disbelieving look.

"We don't even know her," he said before turning back his attention to Tor. "How could you bring someone here, compromising our location and our safety?"

"I—I didn't know she was . . ." Tor stopped and looked over his shoulder at Annie. His dagger remained clenched in his hand, pointed in

Harrow's direction. With slow movements, he lowered the weapon and sighed. "Annie, is Gail your daughter? How come you didn't mention her?"

Annie's body was ramrod straight, the nod of her head almost indiscernible. "When I was taken, she was left behind at the ice skating rink." Her voice was even until Gail cried again, and then Annie unraveled in front of everyone. The tears she had been fighting flowed like a river unleashed.

"Mommy?" Gail cried.

"For Christ's sake, will you let them go?" Jordan stepped forward with Gail in tow, pushing weapons aside as she went. "Harrow, we can't deny the resemblance, and Gail recognizes her mother." As painful as the situation might be for her, she nudged Gail forward.

"Jordan, we don't know who she's affiliated with. She might be a mole or something," Harrow said as a warning, placing a hand on her shoulder.

Rohnert spoke up. "She's not a mole. I suspect she's one of Goran's creations. Just like Jordan."

"Then we're screwed, aren't we?" Harrow gritted his teeth, but he didn't prevent the reunion between mother and daughter.

Jordan let go of Gail's arm and watched the little girl scramble toward her mother. Annie sat on her heels and spread her arms wide, and Gail ran into her embrace.

"Mommy, where have you been?" Gail asked when she finally squirmed out of Annie's arms.

It was clear that Annie had no idea how to answer the question, so Tor came to the rescue. "Your mommy was taken to work at a secret location. She has a very important position, so you can't tell anyone about it," Tor said in a conspiratorial tone.

"Really?" Gail's eyes widened, oblivious to the lie Tor had concocted for her benefit.

Annie nodded in agreement. Tor could see she was unsure of what to make of his embellishments but was nonetheless thankful to be spared from having to answer Gail's question.

"Sweetie, I'm so glad they found you. I have been worried about you," Annie said when her tears receded.

"Mo—um, Jordan found me at the skating rink. She took me home with her. I was crying for you, Mommy. But you know what? I went to my first grown-up party. We went shopping at this big department store, and Allison got me everything I wanted!" Gail was speaking a mile a minute, her earlier woe already forgotten.

"I missed you so much, baby," Annie said, crying into Gail's hair.

"I missed you, too, Mommy. I like it here. Isn't our house beautiful? Daddy paid people to build this fast. I have my own room next to theirs. I guess you can share my room. You'll love it. Allison and I picked out all the colors and the posters." Animated, Gail continued to ramble while her mother held her and listened.

Allison was happy for Gail, but she'd had enough. If she didn't leave the room right now, Lord knew what she'd do next.

With quick steps, she crossed the room to the stairwell, which led to the top level. She was aware that Jordan was following her. They ended up at the patio bar, where the booze sat, taunting her. The two women exchanged a quick glance before Allison walked to the bar, while Jordan settled on the patio chair.

Allison didn't have to rummage long to find what she wanted. She took the half-filled bottle of Kauffman, not even bothering with a glass. Unscrewing the cap, she took one long, satisfying swig, loving the effects of the vodka in her throat. She hoped it would ease the malignant thoughts inside her head.

Striding back to the lawn chairs, she stood over Jordan and looked down at her friend.

Jordan met her gaze, and in all honesty, the vampire looked like she needed a drink herself. Allison offered her the bottle. At first it looked like Jordan would decline, but she reached out to take it.

Jordan took a big gulp, and her reaction was beyond comical. Not used to alcohol, her eyes watered, and she sputtered like a dying engine. "This sucks," she said and handed the bottle back to Allison.

"Jordan, talk."

Jordan got up and walked to the railing, leaned forward, and retched.

"What's wrong?" Allison asked from behind her. She placed a hand on Jordan's back and began rubbing with slow, rhythmic motions.

"I'm fine."

Allison snorted.

"Okay, fine, the whole thing makes me sick."

"I know."

"I will miss her," Jordan whispered. That was an understatement.

Allison knew they all would. Gail had brought color into their world, and her presence made their lives worth living.

"I don't know what I'm going to do without her," Jordan said, sobbing.

"We don't know what will happen. For now, let's hope for the best," Allison murmured, still rubbing Jordan's back. With the other hand, she raised the bottle and drank more vodka. This was, without a doubt, a great time to drown her sorrows.

Questions started lining up, but the most daunting ones made her heart go crazy and the green-eyed monster rear its ugly head. What was Tor's relationship with Annie? Why in the hell had he thought it was okay to bring her here? And why would he choose to break Jordan's and Harrow's hearts by reuniting Gail with her mother?

Allison stopped soothing Jordan to concentrate on the bottle, leaning her head back to take another swig. At the rate she was going, she'd no doubt turn into an alcoholic pretty soon. Did vampires even do that?

The sound of approaching footsteps startled them both. "Is everything okay here?" Tor asked.

Yeah, Allison thought. *Just dandy. Thanks for asking.*

Jordan looked over her shoulder at Tor, but Allison continued to stare into the darkness.

Tor's voice came closer. "Do you mind giving us some time alone, Jordan?"

"Not at all," she said, and she left without another word.

Allison continued her assault on the liquor, downing the last drop with satisfaction. With one powerful swing, she threw the bottle out into the darkness. Judging from the crash, it went pretty far.

"You're probably drunk by now. Maybe I should take you to your room." Tor's tone gave no sign of what he was thinking.

Allison clenched her jaw and remained quiet.

"Turn around so I can see your face."

She shook her head, remaining tight-lipped. Before she knew it, Tor spun her around like a top. He planted his hands on her shoulders in case she planned to bolt, but she still refused to meet his gaze.

"What's going on, Allison? What's with the silent treatment?"

"You don't want to know," Allison said, feeling the effects of the alcohol and suppressed rage taking over.

"I wouldn't ask if I don't want to know." Tor's hands remained on her shoulders.

Her eyes zeroed in on Tor. Her gaze seared through him, and she sneered. "I'm jealous. You brought another vampire home. What did you want to do with her, Tor? I'm sure you weren't thinking about playing Scrabble or talking until the wee hours of the morning."

The humiliation of her admission made her sick. Wanting to escape, she tried to break free from his grip, but Tor just tightened his hold.

"Let me go," she growled.

Tor shook his head, regarding her with what looked like pity. This wasn't what she wanted. Without a word, she stomped on his foot with enough force to leave him howling. Tor's hands released her to cradle his foot. While he hopped and cursed the pain, Allison turned to run.

"Not so fast." Tor snarled. He grabbed her arm and yanked her back.

Allison's blood started pumping, and it felt like her temples were about to explode. She had to get out, and soon. Doing what Lambert had taught her, she flipped Tor like he weighed nothing, and he landed on the ground with a loud thud.

Surprise, surprise!

She ran down the stairs before he could react, faster than she'd ever run in her life, ignoring the stares she got from the others in the hallway. Reaching her room, she turned the knob and was about to slam the door shut when Tor's foot wedged it open.

"You're jealous, huh?" His voice thundered when he slammed the door shut, closing them off from the outside world.

This was a bad idea, she realized, but was too proud to admit it. Allison jerked her chin up and rushed to her desk, picking up a vase to hurl in his direction.

"Enough of your childish tantrums." Tor's hand clamped on her arm and removed the vase from her grasp. "You want me?"

He let out a primal snarl, filled with fury and challenge enough to make her cringe, and swept her off her feet. There was nothing romantic in the gesture; it was pure need. With quick movements, he threw her on the bed and unzipped his jeans.

"Then that's what you're gonna get, princess!"

Melissa knew something was amiss when all the girls piled in the training room. Someone was missing. It took her a while to figure out who it was.

Where was Annie? She was never late or called attention to herself, so there had to be a good reason why she wasn't there. Melissa glanced at Graciela, the one person Annie had associated with since her arrival in the harem, but the vampire looked as innocent as a newborn.

Interrogation at this point would draw unnecessary attention to Annie's absence. Besides, Melissa wasn't sure how Bretania would take Annie's absence. She hoped Bretania would not make a big deal of it. Their technical and tactical expert was smart, sound, and impatient. She almost never engaged in small talk, and her smiles were few and far between. Most of the girls in the harem called her "Creeptania," and Melissa had to agree with the nickname. The instructor eyed her students like they were her next meal. Melissa sat at the last seat in the back of the room, preferring to watch while she listened.

Bretania's formidable presence waited while the other females settled in their seats. They were all dressed in the uniforms Goran had selected: a white cotton camisole and black silk pants under a black silk robe. Anyone who didn't know better would think they were from a monastery.

When the room quieted down and attentions were focused, Bretania did a quick sweep of the room. Her mouth moved, counting heads. As soon as the silent roll call was confirmed, she threw a questioning look in Melissa's direction. Melissa pretended to be reviewing the scribbles on the chalkboard and avoided Bretania's gaze.

It was better to pretend at this point. When the actual fighting instruction began, she would slip out of the room to check on Annie. Maybe she could haul the woman into the training room unnoticed.

"Today's lesson will be on escape and evasion. Some of you may think that escaping is an act of cowardice, but that is far from the truth. Smart fighters know when to stay and when to go. I will show you some evasion techniques, and then we'll have our usual question and answer session right after."

Once Bretania moved onto the finer details of their lesson, Melissa let her mind wander. It always went in the same direction: Demetrius.

Her son still hadn't surfaced, and the longer he remained absent, the more desperate she became. She had ventured out twice already, but she had returned none the wiser. No one had seen Demetrius or his gang. All she had hit so far were roadblocks. There was nothing to even give her a sliver of hope that she would ever see him again.

With each day that passed, she felt more and more like a ticking time bomb, and she was afraid that time would run out. The thought of never seeing her son again brought an ache so great she wanted to cry and scream. However, there was nothing Melissa could do but hold the rage inside her and keep up appearances.

Goran considered weakness a flaw, and if he saw it in her, it could compromise her position. This was not an option. She planned to stay at the top of his whore lineup and had no intention of giving up her position.

Melissa put on the pretense of listening to whatever Bretania was babbling about, but her mind was moving at a fast pace. As soon as the class progressed to the show-and-learn period, she slipped from the room.

She moved in total silence, not wanting to draw attention to herself. When she reached the harem's wing, she stood outside Annie's door. All was still and quiet. She didn't have to pull out her spare key to know that the room was empty.

If Annie wasn't in her room or in the training room as she should have been, where else could she be? There was one place left to check.

With precision of a hunter, Melissa moved stealthily through several hallways, hiding her face when soldiers marched past. Minutes later, she was in front of Goran's door. She took a deep breath before she knocked on its imposing surface.

Normally, if her knock went unanswered, she'd go in, but this time, she waited for Goran to respond. Holding her breath, she walked into Goran's dark chambers. Melissa wasn't sure she wanted to see him with Annie, if she were there. However, the scent in the room did not belong to Annie. She could hear muffled whispers coming from the study.

"Melissa?" Goran called out.

"Yes," she said and made her way into the room. As soon as she entered, Goran and August turned their heads to watch her. The elder vampire looked like he was about to pass out, but he smiled when their eyes met. His skin had a grayish pallor, and she knew that beneath the calm facade, the vampire wasn't having a good day.

"What can I do for you?" Goran asked, clearly not in the best mood. Whatever these two men had been talking about, it hadn't pleased him.

Melissa smiled demurely. "I wanted to see if you needed anything," she lied. Of course, she had to lie. How could she admit to Goran that she had been checking up on him? The head of the Vampire Council didn't need one of his subjects snooping around in his business.

"I'm fine. Is there anything Melissa can get for you, August?" Goran turned to the council member and waited.

Water, perhaps? Melissa almost blurted the words. The faint light coming from the only light source in the room illuminated August's grimace of discomfort, and Melissa felt sorry for the older vampire.

"No, I'm fine. Thank you."

How about I open the nearest exit so you can disappear before you have a heart attack? If Goran had been in a better mood, she might have snorted at the audacity of her thoughts and would tell him later if he asked her.

"Why don't you wait in my bedroom while I wrap things up with August?"

She bowed low and left the study in haste. From the looks of things, she might be in for a long wait. Perhaps a warm shower would help her to relax in the meantime. Once she entered Goran's bedroom, she continued straight into the bathroom and turned on the water.

Stepping into the shower, she let the water pound down onto her head, savoring its revitalizing warmth and allowing it to melt away her anxiousness.

But her worries soon came back. Annie was still missing. What would Melissa say when Goran asked? Why did it feel like she was the one who would get the lashing if Annie didn't return?

Melissa cursed under her breath, unbecoming as it was for her, she couldn't help herself. She fervently wished that Annie was holed up somewhere inside their fortress, because as much as she liked to believe that she was still first in Goran's affections, there would be hell to pay when Goran found out that Annie wasn't where she should be.

When things had calmed down, Harrow found himself in their bedroom. Jordan had returned after tucking Gail in bed. Annie sat in the rocking chair watching Gail, while Peyton stayed close by to keep an eye on her in turn. What a tangled mess the whole situation had turned into.

They settled into bed, both wordlessly pining for Gail and knowing their time with her might be reaching its end.

"Come closer," Harrow said.

Once Jordan was wrapped in his arms, her body began to shake with sobs. He hadn't seen her cry like that since Demetrius had stabbed him. This time it wasn't just fear emanating from Jordan, there was a profound sense of loss. She had nurtured the girl through some rough times, held her when she was scared, and loved her like a mother would do.

Jordan seemed to have confined herself to tears, because she didn't say a word. Not one. This scared Harrow more than anything. *Damn! Gail won't go if I can help it.* There had to be something he could do to change Annie's mind if she decided to take Gail with her.

Unable to fully lay blame on Tor for this turn of events, Harrow tried to rationalize his friend's actions. What had made him decide to bring Annie here? If Tor had no idea of Annie and Gail's relationship, he must have had another very good reason for bringing Goran's creation to them. Maybe nurturing lost souls was part of their purpose. *Shit!* The info scared him. How could he even add to their growing number of responsibilities—plus a vendetta to top it off? Avenging Pritchard's, Dante's, and Leroy's deaths hadn't been forgotten and still was the highest priority for them.

Harrow began to wonder what was behind Goran's sick fetish for redheads. Did he get off on them? If he created Jordan for the same sick reason he'd created the rest, how could she have gotten away? From her story, Goran had left her in the wilderness. Nothing made sense. Goran had to have had a reason for leaving her. He must have known he could track her down one way or another.

Something didn't add up.

"Harrow?" Jordan whispered and turned so they faced each other.

"Yes?"

"Make love to me."

He pulled her on top of him, and she moved without protest. She braced her legs on each side of his body and pushed herself up with her arms. Harrow could see the smudges of tears still dampening the surface of her smooth skin. He pulled her face closer and wiped the tears away with his thumb. He kissed her on the mouth but didn't linger. Instead, his lips glided along her face with featherlight kisses until he had covered the whole expanse.

The moment was sweet and tender. Before he knew it, Jordan's mouth had sought his, and they began to go at it with unmistakable, mutual need. They kissed long and hard, the intensity beginning to unfurl. Their concerns were forgotten for the moment while their yearning took over.

Jordan framed his face with her hands, grinding her body against his. Passion had taken root within them. With their lips fused and their bodies tangled, it would have taken a monumental calamity to pry them apart.

Harrow slipped a hand into her pants, then her panties. He started touching her in the places that he knew never failed to excite her, trying to lift her spirits with every touch and caress.

"Yes . . ." Jordan whispered.

Harrow shifted so he could see her face. "I love you, Jordan," he whispered while working the zipper of her jeans.

Their moment was interrupted by the sound of faint yelling. Jordan and Harrow wouldn't stick their noses in someone else's business, but the yelling got louder, making it impossible to ignore.

"Damn it," Harrow cursed and heaved himself away from Jordan. Some people had no idea how to keep things to themselves. Now that he had his girl in bed with him, the last thing he wanted was to leave her. He strode out of the room, not bothering to hide his disgust, and pounded on Allison's door.

"Keep it down will you? We don't want to hear wh—"

Another scream brought his words to a halt, and he could hear Tor's voice inside.

"What the—? Open the goddamn door!" Harrow shouted through the thick mahogany wood.

"Harrow, please leave." Allison's tone was ragged.

He stood there feeling torn between leaving and putting his foot down. After all, she was his sister, and he felt responsible for her.

"Leave them be," Jordan said from behind him, tugging his arm to make him turn his back and leave Allison and Tor alone.

"You don't have to have sex with me." Allison shrank back as Tor loomed overhead, on the verge of pulling his pants down.

"Isn't this what you wanted?" he demanded.

"Yes, but . . ."

That was all Tor needed to hear. He pulled down his jeans, seeing the surprise in Allison's face while she watched him. She screamed, but he wasn't certain what had pushed her to do so.

This time, he was free of crack, he was in the right frame of mind, and he knew he wouldn't hurt her. Tor would rather plunge a dagger into his heart than hurt the woman he loved.

Fuck! Wasn't that a goddamn revelation? *No, Einstein, this is something you knew all along. It's the reason you fled when you did and why you stayed away to protect her.*

Tor jumped onto the bed with one thing crystal-clear in his mind: He was going to have her, and that was that. Add a freakin' period to it.

Allison's expression became horrified when he shed his shirt and threw it on the floor. Her mouth formed an O when her eyes settled on his chest.

He wanted to laugh, but the throbbing in his boxers kept him focused on his target.

Without a word, Tor spread his legs, trapping her in between his massive thighs. He no longer cared if she saw Godzilla pop out. All he cared about was latching his mouth onto hers and getting his hard-on inside her. He was running on autopilot. Anyway, talking would only waste time.

"Remove your shirt," he said, eyeing the thing like it carried the plague.

Allison shook her head and inched farther up the headboard. Though he kept her trapped between his legs, he allowed her a little room for movement.

After all, she wanted him, and that was all that mattered.

"Remove the shirt." This time, there was a harsh edge to his voice. He breathed through his nose. The more he inhaled her scent, the harder the throbbing got. What was with vampires and scent anyway? It was like all he had to do was take a sniff and his cerebral wires were jacked off the charts, chanting for hot and heavy sex that instant.

Tor heard the rapid pounding of Allison's heart against her ribs, but her expression showed no sign of "don't touch me or I'll kill you."

"Don't make me ask again," he said.

Thank God, she took his threat to heart. Allison might have accumulated enough confidence to show off her newfound knowledge in fighting and self-defense, but this time, no kick or punch would be enough to deter him.

Once the shirt had been tossed to the floor, he let his eyes run across her chest, which was covered by a lacy black brassiere that made his mouth water. Her creamy skin taunted him to run his tongue along its surface. Tasting her would be the ultimate prize.

He smiled, liking every inch of what he could see and imagining what still awaited him. With one swoop, he dove to her breasts and buried his face between them.

Sliding down, he bit the center of her bra, and her breasts jiggled enticingly. With satisfaction, he let his mouth glide down to her stomach. He lingered long enough to place a kiss on every spot that needed TLC. Tor released her jeans buttons and got down to her matching lacy black bikini panties, then pushed himself up and eyed her pants. Instead of demanding that she remove them, he assigned the task to himself, lowering the zipper and sliding the denim off her long, shapely legs.

He was firing on all cylinders now, and no matter how much one inner voice insisted she wasn't his to take, the rest were cheering him on.

Then with the raw desire he had always felt in her presence, he let himself loose and ripped away her panties.

Tor sat up, still trapping her between his legs, and let his eyes feast on her glorious body, noting her creamy skin and finding a birthmark right below her belly button.

You're an idiot. She won't forgive you for this, the lone, crazy voice in his head shouted while the others taunted him to dive in and take his woman. Yeah, the foolish voice should go away, because he wasn't listening.

"Tor?" Allison's voice was raspy. Her scent was giving him the sign that she wanted this as much as he did.

"Allison, you're beyond beautiful." His hands came up to her breasts and fondled them.

"Tor . . . you know this isn't right," she said.

"Why?" he barked.

"I'm not safe," she protested.

"Do I look like I care?"

She whispered, "But I do. You have to protect yourself."

Damn it, he wasn't prepared for this. "I don't have a condom. Never needed one lately." That particular revelation wasn't what he'd wanted to say, but geez, he was never good at the talking part.

"I have one, and I want you to use it," she said. When he nodded, she scooted to her nightstand and opened the drawer. She handed him a foil, and with movement as fast as lightning, he ripped the packet open with his teeth and wrapped himself. Then he went right down to business.

His mouth seized hers for a kiss that was long overdue. Everything about her tasted like honey, and Tor sucked on the nectar like tomorrow hadn't been invented yet.

Allison had been letting Tor lead for the most part, but now her lust took over. There was no taking the reins from her. She moved into position, letting him know she wanted him inside her.

With the movement of a pure seductress, she flipped Tor underneath her and took over. Her body undulated against him when his mouth closed in on her breasts. Their sweat mingled as their bodies rubbed against each other, lubricating their skin like fragrant oil. Without hesitation, she positioned her center over his length.

One touch was all it took to make Tor growl like an animal. This was not just a lover's delight—it was also a battle of supremacy between two aggressive beings. Forcing her off the perch she was enjoying, he flipped their bodies over so once more he was on top. The jungle that was her bedroom was rumbling with raw energy. Her nails dug into his skin when he sheathed himself inside her.

Tor was enjoying the full visual, loving the expression on Allison's face when her fangs elongated, cherishing the ecstasy of filling her completely. Closing his eyes, he freed his mind and let his body take control. Yes, he'd always known there was a tiger inside the kitten, and she was going at it with a primeval hunger that matched his own feral nature.

But with anything good came the bad. When he opened his eyes, the sight that greeted him was Allison lying in a pool of blood. Her body was lifeless, and her eyes looked up at him, glazed and unseeing. Dead.

The sound that followed was an anguished wail, filling the room and startling Allison into fear and confusion.

She scrambled to her feet when Tor pushed her away. He retreated to the corner of the bed, away from her, planting his feet on the floor and rested his elbows on his knees to cover his face with his hands.

"Tor! Tor! What's going on?" Allison demanded, wondering how everything could have ended this way. She moved to him and put her arms around his massive shoulder, feeling his body quake.

"Stay away from me, Allison, before I kill you!" he cried in a strangled voice.

A furious pounding came from the door, and Harrow's voice boomed through the thick wood. "What the—? Open the goddamn door!"

Allison knew Tor was in no condition to respond. Until she answered the door and gave Harrow the chance to see that they were okay, her adopted brother wouldn't leave. Chances were he'd probably break the door down.

Snatching the throw from her bed, she wrapped it around herself, ran to the door, and opened it. Allison wasn't surprised to find the whole house staring at her with expressions ranging from worry and curiosity to suspicion and panic.

"Allison, what is wrong? Are you okay? Where's Tor?" Harrow's words were stumbling over each other while he craned his neck to get a better look into her room.

"I'm fine. We're fine," she said, trying to keep the doorway opening as miniscule as possible.

"Leave them be," Jordan said from behind Harrow, tugging at his arm to make him turn his back and leave Allison and Tor alone.

"I want to see you and Tor when you guys are done in there." Harrow's tone left no room for protest, so she nodded and pushed the door shut.

Hurrying back to the bed, she kneeled in front of Tor. "Tor, talk to me. Tell me what I did wrong."

Tor's sobbing stopped, and he dropped his hand to look at her. "Ally, you didn't do anything. You're perfect. I'm the one that's wrong. You should be afraid to come near me."

Allison reached out tentatively and touched his cheek. Although she couldn't see his face as clearly as she wanted, she could sense his turmoil and the grief he'd been keeping inside.

"Don't say that, Tor. You're beautiful to me." She stroked his wet cheek while he was caught between rivers of torment and heartbreak.

When Tor spoke again, the words flowed like a dam had exploded. He told her about Jessie, his crime, his addiction, his nightmares, his remorse. Tor bared his soul. In exchange, all she could do was make him believe that his past wasn't important to her, even when he tried his best to portray himself as unworthy of her trust.

"I don't deserve you. I'd be better off dead than alive." He buried his head in his hands once more after laying out his litany of offenses.

"That's not true. There is a purpose for you. Whatever you've done in the past isn't going to change my mind. You have suffered for your mistakes. It's time to forgive yourself." Allison didn't falter. She held Tor close and listened.

"I don't want to hurt you. That's why I tried to push you away."

"Tor, would you believe me if I said that these things don't scare me?"

"No. You should run. Now. As far away from me as possible."

"No," she said, shaking her head.

"On the second thought, I should be the one to leave. I'm the outsider here."

"Tor, listen to me." Allison glared at him. "You belong here with us, and more to the point, with me. You killed your wife, and I can see that you have suffered and still are suffering. What you did was a crime, committed by someone who was under the influence of a terrible substance." She paused and pressed her fingers to his lips when he tried to interrupt her. "I know what you're going to say—that you don't want me to make excuses for you. I won't. You went to prison, you served your time. Now it's time to set yourself free from the guilt and allow yourself to move on."

Allison's gaze never wavered. She saw the good man in Tor, just as she had since she'd first laid eyes on him.

"Allison, I want you so much. You have no idea how hard it is to say no to you. But I'm not the man you want to be with. I don't have anything to offer you. I—"

"Stop! Don't tell me who is right for me and who I have to live without. Let me decide what I want. If you don't want to be with me, then be a big boy and tell me. But don't ever tell me what to do."

"I want you and want to be with you, but—"

"I don't want to hear what comes after the 'but.' If you want me, then be with me. We'll work through this together."

"Come here," he said, pulling her up onto her feet and cradling her on his lap. Tor snaked his arms around her waist and pulled her close. Pressing his lips against her hair, he said. "Are you sure you want to ride the tide with me?"

"I'm an excellent swimmer. Didn't I tell you that?"

Sure as the heaven was blue and seawater was salty, Tor and Allison walked out of her bedroom with smiles as wide as the Gulf of Mexico. With hands entwined, they made their way to the meeting room as Harrow had requested.

Tor had showered and sported freshly trimmed hair, courtesy of Allison. Refusing to go to the barber, he agreed to let her try. It was sad that the growth he'd so loved and nurtured for the past three years was gone. He likened it to a teenager's rebellious stage.

"Ready?" Allison asked with a grin when they stopped in front of the door. They could sense, even through the thick door, that Harrow was waiting inside and was seething.

Tor winked and turned the knob.

As soon as they walked in, Harrow eyes narrowed and zeroed in on their joined hands. His mouth thinned in apparent disapproval, but he said nothing. Instead, he motioned for them to sit. The room, although not as big as the I-room, could accommodate twenty or so people. Decked out with a big plasma TV in the front and speakers hovering in all corners, it was used more for additional monitoring of their surroundings than entertainment. If not for the big table in the middle, the room could pass for a lounge instead of a meeting room.

Tor sat at the other end of the table, allowing plenty of space between them in case Harrow was in the mood to instigate a fight. Allison took the seat right next to Tor, showing her allegiance to her man.

Harrow watched their movements with detached curiosity, which was rather amusing. Tor knew his friend wanted to appear uncaring, like the linked hands were no big deal, but the fact was, it *was* a big deal.

"So, what went on back there?" Harrow asked.

Tor glanced at Allison for a moment, trying to convey that he wanted to do the talking. Allison smiled and dipped her head in agreement.

"Nothing much," Tor answered evenly while stroking the absent hair from his shoulder.

"Screaming bloody hell back there isn't 'nothing much.' So start yapping." Harrow pounded a fist on the table.

"Easy there, buddy. No point in getting all huffy," Tor said, making sure the warning in his voice was evident. Harrow might be a friend, but this was his and Allison's business. No one was entitled to know about their private lives except the two of them.

Harrow exhaled and yanked his sunglasses off. He rubbed his eyes before putting them back on. "I know it's none of my business, but I'm warning you—and I'm not kidding here—hurt Allison in any way, and you'll become my enemy."

Well and good,. At least we're both on the same page. Tor nodded in understanding. Harrow was merely protecting Allison, and the deep-rooted caring stemmed from his allegiance to her father. Understood.

"I swear on my life, if there's anyone who'll get hurt in all of this, it'll be me. So rest assured, my friend. She's in good hands."

There was something distracting about the way Tor's hand gripped hers when he uttered those words. Allison, with all her heart, knew he meant every word. She felt a mixture of elation and dread. *No one* should get hurt in all of this.

Tor deserved better after what he had gone through in the past. The way he rubbed her palm with his thumb reminded her of how he'd touched her not even an hour ago, when he finally let his guard down. He'd succumbed to temptation, doing what he admitted he'd always wanted: to feel every inch of her.

She felt a blush rising to her cheeks and looked down, afraid that Harrow would see right through her, even with his bad eyesight. This was something she wanted to keep private, which would be a hard task to accomplish when she was living under the same roof with a bunch of keen-hearing vampires and one mind reader.

"I'll hold you to those words, my friend," Harrow replied, seeming content with Tor's pronouncement.

"I expect nothing less from you." Tor brought his free hand to his heart, as if taking an oath, and bowed his head.

Harrow chuckled, and the earlier edginess dissipated into thin air. "So does that mean you're not going on vacation anymore?"

Tor laughed at the question. He took one look at Allison and squeezed her hand. "I will be around but not *really* around. How's that?"

Harrow seemed to consider the statement. "Whatever. I'll take you off rotation for a few days, but that's all I can give you for now. We're a bit shorthanded with Harding flat on his back. Cyrus is doing double time and training is kicking his rear and, to top it off, he's babysitting five newbies."

"Thanks. I understand."

"Can I join the rotation once Rohnert and Lambert give me a go?" Allison piped in.

"No!" Tor and Harrow answered in unison.

"What do you mean, *no*?" She glared at Harrow, then at Tor.

"You've got to be kidding me," Harrow said, moaning.

"No, Ally. I don't want you going out there." Tor protested softly, for her ears alone.

"Why not? Jordan's out there. Peyton goes out. Why can't I help?" Allison asked, incredulous. This double standard was too old school for her. It was sounding so much like what her father would say if he were alive.

Harrow answered this time. "Because I need you to help me with running the business. There is so much that needs to be done, and I'm just one person. I don't think I can run the facility and worry about the business at the same time."

"But we have trusted employees who can help you." Although Allison understood the complexity of running the business and facility together, her heart was set on going in rotation and chancing it out there with the rest.

"We do, but a business of this magnitude," he gestured, "needs personal attention. We're under the microscope as it is, with Pritchard's absence under close scrutiny, the demolition . . . do you need me to add more?"

Allison shook her head. "No, but Leo is helping us, isn't he?"

"Yes, but Leo can only do so much. We have to take care of the business aspect, the internal matters. I can't do it by myself," Harrow said. Judging by his appearance, the poor guy needed a break.

"Fine. I will help, but you can't keep holding me back."

"Let's not go there," Harrow warned.

Tor jumped in, either to fuel the fire or to diffuse the situation. "Yes, Ally, why don't we talk about this later? When you're calm and thinking straight."

Allison fanned the flame. "Thinking straight? You think I'm not *thinking straight*?"

"No, you're upset, and you're not seeing it from our point of view. Harrow is right. He needs help. Look at him. He hasn't gotten a chance to take a breather since your father passed away. Why don't you give the poor man a chance to rest and do your thing?"

Allison pulled her hand from his and stood up. She paced for several seconds.

"Fine! I'll take care of the business side, but I'll go where I'm needed. I'm not going to hide like a bat. If there's a matter that needs to be addressed, we'll discuss it at the new place. Shutters and all." Yeah, bargaining was good—as long as it went in her favor.

"What the hell? You're not going out during the daytime!" Tor jumped up, grabbed her elbow, and spun her around.

"Yes, I am. That's why we have our armored vehicles."

"Armored, not sun protected." Tor enunciated the words as if she were hard of hearing.

"Tor, we have both. Did you miss the memo?" Harrow laughed.

When Tor shot Harrow a dagger glare, Harrow's expression of delight disappeared and he clamped his mouth shut.

"Fine. If that's the case, I need one more person with me when we're out and about." Tor raked his fingers over his skull in apparent frustration.

"You got it," Harrow said. "If we're done, we need to get the guys in here so we can talk about other pressing matters."

"We're done for now, but don't think that I won't bring the topic up again. Because I will," Allison said and stormed out of the room.

Tor sank into his chair, and Harrow did the same. "That went well," he said.

"Indeed," Tor answered, but he didn't look convinced.

Harrow tapped the intercom, and he called the rest to come in. Rohnert showed up first, revved up for the meeting, followed by Jordan, Lambert and several other fighters.

When everyone took their seats around the table, Harrow stood up and went to the mini bar that housed their favorite beverages. He poured a glass of Armagnac before going back to take his place.

He glanced around, eyeballing Rohnert the longest. Harrow was certain the vampire had already gotten a glimpse of what he was planning to say. *Damn vampire!*

Rohnert arched an eyebrow.

"Got a few things I want to discuss with all of you." Harrow took one fast gulp and set the glass on the table. "One, Tor will be taking a few days off, and I'll take his place in rotation."

The entire group knew the reason behind the break, and the congratulatory hoots were accompanied with some claps and fist pounding. It would be impossible to keep anything a secret within the group—and besides, Tor and Allison made enough noise to wake the dead. Harrow couldn't help but chuckle at the sight of Tor's sheepish grin.

Yeah, the big man had landed a gold mine. His sister sure know how to reel him in. Perfect. Everything is just perfect.

"Two, we have had some incidents involving soldiers from the Vampire Council." He gave a quick look at Tor and Rohnert. "I won't discount the possibility that we will be seeing more action this way. After all, when people go missing, there are bound to be others looking for them."

"I suggest all infected ones in the room steer clear of hunting in the immediate area around the house. If you need to feed, avail yourselves of our supplies here or go in groups. I won't tell you how and when to do this, use your best judgment."

Deuce, a rather bulky vampire who'd been recruited following a bar brawl a few months back, snorted. Under normal circumstances, vampires didn't involve themselves in altercations, especially when the Council's soldiers were involved, but Deuce had jumped in, adding more muscle to Holt, Drake, and Peyton's flimsy group.

"Got no problem hunting me some Council idiots," he said with arrogance.

"I'm sure you don't." Harrow laughed.

Everyone applauded. Put a bunch of egotistical males in a room, and this was the end product. Jordan and Peyton rolled their eyes and waited for Harrow to proceed.

"Next, Leo's men gave us a go for the new Tack Enterprises building. Our offer to buy was accepted and escrow is scheduled to close in less than thirty days. At this point, depending on how fast we can get situated, we're looking at moving within two months."

"I've no doubt you'll move fast, Harrow," Drake said.

"That's the plan. Allison has agreed to step in on the business side, so I can concentrate on the production line and the facility. Our main purpose is still to manufacture guns and, at the same time, do what Pritchard wanted us to do."

"Here, here," Rohnert said.

"Last, but not least, I want extra attention paid to the area surrounding the Rockefeller Center. We have enough intel to support the assumption that the Vampire Council's headquarters are somewhere in that general vicinity. There's a large concentration of vampires there. At this point, we have yet to find their hideout."

"Rohnert should be able to shed some light on this, can't you?" Tor swiveled his chair in Rohnert's direction.

From Rohnert's body language, it didn't look like he enjoyed being asked in front of everyone. He shot Tor a not-so-friendly glare before he cleared his throat.

"You'll find this odd, but as soon as one of the members is kicked out or leaves of his own accord, the entrance that was available to them disappears," Rohnert said.

"Like magic?" Lambert asked, disbelieving.

"I kid you not. Years after I left, I went to check on it just for kicks, and the gateway wasn't there anymore."

Everyone started talking at the same time, offering theories and backdoor gossip they'd overheard during their recon missions. There were theories about Goran who possessed the innate power to mislead weak-minded vampires. Harrow narrowed his eyes but didn't say a word. Whatever reason Rohnert had for keeping this piece of information to himself wouldn't be a secret for long, at least not from him.

Rohnert gave Harrow a sideways glance but acted nonchalant. The group appeared to buy the excuse, but Jordan seemed unconvinced, and, like Harrow, remained in her seat, but her eyes told anyone who cared to look that she remained doubtful.

"Is there anything else you guys want to bring to the table?" Harrow asked as soon as the chitchat died down. No one came forward with additional issues.

The main phone line started ringing just before he had the chance to dismiss them. Harrow picked up the phone, seeing Holt's number flash on the caller ID. He punched a button, and Holt was live on the speaker for everyone to hear.

"What's up?" Harrow asked.

"Zane is gone, boss." Holt sounded frantic, which was unlike him. The others called him a cool dude, but he didn't sound like one at that moment.

"What do you mean *gone*?"

"He is not in his apartment. The place is empty."

Harrow jumped out of his chair. "We're going hunting."

Zane revved the Ducati one more time before turning off the engine. It was a nice night, a great ride away from the city, and a fruitful endeavor to top it all off. With a smile on his face, he slid off the bike in one fluid motion and removed his helmet.

Tucking the helmet under his arm, he strode into the lobby and proceeded to the elevator. While he waited to get to the top floor, he glanced in the mirrors around him and was pleased to see the man staring back. Yeah, Demetrius' blood ran thick in his veins. He had the knack for pursuing and evading, just like his father.

He smiled at his reflection and smacked his lips. There was work to do, and with the new info he'd accumulated during his night out of town, he'd be burning the midnight oil in hopes of getting more answers. After all, his father had, for the most part, relied on his ability to come up with information.

He wasn't your garden-variety vampire for being able to come out during daylight. His father had often referred to him as an anomaly. Life hadn't been so bad growing up. He went to a normal school with human kids. Dated, went to dances, studied, and got into trouble just like the rest. School officials didn't question why there had never been any sighting of his parents outside of evening school activities. The story that his mother was dead and his father was a busy government official made an acceptable excuse. Demetrius had always appeared to be a hands-on parent who tried to balance his responsibilities as both father and public servant, and they bought it, all of it.

Demetrius' disappearance remained suspicious, something Zane needed to find the reason for, and soon. His father had always kept in touch, and this no-call, no-show wasn't something he could take lightly. Just the same, the info he'd gathered tonight would shed some light onto Demetrius' vanishing act.

Good thing he was able to secure some much-needed funds. Slumming it in halfway houses and living in destitution wasn't in his makeup, and until he found his father, he'd have to keep dipping his hands in the old man's account.

Zane pulled the house key from his pocket and inserted it in the lock. As soon as he opened the door, he noticed that the drapes were drawn. Celia, the cleaning lady, had been around at his request and had cleared all the crap in his kitchen, had done his laundry, made the bed, and whatever else there was to do.

One thing she had always commented on was the lack of food in his refrigerator. She often clucked at him in a motherly way that he should eat hearty, home-cooked meals.

His penthouse was pitch-black. Zane walked to the side table and fumbled for the light switch. The living room was bathed in light, and he stumbled into the coffee table when a figure in a dark suit straightened his legs and looked up.

"So glad you finally made it home, Grandson."

What the hell? Grandson?

Goran stood up and glided over to him. Zane felt like he was having an out-of-body experience while he watched, with unbelieving eyes, as the leader of the illustrious Vampire Council moved toward him.

Melissa let go a long sigh of relief as soon as Goran left. She had been with him all day, providing for his needs—not an easy feat. The vampire had an insatiable appetite and the carnal desire of a bona fide sex addict.

She was at his beck and call, serving as his secretary and a host of other roles he wanted her to fulfill.

After giving him a full report on the development of Esmeralda, his youngest daughter with Milla, she went on to recite the progress of his other children. All six of them, to be exact. It saddened her that Goran hadn't even mentioned Demetrius. After all, he was his firstborn. One would expect that Goran would care for his oldest son.

He hadn't asked her about her outings, how she felt, or if her search had produced positive results. No, it seemed like he was just fine and dandy with Demetrius being missing, and it hurt. So damn much.

Melissa ran the length of the hallway as fast as she could, and once she got into her room, she worked fast on getting out of her white silky robe and into a sturdy pair of jeans, a dark blue turtleneck, and boots. After a quick inspection in the mirror, she pulled her leather jacket from the hook behind the door and left to meet those she had called to go out with her tonight.

Graciela was already waiting at the foot of the stairs with Milla and Ruth. They were all dressed in a similar fashion and looked excited at the chance to venture out. After all, they had been cooped up inside the four walls of the headquarters since they'd been abducted, seduced, or whatever their individual case might have been.

With the exception of Graciela, who had been out with her twice, Milla and Ruth were first-timers, and it showed in the excitement that radiated off them.

"Ready?" When they nodded, Melissa led them to the side door by the Blanch Room. The section had been designated to house the many humans, most of them unsuspecting, who were about to undergo the change. A session was in progress, and wails echoed through the entire east wing. Hamilton, Goran's second-in-command, was seated on a chair, looking bored. He glanced up when he heard Melissa approach.

It wasn't a secret from Goran's trusted soldiers that Melissa and some female vampires were embarking on a search mission to find her son. Hamilton shot her a hard stare.

One of these days, her palm would find solace in slapping his face and ridding it of the smug expression he wore nowadays. If Demetrius were around, Hamilton wouldn't be enjoying his current position at all.

They stepped away from the dark, dank patio in a hurry and slipped onto a short walkway before reaching a door that would lead them to the outside world.

Once they had stepped into the loud, bustling city, Melissa advised her group. "We try to fit in. Don't act like you haven't seen this place before or any other place we're going to visit. Keep your weapons close, and be ready to act at a moment's notice. If we're ever separated, go back to headquarters right away."

Milla hesitated, looking a lot like Annie had on their first day out. "What happens if we find a human we want to drain dry?" Stupid question, but a question nonetheless.

Melissa scowled. "If you must, do so without attracting attention to yourself. The last thing we need is exposure. Goran wouldn't be happy if that happened."

Milla nodded. Graciela was pumped and eager, acting very much like she was ready to take on the world. They headed for Times Square at a brisk walk. Melissa was aiming to hang out in a pool hall she'd overheard some soldiers talking about.

Maybe she'd find some noteworthy information this time. She had to, it had been too long.

This time, there were no long lines snaking around the block and no boxy doorman to check their IDs. As soon as they entered the smoke-clouded pool hall, Melissa adjusted her vision in the dark room and started dissecting the mixed beings around her. Plenty of humans. A handful of vampires lounging in one corner, drinking and carousing with women in hooker outfits.

They fit right in. Their attire made them look like biker chicks looking to chill out for the night. After all, New York City was a melting pot.

However, looking the part and acting it were two different things. Some of them would need to play pool to avoid calling too much attention to themselves. As if Ruth had read Melissa's mind, she jumped forward, pulled down two cues, and handed one to her. Graciela strolled to the bar to get their drinks, while Milla cowered in a corner away from the salivating glances thrown her way.

"But I don't know how to play," Melissa hissed.

Ruth laughed. She'd joined the harem a few years after Melissa. Even-tempered and soft-spoken, the well-bred socialite was the epitome of grace.

"Where did you learn?" Melissa lowered one end of the cue to the floor and used it as a walking stick while she surveyed the table, watching Ruth arrange the balls inside the triangular rack.

"My father loved to play pool. Growing up, I used to watch him play with friends. When no one's watching, I play by myself." Ruth straightened up and glanced at Melissa. "Shall we?"

As the night progressed, Melissa got the hang of it and found several strokes that worked for her. Graciela and Milla stood close by, but Graciela was busy scouting the place.

After an hour of playing, several men walked over to the table. "Mind if we join the next game, ladies?" a younger looking man asked, smiling down at them with the tips of his fangs showing.

"I have no problem with that," Ruth answered with obvious confidence, as if playing pool was second nature to her.

"Great," the young vampire said. "Could I buy you ladies a round of drinks?"

"No, I'm fine," Ruth answered and looked over her shoulder at Melissa.

Melissa shook her head when she noticed Graciela waving at her. She handed her cue to the vampire. "Guess you'll be playing sooner," she said.

The young vampire smiled graciously and signaled to his two friends to get their own cue sticks.

"What's wrong?" Melissa asked, following Graciela's line of vision.

"That guy right there, the one wearing the green sweater. I swear I've seen him before. If I'm not mistaken, he used to be part of Demetrius's army."

"C'mon Graciela, how can you tell?" Melissa said but took stock of the man sitting at the bar, looking very comfortable in his surroundings.

"A few times, I snuck out of my room and walked the hallways. You know, boredom can do that to a person. I'm ninety-nine percent sure I've seen his face before," she said, certain in her identification.

"Sure you have. We're in New York City. For all you know, you saw the guy on TV, and you're just mistaking him for one of Demetrius's men."

In spite of her skepticism, Melissa found herself inching in the man's direction. What harm could it do to ask?

When she approached the bar, she rested her elbows on the counter. Making it appear like she was hailing the bartender, she absent-mindedly knocked over the vampire's drink. When the glass toppled over, she started her act.

"Oh, my! I'm so sorry," she said, looking startled. Quickly grabbing a napkin from the counter, she offered it to the man.

He jumped off his chair when the liquid started dripping down from the counter. "It's fine, don't worry." He took the napkin and started wiping the surface. When he looked up at her, his expression went blank.

Melissa took this as an opening and continued her act. "Have we met before?" she asked and mentally applauded herself for her performance.

Recognition dawned on his face, and he smiled. "Aren't you Goran's . . . Wait. You're Demetrius' mother, right?" he asked, wiping off his jeans.

Melissa felt her heart leap at the mention of her son's name. "Yes. Yes, I am." She smiled and offered her hand. He shook it vigorously, an expression of awe lighting his face.

"I can't believe how much he looks like you," he said with a southern twang.

Feeling like she'd unearthed a chest full of treasures, Melissa smiled back warmly. A door had been opened. Someone knew her son, and this was something she could celebrate.

"He does, doesn't he?" When the man nodded, she started the interrogation process, careful to appear indifferent. "How do you know my son?"

"Oh, I was one of his neophytes before."

"What do you mean *before*?"

The man sat down and called out a drink order before answering. "Well, I left because I didn't feel like I fit the group."

"Why is that?"

"Well, they were scouting a lot, and it was boring as hell. I'm way too energetic to sit around and watch for infected vampires to show up. Just wasn't my thing," he explained, sounding like Melissa should know all these things.

"Was Demetrius upset when you left?" she asked, pretending she cared about his answer. Even though she wanted to squeeze it out of him, she knew she was going to get some valuable information from this man, so she kept up the pretense that she was interested.

"To put it bluntly, he cussed the living fuck out of me. But then he got preoccupied with stalking this one place, so I was able to slip out unnoticed." He rubbed his head as though he were embarrassed by the thought of deserting his post.

"Do you know what it was about?" she asked. Her body shook a little. She was getting more antsy by the minute.

"He was talking about this multi-billionaire he suspected of having ties with vampires. Honestly, I didn't see it, but he was adamant, so I guess they all went. How is he, by the way?"

It took a tremendous amount of restraint to keep from shouting that she had no idea how her son was or where he was. "Um . . . he's fine." Tremendous restraint.

"Well, don't tell him you saw me. I shouldn't be out and about like this. Don't want D to find me and do his thing."

"I won't." she smiled and ached to ask one more question. "What was that rich man's name?"

The man stroked his chin, and his eyes rolled up while he tried to remember. "Rich . . . Richard? Oh, Pritchard Tack, I think."

Melissa, for the first time in over six months, began to feel a sliver of hope. It might be misdirected, but she'd be damned if she wouldn't seek out Pritchard Tack. He just might well be the key to finding her son.

"My boy, close your mouth and relax," the stranger urged as he stepped closer to Zane. Illuminated by the soft glow from the lamp, his face came into full view. Despite the smile he wore, the man possessed a malevolent aura about him—something that told you to run for dear life—and that was what Zane intended to do.

He shut his mouth and was poised to make a run for it.

Under normal circumstances, meeting prominent figures didn't faze him. This time, he was at a loss for words, and his body stilled, denying his internal, unspoken desire to bolt out of the apartment.

All of his cylinders were a no-go. None of his body mechanics were able to function while he stood before the stranger with his feet glued to the floor, mouth clumped shut, and feeling awestruck and scared at the same time.

If there were any time he'd wanted to say something smart or witty, this would have been it. The stranger stared at him, and Zane could only stare back, wishing he could sweet talk his way out of this impromptu meeting and run away as fast as he could.

His guest didn't break eye contact, as if he were sizing him up.

"You look just like your father," the man said with the calm assurance of someone who knew what he was talking about.

Zane stood still, struggling to speak without revealing his fear and uncertainty. "Who are you?" He wasn't sure if he should cower, drop to the ground, or crawl under the nearest sofa.

"I called you 'grandson,' didn't I?" The stranger inhaled sharply and tilted his head toward the window as if in response to some unseen movement.

Zane followed the path of the man's eyes while judging the distance between him and the window. He might be able to reach it. *Then what? Jump?*

"It would be better to just stay where you are. I'm not going to eat you. I'm full. And besides, I don't like men."

Whoa! Where did that come from? "You're my father's sire?"

Onyx eyes flickered in confirmation, no words were necessary.

"That makes us family," the stranger said. "Goran." He extended his hand, and Zane reached out to shake it with some reluctance.

One more time, Goran looked at the window, and Zane watched the man closely, taking in the vampire's predatory demeanor, the way his lips turned upward like an aborted smile, the black hair that hung behind his shoulders, and the proud arch of his neck.

In response to something Zane couldn't sense, Goran walked to the terrace and opened the glass door. Cold wind swooshed in through the opening, but the vampire stepped out, showing no signs of discomfort. His stance aggressive, he scanned his surroundings, sniffing the air.

Zane had no idea what dear old Grandpa was up to, but whatever it was, he looked pissed.

Without a word, Goran jumped off the balcony. Zane bolted through the patio doors after him and searched the darkness. There was no sign of Goran when Zane approached the railing and leaned over it to look down. The vampire was gone. He began to draw rapid breaths, not certain if he should be relieved or worried. There had to be a reason for Goran's visit. The big question was *why*.

Goran's movements were fluid as he glided down the side of the building, grasping at balcony railings while he made his descent. He landed with a soft thud on the concrete, mindful of anyone who might be watching.

He made his way toward the parked car with stealthy steps. He knew that the two indistinguishable characters inside were on a stakeout, watching his grandson's every move. He approached the car from behind. When he reached the car, he unlocked the door with his mind.

It was so damn easy. Goran slid into the back seat. Before the occupants could react, he pushed his dagger into the vampire's neck and heard the inevitable sizzling begin.

With one down, he turned to the human behind the wheel, who had been stunned to inaction.

"Now tell me—what you are here for?" Goran whispered. He couldn't smell fear from the man. Instead, there were jumbled emotions, including a healthy amount of anger and surprise.

"You just killed my friend, and you expect me to give you an answer?" the human replied with defiance. Although in a very bad position, he reached inside his pocket for his weapon.

Goran acted quickly, circling his arms around the man's neck and pulling back to trap his head against the headrest. Before the human could as much aim his weapon, Goran pushed his dagger into the man's eyes one at a time with blurring speed.

An ear-splitting cry rattled inside the vehicle, and Goran decided it was time to go.

"Call me merciful. I could have easily killed you," he said before stepping out of the vehicle and slamming the door shut. He lifted the dagger to his face and licked the blood from his weapon. With a grin, he slid the dagger inside his jacket and smoothed the surface of his suit before striding off into the darkness.

It was an hour before sunrise. There'd be more time to visit with his grandson and maybe have a real conversation with him.

Harrow, Tor, and Rohnert traveled at a dead run and reached their destination in two hours. Outside Zane's apartment, the trio paused but did not speak.

A cry came from a nearby vehicle, and Rohnert whipped his head toward the sound. He hurried over to investigate, and Tor and Harrow trailed him. Hands on their weapons, they closed in on the vehicle.

Once they'd surrounded the vehicle, Harrow looked in and cried, "One of ours! Holt!"

"Shit, he's hurt," Rohnert said and opened the driver's door. They found a heap of ashes on the seat next to Holt, who was writhing in pain, clutching his face with bloodied hands.

"Damn!" Tor hollered.

"Holt, my man. What happened?" Harrow asked.

"Someone hacked my eyes," Holt screamed. His body started to shake, and he began thrashing blindly.

"Let's take him home to Shelly," Rohnert said, lifting Holt from his seat and transferring him into the back. "Be careful, though. I caught Goran's scent. He may still be around."

"Go on and take Holt home." Harrow rested his hand on Holt's shaking shoulder. "You'll be fine, buddy. Shelly will help you out." He knew the odds were stacked against their friend. Blindness would be his reality from this day forward.

"Tor and I will stay here and check on Zane's apartment. We have less than an hour to go before sunrise. We'll meet you back at the facility."

Rohnert took the driver's seat and quickly guided the Impala into the street. Once the car had turned the corner, Harrow looked at Tor.

"Be ready.".

Tor smirked. "I'm always ready."

They crossed the street, letting a few people pass by before they began scaling the side of the building. Harrow took the lead, his Kalimetal strapped to his back, and Tor followed.

They ascended with the ease of rock climbers. Their movements were strong, measured, and confident, and each step was precise. They used whatever protruding blocks or bricks they could find to hold onto and pull themselves up.

When they reached the balcony of Zane's apartment, Harrow ran to one side of the glass door, and Tor took the other. A single light illuminated the living room. No one was in sight, but they detected movement coming from the bedroom.

"Give me cover," Harrow said.

Tor nodded. Harrow punched a fist-size hole in the window and disengaged the lock. The noise of shattering glass prompted them to move as fast as they could. Harrow slid the door open, and Tor entered, gunning for the bedroom with his Glock aimed and ready to go.

The movements in the bedroom stopped. Without hesitation, Tor kicked down the door. Harrow honed in on Zane's exact location. As if he could hear a heartbeat, he lunged in the vampire's direction.

"Settle down!" Harrow shouted when the man they believed to be Zane started scrambling to get to the shotgun by the side of the bed. Harrow caught him, and they fell to the floor, struggling.

Tor marched to the side of the bed, tucked his gun into his waistband, and picked up the shotgun. He cocked the rifle once. "If you think your life is worth a damn, stop resisting, and we'll let you live."

By this time, Harrow had subdued Zane in a headlock.

"Who the hell are you people, and what do you want from me?" Zane roared, still struggling against Harrow.

"Zane Drew, we have questions for you. If you want to live to see another day, you will come with us," Harrow said.

It took Zane a few moments before recognition flashed in his eyes. "You," he gasped, looking at Harrow's face while his own paled.

"Yes, me. You and I, we have a lot to talk about."

Zane was by no means easy control, and he kept struggling on the floor. Caution was necessary. Tor appeared to sense Harrow's unspoken concern, and he yanked Zane up off the ground by his sweater.

"Yeah, I need to know what you've done to my father," Zane said, sneering despite the rough handling.

With one clean sweep, Tor backhanded Zane. "Enough talking for now. You'll come with us without causing a commotion. If you so much as utter a word to anyone, I will blow your head to pieces before you even realize what's happened to you." Tor's eyes flashed.

Zane wiped the blood from his busted lip with a finger and spat on the floor. He said nothing. Harrow pushed himself up and strode to the door, his cell phone pressed to his ear. "Cyrus, send a car to this address."

He turned to face Zane, who was being dragged by Tor. "Pray to your God now, because if I find out you had anything to do with the attacks on my people, I'll kill you with my bare hands."

When Allison woke up the following morning, she was afraid to move. She didn't want to risk doing anything that might kick her back to reality. She didn't want to wake and discover it had all been a dream.

Did they really have sex? The memory of how great they'd been together made her flush; even more so, the images of Tor's naked body before her. Even with her bad eyesight, she could grasp how beautiful he was. Her touch and her mouth had made up for her lack of vision.

Her face reddened at the thought like an infatuated teenager. It sure felt like infatuation. In many ways, Tor had been her first: the first man she'd committed herself to, the first one she ever let see the real Allison, the first one who'd made her feel like she wanted to live forever. Yep, she had it bad.

Rolling over, she opened her eyes and glanced at the clock. Tor should be back from rotation—and no, she wasn't dreaming.

But her reality was missing him right next to her, where he now belonged.

She walked straight to the bathroom and started the shower. Glancing in the mirror, she noted the glow around her eyes and the smile that never left her face. However, Harrow's vehement refusal to let her participate in the rotation still infuriated her, as did Tor's agreement with her brother. It left a bad taste in her mouth, even if most of what they said was true.

Allison would just have to prove them wrong. She could help run the business and participate in the rotation just like the rest. If Jordan could do it, so could she. They wanted her to be strong, so she would be that and more.

She walked back to the bedroom and picked up her cell phone, pushed Tor's code, and waited.

He answered on the first ring.

"Hi," she said.

"Hey, baby. We left in hurry, and when I checked in on you, you were sleeping, so I thought it was best to leave you alone," he said.

"I was just thinking about you, and I wanted to hear your voice," she said, pressing the phone closer to her ear and longing to hear the sound of his steady breathing.

"I haven't stopped thinking about you. I'm glad you called. It has been a crazy night for all of us." Tor sounded tired.

"Are you all right?"

"Uh huh," he mumbled. "We're in the facility right now."

She heard him cup the phone to muffle the sound of a conversation in the background. No matter how she strained to make out what was being said, the voices were too faint. It took a minute before Tor came back on the line.

"I have to go, but I'll call you in a bit."

"Okay, I'll be waiting."

The rest of the day was spent training with Lambert and Jordan. It was a grueling session because two equally tough instructors demanded a lot from her. They were patient when showing her numerous fighting forms, but as the day progressed, their expectations rose. She didn't mind the increased intensity, because she was eager to show them what she was made of. Whether it was sparring, shooting, or throwing daggers, they kept pushing her to do better. Every attempt was appraised, calculated, and examined.

Jordan and Lambert were relentless in their push toward perfection, and Allison was happy to comply with every instruction they gave her.

They took a fifteen-minute breather when Lambert excused himself to answer a phone call.

"Are you ready for the Kalimetal?" Jordan asked, handing her a bottle of water.

"I think I am, but I am most curious about the axe." Allison smiled. Twisting off the bottle's cap, she slugged more than half of its contents.

"Why am I not surprised?" Jordan gave her a knowing look before she took a big gulp of water.

"Just saying," Allison said, laughing.

Lambert rushed back into the room, his face grim.

"What's wrong?" Allison asked.

"That was Harrow," Lambert said, sitting between her and Jordan.

She felt Jordan stiffen when Harrow's name came up.

"Is he okay?" Jordan's voice shook.

"He's fine. Holt was injured, and Ray's dead."

Ray had always kept to himself, but Allison would miss the quiet vampire. "What happened to Holt?"

"They were outside Zane's penthouse when someone barged into their car, stabbed Ray, and then turned on Holt. He gouged out Holt's eyes when he refused to answer the man's questions." Lambert looked like he was going to puke. He'd turned pale, and his breaths came in gasps.

Allison reached over and gave his back a comforting rub. She and Jordan had been stunned to silence. These vicious attacks had to stop before more innocent lives were destroyed.

"Who would do such a thing?" Jordan sobbed, unable to hold the grief inside.

Lambert looked up and shook his head. "Holt doesn't know. He didn't even get a chance to see his attacker. The only thing he was sure of was that it was a vampire. It had to be."

"Bastard!" Allison blurted.

"Holt is under sedation now. Shelly has worked on him already. There was no way she could restore his eyesight. Retinas were damaged, and the nerves were far gone."

The gravity of Lambert's revelation settled on them, and they remained quiet for a long time. All that accompanied their silence was Lambert's ragged breathing and Jordan's stifled sobs.

"I think I'm ready for the Kalimetal," Allison said, breaking the long silence. She jumped up and walked over to the cabinet to retrieve four Arnis sticks. She tossed two in Jordan's direction.

"Let's do this," Jordan said.

When the two women were back in the middle of the blue mats, both barefoot and raring to go, Jordan took the lead one more time. Lambert crossed his arms, keeping a close eye on them.

"Here's my take on this whole Kalimetal business. Of course, many of the ideas came from Rohnert, but I added a few of my own," Jordan said.

"Arnis is the original weapon that Rohnert developed into the Kalimetal we use now. Eskrima can be a deadly form of martial art, or it can be purely instructional, for competition and show purposes. For me, it's a form of self-defense, something I revere. It's almost spiritual, with psychological elements. You take it any way you want, but whenever you practice this particular martial art, do it with respect. It's not something to be taken lightly, for it can mean life or death—yours or your opponent's. You follow me?"

Allison nodded, absorbing every word and taking each one to heart.

"Let me show you a few basic moves first." Jordan dropped one stick on the mat and took three steps back. She spread her legs until her stance was wider than her shoulders. "I want you to hold your stick like this, leaving one fist space between the end of the stick and your grip." Jordan demonstrated the grip, and Allison imitated her. "The reason for the space is to give yourself more freedom to twirl it around and execute linear movement, thereby increasing the speed. You can think of a whip and how you'd use it with the same type of grip. Check it out." Jordan demonstrated with fluid movements, whipping the stick faster than the eye could follow.

Watching in awe, Allison couldn't wait to get a chance to try it. She nodded for Jordan to continue.

"When you choke on the butt of the stick, it offers more leeway to hook around the neck to disarm an opponent, or you can clip their sticks away from them. It allows you to move a little faster and get closer to your opponent." Jordan showed Allison several moves while using the butt-end grip.

"We practice with sticks right now because all our Kalimetals are made with Dangeran, but the theory and execution are the same. The Kalimetals are a bit longer than these wooden sticks, so they have longer reach."

By the time their session ended two hours later, both women were soaked with sweat. Allison had learned fast and managed to use both sticks together with fluid grace. Jordan complimented her several times and even joked about Allison giving her a run for her money as they walked out of the training room.

Just as they reached the kitchen to help themselves to some cold water, the front door opened. Deuce, Knox, and Peyton walked in from their hunting expedition. Allison watched them with great interest while Lambert questioned them.

"What the hell are you guys so pumped about?"

"Boss said to hunt in a group, right?" Knox asked.

Lambert nodded, eyes narrowed.

"Well, we were about forty miles out when we crossed paths with two Vampire Council soldiers." Knox paused, cracking his knuckles. Peyton sat on the barstool while Deuce continued pacing.

"And?"

"Well, they were insistent on taking Deuce. You know, being infected and all. We tried to reason with them. We told them he's been clean. I swear I have no idea how they could even tell he's a carrier, but they knew. They wouldn't listen and threatened to take all of us to the Council. Of course, we resisted. The fuckers didn't even make sense." Knox scowled.

"Go on," Lambert demanded. His earlier lethargy had dissolved, and he was looking very much like his old self again.

"So a fight broke out, and we killed them both," Knox said, not even bothering to show humility.

Lambert studied each one of the trio, sizing up their state of mind, and nodded. "Well and good. I'm glad you guys made it out in one piece. We'll keep it that way, but for now, let's all lay low. We'll halt all hunting until Harrow comes back. There are just too many weird things going on."

"Like what?" Deuce asked, eyebrows arching over the rim of his sunglasses.

"Ray's dead, and Holt is . . ." Lambert ran his fingers through his hair, at loss for words.

"Holt is injured," Allison jumped in. "And from what we've gathered, he might not be able to see again."

A deep silence followed. Deuce cursed under his breath, and Peyton wrapped her arms around her body. It was different when one of your own died or was wounded. It just drove the reality deeper that death could come at any time without warning.

"Momma, are you going to stay here with us?" Gail asked during breakfast.

Jordan, Allison, and Lambert looked up, startled by the question. This was something meant to be discussed in private, but Gail wouldn't know that. To her, they were all family, and nothing she said needed to be filtered. They glanced at each other and waited for Annie to answer.

It had been a week since Annie had arrived with Tor, and by the looks of it, she was there to stay. Frankly, Jordan didn't mind sharing Gail with her mother. After all, Jordan was the outsider. Still, Gail had been coming to her instead of Annie for everything she needed, from tucking her to bed, matching her clothes, or consolation after scraping her leg riding her bike. In a way, Annie had remained the outsider, uninvolved with the everyday rituals to which Gail had become accustomed. The little girl treated Annie more like an aunt than a mother, but Jordan had to admit that fear of losing Gail plagued her.

Now Jordan watched Annie squirm in her seat, and she understood the other woman's hesitation. It had nothing to do with not wanting to stay but with the uncertainty of her situation. Annie did not want to make promises she might have to break and cause Gail unnecessary pain.

"I want to, but I might be called upon at any time," Annie said.

Gail pouted, and Jordan knew what was coming. She jumped to Annie's rescue. "I think what your mother is trying to say is that she'll be staying until her employer calls for her."

Just like that, Gail's pout turned up into a smile.

Annie mouthed *thank you* to Jordan while Gail forked up the remaining eggs on her plate, chattering about her upcoming swimming lesson with Lambert. With everyone on mandatory lockdown, the house was filled with people Gail could call on to spend time with her. Once her plate was scraped clean and her glass emptied, Lambert whisked her away, leaving the three women to sit in awkward silence.

Allison spoke first. "Annie, I'm curious. Do you think Goran is looking for you?"

Annie sank in her chair, her head laid back and her eyes closed. She swallowed hard. "He has been calling me," she said with sadness in her voice.

"What do you mean, he's been *calling you*?" Jordan asked, perturbed by Annie's declaration.

"There's no distinct pattern. Waves of air whisper my name out of nowhere. Sometimes it's a sharp, physical tug inside me, clutching at my chest and wrenching it until I can't breathe. I know it's him. It's a nagging pain, and it's getting stronger. He could kill me anytime without laying a finger on me." Annie's eyes reflected her fear.

Jordan was staggered by this revelation. She had experienced similar feelings, but hers had faded over time. It hadn't disappeared completely. From time to time, a nagging pull would manifest itself again. Annie's explanation for the sensation was way past scary—it was something taken from the pages of a horror novel. No matter how freaked out she was, Jordan intended to run and hide until it was time to meet her creator and accomplish what she'd set out to do.

"That is the creepiest thing I've ever heard." Allison said in a shaky voice, her features darkening. She glanced at Jordan before turning back to Annie. "What do you plan to do?"

"I don't know how long I can keep avoiding Goran. I know I must return soon if I want him out of your lives. His summons was unexpected. I thought once I got out, there would be no going back."

"Is there no way you can ignore it?" Jordan finally asked.

"I'm trying. I don't care if I die here, as long as I don't have to return to the harem."

"Harem?" Allison's eyebrows shot up, and she stared at Annie in disbelief. "Is that what he created you women for?"

"What other purpose could he have for creating us? We all have the same features. The most obvious common characteristic is the color of our hair." Annie's eyes flickered in Jordan's direction.

"Could he have some reason other than sex?" Allison grimaced.

"We're all trained to fight. Whatever reasoning is behind Goran's preparations, it is not discussed with us. We're just his puppets. We're called upon to service his sexual appetite, train whenever we're scheduled, and to keep to ourselves. It's a glorified prison, if you ask me."

"Are there many of you?" Jordan stood, her body stiff as a rod, and began to pace.

"There are about twenty-five of us, all redheads," Annie replied. She glanced again in Jordan's direction. "I think you're the one he's been missing."

Upon hearing Annie's statement, Jordan whipped her head around and shouted, "He can miss me all he wants, but he'll never have me! I'd plunge a dagger into my heart before I'd allow him to touch me!"

Annie flinched at Jordan's assertion. "I wish I possessed your strength, Jordan. I don't know how you do it—how you're able to resist his calls—because none of us were lucky enough to avoid him." There was an understated gravity in her voice that revealed a measure of awe, respect, and envy.

Jordan stacked dishes in the dishwasher as if her life depended on it. When she slammed the door shut, her voice was raw, but there was kindness to it. "I will help you in whatever way I can."

The palpable relief in Annie's face was unmistakable. "I know how much Gail has come to mean to you, to Harrow, and your whole family here. I'm grateful for everything you have done for her."

"We love her like she's our own," Jordan said, walking over to the table. She sat down and placed her hand over Annie's. "And you're welcome here with us for as long as you want to stay."

Annie blinked back tears before closing her eyes. After a brief moment, she lifted her lids to look at Jordan. "I will stick around as long as I can, but when the time comes for me to leave, please promise me that you will love and protect Gail as if she were your daughter."

"Don't talk like that. We can all be here for her. You don't have to go back to that bastard."

"Let us help you, Annie," Allison said, placing a hand on Annie's shoulder. "You don't have to go."

Tears trickled down Annie's cheeks. "You don't understand. Something tells me that if I don't heed his call, he'll come for me. I won't take that gamble, knowing what the outcome might be."

Despair hovered thick as clouds while they stared at each other, the fear of the unknown blanketing them.

Zane had no idea where the two men had taken him. He'd struggled against the big vampire inside the vehicle until the butt of a Glock knocked him out. That was the last thing he remembered when he came to, still blindfolded and sporting a raging headache. This time, he was vertical and tied to a chair. Pointing his nose up, he tried to catch a whiff of anything that might give him an idea of his whereabouts.

There was nothing distinctive about his surroundings except a sterile scent, something you'd associate with a medical facility. There were a few distant sounds, but it wasn't enough to give him an idea of where he was or what was going on around him.

He tried to move his legs to get a feel of the space he was in. There was nothing close to him that could offer any answer.

"Hey, assholes!" he shouted.

A few minutes later, he heard the door open and close, and then approaching footsteps.

"Sleeping beauty's awake."

There was a grunt, then something struck him in the head again.

The next time he woke, the first thing that registered was the sound of people talking. It stopped when he raised his head. Damn. If the headache he'd had earlier was bad, the one he had now felt made his head feel like it would explode.

Zane groaned from the searing pain. "Damn it," he muttered before lowering his head and resting his chin on his chest. He winced at the throbbing ache but welcomed it, too. At the very least, it was a reminder that they hadn't killed him yet.

"Asshole's awake again," a familiar voice said from his left.

The conversation ceased, but he was certain there were more people in the room than before. His head moved toward the sound of the voice.

"What do you want from me?" Zane asked, his voice gravelly.

"Let's start the countdown, shall we?" a different man taunted.

Before he could respond, someone behind him yanked the blindfold from his face. The massive ache in his head started pounding like it had a life of its own. Next they removed the rope that bound his wrists.

"Fuck you." He spat and blinked to clear his vision. Once he was able to focus, he found four men surrounding him—the two vampires who'd abducted him and two men he hadn't seen before. Zane was almost sure the bald one was a vampire, but the one with a severe crew cut looked like a human. God, he smelled like a human, too.

"You stay quiet while we talk, or you'll get up close and personal with the butt of my Glock again," the big vampire snapped at him.

The room was stark white, except for the large TV in front of him. Several cameras were pointed in his direction.

The smaller of the three vampires paced the room, and Zane recognized him as the man he'd watched during the demolition. By vampire's demeanor, Zane could tell that he had a lot on his mind.

"Tell me why you came here before. Was it business you had in mind back then?"

Zane leveled a stare at the man but didn't answer. There was no way he'd admit to snooping for his father. He would remain tight-lipped no matter what. They had no way of knowing he was associated with Demetrius.

"Who are you working for?"

Once again, Zane stayed quiet. His eyes darted left to right, contemplating how to create a diversion and escape.

"He won't talk. He doesn't want us to know he was following his father's instructions," the bald one said.

Zane studied the bald vampire, hating that he'd been able to get such an exact read on him. They stared at each other while Zane tried to gauge the man's mind reading prowess. Or had it just been a lucky guess?

"Yeah, you can't keep me out. I know everything your little brain is thinking," the man said, sneering. "So you're Demetrius' son. No wonder he created havoc here."

The vow of silence was immediately forgotten when he heard his father's name. "You know my father?"

"Do I know him?" the bald one said, a mocking tone in his voice. "I *knew* him."

The use of the past tense could mean only one thing. Like a caged animal set free, Zane lunged at the man in a surprise attack and locked his fangs on his shoulder. Too bad he missed his jugular. He bit hard, his jaw locking on the bald man's neck like a pit bull.

The vampire struggled to pry him off. Fueled by anger, Zane bit off a huge chunk of flesh and spit it on the floor. Blood squirted like out-of-control sprinklers while the others scrambled to help the vampire, who was now writhing in pain on the ground.

The human acted fast, cursing under his breath, and hustled the vampire out of the room in a hurry while calling for help.

"You motherfucker!" The big vampire grabbed him by the collar and hurled him across the room. With a loud thud, his back hit the wall, and he fell to the ground. Zane felt aches everywhere. Before he could push himself up, big hands pressed around his neck, yanked him upright, and propped him against the wall.

"Say your Hail Marys now," the big vampire roared.

The air was being squeezed out of him. Zane thrashed and pried at the vampire's hands, but his sheer size made him impossible to budge. Zane's energy started to dwindle, and his lungs burned from lack of oxygen, but he still managed to say, "Fu—ck . . . y—ou!"

"Tor, stop!" the smaller vampire commanded. "There's a more fitting end to this piece of shit."

"Tell me before I kill him," the man called Tor snarled.

"Be nice and turn his lights out first."

Another blow to the head sent Zane back into darkness.

"Shelly, get your ass to the clinic now!" Cyrus barked into the walkie-talkie. Despite Rohnert's protests, Cyrus all but dragged him to the clinic.

Rohnert's shoulder throbbed as he covered the gaping hole in his shoulder with his hand. He took a quick look, and the sight of his bone greeted him through his torn shirt. He wanted to throw up.

"Shit, this is messed up. Pretty boy is a goddamn cannibal," Cyrus said, trying to lighten the mood, but the attempt made Rohnert even angrier. He was angry at himself for not being able to anticipate the sucker's movement.

Blood continued to pour from his wound. Rohnert sat down the moment they reached the clinic, his vision spinning. He wasn't squeamish by any means, but somehow this piranha episode made him nauseous. Cyrus took one quick look at him and rushed to the corner of the room to pick up the wastebasket.

"Puke here. Don't think Shelly would appreciate that stuff on her floor." Cyrus shoved the can between his legs.

Rohnert shook his head, dispelling the gagging sensation. "I think the bastard has poison in his saliva."

The door swung open, and Shelly ran in, stopping short when she caught sight of Rohnert. Although her feet seemed to have forgotten their function, her eyes assessed the damage.

It took just a second for her to regain her wits. She moved, barking orders at Cyrus. "Page one of my assistants in here!"

Cyrus rushed to the phone, punched in some numbers, and sent a facility-wide page. "Cheryl, you're needed at the clinic now."

Shelly reverted to doctor mode and sat on her heels facing Rohnert. She lifted his hand and flinched.

"What happened?" she asked while she surveyed the extent of the injury. "There's massive soft tissue damage, bone seems intact, but I'm worried about tendon involvement. Hmm . . ."

"We were questioning a vampire about the break-in here last year when the bastard lunged at Rohnert and bit him," Cyrus said. His usual calm demeanor was nowhere in sight, and he was hovering over Rohnert like a mother hen.

"Rohnert, get up. Let me work on your wound." Shelly placed a comforting hand on his arm.

He stood and walked to the examination table while Shelly ran to the sink and began washing her hands. Cheryl came rushing in just as Shelly was snapping on surgical gloves.

"What do you want me to do, doc?" the petite brunette asked. One look at Rohnert and the girl sprang into action, gathering the instruments Shelly might need.

"I want some Jeff Beck," Shelly ordered, walking back to the examination table where Rohnert sat, his blue cotton T-shirt soaked with blood. "Cut his shirt."

Rohnert ground his teeth to keep from hollering as pain shot through his arm. Beads of sweat were pouring from his temples by the time he'd been freed from the blood-soaked fabric.

"Give it to me." Cyrus reached out and took the shirt from him. He tossed it in the trash can, and then stood out of the way, preferring to watch from the sidelines.

"I'll give you a local anesthetic before I work on you."

"No . . . no pain shot, please," Rohnert said. He didn't want them to know that he hadn't fed in a while. The pain medication would dull his senses even more.

"It's going to be a hell of a lot better for us both if you're not feeling any pain while I work on you." Shelly's clear blue eyes were filled with compassion.

He knew she thought he was nuts for wanting to feel the pain. "Shelly, just work on me."

"Your call, Rohnert, but I'm warning you now. Even one little movement can jeopardize my work, and I would hate the idea of injuring you any further."

"I won't move. Just get it over with."

Rohnert could feel the silent assessment and fear from Shelly. The injured tendons would never regain the same range of motion they had before the injury. He was lucky that the bastard hadn't gotten his dominant side, or fighting for him wouldn't be the same.

As Jeff Beck's solo guitar reached a crescendo, Shelly began the painstaking task of cleaning the wound.

"What the hell?" She stood back and shook her head.

"What's wrong?" Cyrus jumped from the corner and worked his way closer.

Rohnert turned to look at Shelly and winced at the pain. "What is it?"

"Stay still." She held Rohnert's head to steady him while she pointed at the wound. "You see this?"

Cyrus nodded.

"That is the tendon. They don't heal easily, and the process is long and painful. But look at them, they're repairing themselves."

"That's a good thing, right?" Cyrus asked.

"Yes and no," Shelly said. "The healing part is great because I don't have to do much for him anymore, but they're ossifying. And that is *not* good because it will limit his arm and neck movement."

"Ossi—what?" Cyrus scratched his head in confusion.

"It's a term that means hardening into bone. And that's the point where there's nothing more I can do. It's his body's reaction to trauma."

Something I haven't seen before and would love to study further. The doctor's thoughts didn't surprise him.

"Shelly, no," Rohnert said quietly. "Just stitch me up and be done with it."

If Shelly had any inkling that he'd heard her thoughts, she didn't make a big fuss about it. "I will give you some antibiotics and anti-inflammatory pills to take," she said as she helped him with an arm sling. I don't want you participating in any strenuous activities for a week. Just keep your arm low for now, and I want to see you tomorrow."

Rohnert nodded and Shelly began stitching him back together like a torn ragdoll. After half an hour, she stepped back and inspected her handiwork.

"I guess we're done here," she said, removing her gloves.

Cheryl stepped in to clean the blood off the area around his wound. Cyrus remained quiet, deep in thought until Rohnert glanced in his direction and spoke.

"Will you excuse us, please?" Rohnert asked.

"Sure thing." Cyrus walked to the door. "I'll be waiting outside."

"You, too, Cheryl," he said, offering the girl a grateful smile.

When the door closed behind Shelly's assistant, Rohnert hopped off the examination table, his enormous body blocking Shelly's field of vision.

She remained glued to the spot, her eyes watching him move toward her. He could tell by her expression that she was fascinated by him, and not just for his physiology. The way she held her breath and the anticipation she exuded told him everything he wanted to know.

Thought alteration or insertion was one of the powers he'd rather not use. In Shelly's case, considering the emotions she stirred within him, Rohnert had no other choice. Falling for a human could complicate his already difficult existence. Watching those expressive eyes and knowing how she felt about him, even now he struggled with the urge to hold her and kiss her luscious lips.

Rohnert, you're in big trouble! He tamped down on the desire. Without breaking eye contact, he took control of her conscious and subconscious mind, and he inserted thoughts into her brain.

"You're not interested in Rohnert," he whispered. Everything about him rebelled at doing this, but his better sense told him it was for her safety. He willed her to believe that the compassion she felt for him was nothing more than that of a doctor-patient relationship.

When he snapped his fingers, Shelly emerged from her stupor, blinking several times.

"So, I will see you here again tomorrow. Do you have any questions?" she asked, showing no recollection of the last minute.

"No. I think I'm good. Take the pills once a day, right?"

"Yes, and if you have any questions, just give me a call." Shelly gave him a look over before turning to the sink to wash her hands.

"Thanks, Shelly," he said, slipping out the door.

"Bye." He heard her mutter to herself as he walked up to Cyrus. "Let's get something to drink." He sighed and turned to walk away.

"Sure thing." Cyrus strode alongside him down the well-lit hallway.

Oh, God! He was in even more trouble with this attraction to the doctor. The ache in his shoulder throbbed, but it was no match for the ache he felt in his chest. *Not again.* They made their way to the rec room, where the stash of alcohol, everything that was potent and tight, was waiting for them.

Goran had just stepped out of the shower when he heard a soft knock on the door. He didn't bother answering. Within a few minutes, Graciela appeared in the doorway, garbed in her fine white silk robe, her hair up in an elegant chignon.

"You wanted to see me?" she asked. Her eyes were alert, and her movements were almost edgy.

"Yes," he answered, securing a towel around his waist. "Come . . ."

Graciela moved across the room and stopped a few feet away from him. She looked up and smiled in a sweet, innocent manner. "I'm at your service, my lord." Her hands fell with grace when she curtsied.

Goran seized her unguarded thoughts before reaching forward and lifting her chin so she would look up at him.

"Satisfy me," he said, before offering his hand to her in a gentlemanly fashion.

Taking his outstretched hand, she pulled herself up. Without a word, Goran circled his arm around her waist before lifting her off the floor.

He smiled at how she left herself open for his private scrutiny while he walked to the bed. In Annie's absence, he had expended his restless energy with the other women he'd created to please him.

Feeling a wave of anticipation wash over him, he sat Graciela on the edge of the bed and let the towel drift down to the floor. Her eyes flickered, and she smiled with appreciation.

Liar! he thought, and he nudged her backward. They moved to the center of the bed, and he straddled her thighs and released the tie of her robe. He slid his hand in the V-opening and drew apart the soft fabric.

She wore nothing underneath, which was how he preferred it. Her body glistened in the lamp's buttery glow.

With one quick swoop, he tongued the tip of one nipple, and it jerked to attention. He smiled. No matter how they loathed him, their reaction was always the same. Carnal desire couldn't be denied.

Not going for slow and easy, Goran sheathed himself into her in one fast motion, and her moans exploded in the room.

He chuckled. *This is what I'm talking about. It's time for pillow talk.*

Graciela stiffened, perhaps sensing the venom in his laughter, only for him to seize both her wrists above her head. Trapped, she couldn't do much but take each pounding without complaint. He rotated his hips, gaining more and more access to her core until she screamed.

"Tell me where Annie is." One hard thrust.

She unraveled before him, wet. "Sire, I don't know what you're asking me!" she cried in part ecstasy, part fear.

"Your mind doesn't lie, my dear Graciela. Don't even attempt to shut me out. It won't work. I will penetrate, every single time." He drove his thick length harder into her.

"I . . . don't know where she went," she said.

"Why did you help her get away? Didn't you think I'd find out?" *Cat's out of the bag.*

"Goran, I'm sorry. I didn't know what to do. She asked for my help. She wanted to see her daughter." Graciela floundered like a fish out of water, but she was no match for his strength.

He pounded harder until her body bounced off the mattress, her hands still trapped above her head. She cried and screamed, but Goran ignored her pleas.

"You should know that if there's anything I abhor, it's lying." He continued pounding into her, each thrust more violent than the last.

The ecstasy she'd first felt turned to terror. Her eyes rolled with his unmerciful thrusts, but he wasn't even feeling his high yet.

She attempted to clamp her thighs together to slow him down, but the effort was futile. He was going to give her what she deserved: death.

"Forgive . . . me . . ." she begged, but he was way past listening.

"You have sealed your fate, my dear. I created you, and now, I choose to let you go." His body had taken it to another level. The relentless assault was like a dagger, knifing through every fiber of her body. Killing her.

He lowered his face to her neck. "Please, Goran, forgive me!" she cried one last time before he sank his fangs into her neck and drank from her. He didn't stop drinking while he continued to pound into her, and only reaching his climax when he'd sucked her dry.

Her body went limp. Graciela's eyes were fixed, and her once-beautiful face was contorted in a gruesome expression.

Goran unsheathed himself and sneered. He stood up and picked up the discarded towel. Wrapping it around his waist, he took a dagger from his desk and returned to the bed, plunging the weapon into her chest. Graciela's body began to sizzle, and after a couple of minutes, it had turned into ashes.

"Thanks for the memories," Goran said and gave the heap of ashes one last look before heading back to the bathroom to clean himself.

When Zane woke up from yet another forced slumber, he still had a splitting headache. There was also a piercing pain in the back of his skull that radiated everywhere.

He did a quick inventory to see if he'd sustained injury aside from the nasty bump on his head. It felt like he was otherwise intact. Moving a little, he realized his hands were tied behind his back, and he was in an awkward position—half sitting, half lying down.

His first instinct when he opened his eyes was to struggle, but he soon realized that he had his work cut out for him. He was tied to a lounger at a popular sunbathing hangout in the Hudson River Park, so he had a good idea of what they intended to do with him.

Something moved behind him.

"Well, it seems like our friend has awakened," one man said. Another snorted in reply.

Zane pivoted in his chair, but a crippling pain gripped him once more. Two humans idly sat on the grass, wearing identical smirks. He looked around him. The place was empty in the early morning hour. The city had yet to wake up. There were faint sounds of the first ferry run across the river. When he looked up at the sky, his eyes slid over to the horizon, seeing the sun peeking up to begin a new day.

Zane smiled to himself. Little did these fools realize that he was on friendly terms with the sun. Now, if he could devise a way to break free before daylight hit.

Ackwardly standing up from the chair, he swayed and pretended to stumble forward, allowing himself to fall to the ground. He dropped face first and groaned. Instead of approaching him, the two humans remained seated on the grass like sheep grazing in the pasture. They eyed him with mild interest, most likely wanting to get this "Dracula meets his doom" episode over and done with.

While Zane fought the massive pounding in his head, he rolled over to the edge of the grass, where he was met by cool concrete. He knew this park by heart, having spent time here during his high school days ditching classes.

The sun was making its steady ascent. The glorious hues of orange peeked around a cornucopia of fat clouds, creating a picturesque landscape that was expected to kill him on contact.

"Dude, you can't run and hide. You're going to meet your maker soon." One of the two men walked up to him, holding a dagger while chewing on a piece of gum. He sat on his heels while Zane struggled to sit up.

It took a few minutes for the sun to show its splendor. When the first rays hit him, Zane screamed an ear-shattering howl of a vampire burning.

The man laughed, no doubt pleased by Zane's impending demise. "Do you have any last words?"

The other man walked up to them, while Zane concentrated on looking scared. "Yeah, any last minute crap you want to say before you go buh-bye?"

"Can you . . . ahhh . . . at least remove . . . the binding on my wrists?" he begged, loving the pathetic sound of his voice.

The humans glanced at each other as if coming to a silent agreement before the one holding a dagger pushed him on his face and slashed the tie free.

The sun made its steady climb without mercy, and Zane remained flat on his stomach while he continued to moan in pain, calculating his moves and their positions. When the sun's rays pounded on his back, he made his body spasm with violent movements.

There were cries of pure glee from his captors. They were expecting him to fizzle out soon, but Zane jumped to his feet and lunged for the man with the dagger. The element of surprise meant the fuckers weren't ready for him.

Their looks of disbelief were a picture to see. Zane moved with efficiency, disarming the man and turning his own dagger on him. He thrust the weapon solidly into the man's abdomen, twisted hard, and he smiled. "I'm not done with you."

He pulled out the dagger and pivoted just in time to avoid a knife zipping in his direction.

"Last words? You wanted me to say something?" He released the dagger in one quick motion, sinking it smack dead in the middle of the second man's forehead. "How about, I won't fizzle in the sun like you morons thought I would?"

The man dropped like a swatted fly, blood dripping from the wound in his head. Zane turned and watched the other man writhe in pain.

"Too bad you can't tell your bosses that I'm not your typical vampire. I guess they'll just have to find out later."

Zane wiped the dirt from his jeans and shirt before striding off to the nearest sidewalk. The headache was in full blast now.

Where to go was the question. He'd make a quick run to his penthouse to gather some stuff, but then what?

It had been several days since Allison had seen Tor, but every waking hour had been spent in training instead of moping around. She trudged to the water station after yet another grueling session with Jordan.

Today she'd been able to match Jordan's speed and endurance with near precision. Allison saw the approval in Lambert's face when he handed her a cup of water.

"Not bad, not bad at all," he said, crossing his arms across his chest.

As usual, the first round had been with him. Lambert's skill with daggers was notorious, as was his prowess with a gun, but her session with him had been a walk in the park compared to her time with Jordan. Although she was pleased with her progress, Allison had to admit she was tired to the bone.

"Thanks," she said and collapsed on the chair next to Jordan. "You're a monster, Jordan. I don't understand how you haven't killed me yet."

Jordan rolled her eyes and took a quick swig from her cup. "You are a firecracker, aren't you? Just when I think you're down, you keep coming back for more."

"I don't believe in quitting," Allison said with complete honesty. If her father were alive, he would say the same. Pritchard's mantra was "attain the impossible." The idea of quitting never came up because he didn't believe in failure, and that same belief had been instilled in Allison at a very young age.

Trouble was, she loved pain, too. As crazy as it sounded, she felt nothing had been gained if she didn't sweat, spill blood, or experience some hardship. If she wanted to be a part of the team, it was imperative to earn everyone's respect, even if she had to beat the shit out of them to do it.

"Quitting is a hiccup for losers. And down they go." Lambert laughed. "Ready?"

Allison got to her feet and followed Lambert into the adjoining room, where they kept their firearms. "I can see that you're very comfortable with the Kalimetal now, and your gun aim is fantastic. I think we should concentrate on throwing stars and daggers this afternoon."

Lambert unlocked the dagger cabinet and opened it to reveal rows of weapons Allison hadn't seen before. She examined each one with interest, salivating at the thought of using them on actual targets. Although her vision wasn't 20/20, she made up for that weakness with her intuition and other senses. Because the target on the firing range didn't move, her aim was slightly off, which had made her scream in frustration. Lambert had remedied this by moving the target for her with a press of a button.

"How does Harrow do it?" she asked, twirling a throwing star between her fingers.

"Cyrus told me that Harrow closes his eyes and memorizes the location. When the target starts moving, he reacts using his hearing, marking his target in his head or some shit like that. His aim is usually right on. Maybe you can do the same thing."

She thought about it, and then nodded. "I can try."

Allison took several knives, daggers, and throwing stars and brought them to the table. Lambert stood next to her, inspecting her stance before he gave her a go.

With a joystick, Lambert began maneuvering the target. A mechanical whirring sound came alive, and Allison felt her pulse quicken. Picking up more throwing stars, she took a deep breath, closed her eyes, and imagined her target. She listened to the movement and tracked her target by sound alone. Following with her head, she aimed and released the throwing star with gusto.

A thud sounded when the metal hit the wooden target. Allison opened her eyes and heard Lambert whistle.

"I'm impressed."

He levered the joystick, and the target buzzed closer to them for a closer inspection. Allison couldn't believe her faulty eyes. She'd been a little off, but if her target had been alive, the wound would have been fatal.

The afternoon passed in a blur while she immersed herself in learning about the different weapons. She figured everyone had a favorite, and she found hers. The Ronin throwing star was a perfect fit for her. Its four razor-edged blades sailed to her target like missiles. The stars were lightweight, although a Dangeran-packed Ronin was heavier. Allison spent an hour becoming familiar with the contours of the weapon. It was love at first sight.

"You can take whatever you like. Just make sure you keep them out of Gail's reach, and you know the rest of the drill. Keep your weapons inside the your bedroom safe at all times, leaving one close at your bedside," Lambert said while she gathered half a dozen throwing stars and stashed them in a belt sheath.

As they walked out of the room, they heard raised voices coming from the living room. She and Lambert exchanged a quick glance and rushed down the hallway, taking the stairs two at a time.

"What the hell are you doing?" Deuce shouted at the television screen, although his rage was directed at Knox, who was sitting next to him, eyes glued to the same screen.

"You're dead man. Dead!" Knox hollered and punched the button on his PlayStation controller.

"Idiots!" Lambert muttered at the two vampires involved in a game of Street Fighter. It was an older video game and the reigning favorite in their group.

Like a child, Deuce slapped Knox in the back of the head. "No, I'm not. Take this, you moron." Deuce spun Ken and flipped a Hadouken on Knox's Adon.

The vampires engaged in yet another round of insults and swearing.

"I'm going to take a shower," Allison said, turning toward the stairs.

Back in the privacy of her room, she grabbed her cell phone from the nightstand. When she sat on the edge of her bed, she could hear the shutters retracting for the night. She pressed Tor's number and waited.

He answered with a grunt after just one ring. "Hey, Ally," he said, sounding fatigued.

"Hey there. Can you come home now?" There was no point in beating around the bush.

"What's wrong?" Worry replaced the tired timbre of his voice.

"I have to feed, and you said not to leave without you."

"I can't." There was a slight pause and then some rustling over the phone. "But can you come here instead? Have the Three Stooges escort you," Tor suggested with a little chuckle, referring to Deuce, Knox, and Peyton.

"Sounds good. We'll be there in a few hours." Allison hung up, feeling refreshed after hearing Tor's voice, and went to jump in the shower. She was dying to get on the road as fast as she possibly could.

Annie glanced at the little red neon light on the nightstand. Three o'clock in the afternoon, three more hours before the kindness of "dawn" would be upon them. With a sigh, she rolled back onto her stomach and hugged the pillow closer. She could hear Gail in her room, playing with the dolls Harrow had sent for her.

Listening to her daughter's voice made her smile; Gail was pretending Ken and Barbie were walking down the beach. Jordan had her hands full keeping her daughter entertained.

The thought made her bolt upright into an awkward sitting position. Had she already relinquished her role as Gail's mother to Jordan? When had this happened?

Annie recognized one crystal-clear truth: Jordan had stepped into her shoes while she was away. The vampire had proven she loved Gail unconditionally, had tolerated her daughter's antics, and had given Gail the security of a home while her real mother was nowhere to be found.

True, she was here now—but for how long? Did she expect that escaping Goran's clutches would be easy? The sad truth was it was only a matter of time before Goran exerted his full control on her. She felt his power every day—the pull, the tugging, and the distorted voice summoned her home. It grew stronger with each passing day, turning her into a shaking heap of dread.

It wouldn't be long. She must say her good-byes soon if she wanted these people's lives spared. As much as she hated parting from her daughter again, it was the only choice she had.

Gail was in good hands. She had a bright future ahead of her, surrounded by people who adored her. What more could a mother ask?

Listless, Annie got out of bed, walked to the bathroom, and paused when she caught a glimpse of her face in the mirror. She hadn't changed much during her transition; she looked pretty much the same except for the blood-red eyes. However, it wasn't her outward appearance that she was worried about. It was what Goran had done to the woman inside the body. She belonged to him, and there was nothing she could do to change that.

How had Jordan escaped? Was she the only one capable of such a feat? Was it too late for Annie to find out if Jordan could help her? It felt like her well of time was drying up.

With a sharp exhale, Annie turned on the tap and scrubbed her face under the running water until it felt raw. Her questions would remain unanswered for another day, and her only reprieve was the time she spent with Gail. And by the grace of heaven, she'd spend every minute of her day with her.

Stepping into fresh jeans Allison had given her, Annie experienced another disabling pain in her gut. It wrenched every fissure inside her until she landed on the floor, panting and writhing in agony. Her heart pounded like a gong, deafening and frightening. It took her several minutes to cast the wave of pain aside enough to push herself up from the floor.

As far as she could see, Goran wouldn't stop until he had all his creations tucked away in his sanctuary of collectibles. Wherever her destiny led her, she feared that time was running out.

Allison let the brisk wind caress her face after she rolled the window on the last stretch of their four-hour trip back to the city. Despite Lambert's disapproval, she refused to be denied her time with Tor. It was a known fact within their circle after Harrow's announcement of room changes that she and Tor had already bonded as a pair.

She smiled at the wicked thoughts running through her mind. The ecstatic sound of Tor's groans when their bodies melded replayed over and over. The memory gave her a delicious burst of energy, enough to last her until they found some quiet time to be together again.

Deuce and Knox continued the competitive banter about their video game session, annoying the hell out of Peyton who remained neutral through it all, offering occasional suggestions on how the characters should have been played and how to rack up coveted points.

Meanwhile, Allison was content to let the trio entertain each other while their car made its way through the tunnel that lead to their underground facility.

The demolition crew was still hard at work. At least the noise had tapered off to a more acceptable level and the disgusting wrecking ball was nowhere to be found. What remained were mounds of blasted concrete and pieces of metal ready to be hauled away. The dust clouds still hadn't settled, floating around like a thick fog and giving the whole area an eerie appearance.

After their car pulled to a stop, her door was yanked open, and Tor's thick arms encircled her waist in one powerful sweep. He pulled her into a tight embrace, rendering Allison breathless.

Snickers came from the three others, and Tor shot a look meant to silence them. Instead, the laughter increased, the sound following them as Tor carried her through the massive doors leading to the facility and locked his mouth possessively on hers.

Heedless of the people staring at them, Tor's big strides took them down several hallways until he reached the door to his suite. All he wanted was to taste this woman again. Oblivious to anything else but Allison's response to his kisses, Tor did not hear Harrow's approaching footsteps.

There was the sound of a throat clearing, rudely halting their intimate reunion. "I'm sorry, folks, but I don't condone this type of lewd behavior in public." Harrow chuckled from the end of the hallway.

Tor hissed under his breath, and they both whipped their heads in Harrow's direction. Allison couldn't help but grin at Harrow.

"Impeccable timing as usual, Gates." Tor scowled, cradling her body closer to his.

"Sorry, guys. But can you keep this PDA in check? How about confining yourselves to the bedroom and keeping the noise as low as you can. This is a workplace, for Christ's sake." Harrow turned away before Tor could respond.

"Hell-boy is just upset because he hasn't gotten any love from his woman," Tor muttered and sought Allison's mouth again.

"I heard that!" Harrow yelled before the door closed behind him.

Tor laughed against Allison's mouth and kicked open the door. He walked to the bed, laying her in the middle without allowing their mouths to even part a fraction. She caught the soft glow of candles, and the scent of roses tickled her nose.

"Tor," she said.

"Hmm . . ."

"You got me flowers, too?" she asked. What a big surprise. It went to show how little she knew of her man.

"Yes . . . someone told me you liked them," he whispered.

"Would that someone be named Jordan?" Allison's eyes swept across the room before settling on Tor's face.

"Yes. I wanted something special when you came back here."

"Oh, Tor, I don't know what to say."

He gave her another disarming smile. "Just say you'll make love to me. That's all I ask."

"Yes!" was her enthusiastic answer.

There was nothing slow or romantic about the way Tor removed her clothes. It was pure need—a hunger she hadn't seen before but welcomed nonetheless.

"Woman, if I have to wait a minute longer, I swear I'll go crazy. My imagination has been doing a number on me since the night I left," Tor said, hovering over her like a feral animal.

"I won't keep you waiting." Allison uncurled underneath him, her naked body arching a seductive invitation. "But you need a condom first, before we get carried away."

"Oh, Lord!" Tor groaned but lifted his body away to grab the foil on top of his nightstand. As quickly as he'd undressed them, Tor tore the foil, sheathed himself, and settled on top of her again. "Ready?"

Allison had to smile. His eagerness and the desire in his eyes were all the validation she ever needed. Knowing that they were both on the same page was all she could ask for.

The moment their bodies fused was paradise. She followed where Tor led. He was her anchor.

Tor held her close while they caught their breath, lying together in the darkened room.

Once they'd recovered, Tor said, "Round two," with a wicked gleam in his eyes.

She giggled and jumped on top of him. "I think I'm ready to rumble."

"Perfect. I love a jungle woman."

The ring of his cell phone interrupted them. "Fuck." Tor whipped his head in the direction the sound had come from.

"You should take it," Allison said but her hands remained latched to his body.

"Damn it." He pushed his body out of bed with a disgruntled expression, and she sank against the mattress while he retrieved the phone from his jeans.

Tor punched a button and snarled. "What?"

Allison could hear Cyrus's voice. "Tor, my man. Sorry to interrupt, but we need you in the I-room right away."

"What's going on?" Tor asked, already jumping into his jeans. Allison bolted out of bed and moved to match Tor's speed.

"Just come. Harrow is already waiting for us," Cyrus said before the line went dead.

They were out of Tor's room in a matter of seconds, the remnants of their lovemaking buried under the urgency of the summons. Before long, they had torn down the length of the corridor and into the I-room where the rest of the fighters were already gathered. Harrow shot them a quick glance of acknowledgment before switching his attention back to the news already in progress on the television. Cyrus adjusted the volume, and the newscaster's voice filled the room.

"Hudson River Park officials have found the bodies of two men in the vicinity of Clinton Cove early this morning, the victims of an apparent knife attack. Police are treating it as a double homicide. The identities of the victims are still unknown. Motives in the killing are unknown, but experts are not ruling out gang involvement or a drug deal gone bad."

Harrow muted the volume and faced everyone with a grim expression. "I have a feeling that those victims could be our men."

Allison listened in horror while everyone spoke at once. She learned that the two human fighters, whom she hadn't met, had been assigned to take a captive to the cove and expose him to the sun. The prisoner was believed to be the person responsible for the attack on their facility, and he'd deserved to die.

"The vampire can go out during the daytime?" Tor asked when the room quieted down enough that he could be heard without yelling.

"I've seen strange things that could make your head spin," Rohnert said from where he had been sitting in silence.

"You didn't see it coming?" Harrow turned to Rohnert, his eyes blazing with accusation.

Rohnert stood up and walked to the front of the room. Cyrus and Tor moved fast to avert any possible collision between the two fuming vampires.

"I sure hope that accusation was a mistake, because I swear to God, I won't back down from you, Gates." Rohnert's voice was low and serious.

"Are you going to deny that you knew what that Zane guy was capable of?" Harrow spat in contempt. He moved closer to Rohnert until their noses almost touched.

"Whoa! Stop this shit now," Cyrus barked, moving between Harrow and Rohnert.

Rohnert spoke slowly, his eyes never leaving Harrow's face while he ground out each word. "The vampire bit me, which caught me by surprise. If I'd known what the bastard was thinking, it wouldn't have happened. Think, Gates, think."

Harrow took one step back after a few moments of forced reflection.

Allison rushed over used the opening to restrain him long enough for him to contemplate the facts. "Calm down, brother. I think Rohnert speaks the truth."

Harrow drew a sharp breath before rubbing his eyes in frustration. "Damn it. We can't lose any more people. This has got to stop," he rasped and shook his arm away from Allison's grasp.

"It's a pity we had no idea what the vampire could do," Rohnert said, agreeing with Harrow. His taut body began to relax. "I feel your pain, my brother, but we have to stay focused."

Harrow turned to Rohnert and reached out his hand. "No harm, no foul?"

"It's all good. Just don't pull that shit again." Rohnert clasped Harrow's hand and shook it.

"I'll work on it," Harrow said.

"Okay, now that you ladies have expressed yourselves, what's our next move?" Tor returned to his seat, and the rest of the fighters did the same.

"We remain tight and stay on course. If anyone sees this man," Harrow flicked on the remote, and picture of Zane flashed across the flat screen, "take him. I want him alive so he and I can have a long talk."

Melissa rushed to the door to answer the nonstop knocking. She straightened her white gown and puffed her chignon before opening the door.

Hamilton stood outside, looking impatient. He was not someone she'd ever trust with her life, and Melissa felt her defenses surging to the surface. It was unfortunate that he was one of Goran's faithful servants and someone with whom he conferred regarding important policing activities for the Council. She swore the vampire had it in for her. A kiss-ass in every sense of the word, Hamilton would dance to any tune and give praise where he thought it worthwhile to get into Goran's good graces. So far, he'd been able to charm their leader into giving him prime assignments and command over most of the Vampire Council's soldiers.

Goran could see right through people, so she wondered how in heaven's name he could have missed Hamilton's iniquity. Then again, no one could predict Goran's choices.

"Goran wants to see you," Hamilton said in a scathing tone.

"Thank you." Melissa shut the door in his face and rested her forehead against its surface. She took a deep breath. *What could Goran possibly want now?*

Things had been in turmoil since he'd executed Graciela. No one had been privy to the reason, but Melissa guessed that it was connected in some way to Annie's disappearance.

Scared witless, Melissa took several minutes to muster the courage to head to Goran's chamber. She hesitated before knocking.

"Come in."

A paralyzing fear engulfed her. She took a long moment to summon all her practiced poise before walking through the door and across the sitting room to Goran's desk. He looked up from a book he was reading—*The Art of War.* Melissa's dissipating confidence dropped another notch.

"You wanted to see me?" she asked, adding a dash of extra sweetness to her tone.

"Yes," Goran said with a lazy smile.

He gave her a long look-over, glancing from her perfect, imperial chignon to the white ensemble covering her trembling body. "I want to tell you something, but first come here," he said and patted his lap.

Like an obedient child, Melissa walked around the desk and sat, albeit with hesitation. She wondered what Goran was up to, but wondering wouldn't do much for her. Just when she thought she had him all figured out, he'd do a one-eighty, and everything she thought she knew slid down the drain.

He skimmed his lips over her hair, but then remained motionless, adding to her nervousness. Melissa shuddered when his warm breath blew on her neck, reacting in the way Goran expected. His powers were endless; evoking lust was just one of them.

Goran latched onto her vein and pulled hard, and her body arched in submission. Melissa's head lolled back, and she shuddered while he fed on her. After he drank all he could, Goran turned her around so she was facing him. His slick hair was pulled back in a ponytail, and his face was eerily calm.

"I think there's a pretty good chance that *our* son is dead."

How could he exude calmness when delivering such dreadful news? Melissa stared at Goran with disbelieving eyes, and then . . . her world fell apart.

Melissa had no idea what happened next. When she snapped out of her black hole of anguish, she found Goran watching her. For once, he wore an expression akin to worry. Had she screamed at the top of her lungs or passed out? Had Goran been holding her the whole time? Had she clawed at him in anger for her loss, for his noncommittal attitude toward their son's disappearance, or for all the years when Goran had failed to show Demetrius a father's love?

But Goran hadn't said he was certain. She'd hold out hope, even in its dimmest possibility. Could Goran ever be wrong?

When the last of her tears bled out of her eyes, Melissa raised them, pleading, to make one last-ditch effort. Only a mother would remain steadfast even if time and facts corroborated against her.

Goran watched her without expression as she attempted to put her jumbled thoughts into words. His arms remained around her waist as he waited for her to speak.

"I still want permission to go out to find him. Surely, you won't deny me the satisfaction of a more concrete answer. He is, after all, our son." Melissa's tone held a challenge she'd never thought she'd use on Goran, but the mere idea of losing her son emboldened her.

"You have my permission to go, but I want to make sure you know the repercussions of losing any more of those under your command."

She didn't miss a beat. "Of course." At this point, she'd take whatever she could get.

"Maybe this will cheer you up. It's about time you met someone." Goran took a piece of paper from the drawer and handed it to her.

Melissa glanced at the paper through her tears and committed the address to memory. "Thank you." Feeling the weight of the world on her shoulders, she tried to get up, but her body swayed and she sank back against him.

Goran, in one of his rare displays of compassion, cradled her in his arms. "Hush, my dear," he whispered.

Without uttering a word, he carried her out of his chamber and back to the safe confines of her room. Laying her in her bed, he tucked her in and left.

Melissa lay there, watching the walls close in on her again and wishing it was all a dream. She wanted to wake up and find everything back to normal, with Demetrius back so that all would be well in her world.

"Lambert?"

Annie walked into the training room after she'd sung Gail to sleep. The down time was as a good chance as any to get a whiff of fresh air.

"Yes, Annie. What can I do for you?" Lambert looked up from the stacks of papers he had on the desk and waited for her to approach.

"It's pretty quiet around here, and Gail is in bed. I wondered if I could step out and maybe get something to satisfy my craving?"

"Craving? Isn't the blood we have here satisfactory?" Lambert ran his fingers along his beard and eyed her with curiosity.

"I . . . err . . . actually want some time alone." There, she'd said it. As much as she loved being with these nice, loud, and happy people, she needed some time away to think.

Lambert seemed to consider, still staring at her. After a few seconds, he nodded. "One condition: I will provide an escort. Harrow's orders. No one goes out alone."

It was better than not being allowed to leave at all. She just hoped her companion wouldn't expect any conversation from her because she wanted peace and quiet.

"Yes, thank you." As usual, her voice came out soft and meek, not what she'd intended to project.

Lambert smiled before hitting the walkie-talkie. The thing crackled. "Hey, Dave. Mind keeping Annie company while she feeds?"

"Sure thing. I'll wait for her on the deck," the walkie-talkie buzzed, and Lambert grinned at her.

"He's ready."

"Thanks again." Annie turned to leave, but Lambert cleared his throat, and when she paused, she heard the rustle of the chair being pushed back.

"Be careful out there," he said and produced a little dagger from his cargo pants pocket and offered it to her.

"Thank you." That was all she could say. Yeah, they could be a rowdy bunch most times, but they were all accommodating and caring. Could she ask for her and her child to be surrounded by better people?

As promised, Dave was waiting for her. They departed in silence after he told her that he'd keep his distance if she wanted space to herself. Annie had to smile at Lambert's sympathetic gesture.

The forest was as quiet as it had been the night she'd first set foot in the house with Tor. Closing her eyes and pointing her nose upward, Annie couldn't catch the scent of any human nearby. Not a surprise. The house was situated far from the nearest city, embedded in a forest of giant spruce, pine, and redwood trees. They couldn't have found a better place for serene isolation.

Annie broke into a jog for a minute before sprinting hard, aiming for the east side of the forest. Nothing but the chirping sound of night creatures accompanied them on their run. Dave stayed close but didn't crowd her while they leapt and zigzagged across the damp earth. The cool wind was a welcome caress to her face, and the air was a nice change from the confines of her present accommodations.

As much as she wanted to participate in the animal diet everyone had been raving about, the idea still repulsed her. Only her ingrained manners had kept her from gagging in their presence. What was wrong with good, old-fashioned sinking your fangs in your victim's neck? That was the thrill of feeding—the one thing she looked forward to in her existence.

"Annie, I know what you're looking for, and it's something I haven't done in a long time," Dave said from behind her.

Annie stopped short. Dave did the same, still keeping a little distance between them.

"I want humans. I can't imagine feeding on animals," she replied and turned to run again.

"Do you have any idea why Goran can't reach Jordan?" Dave asked while he trailed her, his breathing as even as the wind blowing around them.

This, of course, stopped her dead in her tracks once more. "Tell me."

Dave pushed his glasses off his face, and what stared at her were whitish pupils and a whole lot of knowledge she hadn't had before. He took one step closer. "It's not a secret. Rumors are swirling that Jordan has never fed on human blood, ever. Leroy, may he rest in peace, always theorized that because she didn't take what Goran expected her to feed on, it negated his power over her."

Annie stared at Dave in disbelief. This was preposterous. No one had ever escaped Goran's clutches. *No one.* This was common knowledge among the inhabitants of the Council walls. Had Goran kept his failure with Jordan a secret to lead everyone to believe that he was foolproof?

Just as she began to contemplate the information Dave had shared with her, a sudden pain overcame her, just as it had before. This time, the pounding pain in her chest was enough to knock her off her feet. She fell to the ground, twisting like a centipede scuttling for cover, and a new deafening roar sounded in her ears.

"Annie, what's wrong?" Dave kneeled beside her. He watched in horror when she began clawing at her chest.

"He's calling me!" she cried, thrashing about when another barrage exploded in her stomach.

Confused, Dave hoisted her up and slung her over his shoulder. "I'm taking you home," he said and started on a mad dash back to the house.

"No, no . . . leave me here, Dave. I don't want Gail to see me like this." Struggling against his hold on her, she tried to wriggle free, but the crippling pain and clashing sound in her ears made it impossible to move.

"I can't." Dave's big strides raced across the distance, trying to make it back to the house as quickly as he could.

After a few more minutes of resistance, Annie succumbed to the pain and hung limply on his shoulder. She closed her eyes.

Then the echoes of Dave's footsteps were joined by several more, and she felt him stop mid-stride.

"We heard the lady ask you to let her go," said a voice she found vaguely familiar.

"She is none of your concern," Dave answered, and Annie felt his body tense.

Annie raised her head to see the owner of the voice. Hamilton stood in front of Dave, preventing him from going forward, while two other soldiers blocked his other exits. They were surrounded.

"She is my concern." Hamilton assessed her with calculating eyes before giving Dave his full attention. "Release her, and I might give you a little leniency and allow you to run before we kill you."

Aghast, Annie lifted her head and caught a glance of Dave's face. She saw defiance in his clenched jaw and the twitch of his eyes.

"Dave, go now," she whispered, "before they kill you."

He shook his head, pulled a gun from his waistband, and aimed at Hamilton, who merely shrugged.

"So be it," he said.

A shot rang out before Dave could pull the trigger. His body shuddered, and they fell to the ground. Annie rolled over while Hamilton and his men closed in.

"No! No!" Annie screamed, watching blood ooze from the small bullet wound in Dave's head. He gave her one fleeting look before the disintegration process started. She scrambled away just as his body exploded into a million dust particles before her eyes.

"You didn't have to kill him! I was on my way back!" she shouted with fury.

"Shut up, bitch." Hamilton yanked her up by the hair. "You've kept Goran waiting long enough."

He dragged her across the ground, and the long arduous journey back to the Council's headquarters began. Annie realized that the inevitable end was near.

Thank God, she'd been able to kiss Gail one last time.

Harrow placed the phone back in the cradle and pondered the information he'd just received. The purchase of the building had been finalized, thank heavens. Escrow was set to close in a few days. Most importantly, his team had installed the wiring and safety devices in the building that were vital to their operation. Rayce was on site to supervise and monitor and to make that sure everything was done according to specifications.

Safety and protection were the biggest concern, not just for them, but for their employees in general. Leo's men had popped in as promised and conducted a quick check. Declaring the location secure, Leo's team wrapped up their visit by approving the structural soundness of the building. With preparations proceeding as scheduled, they should be calling their employees to report for work in as little as one week.

Harrow slid the sunglasses off his face and rested them on the table. The I-room was all his for the time being, since all available hands were out in the field, patrolling and putting in additional time to locate Zane and the others responsible for Pritchard's death.

Harrow ran tired fingers through his hair and inhaled. They would get through this. He so needed a vacation, but there were pressing matters that had to be addressed first.

Damn it. When was the last time he and Jordan had been alone? Like honest-to-goodness quality time? Dilemma after dilemma had kept piling up. It rattled him at times, and he couldn't help wondering if he had what it would take to prevail.

He needed help—all the help he could get. Their numbers had dwindled, and they needed to add more fighters to the group. Trained fighters didn't come easy; it took a tremendous amount of time to train and harness each fighter's aggression and keep them focused on the big picture.

His primary concern was how thin his troops were spread these days. Then there was the incident with Rohnert, Harrow remembered. He couldn't believe he had questioned the vampire's loyalty by assuming he was withholding information from them. Harrow's huge blunder still stung like a bitch. Hopefully it hadn't put a dent on their working relationship, let alone their friendship.

A blaring siren sounded in the I-room, and it could only mean one thing: Something had gone awry. Harrow shot to his feet and snatched the receiver from the table. "What's going on?" he barked into the phone.

"Harrow, Annie and Dave went hunting hours ago, and they haven't returned." Lambert's breathing was loud and intense, even across the vast miles that separated them. "Daylight's going to hit any minute, and I don't know what to do."

"What the hell? Did you try Dave on his cell?" Harrow raked his mind for possible explanations of what could have delayed the two. Their rules were clear-cut: call and check in if unable to return at the designated time.

"Yes. There's no answer. I've called several times." Lambert's tone was thick with worry and frustration.

"Damn it. They shouldn't have gone out." Harrow pounded his fist on the table.

"It was a big mistake on my part to let them go."

There was guilt in Lambert's voice. Harrow felt sudden shame brush over him for giving the man a hard time. Although he wanted to back off, missing vampires were a crisis he had hoped to avoid.

He softened his pitch. "There's nothing we can do now until sundown, unless you and Drake want to go without vampire escort." Harrow paused and thought for a second. They shouldn't gamble with fate. At the rate things were going, they'd drop like flies if they didn't stop to think before reacting. "Get some men and patrol the general area at sundown. In the meantime, just sit tight." Easy for him to say; he was hundreds of miles away. "There should be remnants of their scents you can use to track them."

"Will do."

"And, Lambert, don't worry. Let's just hope those two are bunked somewhere cozy." Harrow faked a laugh, but morbid ideas crept in and told him to expect the worst.

"Yeah. I hope that's the case."

Harrow sunk into his chair, his mind going full tilt.

Zane had just gotten out of the shower when he heard movement in the living room. The first thing that came to mind was another unannounced visit from Grandpa. But maybe that band of vampires was back again. Wrapping a towel around his waist, he moved toward the bureau and pulled a semiautomatic from the top drawer, making as little noise as possible.

Pulling the door open, he listened and waited. With calculated movements, he covered the short, dimly lit hallway to the living room. Zane heard another swishing sound. Ready to pull the trigger, he turned right, barrel aimed in the direction of the noise.

"Don't fuckin' move!" he shouted.

"No!" A woman's high-pitched voice rattled in the room, and she skittered for cover behind the sofa.

Thankfully, Zane was not trigger-happy or he would have blown the unexpected guest to high heaven. At such close range, his gun would obliterate its target, and he'd be sweeping up ashes.

"Who the hell are you?" His aim didn't waver, still pointed in the direction of the sofa where the intruder hid.

"If you promise not to shoot, I'll come out, and we can talk," the woman behind the sofa said.

"Who are you?"

Instead of answering, the woman stood up ever-so-slowly until she was standing at her full height. Flaming red hair fell to her shoulders, and the kindest eyes stared back at him, imploring and seeking some sort of connection Zane couldn't quite understand. He held his ground, gun still pointed in her direction.

"I am Melissa, the mother of Demetrius—your grandmother." Her voice held a steady calm that had been missing seconds ago. She held his gaze even with the nozzle of the gun pointing at her.

"My father's . . . mother?" Zane's voice quivered. He took a step back and realized that sounding like a pansy was not your typical "hey, Grandma" type of greeting. Really, on the weird scale, this one easily took the prize.

"Yes. Why don't you come here and give me a hug?" The woman said and extended her arms toward him. Her smile was beguiling, and her expression was one of longing and relief. Confused, Zane lowered the gun but didn't put it away. Instead, he let it dangle from his fingers while he searched Melissa's face for any sign of a cruel prank. Instead, she waited, watching him hesitate, shifting on the balls of his feet.

Damn it, she wasn't joking. Zane stared at the woman. Here he was, half-naked, standing in front of his grandmother and speechless.

Holy cow! Grandmother? What do you say to your grandmother?

Her arms remained outstretched, beckoning him to come forward.

Zane looked around before he moved close enough and allowed himself to be pulled into her tight embrace.

Family warmth had been missing from his upbringing. Zane had no idea how to respond. Growing up with housekeepers and Demetrius's almost nighttime visits hardly constituted a warm household, but he'd stayed tight. It was just at this moment, wrapped in Melissa's warm embrace, that the realization hit him. He had missed out big-time.

With his father nowhere to be found, he had no one left. No one, until Grandpa had shown up a few days ago. Now Grandma had made an appearance. Wow, talk about winning the damn lottery. Family members had sprouted up like mushrooms in a matter of days.

Not trusting himself to talk, Zane held onto Melissa as if the very thread of life, his existence, depended on her.

"I'm so happy to finally meet you," she said after a long moment.

He gave her a final squeeze before answering, "Same here." His voice sounded hoarse, filled with emotion, and he didn't like it one bit. "How did you find me?"

"Goran gave me your address. He thought it was best that we meet." She looked at him and smiled. Zane noticed that Melissa smiled a lot.

"I'm glad you came." Wasn't that the damn truth? He felt like Billy freakin' Elliot, wanting to pirouette around the room to the rhythm of Kumbaya. The emotions spilling from him made him feel like a different person.

He returned Melissa's gaze and noted how beautiful she was. The complete package, from the beautiful red hair, her kind eyes, and her ethereal outfit, down to the strappy golden sandals she wore. Man, talk about luck with the gene pool. They'd bagged everything in the looks department.

"Why don't we sit so you can tell me all about yourself?" she asked.

Melissa waved her hand toward the sofa. Zane followed her, but then remembered how underdressed he was. He had on nothing except the towel wrapped around his waist. What a way to give a good first impression.

"Let me throw on some clothes on first," he said and backpedaled in the direction of his room, gun hanging from his finger, totally forgotten.

As soon as he got in his room, he employed the fast movement inherent to his kind and donned faded jeans and a white cotton T-shirt. He ran to the bathroom and rammed a brush through his hair, yanking at the roots fast enough to make him wince several times.

After inspecting himself in the mirror, he deemed himself half-ass ready and walked back to the living room. He found Melissa seated on the sofa. Her legs were crossed at the ankles and she looked very much like a prim and proper lady, bred to perfection.

"So, what brought you here?" He tried to sound casual despite the questions running through his mind. *Why now, after all these years? Where was his father? Why would Goran initiate a family reunion?*

"I wanted to meet you, of course." She paused. Her calm and serene expression was replaced by one filled with anxiety.

Zane tilted his head in confusion.

"I also wanted to find out if you have seen your father in the last six months."

"No, I haven't seen him. In fact, I have been waiting for him to show up or contact me."

"You have no idea where he is?" Melissa's face fell.

"No idea. The last time I saw him was half a year ago, if not longer. You don't know where he is, either?"

"I was hoping you could give me some answers." Melissa seemed on the verge of tears.

Zane thought for a moment, and that was when reality struck him. His father was most likely dead. He wasn't certain, but the clues were hard to deny. It was the only logical explanation. Demetrius must have died at the hands of the people who had taken him prisoner.

"I hate to be the one to break the bad news to you, but I think there's a possibility that Dad might be dead." The damning words echoed in his ears.

Melissa's grief was so profound that he didn't have a chance to console himself. He held her with all the gentleness he possessed, knowing it was going to be a long night.

Rohnert knew the minute he opened his eyes that he hadn't been asleep for very long. Groaning at the throbbing pain from his shoulder, he gingerly turned his body toward the digital clock on his nightstand. Hell. He'd been asleep for just a couple of hours, and there was still a lot of time to kill before he could go out and start his patrolling duties.

Nope. No patrolling for him. Doctor's orders.

Ten o'clock in the morning. For Pete's sake, two hours of sleep wasn't going to cut it. He'd be running on fumes if this kept up.

Between the ache in his shoulder, the nagging thoughts that hadn't left him since the small incident involving Zane, and the vision of Shelly, Rohnert realized that he might as well stop trying to sleep. It wouldn't come, and staring at the ceiling wasn't fun at all. Rohnert kicked the comforter off his legs.

It wasn't hot by any means, with the air conditioner firing at full blast, but thinking of Shelly made him warm all over. Yeah, he had taken advantage of his mind-reading abilities and had gotten all the information he needed. The blasted gift came in handy, but he felt guilty as hell. Knowing what she was thinking was exciting, and, well, if he were being honest, it was flattering at the same time. However, his hands were tied. It wasn't that he was saving himself for anyone in particular. The damn decree to which he was bound messed up the possibility of a future with anyone but a purebred vampire. No chance in making a go for the pretty doctor. It wouldn't be possible. Considering his unspoken attraction, he wouldn't trust her safety around him, either.

"Damn it," he muttered. God help him, the woman was getting under his skin.

Hell, ever since Jordan had made it clear that he was just a brother figure to her, he'd vowed to tighten the reins on his emotions. He feared the possibility of looking like a fool again. This type of emotion wasn't healthy. Sure, he was happy for Jordan and Harrow and had no hard feelings toward the vampire who had snagged Jordan's heart.

In retrospect, maybe Jordan had been right. Rohnert watched after her because he felt responsible for her, knowing her predicament when they met. And he, the ass, mistook his feelings of affection for something more profound. He had been so alone then . . . and was still alone now.

Although the solitude had been his choice, it went without saying that it got pretty lonely inside his head. His damn pants weren't faring any better.

Ha! Rohnert snorted, recalling Harrow's question if he was noble. Not by a long shot, but Goran's goals were geared toward personal gain and not the improvement of their race.

Rohnert couldn't live with that, so he didn't want to stick around. It was painful enough to watch the others blindly follow Goran out of fear. Out he'd gone, disgracing himself and his blooded kinsfolk with his betrayal.

He would be a fool to sacrifice his scruples in exchange for a stint at being Goran's dummy. It wasn't the direction he envisioned for the Council, or their race in general. They were headed into hostile territory, and alienating most of their allies was a big mistake. These were the same vampires who had stood by their side during the Great Vampire Revolution. It was such a pity that they had broken the alliance with Goran upon finding out that Rohnert had defected.

He had no intention of further involving himself in unnecessary bloodshed. Rohnert believed in the sanctity of life, be it vampire or human. Force, coercion, and persecution were definitely not his cup of tea, and he would rather stay away than engage in massacres and discrimination. Not to mention Goran's lust for building a personal army was wrong on so many levels.

Then there was the nagging question of how the hell that Zane guy had gotten away with attacking him and escaping the wrath of the sun. While he and Cyrus shared a bottle of expensive tequila from Tor's stash, they concluded that the man could be the by-product of a union between a human and vampire. The trouble was, no one could explain how these anomalies were created.

The theory he deemed likeliest was that Zane knew Rohnert could read minds. He wondered how on earth he'd missed the signs. Looking back, he knew that the bastard was a half-breed based on the color of his eyes. Halflings' eye colors ranged from dull tomato to reddish purple. Zane's eyes were the color of V-8 and could be hidden with contacts. Rohnert, a purebred vampire, had eyes the color of onyx.

Man, how could he have missed the obvious? Was he losing his touch? In hindsight, he shouldn't have waited this long to feed. It was a part of their makeup, part of who they were. Purebred vampires like him needed the blood of another purebred from time to time. Scratch that—they *required* regular feedings to increase their longevity. Why? He wasn't sure, but it had been a longstanding necessity for their race. It was something he'd conveniently *forgotten* to mention to Leroy, Harrow, and even Shelly. Prolonged abstinence from taking pure blood not only decreased their gifts, but also added to their susceptibility to pain and slowed their healing process. Human blood could serve as a supplement to their diet, but it could not replace purebred vampire blood entirely.

Glancing at the clock again, he saw that all this thinking had used up just fifteen freaking minutes. Sighing deep, he swung his legs off the bed and stood up. Sure enough, another bitch of a pain radiated from his wound all the way down to his toes. Yowling, he shrunk back to a sitting position and waited until the throbbing subsided. *Here's hoping the bastard doesn't have rabies.* With caution this time, he pushed his body up and headed to the bathroom. The burning was more bearable. What was the point of lying in bed when sleep was elusive? And there was still a lot of time to kill before he could go out and start his patrolling duties.

Yeah, being on rotation was better than being cooped up in the training area, day in and day out. No wonder Harrow had cracked and demanded to be included in the nighttime grind of walking the beat. The more strenuous the activity, the better.

Casting an eye at his reflection in the mirror, Rohnert noted that the hair he shaved religiously had been growing, creeping out like chin stubble. He ran his palm over his skull and decided to leave it alone. Why the change? He had no idea. Maybe this was better.

Damn, he had been reduced to a dithering fool who spent time thinking about whether he should shave or not. Yeah, that sounded like him, all right —just like the way his resolve to avoid Shelly was wavering. He wanted to see her even if it meant he'd be subjected to her prodding and questions. Perhaps he should start admitting to himself that he enjoyed her silent musings about him. Call it vanity. Either way, Shelly's naughty thoughts made him all too aware that they were an accident waiting to happen. Rohnert would cross that bridge when he got to it. In the meantime, he'd enjoy the sensations she evoked in him.

Yeah, men are pigs.

Since he'd admitted it, there was no point in denying himself a little indulgence. It had been far too long since he'd had a woman. He couldn't even remember the last time.

After he changed into long nylon basketball shorts and a cotton shirt, he fitted his arm in the sling Shelly had sent and walked out of his room.

Harrow was leaving the clinic just as Rohnert was walking in. They nearly bumped into each other. Harrow took a step back and held the door for him.

"Hey, how's the shoulder?"

Rohnert sensed the slight hesitation in Harrow's tone. No doubt, Harrow was still thinking about their exchange the night before. "I'm tight, my man," he answered. They clapped each other's backs, establishing an unspoken truce.

"Here to see Shelly?"

"Yup. Is she in?"

"The question is, when is she ever out?" Harrow chuckled.

Rohnert laughed at the jibe.

Somewhere in the room, the woman bristled. "I heard that. If you guys want me outta here, just say so and I'll go on an extended vacation."

"Hell, no! You can take a one-week break at a time, Doc. You're too precious, and we'd be lost without you." Harrow laughed, winking at Rohnert before he strode away.

"Flattery's not going to get you very far, Gates," Shelly hollered.

Chuckling, Rohnert let the clinic door slide closed behind him and headed toward the little adjoining office where Shelly often parked herself during the rare lulls in activity. Even though she had a big office at the end of the hallway, she spent a lot of time here, closer to her patients. Dedication could have been her second name, as far as Rohnert was concerned.

"Shelly?" Rohnert stuck his head in the open door. The room was no bigger than a broom closet, holding nothing more than a tiny desk and a chair.

"Hi, Rohnert." Shelly looked up from a book. She smiled and bookmarked the page before giving Rohnert her undivided attention.

His eyes slid down to catch the title of the book out of curiosity. *To Kill A Mockingbird.* Great choice. Smart woman. Terrific combo. *Oh, shut it, Rohnert! Don't be a fool.* "If you're busy, I can come back later." He didn't walk inside but leaned against the doorjamb.

"Nonsense," Shelly said. She got up, and her Crocs squeaked across the tiled floor.

Rohnert stepped to the side to give her room to pass. Shelly was in her usual uniform of green scrubs. Her hair was in a bun and her lips burnished with a light gloss. Very professional, he observed.

"Since you're here now, I assume you didn't get much sleep." It wasn't a question. The woman had enough experience with their kind to know their tendencies, anatomy, and even their schedules.

"Well, yeah." What was the point in covering up what she already knew?

"Do you want me to give you something to help you sleep?" she asked, motioning for him to climb up on the examination table. Instead of sitting on it, Rohnert went for the chair in the corner, pulling it closer to the table.

"I'm fine. Thanks." He sat down and saw Shelly raise an eyebrow. She walked to the sink, snapped on gloves, and returned. When she gave him a long look-over, it left him uncomfortable. Damn, the woman had a stare that could make even the toughest of males squirm.

"So, how's the wound?" She tugged on the arm sling from behind to release the clasp.

"It's okay. Some pain here and there, but nothing I can't handle." Why in the hell was he trying to sound like a macho-man?

"Hmm . . ." Without another word, Shelly leaned forward and reached for the hem of his shirt, which instantly caused him to shrink back in his chair. The woman was straightforward—no dillydallying and pure concentration. There was none of the inner monologue that he had been looking forward to hearing.

As soon as he lifted his arms to let her slide the shirt up, he winced in pain.

"Just as I thought. Did you take the pain medication?"

"Didn't get a chance yet." Upon seeing her frown, Rohnert tacked on, "But I took the antibiotic you prescribed."

"Well, good for you." Her tone was patronizing, and she moved closer to inspect the healing wound.

Rohnert couldn't do much, given their close proximity. She poked and prodded, and each time he winced, Shelly's suspicions were confirmed—he was in more pain than he was letting on.

After several minutes, she rubbed her chin. "It's healing well. As fast as can be expected. The stitches are holding up. Given that you're still in pain, don't move your arm if you can help it. Leave it in the sling for five more days. No strenuous activities for you, so patrolling is definitely out of the question."

"Wow," Rohnert muttered under his breath. What in the hell would he do when most of the fighters were out patrolling and he was stuck in the facility?

Shelly lifted her head and looked at him. "And no sparring, either. Allow the wound to heal. I know you want to test movement and rotation, but it's too soon."

"Why don't you just kill me?"

Shelly exhaled sharply and handed his shirt back to him. "A few days, Rohnert. I'm sure you can find something else to occupy your time."

Rohnert put his shirt back on as fast as he could, despite the screaming ache of his shoulder. He tried to hide his discomfort. "There's nothing much for us vampires to do, unlike you humans."

"Well, I'm off tonight . . ." She paused. "Well, not really, but I'm allowed some downtime. I'll let Cheryl take the reins for a few hours. As long as no one shows up with a bullet wound or a cracked head, I can make us a mojito, and we can hang out."

Ah, a date. "Make sure you crush enough mint, because I can drink like a fish."

Rohnert reached for the sling, but Shelly beat him to it. She eased it over his arm. When her hand brushed his skin, he jumped like megawatt voltage had hit him. Another sharp pain shot through him.

"Ow." That was the very word he was trying hard not to utter, but there it was, exposing his vulnerability.

She didn't fuss at him. "Hmm . . . lots of mint. You got it."

"I'm bringing an old samurai movie," he said before jumping to his feet, ignoring the pain, and running out of the room like his ass was on fire. For Christ's sake, he'd agreed to a night of movies and mojitos with Shelly. He hoped he could be a gentleman and leave her alone.

The nightmare had receded over the last month or so. Tor couldn't fathom how in the hell he had gotten off so easily. He deserved much more for killing his wife. The worst. The wrath of hell wasn't even enough to cover what he'd done.

Then there was Allison sleeping next to him, so trusting and always giving. Tor cursed under his breath. He wasn't worthy of her. No second chances were given to murderers. A prickle of panic passed over him. He had always believed in the calm before the storm. Even though he had no idea what was coming, he was certain it was just a matter of time.

"A penny for your thoughts." Allison snuggled closer, and her sweet scent drew him out of his silent ruminations.

"You." Tor lied, not willing to drag her into his cesspool of thoughts.

"Liar." Allison smiled and snuggled closer.

He slid his arm around her naked body and felt her body shudder. Ahh . . . the result was always good. Why were vampires attracted to scents like the moths to light? It was always her scent that drew him out, every single time.

"We'd better get ready. My five o'clock meeting was confirmed." Despite her words, her hands were already gliding south, and Tor knew that her five o'clock would just have to wait.

With a huge grin, he sunk his face into her neck. She arched to give him full access. Delighted, he let his tongue glide over her creamy skin. Wherever this led them, the possibilities were endless. This was just a warm and eventful start to their evening.

The now-hardwired office building had begun operation as scheduled. Two weeks after opening their doors for business, everything was running like a well-oiled machine. Employees of Tack Enterprises had been more than eager to start working again and get back into the swing of things. Although their weapons production didn't cease during the darks months following Pritchard's death, the demolished office building had to shut down its operations.

The production line had continued processing orders for long-standing clients. Now that the offices were operational once more, meetings were scheduled and new business was being conducted. All of this was done under the watchful eyes of Harrow.

Allison put much of her time into the business to alleviate some of Harrow's workload. This meant that Tor's responsibilities had also increased. He remained the head of Allison's personal security and continued to participate in the regular patrolling rotation.

The sudden disappearance of Dave had put a dent in their manpower, since he had been part of Allison's security team. Deuce had taken his place, thus breaking up the playful trio of the three stooges. The facility's leaders had been spreading the fighters a little thin, with Harrow, Rohnert, and Cyrus logging countless hours training new recruits.

Tor and Allison usually retreated to her room for a short nightcap before Tor had to leave for rotation. Jordan, on the other hand, divided her attention between Gail and the added tasks of helping with recruitment and training. She and Harrow, sometimes with Rohnert, would venture out to find suitable members for the team. The process was slow and intensive, considering Vampire Council soldiers were visible and active throughout the city.

A few weeks after the grand opening, despite Harrow's insistence on keeping the operation on the down-low, Leo made a valid argument for increased visibility. Current clients, as well as prospective ones, needed the assurance that Tack Enterprises remained at the top of its game. As much as Harrow detested the fanfare even for a few hours, Leo's suggestion couldn't be ignored.

The ribbon cutting ceremony, spearheaded by Leo, had been successful. He brought in more prospective clients, more than what Harrow and Allison had expected to land, in just one attempt. Several big-time private company owners attended the grand opening, and the short presentation of their products immediately garnered attention. Contracts were offered and signed in a matter of weeks.

This also meant that Allison had been a strong fixture in most transactions. She attended business meetings and was an active participant in introducing new products. She had emerged as the new face of Tack Enterprises. Questions about Pritchard's absence had tapered off after her convincing lie that Pritchard had become an avid diver and had decided it was time to hand over the reins of the business to his daughter.

This, Harrow had reiterated, might backfire if anyone decided to take a closer look at her, her lifestyle, or even just her schedule. Of course, he tended to lean more toward paranoia and worry. However, precautions were taken, and any threat would be taken seriously.

"We're thirty minutes late," Allison complained as they made their way to the elevator in the underground parking garage. Deuce followed them after parking the bulletproof, sun-resistant Lincoln Continental. As usual, Deuce had opted for taking the stairs out of habit, although Tor suspected he was trying to give them privacy.

"You weren't complaining earlier." Tor grinned and pressed the button for the top floor.

All forty floors were fitted with metal shutters inside the bulletproof glass windows. Harrow didn't even blink twice before doling out the money to install the added security. If it meant safety for all concerned, it was an easy decision on his part.

"You make it difficult for me to say no to you," Allison said, her voice purring.

Yeah, the woman knew how to please him. This was one of the surprises he'd unraveled as their relationship progressed, and he wasn't complaining.

As soon as the elevator door closed, Tor pulled her into his arms for one final caress before they had to get to work. "Give me a kiss." He flicked a middle finger into the camera before his mouth descended upon hers. It was his silent but strong message to Rayce, Harrow, or anyone else who might be watching their every move.

When the doors opened, businesslike conduct was observed at once. This meant they would keep their hands off each other until they were back behind closed doors and alone.

Tor stayed a few feet behind Allison once they emerged from the elevator. Allison's secretary met them at the door to her office, papers in hand and a cup of jasmine tea made just as Allison liked it.

"I told the clients that you're running thirty minutes late. They are waiting in the conference room." Allison's secretary glanced with awe at Tor, just like she did every time she saw him. Tor gave her a tight smile.

"Thank you, Samantha." Allison went to her desk and glanced at her papers. "I'll take the documents home to review them. Let the clients know I'll be there in a few minutes."

Samantha smiled before closing the office door. Tor remained standing while Allison gave him a knowing look.

"You're quite a charmer."

"Don't start." He shook his head. This teasing had gone long enough. He'd make sure she got her payback when they were back in bed.

Allison laughed. "Oh, I've been a bad girl for teasing you? Will I be punished later on?" She batted her eyelashes, making it impossible for Tor to keep a straight face.

"You're going to get a lashing and some honest-to-goodness spanking, woman." Tor squirmed at the sudden hardening in his pants. "It's time for you to work," he reminded her, hoping Allison didn't catch a glimpse of the wood he was now sporting.

By the way Allison giggled, she'd seen what he was trying to hide. She took a stack of documents and stashed everything in her briefcase, and they headed out of her office. While they trekked down the wide hallway to the conference room, Tor couldn't help but glance at Allison's very professional outfit. The smart-looking jacket and skirt ensemble suggested power, making him ache for her. Tor blew out a lungful of air. She was driving him crazy without even trying.

Burns, get a grip, he scolded himself. Deuce appeared just as he and Allison entered the conference room.

Tor and Deuce walked to their designated posts in the room. Tor was on the right, his attention split between Allison and the guests, while Deuce concentrated on the attendees.

Once the meeting was underway, two crates of Tack's newest sniper rifles were opened and placed on the table for inspection and demonstration. Allison was in her element. Her newfound knowledge of guns came in handy now.

She picked up a rifle. "As you can see, this," she pointed to the body of the rifle, "has a new, improved muzzle brake to reduce recoil. We have also increased the effective range, which now reaches up to three miles. We're talking accurate, boys. Dead accurate."

When the excited ahh's rippled across the room, Allison turned her head and gave Tor a very satisfied smile.

The entire presentation lasted less than thirty minutes, followed by questions concerning the production schedule and delivery. Almost all of their clients were from the military, including those from the United States and Canada. There was no doubt that this latest offering would garner interest from other nations.

While Samantha handled the rest of the basic questions, Allison excused herself from the room amid appreciative glances from the men. Their obvious awe was not just directed at the beauty of the woman who had given the presentation but also her impressive knowledge of the subject matter.

Tor's chest puffed with pride. Allison had come a long way. She was no longer riding on her father's coattails but was now a confident businesswoman in her own right, ready to take on the world.

"If your grin gets any bigger, your cheeks will burst," Deuce commented while they walked behind Allison on the way back to her office.

Tor glanced at Deuce and snarled. "Shut your hole." What a buzz kill.

Deuce chuckled and playfully socked him in the arm.

When nine o'clock arrived, Deuce went down to the parking garage to get the car ready. Allison returned a few calls while Tor waited for Deuce's text.

Most of the staff had gone home. Harrow had implemented work hours from noon until 8 p.m., utilizing late-scheduled meetings to take advantage of sundown hours. Security and cleaning personnel lingered in the nearly deserted building. When Tor and Allison stepped out of the elevator into to the underground garage, Deuce had the car waiting on the curb.

"That was a kickass presentation, boss," Deuce said from the driver's seat. He tipped his black cap and got the car moving.

"Thanks." Allison smiled.

Tor glanced at her while their car exited the secured parking garage. She was beaming. Yeah, he would beam, too, if he could. He wouldn't in Deuce's presence, since the man was becoming more and more annoying.

"You've done good, woman," Tor complimented Allison. Eyes alert, he surveyed their immediate surroundings once the car cleared the roll-up gate. When the car was preparing to make a left turn, Tor noticed a black sedan with heavily tinted windows parked just outside the exit.

He turned his head when they passed the car and memorized the license plate. He'd have Rayce run a check on it once they got back to the facility. For some strange reason, Tor's gut was telling him something. He switched his attention back to the windshield and felt for the Glock underneath his leather jacket. Deuce caught his movement and ran his fingers along the shotgun resting next to the driver's seat. He, just like Tor, was ready to fire at a moment's notice.

Melissa and Zane spent the better part of the night talking in his penthouse. Yeah, it was just like your average *Leave it to Beaver* type of deal. The reunion brought with it the agonizing realization that Demetrius might never come back. It had been far too long without any form of communication from him, and Melissa, as much as it pained her, had to accept the likelihood of her son's demise.

Her tears dried up, to be replaced with indescribable rage. Zane stood by the picture window and glanced outside, and Melissa was acutely aware that her grandson was holding his grief at bay. Anguish, no matter how hard you masked it, had a damning scent. She could imagine how much Zane missed his father, but he kept his emotions in check for her sake. After all, Demetrius had made it clear that showing weakness was unacceptable. She remembered him saying that such displays meant you had accepted defeat and had lost the fight even before it began.

Melissa dabbed her eyes and set her features to a neutral expression. "What made you think Demetrius was killed by *them*?" Melissa asked one more time, and Zane turned to look at her.

By "them," Melissa was referring to the people who had abducted Zane and taken him to some facility for interrogation. Afterwards, they'd relinquished him to the sunlight, expecting his death.

They had been sorely mistaken.

"All evidence points to them and no one else. I wish I could name names, but all I can give you is a location where I think they're holed up. It's the same place I showed pops."

She slammed her eyes shut, feeling another blast of tears coming. Whenever her son's name came up, a brand new ache tore at her shredded heart.

"Tell me more." Melissa walked over to stand beside her newfound kin. The night was quiet and somber, matching their gloom. The sky was devoid of stars, and the threat of rain loomed.

"I arranged for a meeting with the owner of the company when Demetrius asked me to give him some intel. Nothing at that time appeared suspicious, until we encountered vampires in the general vicinity—"

"Vampires?"

"Yes, vampires. Not your garden variety, but the diseased ones Pops claimed they were hunting down. So we killed 'em all. Well, Pops did. After that, we took some ankle bracelets we found on the scene, and that was the last I heard from him.

"To tell you the truth, I think there's a big connection. My gut tells me they're responsible for Pop's disappearance. God, I miss the man." Zane ran his fingers through his hair, getting caught in a whirlpool of emotions.

Melissa's eyes shot up to meet Zane's. This was the first time she'd heard him call Demetrius "Dad." The word was endearing when uttered with such longing and reverence.

Her hand reached up to touch his face. Truly, he was Demetrius' son, for she could see him in Zane. There was the striking similarity of their eyes, the lazy way their eyebrows quirked up, the angular jaw, and the one-sided smirk. But the most damning likeness had been and always would be the color of their hair.

"We'll kill them all," Melissa whispered. Her eyes blazed even though her tone was soft. Her voice was edged with blistering contempt and pure vengeance. "Just point me in their direction," she added and pulled his face closer to give him a tender kiss on each cheek.

Melissa departed Zane's place with a heavy heart but an iron-clad determination to kill every single one of the people who had taken Demetrius from her. Returning to the vampire headquarters brought minimal relief, for the itch to go back out was too distressing. She had to do it. Goran had to have known that she'd come back. There was no point in aggravating him further. The incident leading to Annie's disappearance had tarnished her reputation, and regaining Goran's full trust was necessary.

Melissa hurried to her room to shower and change. She needed to be fresh and clean if she wanted to see Goran. Pushing all thoughts away, she tried to enjoy the pounding warmth of the water on her back. After taking great care in applying a little makeup, Melissa studied herself in the mirror.

She was ready to haul ass, so to speak. Nothing mattered anymore but punishing the people responsible for her son's death. Her breath hitched, and a cry escaped her lips. Had she really accepted that Demetrius was never coming back? Melissa grasped the edge of the sink as a terrible ache swept through her.

Deeming herself ready to face Goran, she walked out of her room with the confidence of a soldier leading a battalion into a street scuffle. She was about to knock on Goran's door when she heard whimpering inside.

After looking around the hallway, she pressed her ear on the door to listen. She knew right away who was involved.

"No . . . I just wanted to see my daughter. I had every intention of coming back." Annie's voice was frantic. She was, without a doubt, scared shitless.

"You ignored my summons," Goran said.

"Be–because I wanted to be with *her* a little bit longer." The fear in Annie's voice sent chills down Melissa's spine.

They couldn't suffer another loss because of Goran's anger. It was understandable that he was upset when his creations deceived or deserted him. Graciela had been taken down just for being an accessory to a crime he considered unpardonable.

"And you were with another man!" he accused. Goran never shared. Once you were branded, you stayed branded.

"It wasn't like that, it—"

"Silence!" A strike echoed, followed by a loud thud and a piercing wail.

Operating on instinct, Melissa sprang into action. If she wanted Annie alive for interrogation, she had to stop Goran from killing her. It wouldn't be an easy task, but she had to try. She didn't even stop to think twice about how Goran would interpret her intrusion.

"Goran?" Melissa pounded on the door.

Stillness followed, and then the sound of heavy, determined footsteps approached the door. Goran hurled it open, and Melissa took a step back when a pair of blazing ebony eyes greeted her. This was no joke. He was livid.

"Goran . . ." she whispered. Melissa held herself together and tried to ignore the screaming voice inside her head to flee. She used her most placating tone, which had always worked in the past. "I found Zane."

Goran's face had an eerie, calm expression when he focused on her. Alarm bells in her head banged loud, screaming for her to run away and not return until he sent for her.

"You did." It was a dead statement, enough to make her want to scramble for cover.

Yet, she didn't run. With courage she didn't know she possessed, Melissa forced a meek smile and spoke in an innocent tone. "We're going to see each other again—that is, if you agree." Yeah, might as well hand him her head on a silver platter. This could very well be the dumbest thing she'd ever done. She might as well be talking about the weather with someone about to commit murder.

The menace rolling off Goran came in thick waves, and she could see Annie cowered in the corner. There was no doubt in Melissa's mind that the sound she'd heard earlier was a mean wallop across Annie's face.

"I want to tell you all about it." Melissa took a tentative forward, reached out, and touched Goran's face, which at the moment was directing a death glare at her. Her intrusion might cost her not just a punishment but her life. Her newfound boldness empowered her, but Goran's continued stare was disarming, if not downright threatening. Melissa ignored the symphony of warnings in her head. "Let me take your mind off your worries."

Goran whipped his head in Annie's direction instead of answering. He took a few steps, but stopped. "You. Get out of here and make sure you come next time I call for you," he spat out, his eyes flashing a venomous warning. "If you as much as step foot out of these walls, consider yourself departed."

The threat hung in the air. There was no mistaking that Goran meant business. This was not the typical intimidation he often used with them. This was loaded and real.

Annie, despite her palpable fear, bowed low before scampering out of the room.

Goran turned his attention to Melissa. The predatory stance was nothing Melissa had seen before. This was pure domination with a massive dose of terror. She winced when he forcefully took her by the waist. Running was out of the question now.

"You never should have interrupted me. You asked for this," Goran whispered in her ear. His cold breath caressed her neck. He was not going to make it easy on her. Whether it was lashing or binding that would be on the menu tonight, she knew that she would have to make it out alive.

"Yes . . ." Her voice was a mere whisper. "What do you want tonight?"

Melissa could only guess what would happen. Goran wasn't one to mince words or go light in the action department. In a way, she had enjoyed every minute with him, as sick as it sounded. Instead of giving an answer, Goran picked her up and marched straight to the bed. It wouldn't be romantic by any means, something Melissa knew from all the years she'd been with him.

He threw her on the bed and reached into his nightstand drawer. A jingling sound alerted her to what was to come. Her attention shifted to his face and noted his set jaw and his burning eyes. Although he wasn't cursing her to high heaven, she knew better than expect anything but punishment. As his body heaved toward her, he positioned himself in between her legs, spreading them apart.

"You wanted this," he said again. In his hand was a pair of handcuffs, an all-too-familiar accessory.

"Yes." Her answer was clear. She'd do what he wanted. Like a child, she had been out of line, and she deserved this. A shudder rolled through her body when he snapped the cuffs on one wrist, wove the chain through the bedpost, then cuffed her other wrist, and raised her arm.

"Good girl," Goran hissed under his breath. He yanked on the chain, pulling hard until her muscles burned. He produced a blindfold and covered her eyes. All that was left to do was accept what was coming to her.

With a snap of a finger, lights went off and the whipping began.

After Melissa left, Zane had gone knee deep into research on Tack Enterprises. He wanted to keep tabs on whoever was running the show and take notes on the appearances of the billionaire's reclusive daughter. Shifting the mouse, he glanced at the computer screen again and checked the photos his paid cohort had taken for him. He thumbed the pen he was holding before scribbling on the notepad on his desk. He timed the comings and goings of the entire staff but took more interest in the bulletproof vehicle his snitch had reported.

He'd been doing his homework with fevered determination. After all, the talks he had with his grandmamma—damn, the title didn't seem to fit such a beautiful, young woman. It would be an understatement to say that he was glad she found him. The loss of his father was a heavy burden. The sooner he found answers, the better he'd feel.

Drumming the pen with restless energy on the pile of notes he'd put together, Zane realized he was onto something. Those people in that holding room where he had been taken had a definite connection . . . but to what? He had yet to find out, but he would.

In the meantime, he was going to do some hard-core surveillance himself. Employing several good team members was necessary. That wouldn't be easy, considering he was strapped for cash. A lazy smile worked its way across his face. Maybe Grams could help. After all, they had the same purpose. They were both aiming to find out who had taken his father away from them.

Pulling his cell phone from his pocket, he took out the paper Melissa had left him. "Call me if you need anything," she had said. Yeah, now was the right time to pull those strings. He punched in the numbers and stored them in the phone's memory before hitting send. After five rings, his call went to voicemail.

Melissa's soft voice chimed on the other line, asking her caller to leave a message. "Hello, it's Zane. Call me when you get a chance." He pushed the end button and inhaled, and then his eyes caught something on the screen.

Staring at the photo of the car, he zoomed in closer. The window tints were dark and impenetrable. One could guess that whoever was inside was allergic to the paparazzi or to the outside elements. Hmm, wasn't that a doozy? He just might have the answer right at his fingertips. Zane laughed out loud.

"Now, will the real Slim Shady please stand up?" he sang in a mocking fashion. The wheels inside his head were already going full speed.

Minutes later, his phone rang. "You wanted me to call you." Melissa's voice was hoarse and weak, as if she had been crying.

Zane found himself gripping the phone. "Grams? What's wrong?"

There was a pause, and he heard rustling followed by what sounded like throat clearing. When Melissa came back, her voice was almost back to normal. "I'm fine. Just some cold I caught somewhere."

He knew an outright lie when he heard one. Vampires were sturdy. They never succumbed to the normal maladies humans had to constantly deal with. They didn't get sick. He was not fool enough to believe her, but he held his tongue.

"What can I do for you, my boy?"

"I need your help. I'm onto something, but I can't pay for it. I need a couple of people to help me out. I'm strapped for cash, so I can't hire private guns." The words tumbled out of his mouth.

"You need manpower? Does this have anything to do with Dem . . ." Melissa's voice trailed off.

"Yes."

"Then you shall get it. Give me a little time. I'll call to let you know when to expect them. I'll send some spending money with them."

The silly grin on Zane's face lasted long after the phone conversation was over. Perfect. Now, all he had to do was make sure that his assumptions were correct and no fuck ups occurred.

"You know I'd never tell you what to do, but enough is enough. You have pushed yourself to the limit," Jordan said in a stern voice. It was a tone she reserved for Gail, when the girl was being unreasonable, just like Harrow was being at the moment.

"Jordan, there is much to be done—"

"Yes, there's much to be done here, but you don't have to do all of it. You have enough extra hands to help. You have driven yourself to exhaustion, and it's time I said something about it."

Harrow knew from experience that he wouldn't win this argument, no matter what he said. A pounding in his head continued to ravage his resolve, but he kept his expression tight. A damn headache was the last thing he wanted to deal with right now.

"But, I need—"

"Stop it. Just stop. Live a little, Harrow. You have been through a hell of a lot in the last year. Don't worry about the business. It's a well-oiled machine, now that Allison is in the driver's seat. Cyrus, Lambert, and Rohnert can worry about the facility. Come away with me. Let's take a few days." She paused and smiled demurely in an unJordanlike way. "Hell, let's make it a week."

Harrow had to laugh. "Fine, we'll go."

He scooped her up from the chaise and seized her mouth with his. When he set her down on her feet, Jordan's arm snaked around his waist. Yeah, this had been a long time coming. The business had taken up even his sleeping time, which meant he'd had very little time to spend with his two favorite girls. He knew he had been missing out, but the idea of just kicking back and leaving left a sour taste in his mouth. But then, there was always a first time for everything. With a wicked gleam in his eyes, he crushed his lips against Jordan's mouth, and she latched onto him as if their lives were connected by this one thread.

They held on fiercely and tried to make up for lost time. Lost in exploratory touches, they felt as if they hadn't seen each other in decades. He'd been buried in work and whatever new dilemma had sprung in their faces, and Jordan had been busy with Gail, being the mother the little girl needed.

The disappearances of Annie and Dave still hung over them like a dark cloud. The pair hadn't been seen or heard from. That, in and of itself, was alarming and devastating. Harrow didn't have the guts to tell Gail. Was he glad when Jordan had stepped up to the plate and broke the news to their little girl? Heck, yeah. Jordan held their baby while she wept.

"Earth to Harrow, calling Harrow," Jordan whispered, cupping his face. "You're not the only one who has to do the legwork. I'm here, I can help you out."

Harrow blinked, shutting out that train of thought. He'd been so caught up with everything around him that he was failing to pay attention to their relationship. He must have been neglecting Jordan far too long if she had to ask that they get away. It was sad, really.

"I apologize for neglecting you. Let me make it up to you. Why don't we go out for a drink tonight?"

"Wow, that's a first. You know I don't drink." She tugged on his belt loop, coaxing him to sit at the edge of the bed.

"Well, we can enjoy each other's company, and you can be the designated driver." He cupped his palm across the base of her neck and pulled her closer. "You know, like a date."

Jordan laughed. "Sure, like a date. We can ask Tor and Ally to double-date, if you want." She nuzzled her mouth against his neck, a sign that she was aching to drink from him. Her mouth grazed his jaw, tracing the contours with her tongue. Jordan knew where to touch him. His muscles tightened from his legs upward, and she smiled. She'd always enjoyed her effect on him.

"Sure . . ." he answered with a strangled breath. "If we want to go out, we'll have to continue this later." He groaned, knowing it was going to be hard to pry himself away from her.

"I don't mind staying in." Her hand moved to dangerous territory. Harrow groaned, and then bit his lip. Jordan was going for the kill.

Before he could respond, the intercom chimed, announcing an important call. Muttering a curse, Harrow rose and went to the little machine he longed to strip off the wall. It seemed like all he did nowadays was answer calls and troubleshoot. The damn dominoes hadn't stopped falling ever since Pritchard's death. It was always one step forward and three steps back. Everything rested on Harrow's damn shoulders.

Ramming the button with a finger, he grunted. "What's up?"

Rayce's voice filled the room. "Hey, boss, thought you might want to know. Tor gave me a license plate to run an ID on, and the car was registered to a Gralnik Lilic."

"Why did he want you to run the plates?" Harrow turned to look at Jordan with an apologetic expression, wishing there was more he could do rather than making her wait all the time. Jordan nodded her head in understanding before leaning forward to rest her elbows on her knees to watch him.

"He said the car was parked outside the office building when they got there and was in the same spot when they left. You know our man is a little twitchy when it comes to Ms. Ally," Rayce commented with a chuckle.

Harrow thought for a moment. Should he increase security for Allison? Add the newbies they had recruited who were ready to be thrust into the arena? Jesus, the decisions were making his head spin.

"What else can you tell me?" He knew Rayce thorough and would have the pertinent details at his fingertips.

"This is where I think there's some suspicious connection. The car's owner has offshore accounts connected to the defunct company Zane used when he first made an appearance here. Dante saved the info in an unmarked file, and I connected the dots."

This was where Rayce shined—offshore information was difficult to prove, but the hacker in him had a way of breaking every single code and finding that one needle in a haystack. If your life depended on one little piece of information, it was wise to consider what Rayce could discover. The man was a pure genius when it came to technology and everything that came with it.

"Good job, man. I want you to keep monitoring." With a press of a button, the line went dead. Harrow sank into the chair and pressed his thumbs to his temples. The little headache had turned into a full-blown, pounding pain.

"Harrow, is everything okay?" Jordan asked, even though she'd heard everything. "I mean . . . are *you* okay?" She started massaging his temples. The relief of her touch was instantaneous, and Harrow's breathing became more even.

"Yeah . . . been having these damn headaches."

"Have you seen Jones or Shelly?" Jordan moved her fingers in a circular pattern along the side of his face, moving toward the back of his head.

"I was planning to do that soon." The tenor of his voice carried the weariness he'd been experiencing. "Let's get ready. Call Ally and tell her to join us."

Harrow wasn't sure that painting the town red was what they needed at the moment, but it was a start. He needed to take his girl for a night out, away from the facility and the troubles that kept piling up around them. If going to a bar for a few hours would help, he'd be glad to have a little bit of distraction.

The club was almost bursting at the seams by the time they arrived. The electric atmosphere was hopping with each pound of the booming bass, highlighting the promise of a fun night. The group took their seats in the VIP section of the crowded room. Getting a prime spot was easy if you didn't mind paying the outrageous price for bottle service.

"What can I get you boys and girls?" A waitress with the reddest lipstick and shortest skirt stood right next to Tor, appraising him with ravenous eyes and seeming to enjoy what she saw. Harrow snickered at Allison's sharp hiss under her breath.

"Bring me a bottle of Kauffman," Allison ordered in a dismissive tone.

Tor noticed when Jordan flinched. It wasn't a secret that everyone had been having trouble adjusting to the changes in Allison's personality. Ever since she had begun taking lessons and had stepped forward as an integral and outspoken partner of the organization, her behavior had undergone a slight transformation. Not for the worse, but just . . . different.

"Sure thing, chica," the waitress replied in a thick Puerto Rican accent.

Allison would have jumped the woman had Jordan not clamped a hand on her arm to stop her.

"Did she just call me chica?" Allison hissed under her breath, inaudible to human ears.

"Hold your temper, sister." Jordan kept a tight hold on Allison while Tor shuffled uncomfortably where he stood.

"He and I will share a bottle of Patron Silver." Tor pointed at Harrow. The waitress smiled in approval, as if her consent were necessary to process drink orders. "And keep a tab open."

"Anything for you?" the waitress asked Jordan.

"Just a glass of water."

When the waitress walked away and was out of earshot, Tor slid next to Allison in the booth and pulled her close to him by the waist.

"Honey, you know I love it when you're all territorial about me, but take it down a notch with those humans. We don't want to get into a fight over nothing."

Allison snaked her arms around his neck and seized his mouth, not bothering to answer.

After their long PDA session, Harrow cleared his throat. "Um, kids, your CPR practice is disgusting. Do you mind behaving in public? We don't want to catch anyone's attention here."

Why does Harrow have to be the designated party pooper every single time? Tor growled before breaking free. Allison grinned, seeming pleased by her effect on Tor.

Their waitress returned and placed the bottles and glasses on the table. "Is there anything else I can get you?" she asked, her eyes resting on Tor.

"We're good," Tor answered, squeezing Allison's hand.

Harrow jumped in as the waitress walked away, directing a question to Allison. "Hey, what's going on with the ammo orders?"

Tor downed one shot of tequila right away, but Allison took her sweet time sipping the first of many for her before replying.

"Cyrus called earlier and confirmed that we're on schedule as far as delivery. I called Leo, and the rest of the payment will be wired upon receipt of the goodies. So rest your mind, brother, and have some fun."

This was a far cry from the once-timid woman she had been before. Tor marveled at the changes in Allison. Where had it come from? Must have been the confidence from her martial arts training in addition to her increased responsibility within the business. Harrow had boosted Allison's ego and drawn her out of her shell by assigning her more important functions within the company. Brownie points for the party pooper.

Tor couldn't help but stare at Allison. He'd come a long way because of her and the enduring patience she managed to maintain despite the rejection he'd showered on her before they got together. Boy, was she glad she'd persisted and won him over.

"I wanted to let you guys know," Harrow's voice interrupted Tor's reverie, and he swung his attention back to his friend. "I'm going on a short vacation."

"Where are you going? Is something wrong?" Allison leaned forward, her face marred by a worried frown. Her eyes shot back and forth between Harrow and Jordan.

"There's nothing wrong. I need a vacation." Harrow laughed, and although Tor believed it, he couldn't get over the idea that Harrow would actually leave, even for a short time. Tor had always thought it would be impossible for Harrow to take a break from his responsibilities, but he applauded the decision. It was about damn time the vampire got a breather.

"Where are you going?" Allison asked one more time.

Harrow's eyebrows shot up behind his dark lenses before he took Jordan's hand and kissed her palm. "I'm just going to take my lovely girlfriend for some much-needed R and R. I don't think I have to tell you where we're planning to go, but rest assured, we'll be reachable if you need us."

"Fine—be secretive. But make sure you are both armed and watching your backs." Allison demanded, sounding as if she had been running the show all along. In true Tack fashion, she had begun to sound like her father: businesslike and direct.

"If I may put my two cents in, please remember to behave yourselves," Tor said. He took a quick swig from his shot glass before pouring another round for him and Harrow. "As much as I want to say 'no' to your little planned getaway, I have to agree that my friend and his lady needed a vacay. We'll take care of the little rascal, don't you worry about her."

"Thanks." Jordan smiled, and a sigh escaped her lips at the same time. Her amber eyes were sparkling.

"Don't mention it. She's like our own chi—" Tor stopped mid-sentence and swung his head in the direction of the bar. A fight was breaking out, and most of the humans were screaming during the maddening rush to the door. In a matter of minutes, the bar was transformed into a UFC arena.

Without preamble, Tor and Harrow bolted out of their seats and unzipped their jackets for access to their weapons. Allison and Jordan did the same with their purses, where they had stashed their little daggers. They all rushed to the bar, where a group of more daring people had circled the duo grappling on the floor.

Human and vampire. Not a fair match by any means. Because this was not their fight, Tor's group hung back and waited. He was twitchy as hell, palming his Glock while they watched the ongoing fight with interest. Most of the people left in the club were men. None of the human idiots who had any clue to the beings around them were vampires.

The club's muscles were swift to break up the fight. The vampire offered little resistance; he was probably planning to take out the human once they were both out of the public eye.

"Well, well . . . if it isn't Ms. Allison Tack."

All heads turn in the direction of the voice. Allison's face lit up upon recognizing the speaker. Tor squirmed, feeling blood rush to his face with jealous rage, and he stifled the urge to hit someone. Yeah, three shots of Silver, and he was already revving for a fight.

"Mark? Mark Levinson? Oh my God! How long has it been?"

Tor sized up the man. He was of medium build, about three inches shorter than Tor, and would get shorter when Tor was through pounding his ass into oblivion. The stranger was also extremely attractive, if a woman preferred a man who looked like Brad Pitt. With difficulty, Tor diffused the growl emanating from the back of his throat.

"Dude, don't even think about it." Harrow's whispered warning was meant only for him. "Not worth it."

"Hey, give me a little credit. I'm not intending to kill the bastard, just planning to show him to the door." A potent, distinguishable hatred oozed from Tor's every pore.

"Don't be jealous. You know my sister is smitten with you."

Whoever coined the phrase "payback's a bitch" could relate to Tor's plight. Harrow had taken it upon himself to irk the hell out of him, just as Tor had done to him in the past.

"Shut your hole. I'm not in the mood." Tor downed another shot and glumly looked around. The speakers started pumping out a techno beat, and people trickled back into the club again.

A new group caught Tor's eye, but not because they were all beautiful beyond words. One of the women was the same person who had called to Annie the night he first met her. Despite the crazy activity happening all around them, they locked eyes.

Tor studied the woman's features, and a sudden idea struck him. "Damn," he muttered.

Harrow was in his grill in an instant, demanding an answer. "Tor, what's up?"

Tor turned around, avoiding further eye contact with the woman. He hissed under his breath, "I gotta take a piss."

Harrow lifted an eyebrow before it dawned on him what Tor was trying to do. He eyeballed Jordan and gestured in the general direction of the restrooms. He followed Tor, who was already walking away.

When they were inside the dark and dingy men's room, Tor gave him a quick outline of his idea.

"You really think she's connected with Demetrius?" Harrow stroked his chin, deep in thought while he leaned against the chipped white tile.

"Annie said they were looking for Demetrius the night I met her. She never got to say what that woman's connection to Demetrius was, but that's beside the point. She's the one we need to talk to if we want to crack this mystery bullshit once and for all.

"Okay, why don't you get the ladies out of here, and I'll follow the group. Call me as soon as they're safely back home, and we'll meet up."

Harrow went to push out the door, intent on carrying out his plan, but Tor stopped him.

"Hold it. Change of plan. You take the ladies home, and I'll follow the group. You're not good to go, not with you having all those shitty headaches. You're a freakin' liability, and you know it."

Harrow swung around and Tor braced himself for some bitching. But none came. Instead, Harrow smirked.

"It sounds like you're telling me what to do."

"Damn straight, I am. Now, scram and call me as soon as you're good. Bring Cyrus with you. That dude is dying to get in the thick of it," he said, referring to Cyrus's repeated complaints about not seeing any action.

"We're just following a group of women. I don't expect a lot of action." Harrow proceeded to the bar, where Jordan and Allison were in an animated conversation with Mark who turned out to be an old friend of Allison from NYU.

Tor snorted in disgust, but he had more pressing things to do than introduce Mark to the nearest exit. This was not how he'd envisioned their evening. Too bad nothing ever happened as planned anymore.

"What is this about us going home?" Allison asked when she walked up to Tor.

"I'm going to follow some good leads, and I don't think it's safe for you and Jordan to go." Tor snuck another glance in the woman's direction.

Allison narrowed her eyes and folded her arms across her chest. "Hold up! You're not going anywhere without us. We came here as a group, we'll leave as a group."

Tor didn't enjoy hearing this. He gave Harrow a pleading glance, hoping he'd jump in to help him out. Harrow shrugged his shoulders; it was obvious he was getting a little pressure from Jordan.

"Damn, this is not a joke, Ally. I don't want you going out there." He shoved a hand through the hair that wasn't there anymore and blew out a frustrated breath.

"I can hold my own." Allison jutted her chin. The woman was freakin' stubborn.

"Ally, it could get rough. I don't think we're dealing with regular vampires here," Harrow said.

And then Jordan jumped in. "There's strength in numbers. We're here, and we're tough. Use us."

"Damn it. You women are too stubborn. Whatever! It's Harrow's call." Tor snorted in disgust.

He shot another glance in the woman's direction and was surprised to see her watching him with interest. Looking away, he twirled the empty shot glass between his massive fingers, trying to appear nonchalant.

"Fine. Just make sure you don't do anything stupid. Stay behind us all the time." Harrow took a last swig from his shot glass and slammed it down on the table.

Allison clapped her hands. "In the meantime, let's have fun. Don't be so uptight!"

The techno beat had made way to more bouncy music, and the small dance floor was filled with couples jerking to the rhythm. Tor continued his observation of the woman and her companions while Harrow talked with Allison and Jordan about Jones's research on the disease. Listening with half an ear to the conversation, Tor continued to study the woman's movements.

She was beautiful. *If you're into redheads,* he thought. Then the pieces began clicking into place. He wasn't sure why he hadn't made the connection right away. Jordan, Annie, the unknown woman, and her female escorts were all redheads. They had all been created by one man: the father of Demetrius and the leader of the Vampire Council.

"Damn!" Tor exclaimed.

Rohnert was having a good time despite his earlier qualms about spending an evening alone with Shelly. As promised, her mojitos were to die for. They were loaded with mint, just the way he liked them. The movie he'd brought sat forgotten on the counter, and their conversation drifted from inane chatter to a more rigid inquisition about his life before coming to live at the facility.

After a few more drinks, Shelly seemed to relax around him, moving into touchy-feely territory. Her smile was going to land her in a heap of trouble if he didn't keep himself in check. To avert any impending disaster, he had the quick sense to usher her to the sofa and create a safe distance between them.

"Why don't I pop in the movie?" He got up from the easy chair where he'd parked himself and walked to the entertainment center.

Shelly's eyes narrowed when she clued in to his evasion tactic. She smiled and rolled her eyes. "But I'm enjoying our little chat. You haven't told me what made you leave the Council."

Rohnert shook his head. No more questions. "We're supposed to be watching a movie, not doing a blow-by-blow rehashing of my life." He inserted the disc in the player before Shelly could answer. The less she knew about him, the better.

"We're watching a Japanese movie?" Her words slurred, and she lifted her legs onto the coffee table in front of her.

"Yes. It's an old movie, black and white, and it has subtitles. I have a feeling you'll enjoy it." Rohnert adjusted the volume until he was satisfied.

Shelly gestured for him to sit next to her, and he hesitated. He was far from drunk. It would take more than four mojitos for him to get hammered. However, Shelly looked tipsy. She was still upright but seemed close to her limit. In hindsight, he should've watched her alcohol intake. Rohnert sat down next to her on the sofa, leaving a little gap between them.

"If you say so," Shelly said, sliding closer.

The black and white film was one of his favorites, and he'd seen it many times. Given that Shelly was so close, concentrating was out of the equation. Her warm breath caressed his skin, and each whisper of her breath was like an inviting sonata to his ears. He kept his eyes glued to the television, his own breathing coming in ragged spurts. The doctor had better remain where she was if she wanted her clothes to stay where they were. Rohnert's body was throwing off signals that his control was beginning to slip away. He inched toward the end of the sofa, but Shelly laid her hand on his arm, stopping him.

"Why do you keep inching away? Is there something wrong with me?" She sniffed the air before lifting her hair to her nose. "Do I offend?"

Rohnert hated that he knew what she was thinking. "Shelly, no . . . you're fine. I'm sorry. I'm just a little distracted." He lied. It was better if she had no idea how much she affected him.

Shelly looked doubtful. "We're adults here. I don't think we have to dance around the preliminaries." *I think I'm attractive enough. Why can't you see that I'm interested?*

Knowing what she wanted might be the death of him, because he wanted her just the same. Rohnert had known this was coming, but instead of running away like any sane vampire would have done, he'd kept coming back for more.

Pursuing anything more than friendship with Shelly wasn't a good idea. How could he break the news to her?

"I know, but there's so much you still don't know about me—"

"Which is the reason we're here." She scooted closer, until he was pushed to the end of the sofa.

"Shelly, you're not thinking straight. You're drunk." He had nowhere to go.

"I'm not as drunk as you think I am. I'm a doctor. I know about alcohol intake in relation to body mass index." She smiled demurely.

That's it, Rohnert thought. *She's getting what she asked for.* A surge of boldness coursed through his veins, and he grabbed her by the waist. "You're going to be sorry, woman."

The smile spreading across Shelly's face should have given him pause. He read her mind, but his out of control libido was throwing him off and scrambling the once clear signals.

"I'm not a child. You're not scaring me." Her admonition was downright annoying.

Let's see how long you last, Rohnert thought. Without ceremony, he picked her up from the sofa and marched toward her bed. Shelly made a purring noise, which sent him spiraling to the point where sane thoughts were but a mere memory.

Rohnert lay her down on the bed. In her tiny shorts and cotton T-shirt, she might as well be naked. Without a word, he shed his clothes and boots. It had been such a long time for him that his self-control had worn down to a dangerous level.

Then he stopped thinking altogether when she pulled free from her shirt to reveal rounded, taut breasts. Her need was palpable, and his body shuddered in response. Her little shorts came off next, showing off creamy skin.

Sweet heavenly king! The woman doesn't play games. How would he survive the days and months ahead? He just wanted to scare her, but this had been unexpected. Her eyes glowed with excitement and a kind of wanting he couldn't understand.

"Stop thinking. Take what is being offered," she said, reaching for him.

He didn't take the bait just yet. Hovering over Shelly, it was his intention to cultivate fear, but her response was nothing like what he'd expected. She flashed an enticing smile, undeterred, and languidly arranged her body on the bed, spreading her legs further apart to give him a glimpse of what awaited him.

"You're not going to let this go, are you?" he said slowly, unable to take his eyes off her body.

Shelly shook her head vehemently and began running her fingers along the side of her thighs. Her eyes fluttered to a close, and little moans played on her lips.

His body's response to her invitation was immediate. He jumped on the bed, landing on top of her, his legs trapping hers. He ignored the pain shooting from his shoulder. "You're going to be sorry you ever asked."

"I know not the word."

She was warm against him, her skin flushed either from the alcohol or from her raging lust. Rohnert suspected it was the latter. He could practically smell it. His eyes latched onto her beautiful breasts.

"You're exquisite," he said, feeling himself harden.

"And you're magnificent. You're like one of those wild stallions. I want to tame you . . ." *And I want to keep you.*

Shelly had no idea what she asked of him, but at this point, he was powerless to make her understand the peril of being associated with him. With fire raging within, he captured her breast with his mouth. It was pink, perky, and oh-so-sweet. He devoured her with unbridled hunger, moving his palms over her curves. She responded by arching her body into his every touch. Rohnert continued to lap and suck at her breast.

This human had no idea what the scent of her lust was doing to him. It was making him unravel. His years of forced abstinence came undone right in front of her eyes. Like a rabid dog, he greedily took what she had to offer.

"You've deprived yourself long enough," she whispered in his ear.

He froze. Had she known all along? "We're not protected." It was a warning for her.

"I'm on the ring," she said, her breaths coming ragged pants.

Whatever that meant. He was beyond rational thought. He locked eyes with her, but she pulled him back and took over. Her hands glided to his ultra-sensitive skin and guided him inside her.

Shelly cried out when he filled her, stretching her. Rohnert pulled back, but her legs wrapped around his waist, trapping him.

"No more running away. I'm here. Take what I want to give you."

He rested his face in the crook of her neck, inhaling her. She was gloriously wet and delicious.

"Why are we doing this?"

"Because we are attracted to each other. I've wanted you all along. I think you know it. But . . . no more talking."

A low growl rumbled through his chest and echoed in the room. Like a child given free rein to ransack a candy store, Rohnert let his instincts take over. It had been too long for him. The human was willing, and he wanted her like no other.

He pounded, licked, and took everything she had. He pumped into her hard, creating a delicious friction as his shaft rubbed against her walls. Closing in on his release, he ground himself against her while she clung to him, whimpering. He could feel her nails digging into his skin.

"I can't hold on any longer," she cried.

"Then let go," Rohnert murmured. Increasing his pace, he felt Shelly shatter around him, screaming his name. A second later, he came in an ecstatic rush, sending them both into a delicious paradise. When the hazy euphoria cleared, they lay in a tangled heap of overheated skin, staring into each other's eyes.

"See, that wasn't so bad." Shelly smiled.

He shook his head. Why must she ruin his high with her sassy mouth? It wasn't bad at all. In fact, it would forever be etched in his mind. He smiled back before letting reality destroy the bliss they'd enjoyed. "But this is not what I want. You and I won't happen again."

Her smile fell away, replaced by a rigid mask of determination. She rolled her eyes, her spirit undaunted. "Let's see if you can keep yourself away."

"I'm a man of my word. I think I can stay away."

He tried listening to her thoughts for anything that would give her emotions away, but it seemed like she'd closed him off. The smile she gave him was not as brilliant as the ones before. Not bothering to cover her body, she got up and walked toward the bathroom.

"It's time for you to go. Thanks for giving me what I wanted. I'll see you in three days in the clinic. Remember, you're still off rotation." With those words, she closed the bathroom door behind her.

He'd wanted this—no hard feelings, no strings. So why did he feel like such an ass?

Zane sat in the posh lobby of the Tribeca Grand Hotel, tapping his elegant, long fingers to the beat of the jazz music playing in the bar. He swirled the wine in his glass, looking comfortable with his surroundings.

He knew when Gralnik Lilic stepped through the lobby doors. With an air of confidence, he tilted his head and watched the man approach. Gralnik was in his late thirties, sporting a thick beard but was otherwise clean-cut in his tailored sports coat and beige trousers. This was a man who was used to a life of luxury, thanks to the affluent members of New York society who employed his services.

Gralnik extended his hand to Zane, who promptly stood to shake it.

"It was nice of you to meet me on such short notice," Zane said and gestured to the chair opposite his.

They took their seats before Gralnik spoke in his thick Eastern European accent. "I'm a sucker for expensive assignments." He sank back into the leather seat and crossed his legs. "How did you hear of me?"

"Would you care for a drink?"

Gralnik peeked at the wine on the table and nodded. "I hope you don't mind if I get my own bottle."

"Not at all." With the funding from Grams, he was feeling rather generous. Zane summoned the attendant standing nearby, and Gralnik ordered an opulent bottle. The man knew his wine.

"Your name was mentioned by a business associate," Zane lied. How Melissa had known of this man was something he'd been afraid to ask. He retrieved a manila envelope from his briefcase and slid it across the table. "The particulars are all in there, as well as half the payment we agreed on."

The mercenary took the envelope, a smile spreading across his face. He glanced at the money before he read the specifics of the assignment. Zane knew he could afford not to count it; people who tried to cheat Gralnik tended to wind up dead.

After a moment, he looked up at Zane once more. "What is the time frame on this?" he asked, stroking his beard.

"The faster you get me the information I need, the better." Zane leaned in close. "You have good men working for you?"

"The best Serbia has to offer." Gralnik looked around, and then leaned forward. "I had my men survey the place already. I like to know what I'm up against."

Zane liked the way the man operated. He'd heard that Gralnik was thorough, and that was just what he was after.

"I'm going in with you. Save the best for me. Infiltrate, and then come back with the information. Call when you have it."

Gralnik nodded, seeming too relaxed for his own good. Zane smiled, the human had no idea what was in store for him.

Harrow planted a firm grip on Tor's arm when he jumped. "What's wrong?" Harrow asked.

"How in holy hell did we miss the connection?" Tor asked himself out loud.

"What in god's name are you talking about?" Harrow pulled him closer. "What is going on?"

Tor pointed at the woman he'd been watching for the last hour. "I can't believe we didn't see it right away."

"Who is she?"

"She's the one I told you about," he whispered. He shot a quick glance at Allison and Jordan. Good thing they were caught up in a discussion about throwing stars and quite oblivious to everything else. "I'm sure they're all created by Goran. Look at them. They're all freakin' redheads."

Instead of looking at the ladies, Harrow turned his head to watch Jordan. Tor saw the pain in his eyes and understood how Harrow felt about the reason behind Jordan's creation.

Harrow took a deep breath. "I think you're right."

Just as a new energetic tune started, the group started to leave. Tor took one last swig of his tequila and got up. "Let's bounce," he said to no one in particular.

One by one, Tor's group left out of the club through the back exit. Biting, frigid air greeted them as soon as they stepped out of the doorway. Tor immediately broke into a jog, anxious to trail the women. Turning onto the busy street, he spotted the group walking toward the subway station.

Great! He groaned. *Not the subway.*

Harrow was right behind him. "Be alert. We have no idea what these women are capable of doing."

Tor snorted. "I'm on it." He increased his pace while palming his concealed axe and throwing stars.

The women were walking faster than he wanted. They stopped on a platform just as one train stopped. The distance between the two groups became a problem. Before the pursuers could bridge the gap, the vampires boarded the train. The one in braids looked over her shoulder and locked eyes with Tor just as the doors closed. Her smile taunted him as the train eased out of the station.

"Damn it!" Tor scanned the crowd and listened for the next train.

"Hey, don't worry. We'll catch the next." Allison patted his arm.

Tor looked down at her and nodded. His desire to catch her father's killers grew with each passing day. Somehow, Harrow's obsession had rubbed off on him. He took Allison's hand and led her forward to the platform, standing shoulder to shoulder with Harrow and Jordan. When another train came to a halt, they piled in and tried to blend in with the evening crowd. Since they had lost the group, they would have to guess where they should get off the train.

"Tor, let's get off at Rockefeller Center. That's where most of our intel on vampire sightings have been reported. It sounds like an ideal starting point," Harrow said as if reading his mind.

"Yeah."

Riding in a subway car crowded with humans was excruciating. With every breath he took in the enclosed space, the scent of human blood assaulted him. Tor had recently learned to curb the bloodlust, but the temptation was still great. After several torturous minutes, their stop was announced.

He couldn't wait to get out into the open. No matter how much he tried to control his urges, every damn day continued to test his restraint.

Tor stumbled out of the train and ran for the nearest exit, nearly trampling several people in his haste to find clean air. Allison, Harrow, and Jordan were right on his heels. Once outside, he stopped and pointed his nose up in the sky, filling his lungs to the brim.

"Aren't you over the blood-craving shit?" Harrow hissed in his ear.

"Lay off, will you?"

Harrow shot him a disgruntled look but said nothing more.

"What's wrong, honey?" Allison began rubbing his back.

"Most days I'm good, but that train ride just pushed me to the edge." He took her hand and brought it to his lips.

"Are you going to be okay? You've been acting weird tonight."

"Don't worry." He tugged at her hand. "Let's go."

Pushing through the throng of people, Tor led them, with Harrow bringing up the rear. When they reached the crowded area surrounding the skating rink, the scent of vampires was strong. Tor and Allison separated from Harrow and Jordan to scour the area. There was nothing out of the ordinary. If the subway station had proved to be difficult, this place made finding anyone damn near impossible. People filled every space, and even if the vampires followed their noses, the task would be tedious, if not futile.

Tor's cell phone rang. Grudgingly pulling it from his pocket, he glanced at the luminescent display. Allison stayed close by, watching the people around them with childlike appreciation.

"What's up?" he grunted into the phone.

"I got a call from Rayce. Someone tripped the alarm at the office. We're going back to the facility. I suggest you do the same. I don't want Allison so exposed without additional backup." Harrow's tone made the words an order.

" 'K," Tor responded. As much as he hated being told what to do, Harrow was right. In a public area, someone was bound to recognize her, even if a Council soldier didn't get to her first. He flicked the phone off and turned to Allison. "Let's head back to HQ."

"Can't we stay a bit longer?" She implored him, and it was damn near impossible to refuse her. "I haven't been out for a long time."

Tor vacillated between carrying her out of there and giving her a few minutes more. "Ten minutes. I don't want Harrow biting my damn head off," he muttered, more to himself than her.

Watching Allison was like watching a child in a toy store. Every so often, she would smile over to something that had caught her eye. Her fascination with the children learning to skate made him smile, and her eyes shone with happiness. This was something he hadn't seen from Allison since his arrival at the facility.

As much as it pained him to put an end to her fun, it was time to go. He took her hand. "It's time we head back."

Allison's smile disappeared, and he could see that she wanted to bargain for more time but thought better of it. She grinned before standing on tiptoes to plant a kiss on his lips. "I love you."

Taken aback, he ran his fingers through his absent hair, searching for the right thing to say. Then he realized what would mean the most to her.

"No one will ever love you the way I do." And he meant it.

Her answering smile was the brightest she'd ever given him. She looped her arm around his, and they waded through the thick crowd, back to the place they called home.

"Are we still being followed?" Melissa glanced over her shoulder at the large crowd with wary eyes to screen the faces of the people around them.

"We've lost them," Milla answered, sounding smug.

"Good." Melissa summoned the gate. A cloud of smoke appeared, and the concealed entrance materialized. One by one, she let her companions walk in, making sure no one was watching before she slipped inside after them. The gate disappeared, and they were once again within the Council walls.

Cries echoed in the furthermost section of the house, and Melissa's curiosity spiked.

"Go, return to your rooms. Talk to no one, and don't come out until it's time for your morning training."

Milla gave her a fleeting look before turning away, but Melissa didn't have to explain herself to anyone—least of all, a vampire beneath her. After Melissa secured the door to the women's chambers, she darted to the section reserved for the Council guards. The walls were thick and intended to hide room's secrets, but she already knew them. Demetrius had told her stories about what happened in the Blanch Room, but she'd never bothered to check for herself. It was off limits to almost everyone.

Another round of terrified pleas sounded. Melissa slipped through an open door and found a hallway that led to the stairs. She took them two at a time, at last reaching another hallway with windows overlooking the room below. It was the perfect spot to satisfy her curiosity. Mindful that she did not want to be discovered there, she hid behind a curtain. Her eyes grew wide while she witnessed the proceedings below.

The space was filled with humans, men and women. Some were as young as their early twenties, all were bound at the wrists. Terror marked their tear-stained faces while several guards walked around them, inspecting them like pieces of meat, and slamming their bodies together with high-pressure water hoses.

More guards entered, and then, without warning, the turning process began. Horrified at what she was seeing, Melissa slid down against the wall to catch her breath. She had always known this was happening—how else would their numbers grow if they didn't use humans?

The pureblood vampires were dwindling because they didn't churn out babies the way humans did. The vampire females could only have a child every ten years. Melissa had not been able to convince Goran to disclose further details, but she understood one thing: Goran had to produce a full-blooded heir with a female vampire. When this happened, his harem would cease to exist, and she and the other women would be destroyed. No royal female would want to share her mate with another.

Melissa pushed herself back up to watch the remainder of the human conversion. The bodies were now hanging limply, their hands still bound above their heads while the people continued to writhe in pain. Whimpers rose up when the slow and painful process of transformation began.

She cupped her mouth in revulsion. Although she'd known the truth all along, the reality was still a tough pill to swallow. Innocent lives were being taken, and most of them against their will.

An unfamiliar voice spoke from behind. "I would be quite honored to snitch on you."

Melissa's screamed of surprise was muffled by the rough hand that covered her mouth. She was slammed against the wall. If she had been a human, her bones would have cracked from the impact. She still felt pain but was quick to hide it.

"What are you doing here?" asked a palace guard she recognized as Hamilton's second-in-command. He looked her over from head to toe, pausing at the low-cut neckline of her shirt.

"I— I just came to check when I heard the screams." What was the use of lying when she had been caught in the act? "I was about to leave."

"This place is off-limits. I'm pretty sure Goran would love to hear that his prize bitch has been snooping around this section." The vampire stalked toward her in a predatory manner.

"Who are you?" Melissa eyed the exit, which was blocked by the man's massive body, and her heart sank.

"Name's Stephan." He grinned, his ruby eyes expressing interest.

Melissa wracked her brain for something to say or do. She needed to get out of there alive and in one piece, so she decided to take a gamble. In a syrupy voice she rarely used, she coaxed him closer, her hand resting on his rigid arm. "I'm sorry. I got lost . . ." She sounded convincing enough.

Stephan's eyes flickered with caution, but there was also something akin to curiosity. "I don't believe you. I'm going to take you to Hamilton." He came close enough for her to feel the strength of his body underneath the dark trench coat he wore.

"Please . . . there must be something I can do in exchange for your silence."

Snaking her arm around his neck, she summoned herself to do the unthinkable. She'd be dead anyway once Goran found out about her wandering in this part of the Council walls. What did she have to lose? She pressed her body against the guard's, and his reaction was predictable.

"Like what?" he asked, falling under her spell.

Instead of answering, she ran her fingers through his unkempt hair, hating every second of it. He licked his lips in anticipation.

"You want a little action?" She unleashed a seductive smile.

The vampire eyed her with unconcealed interest and was quick to bury his face in her neck. He skimmed and grazed the expanse of her skin with his fangs. Arching her body into his exploring hands, she led him on, letting him enjoy the few moments he had left.

Melissa ran her hands along his tight body until she found what she needed. With one slow, deliberate sweep, she pulled the dagger from his waist holster. Getting a firm grip on the weapon, she pulled back a little.

"Hey," she purred. When Stephan looked up in a daze, she gave him a saccharine smile. "I think the Council can do without a character like you."

"What?"

She plunged the Dangeran weapon deep into his back and twisted, leaving it there to do its damage. He stared at her in surprise and staggered backward. Melissa watched while panic spread across his face and he tried to pry the dagger from his back.

"Four . . . three . . . two . . . goodbye!" She lifted her hand and waved at him. The fizzle, sizzle, and pop followed, and his body folded in on itself. By the time he hit the ground, most of him had already turned to ashes.

Looking down at the detritus, Melissa felt an enormous amount of satisfaction. "That's for thinking I'd be interested." She smirked and took the dagger and his badge from the pile of ashes before walking away,.

Navigating the busy streets of the city was a pain, but nothing could beat taking the way back on foot. Tor glanced at Allison, who was running beside him, her blond hair floating like a cape behind her. Late-night traffic had snarled, and people slipped through the gaps. Within minutes, they had crossed to the other side of the Hudson River and were making their way to the underground tunnel. The gates opened just as they reached the lip of the long passageway. Tor saluted the camera, knowing Rayce was watching them.

When they walked into the facility, the atmosphere was tense. Tor braced himself for bad news. Rohnert and Cyrus were walking into the I-room just as he and Allison arrived. Harrow was already seated at the head of the table, but Jordan was nowhere in sight.

"Where's Jordan?" Allison asked, as if she'd read Tor's mind.

"She went upstate." Harrow's answer wasn't too enthusiastic.

"Why?" Tor settled into his seat after pulling up a chair for Allison.

"Lambert called saying Gail has been crying and unable to sleep."

"You shouldn't have allowed her to go alone," Rohnert said, standing at the other end of the table, his arm still in a sling.

Harrow's nostrils flared, a sure sign that he wasn't in a good mood. "The woman is stubborn. I think we all knew that already." He blew out a heavy breath. "I wanted her to come here with me first and find someone to go with her, but she wouldn't hear of it."

"I could've gone with her," Rohnert said.

Harrow shot him a glare. "I believe Shelly ordered you off rotation for another week."

"Whatever."

Harrow cleared his throat, and everyone waited for his update. "Okay, here's the deal. Rayce detected a breach in our office building. The cameras didn't show anything, but the alarm in the west section had been tripped."

"Which means?" Tor leaned forward, resting his arms on the table.

"Nothing happened, at least not yet. It could be anything—short circuit, faulty wiring. He's going to head over there right now, and I'm going with him."

Tor stood up. Placing a hand on Allison's arm to forestall any argument she might make, he said to Harrow, "I'll go with you."

Allison looked up at him but didn't say a word. Her tight shoulders told him that she didn't want him to go but she wouldn't tell him how to do his job.

Harrow nodded and pushed back his chair. "Let's go. Martin is going to sit in the control room while Rayce is out." He turned to Rohnert. "Do you mind keeping an eye on him?"

Martin was a human who had been recruited by Rayce. He was a single man without associations or ties, which made him a perfect addition to their little group of misfits.

Rohnert nodded. "Sure thing," he said before stepping out of the room.

Tor brushed his lips along Allison's neck before straightening up and turning to the rest. "Shall we giddyup, ladies?"

Harrow snorted, and the men began filing out of the room. Within minutes, they were inside the vehicle. The drive wasn't bad. The usual city crowd had dispersed for the night.

The office building was deserted, with just the skeleton security crew on duty. Once they parked in the underground garage, Harrow, Tor, Cyrus, and Rayce emerged from the car, weapons drawn. Tor took the front, while Cyrus stayed close to Rayce, and Harrow brought up the rear of the group. As soon as they entered the darkened building, the alarm started to wail. They ran the hundred feet to the control room, and the clicking of guns engaging greeted them.

"Put the fuckin' guns down," a venomous voice filled with honest-to-goodness authority stopped them in their tracks.

They all stopped. Harrow raised his hands above his head, his Kalimetal pointed in the speaker's direction.

"Drisco, you make me so damn proud." The laughter in Harrow's voice was evident.

The man Harrow had addressed sputtered for a few seconds before gathering himself together. Tor watched in amusement as the stocky head of evening security walked toward Harrow, looking contrite.

"Sir . . . Mr. Gates, my apologies. I wasn't expecting you." Drisco smiled at him and Rayce before waving his men off.

Harrow sheathed his Kalimetal. "No harm done. We're only here to check on the tripped alarm and look around."

Drisco smiled at his employer. "Is there anything you need from me?" he asked, eyeing Tor and Cyrus with curiosity.

"Nothing. Just keep doing what you were doing," Harrow said, and then motioned for Rayce to disable the alarm. "We'll be out of your hair soon. Anything out of the ordinary going on around here?"

"No sir. Everything is a-okay." Drisco walked toward the door and grinned. "My men are all over—just holler if there's anything you need."

"Thank you. You're doing an excellent job." Harrow went to sit at the rows of monitors, perching himself at the huge workstation.

Rayce went to work quickly, and the blaring noise stopped. He gave Harrow a thumbs-up and sat down at the workstation. He punched in some codes, and the monitors came alive, each showing different areas of the office building, the parking structure, and the general area surrounding the building. Harrow, as usual, turned his head sideways to get a better view.

Tor was growing antsy. He had been ever since they'd lost the redheads they were trailing the night before. "While you guys are being nerds, Cyrus and I will make rounds and see what we see."

"Harrow, just ring us if you need anything." Cyrus headed to the door, opening it wider for Tor.

"We're good. Plan on leaving in half an hour." Harrow didn't even look up, much too engrossed in the flickering monitors.

"Yes, boss." Tor piped in before the door closed behind them. Still holding onto the Glock, he gave Cyrus a quick glance. "You tight?"

"As ever," Cyrus answered in a clipped tone.

They covered the long hallway with long strides until they got to the elevator. While waiting for the doors to open, Tor focused on the murmuring voices of several men in the vicinity. Although he couldn't see them, he knew they were nearby, patrolling as they were paid to do.

The ding of the elevator brought him back, and they boarded. Punching a random number, they waited until the car stopped on the eleventh floor. Once they stepped out, Tor let his instincts take control.

Cyrus walked beside him in silence while they breezed in and out of offices, trying to see if any clues would jump out as to whether the alarms were set off intentionally or if the wiring was just defective. Once they reached the top floor, they took the stairs to the rooftop. Once outside, they spotted Drisco smoking. At the sound of their footsteps, he bit his cigarette and aimed his gun in their direction.

Harrow may have trusted the guy, but Tor was getting tired of having a gun pointed at him. He aimed his pistol at Drisco.

"Hey, hold up. It's just us." Cyrus raised his hands.

"I didn't recognize you." Drisco lowered his gun and pulled the cigarette from his mouth.

"You're a little trigger happy, aren't you?" Tor snarled.

"Just doin' my job." He sized Tor up and blew out thick smoke, clouding the air between them.

When they got closer, Tor couldn't help but notice the way the human's shoulders tensed. Drisco threw the cigarette on the ground before crushing it with his shoe. Cyrus stood next to head of night security, pretending to admire the view, but Tor kept his distance. He kept walking, keeping tabs on the human's emotional grid. He could sense the man was trying to keep calm. Why, he had no idea.

"So, tell me, what's the patrol schedule in the evenings? How many men do you have on any given night?" Cyrus asked, and Tor could tell he was trying to make small talk.

"There are twenty of us every night, give or take, unless someone calls in sick." Drisco sounded anxious and not up for a little chitchat.

Tor grinned. There was no denying that he didn't like the human. Whatever the man knew of them and their operation, this guy was not to be trusted. Tor wondered which sewer Harrow found the bastard in, because Drisco seemed suspicious.

"How many cigarette breaks do you take each night while you're on duty?" Tor decided to annoy him.

Turning around, Drisco shot a glare his way, which Tor returned with nonchalance.

"I take the allotted break, which is ten minutes every four hours. Is there anything else you want to know?"

Tor chuckled and shook his head. "Nah, we're good. That ten minutes is up, I think."

Cyrus turned and gave him a pointed look. Tor snickered. It wasn't in his nature to ease up on anyone, much less a person who threw off bad vibes like Drisco did.

"I'll see you gentlemen in a bit." The sound of Drisco's footsteps was heavy as he took his leave.

Cyrus huffed and shook his head the minute the door closed. "You're such an ass."

"Well, thanks. Just making sure I got what I wanted from him," Tor replied.

"And what was that?"

"He's suspicious and jumpy as hell. How many times does he have to point a gun at us?" He moved to Cyrus's side and glanced at the light display.

"As he said, he's only doing his job. I think I'd rather have them on alert instead of sleeping on the job. You're much too paranoid for your own good." Cyrus placed his gun in his hip band.

"If you say so. But I'm not too crazy about that character." Tor pursed his lips. *Am I really paranoid?*

"Let's get going." Cyrus looked at him and smiled. "And yes, you are."

If the human was yanking his chain, Tor wouldn't know. He hadn't spoken out loud, so Cyrus had to be guessing.

"What's the verdict?" Tor asked, as soon as they were all in the car en route to the facility.

Rayce answered. "All systems checked out all right. No tampering, nothing suspicious."

"How about you guys? Find anything worth shit?" Harrow asked, resting his head against the leather headrest of the Humvee.

"It's all clear. The place is clean." Tor still had doubts about Drisco, but decided to keep them to himself. If Harrow trusted the SOB, then he'd just keep his mouth shut for the time being.

"Good. Let's head home. I want to see the girls."

The girls meant Jordan and Gail, whom Harrow hadn't seen since he'd returned to the facility weeks ago. Even though tonight's visit would be over videophone, it was good enough for their leader. Tor could see why Harrow had wanted to slow down. Even the mighty Superman required a rest.

Jordan ran for a good three hours at top speed, anxious to get to her little girl. It had been a few days since she had seen Gail. She was safe with Lambert and the three stooges in their upstate home, but Jordan had to see for herself. It was a mom thing.

Jordan abruptly stopped. Mom? Had she gone nuts? Annie was still in the picture, and Jordan would be damned if she'd keep dreaming that Gail would stay forever, even though her mother's disappearance might very well be "for good."

She blew out a ragged breath and resumed running. A few more miles and she'd be home.

The familiar scent of her kind caught her attention, and Jordan was quick to pinpoint their location.

Two vampires were walking toward their house, and hell would freeze over before she would allow them to get any closer. With as little noise as possible, she unsheathed her Kalimetal and attacked.

Caught off guard, the vampires had no idea what hit them as she sliced through their neck from behind, slashing one after the other clean through the neck. They fell like mosquitoes zapped by electricity.

"I think you guys are in the wrong neighborhood. No one comes near my baby," Jordan growled while she watched the vampires struggle.

Crackling and popping sounds followed, and both disintegrated. When their ashes fell to the ground like snowflakes, she sneered at the VC seals. She stopped to pick up the seals and placed them in her pocket.

A rustling of leaves sent her into a defensive position. Jordan listened for the slightest noise and pointed her chin upward to catch the scent of anyone in the general area. Nothing raised her suspicion, so she sheathed her Kalimetal and dusted off her coat.

With great effort, she willed herself to calm down before striding onto the property. When the motion detector was triggered, the area was bathed in high-wattage lighting. Jordan waited at the gate instead of climbing up the wall or scaling the wrought iron gates.

Peyton walked out, a throwing star in hand.

"It's me," Jordan called out. Her voice shook a little, and she had to take a deep breath. There was no reason to share her experience with anyone. It had been a clean kill. She'd love to get her hands on more Council guards. The kill filled her with a sense of purpose that had been missing since she and Harrow had gotten together.

"Is everything okay?" Peyton asked, giving her a doubtful look.

"Everything is just dandy." Jordan smiled. "Couldn't be better."

Goran stepped in the shower, still feeling the tingle of Annie's touches on his skin. Her disappearance had fueled his rage—and had exacerbated his lust for her. Although destroying her would be the best punishment for disrespecting for his orders, he wasn't ready to lose her yet. Annie had already cost him Graciela's life, and he'd be damned if he would let her off the hook by killing her so soon.

Walking into the scalding water, he stood under the spray without moving, letting the water soothe his screaming nerves. He had intentionally let days pass without summoning her to get his emotions in check. If it hadn't been for Melissa showing up when she had, Annie would be dead.

He expelled a long sigh and started massaging his temples. There were some things Annie had said that stood out. She'd stayed with her daughter. Where? Who had been keeping the little girl since he'd abducted her mother? How did Annie find her daughter? And who was the vampire with her when she was found?

It was hard to think straight in the face of her disobedience. Although the other vampire had been killed, it didn't bring Goran comfort. He closed his eyes when his muscles began to loosen up. Running the Council had sucked his sense of humor out of him. The constant reminder to produce an heir played in his head like a broken record. Whoever had penned the damn rules must have thought their pureblooded kind was sufficient. The fools had no idea how the passage of time would alter the situation.

There were many aspects of the rules that needed to change. There were more pressing concerns than breeding a pureblood vampire to satiate the long-standing requirements of their ancestors. If they could find him a redheaded vampire, then by all means, he'd fuck the hell out of her and produce enough little squirts to satisfy the flawed system.

For now, he needed to pay more attention to the growing number of Council guards disappearing without a trace.

Goran heard a tap on the door before Melissa's scent wafted around him. Glancing up, he found her standing naked before him. He raked his eyes along her elegant figure to the crown of red hair coiled at the top of her head.

"My lord, would you care for some company?" she asked, her voice husky and inviting.

He wanted to be alone, but he had been neglecting her. Distress showed in her face. So he mustered a fake smile and ushered her in. He took her hand and kissed it.

"You're as lovely as ever." It wasn't a lie. Melissa was a rare gem, a thing of beauty.

"Thank you, my lord." Melissa bowed before stepping into the water with him. She flinched at the hot spray against her skin but still gave a gracious smile. Taking the loofah and pouring a generous amount of body wash onto it, she began to lather his body, caressing every inch of his skin.

"What did your venture outside procure this time around?" he asked. Goran tried to capture any trace of her memories from her outing, but nothing came up. He was either losing his touch, or Melissa had caught on to his silent intrusions into her mind.

"Not a trace of our son," she murmured.

Goran shook his head but bit his tongue. When would she give up on finding Demetrius? It had been too long. If he were a betting man, he'd wager the bastard's ashes were already blown away. No one, not even his son, was allowed to desert his responsibilities and leave without a word. Demetrius had been well aware of this.

He tilted Melissa's chin so she was gazing into his eyes. "Melissa, you have spent countless days and nights looking for him, worrying, and crying. Don't you think it's time to give up hope?"

Her lips quivered, and her eyes welled with tears. Goran knew there had been more to her relationship with Demetrius than that of mother and son. The thought made him see red. Right under his nose, his son and his mistress had been going at it, and yet he'd allowed it. Who in their right mind would consent to such crime?

Someone with a hidden agenda.

"Answer me!"

Melissa looked down, despite his firm grasp on her face. "My lord, a little more time is all I ask."

His jaw clenched, but once again, he restrained himself. "If I gave you the people who claimed his life, would you find peace?"

He had no idea why he'd said what he had. There was no reason for him to think that Demetrius had been killed, but if it would end her madness, he'd be happy to find the answers. Melissa's moping around was beginning to wear his patience thin.

Melissa nodded, and tears trickled down her cheeks. "It would give me the closure I seek." She held his hand and kissed his palm in reverence.

Before he could respond, there was rapping on the door. Goran knew who it was. Hamilton wouldn't disturb him unless the matter was important.

"Wait here. I'll be back."

Not bothering to dry himself, he wrapped a towel around his hips and dripped all the way to the door.

Melissa dashed out of the shower, pulled a towel from the rack, and covered her body with it. Pressing her ear against the door, she heard a familiar voice, and her fist involuntarily clenched.

"My lord," Hamilton said, followed by the sound of the door closing.

"What brings you here?" Goran's response was curt.

"I have two things I need to discuss with you," she heard Hamilton say.

"Go ahead."

"Stephan's gone missing. From what I've gathered from the other guards, they were in the Blanch room with a bunch of new recruits when he left to check out a noise he'd heard. He hasn't been seen since. I've checked everywhere, and there is no trace of him." Judging from the tone of Hamilton's voice, Melissa was certain that the vampire was feeling a bit melancholic over losing his second-in-command.

"Hmm . . ."

Melissa could guess that Goran was dissecting the information given to him. There was a long silence before Goran spoke again.

"What is the other news?"

"Three guards were on patrol upstate, and two were obliterated by a fighter who was sporting the Kalimetal you mentioned to me."

Melissa pressed her face harder against the door, not wanting to miss the rest of the information.

Goran voice raised a pitch. "How do you know of this?"

Melissa knew that losing Council guards was cause for concern, and it always dampened Goran's mood whenever their numbers were affected. But what was this "Kalimetal" Hamilton spoke of?

"One guard was able to escape detection. He said the woman didn't even notice him. He was hidden in thick bushes when she attacked the other two unprovoked."

"A woman?" Curiosity replaced the earlier irritation in Goran's voice.

"Yes, sire. A vampire with red hair."

Goran didn't respond for a few moments, and when he did, he sounded riled—almost hostile. "What did she say?"

"These were her exact words: 'I think you guys are in the wrong neighborhood. No one comes near my baby.' She was fast, lethal, and definitely angry." Hamilton sounded ruffled.

Melissa snorted. So the mighty Hamilton wasn't infallible. She would have loved to see his face and witness the dread in his eyes.

"Upstate? Isn't that where you found Annie?"

"Yes. And we've lost several of our men in that area, including Gentry."

"I remember." There was another long silence. "Leave now. I shall summon you once I'm done with my shower."

Quieter murmurs followed, and Melissa skittered back into the shower. Belatedly, she remembered the puddle on the floor, but it was too late to do anything now. The bathroom door opened, and Goran entered.

"Are you done with your shower, my lord? Or do you wish for me to wash you some more?" she asked, keeping her voice even.

"I'm finished. If you don't mind, I would like to be left alone," Goran said, his face rigid and his expression grim.

"Call on me if you need anything." She stepped out of the shower and retrieved the towel she'd used earlier. Goran was standing by the mirror, his magnificent body taut with unspoken fury.

"Stay close. I will call on you," he said, dismissing her.

Melissa rushed out of Goran's chambers. She had been frightened he'd see right through her or that he might take out his anger on her. From the look on his face, the likelihood of him lashing out was strong.

Instead of staying close by as he'd asked her to do, she went down the hallway and knocked on a door. When it opened, Annie seemed startled to see her.

Melissa pushed past Annie without a word. She glanced around the room before turning around. "You owe me, so I'm here to collect."

Annie shrank back, but quickly composed herself. She closed the door and moved closer to Melissa with tentative steps. "What do you mean?" she asked, her beautiful face laced with uncertainty.

"Sit and talk." Melissa gestured to the bed. Ignoring the damp towel covering her body, she sank onto the mattress and waited for Annie to do the same.

"What do you want to know?"

"Everything. Start from when you left. If you must know, Graciela was killed because you used her. So do right by her."

Melissa would use anything in her arsenal. There might be a connection between these Kalimetal-wielding vampires and Demetrius's disappearance. She'd take any piece of information she could pry out of Annie if it would lead her to the answers she sought.

Annie appeared grief-stricken at the mention of Graciela's name. "I didn't know."

"No one was supposed to know, but I have my ways. Now spill, my girl."

"I met a vampire in the club, and he said he could help me. I left because I wanted to get out. I don't have what it takes to stay here forever."

"Are you attracted to this vampire?"

Annie shook her head.

And then?"

"Well, when we got to their house, I found Gail there. I have no idea how they got her, but they did. She's well and very happy."

"Who is he the vampire that Hamilton killed?"

"Dave. He was taking me out to hunt."

Melissa raised her eyebrows. "Why did you need an escort?"

"They said there were a lot of sightings of Council guards in the area, and they felt it would be safer for me."

"Who are these people?" Melissa was getting impatient. There had to be a connection somewhere.

"I don't know most of them. All I know is they are working on helping the sick vampires. I . . . I'm not really clear on that part."

Melissa body shook. "Sick vampires. You saw them?"

"They're not sick anymore. From what I gathered, they found a semi-cure. They're good people. They took Gail in, and they helped me without question."

"Don't be so naïve. Vampires and humans couldn't coexist. They are fattening the humans for consumption later."

"What are you trying to say?" Annie's demeanor became nervous.

"Vampires need humans. They cannot live without their blood. You know that."

"But they—"

"Hush! You're not going to speak of this with anyone. Clear your head the next time you're in Goran's presence. Do you understand me?"

Annie fumbled, and tears formed in her eyes before she nodded. "I want to see her again."

Melissa sneered. Weren't they a pair? Both would do anything to see their only child. "In due time, you'll have the chance to see her again."

Annie buried her face in her hands, and sobs racked her body. Melissa wanted to console her, but there was no room for pity now. She had better things to do and plans to fabricate. Without a word, she stood and left Annie's room.

She'd have her revenge, and Goran had better not stand in her way.

Gail was fast asleep in her bed when Jordan came to check in on her. Her cherubic face showed traces of smile, and Jordan stood at the foot of the bed, watching her for a long time. It was such a shame that she had to leave Gail with Lambert and the two other vampires in order to spend time with Harrow. Although Lambert, Peyton, and Knox did well, considering their inexperience with children, Gail hadn't been calling her as often as she did at first.

Annie had been missing for weeks now, and Jordan was beginning to suspect there was a possibility they'd never see her again. How would Gail take this news? She had been asking about her mother, and she had spent an entire evening crying when Annie disappeared. Jordan was running out of excuses.

The door opened slightly, and she turned to see Lambert peeking through the crack. "I'll be right out," Jordan whispered.

Lambert nodded his head and closed the door, and she returned her gaze to Gail. Walking closer and dropping to her knees, she laid a tender kiss on the girl's forehead. "I love you, baby girl," she whispered.

Gail stirred in her sleep, so Jordan stood up and snuck out of the room. She wandered the hallways, tracing the sound of Lambert's heartbeat until she found him in the training room. It was amusing how their human counterparts mimicked the vampires' sleeping schedule, awake at night and snoozing during the daytime.

Lambert looked up and smiled when she walked in. "You look like you've been through the wringer."

How astute. She flashed her fangs, feeling the remnants of aggression still tugging at her insides.

"What brings you here at this unholy hour?" he asked, putting down a throwing star he'd been polishing.

"I wanted to see Gail." She unstrapped her Kalimetal and collapsed in the chair opposite his.

Lambert leaned on the desk and eyed her. "Anything else have you been up to?"

Jordan never felt the need to explain to anyone, but this was Lambert. The man had been bailing her out of parental duties too often for her to brush him off. "What do you mean?"

"You look a little high-strung to me." His steady, appraising gaze made her want to squirm.

She stood up. "I'm always high-strung." Grabbing the cloth from the table, she started wiping the grime off her Kalimetal blades.

"Nope. You've been tame since Harrow."

The statement made her wince. She had, hadn't she? "And your point?"

"For one, you had some action tonight, and you're not sharing. Two, you're going at it alone, which is a no-no. Three, you're—"

"Okay, I got it." She lifted her Kalimetal and started swinging the weapon.

Lambert ducked and laughed. "Easy there." He chuckled when she glared at him. "Spill!"

"It's no biggie. I saw two Council guards in the area, and I made sure they kept quiet," she said, sliding the weapon back in its holster.

"So you eliminated them?" Lambert's eyebrows were cocked so high, they made him look like a cartoon character.

"Something like that. I hated the idea of them being close to the house."

"So you took matters into your own hands." It wasn't a question.

"If I see more of them, I would be happy to do it again." She huffed in annoyance.

"I think you need to see a shrink," Lambert commented dryly.

"That was my therapy. I think I'm good." Jordan snickered. Now, one question remained: Would Lambert blab to Harrow?

Stretching his arms upward, Lambert cracked his neck, and then leveled a gaze at Jordan. "I know what you're thinking, and I won't say anything before you do. But you broke a cardinal rule. We go in groups, or at least in pairs. You know that." Jordan could tell that he meant every word.

"I'm going to bed." She stood and walked toward the exit. Before she closed the door, she heard him chuckle.

When she reached her bedroom, she removed her weapons and hid them in the secret vault. It was a necessary process for Gail's sake. The last thing they needed was for her to start asking questions again.

After cleaning up, Jordan buzzed the facility. Harrow was expecting confirmation that she'd made it in one piece. Rayce picked up. While she waited for him to connect her to Harrow, she glanced out one of the windows overlooking their land. The night was clear and quiet. It was a shame that Council forces seemed to be in abundance in their area. They needed peace after the slaughter at the facility almost a year ago.

"Jordan?" Harrow was in front of the camera, looking bedraggled. He wasn't wearing his sunglasses for a change.

"I'm here. I got in about an hour ago. Gail is fine, sleeping like an angel." Jordan smiled, attempting to mask the guilt she felt. She couldn't believe she was hiding something from him.

"Is everything all right?" Harrow was squinting. She knew too well he was trying to get a better look at her. Damn camera had to be high resolution.

"Everything's just fine. How are you doing? What happened in the office building?" She touched the screen, feeling the need to be with him.

"Looks like faulty wiring. Everything's fine." Harrow looked down, and then back to the camera. "It's almost sunrise. Are you headed to bed soon?"

She nodded. "I miss you."

"Then come home to me." His voice was thick with need.

"What about Gail?"

"She's safe with Lambert. I think she's better off there. It's not healthy for her to be around so much commotion."

Jordan had to agree.

He paused and ran his elegant fingers through his hair. "Should I send a car for you?"

"No. I'll be okay. I'll see you at nightfall." She blew a kiss at him.

Harrow smiled. "Take care. You know I love you."

"As I love you," she replied before flicking the off button.

The bed would be empty without him. She'd been so used to having him next to her. An idea popped in her head, and she walked to Gail's room. As usual, the little girl was sucking her thumb, a habit Jordan wanted her to break.

Inching quietly into the bed, Jordan lifted the sheets and joined her little angel. Who said she had to sleep alone? She wrapped her arms around Gail and snuggled close, letting the scent of innocence lull her to sleep.

She was a bona fide softy. No doubt about it.

"Tor, wake up. I don't want to be late for my meeting." Allison leaned down and shook him awake.

She was already dressed in her power suit, a gray pants-and-jacket ensemble that made her look more mature than her actual age. Her hair was swept back in a graceful, loose ponytail, with soft tendrils of hair cascading down the sides of her face.

Tor stirred and stretched, and then snaked his arms around her waist to pull her down. She shrieked, worried her suit would crease.

"Tor, I'm going to be late. I don't want to adjust my schedule again." She nudged him, but he answered with a lazy smile.

"Baby, don't worry. I can be ready in minutes. Why don't you let me kiss you first?"

Allison shook her head, knowing her suit didn't stand a chance. Pecking him on the cheek, she giggled when he groaned.

"No way I'm going to forgive you for that!" He ruffled her ponytail then twisted their bodies until he had her pinned against the bed. His hard body was too close for comfort.

"We're going to be late—"

Her words were cut off by the pressure of his mouth on hers. It was difficult to deny him when her entire being screamed for him. With the heated passion feeding the raging fire in her belly, Allison followed Tor's lead, and they spent the next hour caught up in the rapture.

After the unscheduled romp, Tor kept his word and was in and out of the shower in record time, groomed and somewhat menacing in his leathers. After conferring with Harrow, they left the facility with Deuce in tow.

The building was bursting with activity when they arrived. As usual, Allison went straight to her office to retrieve her messages and get the details about her clients for the day. Her first meeting was with private investors from a foreign firm that manufactured guns in Europe.

Tor stayed behind the scenes, watching each of the gentlemen with guarded curiosity. Deuce was more relaxed, but Allison had nothing to fear with these two vampires looking after her.

The clients knew what they wanted, and playing hardball wasn't even necessary on her part. Once the orders had been placed and the initial payments wired, they concluded their business meeting with a firm handshake and the assurance of prompt delivery.

A few hours later, the trio piled back in the armored vehicle for the journey home. They exited the underground parking as usual, but then Tor cursed.

"Deuce, stop here. Let me out and lock the doors."

"Tor! What's going on?" Allison asked.

Tor was already out and running. The locks engaged, and the car accelerated. She couldn't do anything but watch Tor through the rear window, his figure getting smaller with each passing second.

"Deuce, stop the car!" she ordered, pulling at the door handle.

"No ma'am, I can't. I'm following standing orders." Deuce grunted, then stepped harder on the gas. The vehicle lurched forward.

Helpless and angry, Allison banged on the bulletproof window. How could Tor even think of going alone? What if . . . what if something happened to him?

Hysteria bubbled to the surface, and she fought the urge to cry. *Nothing will happen to him. He'll be okay. He'll be okay.* Once he was safe, she'd wring his neck with her bare hands for scaring her like this.

Deuce was on his cell phone, reporting the incident to Harrow. Allison listened, but she kept the silent chant going. The gates were already open by the time they reached the lip of the tunnel.

She raced to the control room and found Rayce tracking down Tor with the building's camera. Harrow burst into the room a few minutes later, looking like he had just gotten out of bed.

"Ally, are you okay?" he asked, giving her a fierce hug.

"I'm not okay! Tor is out there alone!" she screamed, but she welcomed the strong arms that held her upright.

"He's going to be fine. Don't worry about the bastard," Harrow said with a confidence Allison didn't feel. His eyes searched her face before he let go. "He's going to be back here before you know it." He focused on the monitor, angling his head to see more. "Rayce, where is he?"

"He's in pursuit. One man. Looks human to me. There's no way to tell if he's packing heat." Rayce continued tracking Tor, tapping the keyboard to pull up different angles from the building's exterior cameras.

Allison watched Tor, looking so self-assured and gaining on his quarry. He jumped at the man, and the struggle began. She watched while the man pulled a weapon and the fighting intensified. They rolled on the ground, kicking, punching, and trying to best each other.

Then Allison heard the sound of a gun discharging. She jumped, pushing Harrow away from the monitor and pressing her nose to the screen. Both men fell backward, and her heart jacked up her throat.

"Please, God, please. Don't let it be Tor!"

The moment Tor jumped out of the car, he was in his element. He loved this: the exhilaration, the action, and most of all, the prospect of a kill. With steady footing, he landed on the pavement with a loud thud and pursued the suspicious character he'd seen standing by the lamppost. When the stranger met Tor's eyes, fear reflected back before he turned to run.

Tor loved the scent of fear. It fed his inner machismo and promised a chance for release of his pent up aggression. For a human, the man was quick on his feet, presenting Tor with a good enough challenge. When Tor heard the telltale sounds of exhaustion, he smiled. He jumped and grabbed the man by the collar, and they fell to the ground.

Surprisingly, the human put up a good fight. They struggled with each other, rolling, punching, and kicking.

"You have a death wish or something? What are you spying on?" Tor rumbled, grabbing the man.

"Son of a bitch!" the human yelled.

"You're going to get yourself killed."

"Not if I kill you first."

Tor felt a gun being pointed in his gut. Twisting his body, he struggled to get a hold of the weapon, but then a blast rang in his ear. The recoil pulled the two men apart, and they fell backward. Tor did a quick inventory for pain; there was none. The motherfucker had shot himself instead.

Jumping to his feet, Tor walked over to the human. He wasn't bleeding, but he seemed stunned, even though he managed a sneer. Anger pumped through Tor's body like adrenaline.

"What the hell are you nosing around for?" He grabbed the man's shoulders and pulled him upright, ripping away his jacket with one stroke to reveal a bulletproof vest.

"Speak up, asshole." Tor hurled him to the ground and retrieved the gun.

The poor excuse for a human smelled like he had enough alcohol in his system to last him a lifetime. The impact had been hard enough to crack his ribs. He'd be nursing messed-up ribs for days. Despite his obvious pain, he laughed.

"Drisco owes me money. I know he works in the building. I'm here to collect."

"I'm going to take you to him, and I will let you bastards settle the debt. Thank your lucky stars that I'm feeling merciful today." He pulled the man up by the collar and dragged him toward the building.

"I don't want to mess with anyone else. I just want what Drisco owes me." There, the fear was back in his voice. It made Tor proud.

"Make sure you never come back after this. I won't be as forgiving next time."

Tor went to the front entrance, which was opened promptly by remote control from the inside. Drisco was waiting in the lobby, his gun drawn, and surrounded by five men.

"This punk is here to collect some money." Tor growled and threw the hapless man toward Drisco. "Clean up your mess."

Drisco glowered at Tor before turning his attention to the man, who was trying to crawl away.

Stepping back into the cold and quiet night, Tor sniffed the air and made a run for the facility. What a wasted effort. He'd been itching for a fight tonight. Fewer cars and crowds made his trip back to the facility easy.

Rayce's voice came through the speaker system just as Tor entered the underground hideout. "Come into the control room. Stat!"

Tor flicked a finger at the camera and chuckled. Damn Harrow was probably going to give him a long lecture. He was tired and hungry. All he wanted was to go to his room and have a glass of blood.

"If you're going to give me a lecture, save it!" he said the moment he walked in, only to find that Harrow was not in the room. Instead, he found Allison and Rayce. The latter stood up, nodding in Tor's direction before disappearing into the hallway. Allison stood with her back to him.

"Hey, what are you doing here?" Tor asked, walking closer. He reached out and touched her shoulder. Her muscles were tense and hard.

Allison pivoted, and her eyes gave her emotions away. Without answering, she launched a mean, right-handed slap across his face, and he staggered backward.

"That's for leaving, you stupid, stupid man!"

For once in his life, Tor was out of wisecracks. He stared at her, stunned and at loss for words. Touching his cheek, he could still feel the sting. He'd screwed up.

"I'm sorry . . . I didn't mean to leave just like that. I—I got a little carried away." Tor had no idea how to do the whole apology thing, but he tried.

Allison shook her head. "Do you know how it feels to think I might lose you? I lost Daddy already. Please don't put me through that kind of hell again."

Her plea tore at his heart. He had forgotten to consider her feelings.

"Ally, I apologize . . ." He moved closer, aching to touch her.

"I don't think I'd live if I lost you." Allison closed the distance between them and wrapped her arms around his waist.

Closing his eyes, Tor breathed in her scent and thanked his lucky stars he hadn't blown his chance with her. "You won't. I'll be with you until you're sick of me."

"If you ever pull a number like that again, I swear I'll kill you myself."

Atta girl! That was the Allison he had come to love.

"I won't give you a reason to get rid of me." He tugged at her arm and directed her to the door. "I want to show you exactly how sorry I am. Let me make it up to you."

Allison stopped walking and turned to face him, her eyes narrowing. "And how exactly are you going to do that?"

He waggled his eyebrows and grinned. "You'll find out . . . in the bedroom."

Goran paced his chambers long after Melissa had left. The news from Hamilton continued to gnaw at him, although he wasn't disturbed by upsetting information. The report was clear. It had been a redhead sporting a Kalimetal. Could she be the one who'd gotten away?

Where did Rohnert fit in all of this? The name was like acid scalding Goran's throat. His old friend had severed ties with the Council just to rise up against him. And now, Rohnert even had his woman—his creation.

Rage welled within Goran as the thought continued to taunt him. No one ever got away, and no one should go against him. The whole idea was ludicrous.

There was a knock at the door, but he ignored it. He wasn't in the right frame of mind. Anything or anyone he touched would suffer at his hands, so he was better off alone. However, the rapping persisted. With a burst of anger, he flew toward the door, his feet barely touching the floor, and yanked it open.

"If I don't answer my door, it means I don't want to take caller—"

"Pardon me, sire, but this couldn't wait." Hamilton bowed low, the tip of his scabbard rising with his movement.

"What is it?"

He liked Hamilton. The man got the job done and was astute and loyal, but Goran was getting sick of his bad news.

"I have a theory. With all the disappearances in our ranks, I think we can assume we are being hunted."

With Hamilton's proclamation, Goran's fangs elongated, and he hissed in anger. "*We* do the hunting. We are never hunted. Do you understand me?"

Hamilton never cowered, so it made Goran happy when Hamilton dropped to his knees. Goran was now beyond pissed. No one made a mockery of him or his rule. Hamilton's head remained in a bowed position while Goran paced the room.

"Round up some guards and kill as many infected ones as you can. I want them dead! If you see anyone so much as questioning it, kill them, too."

"As you wish, sire."

"Anyone showing up with a Kalimetal, shoot them and burn them alive."

Seeming overwhelmed, Hamilton bobbed his head several times. There was no room for mistakes at this point. Insurrections, treason, and blatant disrespect for the Council would not be tolerated.

"Yes, sire."

"If you see that redheaded woman, shoot her with tranquilizers and bring her to me. I want her alive so I can kill her myself."

"As you wish." Hamilton bowed his head again and left the room.

Once alone, Goran started pacing again while he racked his brain for a clever solution to this damned development. He needed to talk to the others and round up as much support as possible.

He walked to his desk and picked up the phone. "Bretania, call on the Council elders. I want an audience with everyone right away."

Not even an hour elapsed before the Council was ready to meet. Goran wore his finest robe of black velvet and gold trim, one that emphasized his leadership status. Unscheduled meetings like this would raise eyebrows, and he wanted to establish that he was still very much in control.

When he walked in the assembly room, he noticed a few empty seats. Iden, Alphonsus, and Serena were absent. Ascending to his seat, Goran smiled with confidence and raised his hand in greeting.

"I appreciate your coming here on such short notice."

Randolph coughed. "Why the sudden call?"

Goran leveled a steady gaze at Randolph but was met by the confident gleam in the other vampire's eyes.

"I want to inform the council members that I have ordered a slaughter of the infected ones."

There were murmurs of both agreement and concern. Randolph stood up, and August seemed anxious, his wafer-thin skin looking more fragile than usual. Goran smirked. The finances must be keeping him on his toes.

Goran gestured for silence, and everyone quieted down. "Randolph, do you have any objections?"

Randolph dipped his head in deference before he spoke. "Why a slaughter? Are they truly a menace to our existence?"

Goran clenched his jaw. "We've been through this before, my friend." He stressed the last word. "Yes, they are. The spread is rapid, and I'm concerned that we risk exposure to humans if we don't eradicate the parasites."

Randolph sat down and appeared to digest this proclamation. Goran was getting tired of his contention. Why couldn't the damn vampire accept his rulings without the constant demand for explanations?

"And our old friend Rohnert has been actively campaigning against us," he added. "I have proof of his doings. Kalimetal wielding rebels are in abundance, killing our soldiers."

There was widespread hissing among the Council members at this news. Marania shook her head in amazement. "Rohnert? He is a firm believer in the Council's cause and the prosperity of our race. How could this be?"

Ah, Marania. They didn't come more loyal. As the keeper of their record, she had the tendency to cling to old ways more than anyone else he knew. She was also known to have a tight connection with Rohnert. Goran would need to keep a close eye on her if he wanted to avoid dissention in the ranks.

"I have reports that a Kalimetal-wielding vampire murdered two of our Council guards, unprovoked. Do we know any other practitioner of the lost art?"

There was a collective gasp inside the assembly room, and Goran leaned back in his chair with satisfaction.

"If this were true, does it mean Rohnert had turned his back on us?" asked Bretania, Rohnert's replacement, in disbelief.

"I have no reason to doubt it. Therefore, I'm decreeing as of today, Rohnert is the Council's enemy. Any leads on his whereabouts must be reported without delay. And . . ." He paused and stood up. "You are all responsible for bringing him to justice. He must be taken down without question. Your personal guards must also be utilized for this purpose. Anyone found to be conspiring with him in any way will be considered an enemy of both the Council and our race."

He paid close attention to the Council members, feeling their conviction, but most especially their loyalty. After adjourning the meeting, Goran had made a mental note of names of those under suspicion. However, his first move would be to pay someone a visit.

Allison was stepping out of the shower when the intercom buzzed. Reaching for the towel, she dried herself and went to the bedroom where Tor was sleeping, dead to the world. Her face softened into a smile, remembering the beautiful time they had shared.

She pressed the intercom button. "Yes?"

"Ms. Tack, it's Jones. Could you please come and see me in the lab when you have a chance?"

Jones had been hard at work on the experiments his predecessor, Leroy, had left him. He'd also been instrumental in bringing most of their infected comrades back to health. Still, he continued to be backed up with the influx of diseased newcomers, which had been the priority of their operation.

"Sure. Give me a few minutes. Is there something wrong?"

"No ma'am. I just want to touch base with you. It's been a while since we last saw each other." She detected a smile in his voice.

"I'll see you in a bit." She hung up and dressed in her usual jeans, boots, and black turtleneck.

Tor was still sleeping, and his snoring could have woken the entire facility. She wanted him with her, but she decided his long hours on rotation earned him an extended rest. After she finished towel-drying her hair, Allison left her bedroom and took the stairs to the laboratory.

"Jones?" she called out as she walked into the quiet room.

Nothing had changed. Jones had left the laboratory the same way Leroy had kept it. He looked up from the microscope.

"Good evening, Ms. Tack."

Allison smiled at him. "Call me Allison, please."

Just as Jones was shoving his microscope aside, Harrow sauntered in, looking like he'd just come from a tough workout. His face was flushed, and beads of sweat still trickled down his cheeks.

"Hey guys," he said and sat next to Allison, opposite Jones at his desk. "What's this about?"

Although Jones was Allison's age, he seemed much older than his actual years. The long hours spent on research were beginning to show on his face, creating frown lines on his forehead and dark circles under his eyes.

"Before you start with your report, as your employer, I'm telling you to get some sleep—at least eight hours a day."

Jones raked his fingers through his hair with a sheepish grin. "I- ah, once I'm done with my latest research."

"Jones, no. After this meeting, you're going to march to your room and catch some Z's. Are we clear?" Allison said, sounding a bit more forceful than she'd intended.

Harrow chuckled. "The boss has spoken, Jonesy. You must follow," he said, teasing.

"Okay." Jones nodded his head, then pulled out a stack of papers from his drawer. He leafed through the papers before looking up at his employers. "So, I've been tallying the results of some of the feedback I've gathered over the past six months from you and the others. These are some of the common factors—enhanced senses, even doubling the usual vampire levels of hearing and touch. Eyesight remained poor for those who have been afflicted longer, like you, Harrow. Allison's didn't worsen because she hasn't had the disease for long. The echolocation theory I mentioned early on has only been experienced by you and Allison so far. I need more time to find the reason behind it."

Jones shifted in his chair to make himself more comfortable. "Harrow, I think this could work to your advantage with fighting. All you have to do is concentrate on the sounds your opponents make—their breathing, even the slightest movement—and you can attack before they do. The gene mutation, in addition to the animal diet, has spawned characteristics that are similar to animal behaviors and abilities. The aggression and other instincts are very common to infected vampires."

"Whoa! Stop there. So we're just like animals, is that what you're saying?" Harrow rubbed his chin. His expression made it clear that he considered the idea far-fetched.

Allison rolled her eyes at her brother. "I think we should be thankful that we've gotten a reprieve. We're much better now than before. I can't even remember the pain of the lesions anymore." She shuddered at the thought.

"Well, that's true. I just can't grasp the idea of mutating into another species, however unique."

"If I can put my two cents in?" Jones waited for permission to continue. When Harrow sighed and gestured for him to go on, he produced a graph. "These are my findings on that vampire who bit Rohnert. If you think *you're* a freak, you'll find this guy quite interesting."

Allison and Harrow leaned forward and stared at the graph Jones had drawn. Harrow sighed sharply. Allison realized it had become almost impossible for him to read little scribbles, so she read out the written information and placed her hand on his arm.

"According to Jones's findings, the bastard seems to have a hint of pure blood in him. In other words, this guy came out the way he did because of that untainted blood in him, no matter how miniscule the amount."

Harrow snorted. "Are you telling me the bastard might be related to a Council member?"

"That's what it seems like," Jones confirmed.

"And you got all of these theories from the DNA you took from Rohnert's wound?"

"Yes." Jones nodded. "It explains why Rohnert was susceptible to his attack. The vampire surprised him, and besides . . ." Jones leaned closer. "I'm going to tell you this in strictest confidence. Please don't nag Rohnert."

Harrow narrowed his eyes and nodded. Allison's interest was aroused. Although she wasn't very close to Rohnert, Tor was, and he had spoken highly of the vampire. Rohnert was man of few words, loyal, and straightforward.

"Pureblood vampires need to take the vein of another in order to survive and keep their talents sharp. He admitted that might be the reason the bastard was able to jump him the way he did."

Harrow huffed in disbelief. "Why wasn't I informed of this? Jesus, he's been with us for almost a year."

In light of Jones's explanation, Allison had to agree. It was irresponsible of Rohnert not to take care of himself. It now boiled down to how Harrow would proceed with the information. Allison shook her head at the thought of the probable showdown.

Jones seemed embarrassed, guilty even. "I'm sorry. I just found out not too long ago. You were so busy that I thought it wouldn't hurt to wait a little longer."

Harrow's eyes softened, even if his tone still sounded uptight. "Thank you for bringing it to our attention. Next time, don't hold anything back."

"Yes, sir. I apologize. It was foolish of me to have waited."

The laboratory door squeaked, and they all looked around to see Jordan walking in. Allison beamed at her adoptive sister-in-law, and she noticed the way Harrow relaxed the moment he saw her.

"Sorry that I took an extra day to return. Gail is persuasive." Jordan stopped when she realized that she had interrupted them.

Harrow stood and closed the gap between them in a few quick strides. "I'm glad you're back." He kissed her long and hard. Allison and Jones stared at each other, then laughed. When the lovebirds finally surfaced for air, Harrow said, "Tell me about the little squirt later, but for now, we have to see a friend." Harrow pulled at Jordan's arm and turned to Jones and Allison. "Thanks for the information, Jones. Good job. Sis, I'll see you later."

Allison waved, thinking the showdown would be happening sooner than she had expected. Good thing Harrow had decided to take Jordan with him. She'd be a good mediator in case both vampires flew off the handle. She wondered if Shelly knew anything about this. Maybe a little trip to see the good doctor was in order.

Rohnert got up from behind the desk as soon as Harrow and Jordan walked in. He had been looking for things to do since Shelly informed everyone he was out of rotation.

He caught Jordan's thoughts about her little secret and looked at his friend with a calculating stare. She blinked, catching his perceptive glance, and shook her head in warning. Her eyes flashed with guilt.

"What's up?" Rohnert sat on the edge of the desk while they approached. The set of Harrow's shoulders alerted him to trouble.

"Go ahead, you can read my mind, and you'll see how stupid you are for depriving yourself of what is necessary for your existence." Harrow walked up to him, a little too close for comfort. Jordan stayed back and rocked on her heels, looking uncomfortable.

"This is where I say, 'mind your own business'," Rohnert said, refusing to be baited into a full-on argument.

"I can't, and I won't. You're a valuable member of our team. When you're fucking up, we're all going to breathe down your neck. And don't even think of confronting Jones on this. He did what is right."

"And what is that?"

"Bringing the matter to my attention."

"I'm fine," Rohnert insisted. On the contrary, his healing had been at a snail's pace. What would have taken a few days before was now dragging out over weeks, and he knew it was due to his lack of proper nourishment.

"You're not. Look at you. You're off rotation because that damn shoulder isn't healing as fast as it should."

"What do you suggest I do?" He ought to pay Jones a visit and smack him hard in the head.

"Get yourself whatever you need," Harrow answered.

"You're suggesting I call the very people I'm avoiding and beg for some blood so I'll feel brand new again?" Rohnert leveled a gaze at him, then stood and walked to the middle of the room.

Harrow's tone rose a notch. "Do whatever is necessary for you to survive."

"Yeah. You make it sound so simple. Why don't you put your money where your mouth is and spar with me." He removed the sling and tested his shoulder. The pain was minimal, but he was still sore.

"I'm dead serious, Rohn. You will drag your ass wherever you can to get what you need. It's an order."

Harrow's threat sounded real. Rohnert whistled and laughed.

"I will go whenever I think it's time. For now, leave if you're just going to talk. I'm not in the best mood. I'm bored out of my damn mind."

"Suit yourself, but you won't be on rotation until you've fed." Harrow turned to Jordan. "Shall we?"

Jordan considered Harrow's invitation, glanced at Rohnert, and then back to Harrow. "Do you mind if I spar with Rohnert?"

Harrow sighed. "Whatever," he said and left.

Once the door closed, Rohnert laughed. "You're losing your touch, girl. You look like you're going to burst from guilt."

"Stop it." She unstrapped the Kalimetal holster and placed it on the table.

"Are you planning on telling Harrow what you did?" he asked, pushing the issue.

"I don't see any reason why I should." Jordan assumed a relaxed position at the end of mat.

Rohnert walked to the opposite end and placed his fists together. After they bowed, they met in the middle. He threw the first punch, which she blocked. Okay, that hurt. He winced but said nothing. They went at it, stepping, punching, blocking, and throwing roundhouse and axe kicks.

"You killed Council guards. Don't you think that that's information worth sharing with Harrow?" he grunted when her fist connected with his stomach.

Jordan laughed before evading his kick. She bounced on the mat, inviting him to move forward. He knew better—he'd taught her everything she knew, after all. It was time to use some of the old tricks on her.

Rohnert went closer, not close enough for her kick to connect, and gauged her movement. He threw a right punch toward her chest that she blocked with her left arm, which gave him a chance to loop his arm around her and flip her over, pinning her facedown on the mat.

"You're going to tell him soon. It's not healthy to keep secrets, especially of that magnitude." He pushed her face into the vinyl.

Jordan struggled against him, her body straining. "You should feed soon."

"Fine! I will, but when I'm good and ready. You, in turn, will tell him soon." Rohnert let go of her head, but his knee was still in her back. "I'm not kidding. If you don't, I will tell him myself." He released her and jumped back in case she had tricks up her sleeve.

Jordan jumped to her feet without effort. "You and Lambert make a great pair. You're both crybabies." She shook her fist at him.

"Say what you want, you know I'm right."

Instead of answering, she bowed, picked up her Kalimetal, and left without a word. Rohnert chuckled. Jordan was a piece of work: a tough woman, and irritating to boot. An image of Shelly flashed in his mind. *Women.*

Sometimes, you can't thank your lucky stars enough, Melissa thought giddily as she got ready to step out for the night. Goran had called for her to service him just before he left. She hadn't asked questions; no one ever questioned Goran. She gave in to his whims with enthusiasm, maneuvered into the positions he requested, and did whatever she could to please him.

Glancing at herself in the mirror, she realized her days were numbered. It hadn't escaped her that Goran was quiet at times. She suspected he was ripping recent memories from her mind, to be used against her in the days to come.

All she cared about now was revenge. Nothing mattered anymore. She was sick of Goran—his wandering eye, his treatment of her, and his careless disregard for Demetrius's disappearance. Melissa smoothed a few tendrils of hair that had escaped the bun on top of her head and tucked them behind her ear. She felt good . . . and ready to fulfill Goran's bidding.

The living arrangements within the Tack facility remained the same, even after the demolition of the office building had taken place. Harrow and Jordan opted to stay in a suite in the facility to be more accessible. Tor had moved out of the room he'd once shared with Harrow and parked his ass in one of the vacant suites. This arrangement had continued until recently. Nowadays, Tor stayed with Allison in the underground home her father had built for her when she was infected.

Despite how seldom he used it, Tor still maintained his own room, but Allison was hoping all of that would change soon. The prospect of the two of them sharing everything made her smile. That same smile disappeared once she walked in the front door and she heard his helpless groans as he wrestled with another nightmare.

Running as fast as she could, she tore through the foyer and hallway and burst into her bedroom. Tor thrashed in desperation, his face peppered with beads of sweat and his expression pitiful. Without a moment's hesitation, she sat and reached forward to caress his cheek. With all the tenderness she felt, she wiped away the perspiration from his face and kissed his mouth.

She whispered, "Darling, wake up. You're just dreaming. Everything is all right."

His arms flailed, and he almost landed an errant fist on her jaw. She ached for his pain and longed to relieve him of his invisible torment. "Tor?" She shook him gently. "Wake up . . . it's just a dream."

More thrashing and tortured groans came, so she shook him harder. His lids fluttered, and he stared at her with a blank expression. Guilt studded his eyes while he reconciled the nightmare and reality.

Tor reached for her face, searching, as if to check if she was not a figment of his imagination. "Jessie . . . she seemed so real." He pressed his eyes shut, his hand still touching her. "She's fading away. I don't know what it means." The anguish was thick in his words.

Allison pulled him into an embrace. "Shh. You're going to be okay." She held him tight. "She's probably telling you that it's time to let go. She's happy for you."

Tor's massive body quivered at her touch. "I don't know what to think. I feel guilty for taking her life, while here I am, living. It feels like I have no right to be to be happy."

So much pain, so much remorse. "You have to let the guilt go. Things happened for a reason. I'm not saying she deserved to die, or that what you did wasn't awful. But you've suffered long enough. Let it go and accept the past. You've paid your dues." Allison hugged him harder.

Tor buried his head deep into the crook of her neck. Rubbing his back in soothing circles, she felt tremors rack his body. How could she make him understand? While she rocked him back and forth, they sat in silence for a long time before Allison decided to change the topic.

"Hey, I'm going to see Shelly. Want to tag along?"

"Why do I sense that you're not going for just a social visit?" Tor lifted his head. Although his eyes sparkled with unshed tears, he gave a weak smile.

Allison smirked at his presumption. "I have my reasons." She stood and offered her hands to help him rise.

"I know you, woman."

His mood seemed to have shifted, and she congratulated herself. When he took her hands and let her pull him to his feet, she wasn't surprised to find him naked. But what *did* surprise her was her reaction to seeing his unclothed body—she couldn't tear her eyes away from the sinewy outline of his hard chest muscles. Even though she'd lost herself in his glorious body so many times, the need lingered. She could never get enough.

Allison shook her head to dispel the thoughts. There were things to be done and people to see.

Tor watched her, his eyes gleaming with knowledge. "I think we have to satisfy a girl's craving," he said, winking.

"I think you should get dressed. Quick!" She slapped his butt and pointed him in the direction of the bathroom.

He chortled, enjoying her discomfort. Then he took her hand and kissed it, his expression somber. "I—I want to thank you for everything. For giving me a chance."

Tor seemed uneasy, and Allison knew that he was not comfortable expressing his emotions, so she just smiled and shook her head. "You owe me."

"That I do."

"Then start with getting your ass dressed and ready in five minutes."

Within three, Tor was freshly showered and dressed in jeans, a black shirt, and leather boots. They walked to the clinic in silence. Shelly's music was playing at full blast, filling the deserted area with its booming bass. She had her legs up on the little table in the adjoining room and was enjoying a novel. Her foot was bobbing to the rhythm of "Brick in the Wall." She looked up and flashed a pleased smile of welcome.

"Hey guys! What brings you to the fun side?" She lowered her legs and dropped the book on her desk. Her eyes searched theirs but stopped when she met Allison's gaze. "Is there a problem?"

Allison sat down on a chair, and Tor shifted to stand behind her. "What makes you think there's a problem?"

Shelly rolled her eyes. "C'mon, you've never come to see me without news of some sort or to consult on something. 'Fess up, girl."

"I guess there's no point in beating around the bush."

"Nope. So what *really* brings you here?" Shelly asked again.

Allison sighed. "I was in to see Jones earlier, and during the course of our conversation, he mentioned something about Rohnert."

If human's ears could prick upward like animals' did, she would have sworn the doctor's ears did when she heard Rohnert's name. Shelly leaned forward and rested her arms on the table. "What about him?"

No doubt about it—there was something going on between the private vampire and the beautiful doctor. "Jones reported to Harrow that Rohnert hasn't fed from his kind, which explains why he isn't healing as rapidly as he should. You know we have the ability to repair ourselves faster than humans, but the purebloods are even faster. Do you know anything about this?"

Shelly's nostrils flared, but she hid her emotions quickly. She shook her head. "He's been here for almost a year now."

"Which is a cause for concern. I think Harrow already had a talk with him."

Clasping her hands, Shelly snorted. "Good luck with that. He is the most stubborn man I've ever come across." She pursed her lips.

"Um . . . I wouldn't say that. I know of another one." Allison giggled, and Tor shifted behind her.

"Standing right here," he muttered through gritted teeth.

The women burst out laughing. Despite Shelly's attempt to hide her emotions, Allison could see right through her. Allison felt the urge to ask what the deal was between her and Rohnert but decided against prying.

"I'm here in the hopes that you might be able to help convince him to feed. I don't think Harrow can persuade him, but you might."

Shelly's brows drew together. "What makes you think he'll listen to me?"

"I don't know. You're his doctor. Maybe he'll listen from a professional standpoint. I don't know." In all honesty, Allison wasn't sure what any of them could do, but she'd be damned if she let Rohnert destroy himself.

"Well, if he comes to me, then maybe I'll say something. He's different. He's wired in a weird way, you know." Shelly stood and retrieved a bottle of water from her little refrigerator and took a long pull. "I'll see what I can do."

"That's all I ask."

There was a soft rapping at the door. "Come in," Shelly called out. Rohnert stuck his head in, and his smile was replaced by puzzlement.

"Did I catch you at a bad time?" I can—"

Tor interrupted him. "We were just leaving. Ally?"

"Yes, we're on our way out," Allison said and got up.

"Have a seat Rohnert," they heard Shelly say just before they closed the door behind them.

Shelly gestured for Rohnert to sit in the now-vacant chair. God knew that watching him made her weak in the knees. It wasn't fair for a man to be so confident, virile, and attractive. Rohnert smiled and sat.

"What can I do for you?" she asked in her most professional tone.

"I was wondering if you could clear me to go out—"

"Absolutely not! Are you nuts? You haven't fed for a long time. Do you think the human blood you're taking is sufficient? If you think I'd be instrumental in your demise, you're dead wrong!" she blustered without stopping to give him a chance to speak. Shelly tried to hide the accusation in her voice, but it proved too difficult. She cared too much for him.

"Where is this coming from?" Rohnert stood and planted both palms on the desk, towering over her.

"You want to go on patrol. You want to fight. The answer is no. I won't give you medical clearance," she snapped.

"If you hadn't cut me off, then you would have learned that I was going to ask if it was okay for me to go and find someone to feed from." He was indignant, but there was a gleam in his eyes she couldn't quite place.

"You were?" Her hands rose to her cheeks, which were flushed with embarrassment. *Oh, dear. How stupid she must've sounded, firing an unloaded gun.*

"Yes," he hissed under his breath. "But since you *have* interrupted me, I think I won't even wait for you to give me a go."

 "Just make sure you close that door behind you," she said.

Rohnert glared at her in disbelief. "Your sassy mouth won't get you very far, Dr. Anderson," he muttered and turned to leave.

Shelly wanted to kick herself, but she couldn't bring herself to apologize for jumping on him. She watched him disappear, the door shutting with a decisive thud behind him, just as she'd ordered.

She collapsed onto her chair, feeling mortified and more than a little sick to her stomach. Her father had always said her mouth would land her in trouble.

Zane found great satisfaction in pushing his roadster to the limit. There weren't many places in the city where he could test the horsepower, but outside the city, anything was possible. Zane sniffed the sweet air contentedly and shifted into fifth gear.

"You're going to attract attention to yourself," Melissa said, glancing in the side mirror to check whether they were being trailed by a black-and-white.

"Grams, relax. Those squad cars have nothing on this baby." He patted the dashboard with utmost reverence.

Melissa's laugh blended with the swishing sound of the wind on their faces. Granting her request to be taken to an upstate location was the least he could do in return for her generosity. Besides, he was getting claustrophobic in the city. He'd been cooped up in his penthouse for much too long. It had taken him some time to determine there was no one staking out his place anymore. Zane wondered why the stakeout had stopped, but he wasn't complaining. It cramped his style to be unable come and go as he pleased.

His grandmother hadn't disclosed her reason for wanting to go for a drive, or for heading upstate in particular. Not that he cared. They drove in comfortable silence, the wind providing soothing background music.

The road was empty, and he floored it. It took him a little more than two hours to reach the area Melissa had mentioned.

"Stop here," she requested.

Zane eased the car off the road and parked next to a row of humongous junipers. He turned off the engine, and darkness loomed once the headlights went off.

"What are we doing here, anyway?" He looked around and caught a sudden shift in her emotions.

"Goran sends guards here all the time, and there's a particular one I needed to talk to." She craned her neck to follow a rustling sound to their right.

"Why can't you talk to him somewhere else? Like where you live? This is hardly the place for a woman like you."

The way she regarded him then made him want to swallow his words.

"I'm almost seventy years old—I can take care of myself. I appreciate the concern, but I want you to refrain from asking me questions. Also, I expect you to say nothing to anyone else about this errand."

Her reprimand felt like a slap across the face. Zane pressed his lips together and nodded.

Melissa opened the car door and slipped out. "Wait here. This will only take a moment."

Before he could respond, she was gone. He leaned back against the leather upholstery and tapped his fingers on the steering wheel. Okay, if he was going to wait, he might as well entertain himself. Cranking up the volume on his stereo system, he let the music lull him and closed his eyes.

He'd probably dosed off, because the next thing he knew, Melissa was nudging him on the shoulder. Zane straightened and blinked several times.

"I'm ready to go," she said, looking straight ahead.

"Everything okay?" he asked, turning on the ignition.

"It went well."

Remembering her earlier reprimand, Zane didn't ask further questions. He pressed a button, and the soft convertible top came down. The drive back was quiet, yet comfortable.

When they reached Rockefeller Center, Melissa took his hand and held it. She had a wistful expression on her face.

"I'm going to wire more money to your account. It might be a while before I can do it again."

"Thanks." He squeezed her hand. "When do we see each other again?"

"I'll call you." Melissa leaned closer and kissed him on the forehead. Trailing soft fingers along his cheek, she said, "Now, take my vein before you go. I can sense your need." She angled her neck to expose her creamy skin.

Zane's mouth gaped. The suave smooth-talker in him was at a loss for words. Stumped, he just stared at Melissa while she waited for him to take her offering. On any given day, he'd have jumped at the chance to take a vein, but this was his father's mother. It was just plain weird, and it made him uncomfortable. But then again, who in their right frame of mind would turn down such sweet offer?

"I don't have all night to wait," she whispered and leaned closer.

Zane inched closer, still hesitant. The offer was too tempting to resist, and he did need to feed. He lifted his eyes to hers before focusing on the vein in her neck that was pulsing and inviting him to take the plunge. Leaning forward, he inhaled deep to let her scent saturate his senses.

She smiled and pressed his head to her neck. He licked her skin, trailing his tongue along the outline of her vein, marking the spot. Melissa moaned, and he felt something in him come alive. Eroticism and feeding went hand-in-hand, and before he could develop a conscience, he latched on with his razor sharp teeth and pulled, hard.

When the first drop of blood trickled down his throat, the heady scent of lust wafted in the air. He drank deeper, letting her sweet life force surge inside him. She held his face, caressing his cheek while he fed.

Zane was going to lose it. He wanted to take her, right then and there, in his car. Abruptly, he pulled his mouth away from her neck, licking the errant blood off his lips before kissing her. She kissed him back, then pulled away.

"That shall be all for tonight." She wiped his mouth with her finger, and then sucked the small trail of blood off her finger.

Stunned, Zane sat unmoving. He'd met many women, bedded them, and taken everything they had to offer, but Melissa stole his breath away. To say she'd satisfied him would be a gross understatement. She tasted like the sweetest wine, and she was as addictive as mounds of heroin. There was no denying he wanted her.

"No, that is all I can give you. Your father left with me with a broken heart. I must find him. And you shall live to take our place. Give us reason for our existence. Do right my boy, and do right by your father and me."

Melissa walked away. Soon after, the throng of passersby swallowed her. Zane sat in his car, unmoving, unable to fathom how things had gone from casual to complete abandon so quickly.

His phone rang, startling him back to reality.

"Gralnik," he whispered, still in shock.

"You and I need to talk," the smooth voice of his associate demanded.

"So start talking."

"What kind of people are we tracking down?" The question was direct, and Zane knew what Gralnik was referring to.

"You're paid to do a job. Questions are not welcome in this transaction. You finish the assignment, and your reward will be enough to allow you to retire early."

"I don't like this," Gralnik muttered.

Zane smiled. Gralnik didn't have to like it, he just had to do it. "Did you get the crate I sent you?"

"Yes. We've got everything pegged, and the schedule is predictable. We're going to move in soon."

"The plans have changed. I won't be joining you. Go to it whenever you're ready, but buzz me before you make your move." With that final instruction, Zane ended the call.

Melissa's words had affected him. They'd created a rift in his head, isolating thoughts and separating the insipid from the significant. It made him think that there must be some deeper explanation as to why he came to be the way he was, unique and categorically vital to the future of the vampire race.

Zane sat inside his car, pondering what he had to do next. One thing was for certain: He was looking forward to seeing his grandmother again.

Jordan found Harrow in the training room, beating the hell out of the punching bag. She slipped in quietly and waited. As usual, Harrow was barefoot, shirtless, and wearing his favorite raggedy sweat pants. Her eyes wandered along the lines of his powerful shoulders, his well-defined arms, and his glorious chest muscles. The past year had done wonders for his overall well-being, as well as his general physique. He'd been training hard with whatever was left of his free time, and it showed.

Harrow continued going at the punching bag like the fate of the world depended on it. Jordan watched him, marveling at his endurance, his passion, and her luck. When her life had only consisted of endless plots for revenge, Harrow had showed up and changed her outlook. There was more to her existence than her visions of retribution. She had a family to live for, and now there was Gail, who needed a mother.

This was a good excuse to use as an opening line. Hopefully, she could make her news as painless as possible.

"Hey," Harrow whispered in her ear.

She'd been too caught up in her thoughts to even notice that he was standing next to her.

"Hey," she echoed. "Are you finished?"

He pulled her into a quick hug. "Mmm . . . yeah. What did you have in mind?" He was smiling.

Good. It'd be easier to talk when one was in a good mood.

"I want to tell you something." Jordan kissed him on the lips before leading him to his desk to sit down, taking the chair across from him.

"Shoot."

She knew Harrow well. His eyebrows had disappeared behind his sunglasses, which meant he was already thinking a mile a minute.

"You know how protective I am of Gail, right?"

He nodded, removing his sunglasses.

"When I went to check on her the other day, I spotted two Council guards not too far from our home. I acted on impulse and lashed out."

Harrow was suddenly still, all the life and fun sucked out of him.

"Then what happened?" His pitch rose, and he glowered at her.

Jordan shrank back into her chair. "I took them out. No words, no exchange."

To her amazement, Harrow breathed a sigh of relief. He moved so fast, she was surprised to find herself wrapped in his arms.

"You're a stupid, stubborn woman. Haven't you been listening to anything I've said? No one works alone. If anything had happened to you. . ." He shuddered.

Jordan squirmed in his embrace, shifting to wrap her arms around him. "I didn't mean for it to happen that way. I'm sorry. I just freaked out when I saw them so close to our house and to Gail."

"I understand. Next time—hell, there won't be a next time."

Harrow seemed shaken. Jordan felt she'd subjected him to unnecessary worry. He had enough things to worry about, as it was.

She fished inside her trench coat pocket and produced two Vampire Council seals. "I got these from them. No traces, no witness. It's all clean."

Harrow picked up one seal and fingered the embossed symbol. "Woman, if you ever pull a stunt like that again, I'm going to take you off rotation."

Jordan knew Harrow wasn't bluffing when he made the threat. He'd pull the rug out from under her without batting an eye. She gave him a defiant look but didn't say a word.

"I'm going to call a meeting. I think everyone needs to know and be extra vigilant. The concentration on that area is a cause for concern." Harrow kissed her forehead before getting to his feet.

"Um, Rohnert already knows. Well, he read my mind and shoved my face into the ground until I promised to tell you. I'm glad Lambert wasn't half as bad."

Harrow grinned. "We have good people surrounding us. I'd better thank Rohnert for his subtlety."

"Oh, you think you're so funny." Jordan stuck her tongue out at him. Deep inside, she was relieved that he'd taken it so well.

Since it was the middle of the afternoon and patrols weren't deployed until a few minutes after sundown, it only took few minutes to round up the group. Old and new faces waited for Harrow to speak. The I-room was filled to capacity. Rohnert preferred to stand, while Allison took her usual spot, Tor standing behind her. Cyrus walked in, looking rather uncomfortable in a suit instead of his usual duds of jeans and cotton shirt. Snickers flew across the room when he opened his suit jacket to reveal several weapon holsters. Since he was conducting most of the daytime business operations, Allison had talked him into dressing the part. Cyrus had agreed with reluctance but warned her that he'd keep packing heat wherever he went.

Harrow eyed Cyrus, one of his most trusted men, and chuckled. "Glad you made it, my friend."

"Kiss my ass," Cyrus retorted and flashed his uneven teeth. "Why don't you stop pansy-dancing and give us the details?"

"Okay, listen up." Harrow raised his hands for silence. "We have evidence that the Vampire Council is concentrating on our home base upstate."

He threw the seals on the table for everyone to see.

"Kudos to the brave one," Tor cheered.

Harrow threw a knowing look in Rohnert's direction and smiled.

"I'm afraid we'll have to be more cautious during our daily duties. Travel in pairs, if not in groups. The Council isn't letting up. I have reason to suspect they're going to come down harder on anyone who shows even the slightest hint of being infected. I also think that if you show resistance, they are going to strike. So, I'm going to remind you to please, please be careful. Always bring an extra knife with you in case of an emergency."

All the times she'd gone out, Jordan had forgotten about doing that. Despite the Dangeran's rapid and fatal effect, if a vampire was hit in a part of the body that he or she could do without, it was necessary to amputate that body part but the vampire would live.

An unhappy wave of muttering passed through the group.

Then Cyrus stood up. "I did some damage to one vampire a year ago. I guess he was able to live, because I saw him again with his arm gone. It goes to show that you can survive the Dangeran's wrath."

Another round of buzzing spread across the room, and Harrow hushed their concerns.

"Cyrus is right. Just react fast enough; it can be done. On another note, our research continues, but it's going a little slower because Jones is fairly new but he's relentless, and we're hoping we'll find a way to stop the disease completely."

"I'm counting on it," one new member quipped.

"Don't worry. Just continue to do your work and keep your noses clean." Harrow looked at each person one by one until he got to Jordan. He smiled before turning his attention back to the vampires and humans before him. "I will rotate your assignments right now. I believe some of us need a change of scenery, right?"

Whistles and hoots sounded across the room in response.

"A few of you who have been patrolling the city will be switched to our upstate base, while the ones from there will be given the city assignment. This will go into effect in two days. Those interested, please raise your hands."

Several vampires and humans volunteered, and Cyrus began jotting down names.

Jordan watched everyone's reaction to Harrow's pronouncements and marveled at Harrow's easy-going rapport with the group. Her gaze traveled to Rohnert, who sat quietly in the corner.

She walked over to him. "Is everything all right?"

Rohnert nodded. "I'm taking your advice. I'm going to see an old friend."

Her face lit up. "Are you fit to travel by yourself?"

Rohnert considered her question. "You think our boss will let you out of his sight?"

"I believe he will. As long as I don't have to sit and watch." She playfully jabbed him in the arm. It was thrilling to get the chance to help an old friend who'd given her so much.

"It's a promise." Rohnert flashed a scout sign.

When you wanted something done right, you had to do it yourself. To avoid any slip-ups this time, he set out to do the deed himself.

He pulled his favorite sword from the display case. It had been a while since he last held it. Trailing his finger along the exquisite metal, he vividly remembered the first time he'd used it, in a rite dictated by the Council before he ascended the seat. His father had given the weapon to him, a legacy from his father's father. It had been a rainy evening, and he had to track down a vampire from another clan under the sky's vengeful downpour.

Renegade families were in abundance then, back before he took his rightful seat. He'd stormed the vampire's dwelling with courage and confidence, cornering the repugnant excuse for a night crawler. That first strike had been the sweetest and was forever carved in his memory.

For years, he killed with his grandfather's blade, savoring each moment of carnage with pride. The last time he'd used it had been during the Great Vampire Revolution. Together with Rohnert, he had eradicated the insurgent vampires, ushering in his impressive reign.

Those were the days.

Looking at the sacred words on the polished silver metal, he uttered them out loud: "We will prevail."

The heavy, thick sword was the pride of his family. It was a shame he wasn't ready to relinquish his seat to anyone, not even to his own blood kin. Sheathing the sword in its scabbard with reverence, he took an exit he alone knew. While he traveled through the invisible passage between their sanctuary and the world of the humans, he pulled his long black hair into a tight ponytail.

Emerging at the foot of an unmarked building, he sneered at the glaze his comrade's spell had cast around the area. If Alphonsus had hoped to hide from Goran, the effort had been futile. The spell did work on humans, however, sparing them the realization they weren't alone in this world. Illusions such as these protected the vampires' furtive existence.

Not bothering to announce his arrival, Goran scaled the walls until he found the right place. Peeking through the window, he watched Alphonsus in his study. The elder was deep in thought, staring at a blank sheet of stationery. Goran had learned that it was best to catch an opponent when his guard was down and his mind was exposed.

Listening to his friend's rambling thoughts, Goran slid through the open window until he was standing behind the vampire. The pen dropped, and Alphonsus turned around, his face ashen.

"Goran." It was a whisper.

"Great evening, isn't it, Alphonsus?"

The vampire stood. "To—to what do I owe this surprise visit?" Alphonsus inched toward the left, his hand clutching the handle of his desk drawer.

Goran dusted invisible lint from his black suit jacket. "It's a perfect night to start ridding the Council of scum."

Alphonsus's eyes flickered with guilt. "Whatever are you referring to, my friend?"

Goran laughed and shook his head. "You've already told me what I needed to hear, *my friend*." The emphasis on the last words made the other vampire wince.

"I—I haven't done anything. I wasn't planning on corroborating with the others—"

"Yet, you entertained the idea. Too late, Alphonsus. Some things cannot be taken back, and lives won't be spared."

With those words, he stepped back, drew his sword, and slashed Alphonsus before he could flee. Goran's technique was precise, cutting a diagonal line from the shoulder down to the opposite hip. He took a moment to enjoy the fear, loathing, and rage in Alphonsus's eyes.

"You're not going to succeed," Alphonsus cried, holding his head as if to prevent it from exploding.

"I will. Too bad you won't be around to see it." Goran laughed and turned away.

The crackling and popping sounds began. Goran climbed out the window, turning around just before he climbed down. Ashes littered the floor.

He had forgotten the exhilaration of a kill. It had been some time since he had made private visits to Council members. This trip had produced results, he'd intended. Crossing the city in a blur of speed was stimulating. When was the last time he'd stalked a victim? Milla had been the last one, and that had been a year ago.

In a matter of minutes, he reached Iden's residence. Tucked into a row of expensive townhouses, the youngest vampire's home was bustling with activity.

Goran climbed the towering structure in search of his next victim. Servants were nestled in one room.

No thoughts pointed to Iden's whereabouts. Not even his mate's mind allowed Goran to pinpoint his location. Goran could wait, but it was too sensational a night to spend just hanging around. He'd return and collect his dues later.

Goran jumped to the nearest ledge to gather his thoughts. He gazed at the night sky and inhaled deeply. Although he wasn't planning an all-nighter, another kill would be exceptional. He watched the sprawling city and considered his next target.

With a burst of renewed energy, he jumped down from the multistory building to the almost deserted street, his sword clinging to his side. He broke into a run, taking less-traveled paths through deserted alleys and back streets.

This time, he was going to be a gentleman. Ladies wanted to admit their guests by way of the door. Goran acknowledged the doorman's greeting, tossing a spell to erase his memory of the visit. He took the elevator to the thirty-fifth floor of the high rise. It remained a mystery why most of his peers opted to live around humans. He couldn't quite understand their fascination with the lesser beings, but to each his own.

The elevator announced his arrival with a loud dinging sound. He strode out and casually approached Marania's front door. The keeper of their ancient documents needed some help with keeping the records straight, and he was be happy to extend all the necessary assistance.

He held the brass knocker between his fingers and rapped hard. The door was answered by a male vampire in a butler's uniform. Surprise and recognition flashed across his face, but before any questions were asked, Goran silenced him permanently with a dagger to the chest. Once the butler fell to the ground in a heap of ashes, Goran advanced inside.

"Hector, who is it?" Marania's melodious voice drifted through the house, alerting him to her exact location.

Goran walked in silence to her bedroom. "It's me," he answered in a low tone.

Marania was seated in front of her dresser mirror, brushing her raven hair. She whirled around, fear spreading across her face.

"Goran?" Her voice was even, despite her frightened expression.

"How are you this lovely evening?" He walked closer while sneaking glances at the lavish Victorian furnishings. She had always had great taste, especially in clothing. He raked his eyes along her flimsy, black nightgown, feasting on the robust breasts peeking from the low-cut neckline.

"I'm well. What brings you here? Are we talking business or pleasure?" she asked, masking her discomfort with a shift in tactic.

Goran chuckled. "You're well aware that my interest lies elsewhere." He paused and dropped his gaze to her thighs. "But I'm willing to make an exception tonight."

Marania let out a throaty laugh. "You've always been brutally frank. I adore your honesty."

"And I would have loved to have you around for much longer, my dear." He dropped his sword to the floor and walked behind her. Marania flinched the moment he placed his hand on her neck. "Turn and watch yourself in the mirror."

Marania did as she was told. Goran felt her fear and could almost smell it. He looked at her in the mirror and began rubbing her back. The feel of soft silk sent tingles down his spine while he explored the curve of her neck and the proud set of her shoulders. She moaned a little when his hand glided down to the small of her back.

He smiled, not breaking eye contact. "Tell me, my dear Marania, what would you do to keep yourself alive?"

She hesitated, her eyes grew big. "I . . . don't know. What do you want me to do?"

Instead of answering her, he reached forward and caressed her neck with his tongue. Her body swayed to meet his touches. He trailed little kisses everywhere he saw creamy skin. "Keep watching yourself," he commanded when he took a breather.

Her body straightened, and he smirked. Marania was all right—still perky, younger, of exquisite bloodline. She would have made a good mate, if he'd been into gothic beauty. He continued assaulting her with kisses until she lowered her guard.

Bingo!

Marania gave him more than he'd ever thought possible. Flashes of her life, her associations, and her betrayal swam in his mind, shocking and revolting him. She had been secretly conniving with a few members of the Council to oust him. They knew of his escapades, but what they didn't know was that he was always one step ahead. The final, most surprising revelation made him pause.

All these years, Marania had been pining for Rohnert. This was too good. Unrequited love gave him goose bumps. She had been in contact with him up until a year ago, and she had always believed that Rohnert was a better leader.

Goran had wanted the truth, but now that he'd gotten it, he wanted to throw it out the window. All these years, after all he'd done, this was the best she could do for him? He drew a sharp breath, halting his exploration of her body.

"Give me the record," he hissed under his breath.

Marania pressed her eyes closed, seeming to realize that the cat was out of the bag. "It's under my pillow."

Goran was gone and back in a flash, the old, black book clasped in his hand. "Thank you. I never thought you'd be this cooperative. I was mistaken about you. You're a smart vampire, deserving to live forever." The relief in her face was almost comical. Goran laughed with pure glee. "I'm so sorry, my dear. I'm lying."

With one quick thrust, he plunged an ordinary knife in her back, intentionally missing her heart by a hairsbreadth.

She gasped, knowing what he'd done. "Why?"

He held her shoulder to keep her from slumping. "Slow, painful death is what you need. That pure blood will be good for nothing." Goran picked up his sword from the floor. "You would have gone very far if you hadn't been so righteous. You should have done what I asked you to do and rewritten the laws. You didn't have to die."

"Goran . . ."

He could barely hear her voice. Her heartbeat slowed, and blood oozed from her stab wound. Goran yanked out the knife and was tempted to taste her. Licking the blood from the blade, he said, "You taste divine."

The moment he let go of her shoulder, she slumped to the ground. Her black hair splayed all over, covering her face. Blood stained the once-immaculate carpet.

"Goran," she kept saying, and yet he couldn't get any coherent thoughts from her.

"Sorry, my dear. We all need to make some sacrifices. This is yours, for the sake of our continued existence. I shall see you in the latter life." Spoken like he meant it, he gave her one last look before turning away.

"Are you sure this is the place?" Jordan asked as they entered the luxurious building.

"Yes." Rohnert threw a quick glance her way.

Once they reached the top floor, he could sense that something was amiss. He released the buttons of his trench coat and gripped the Kalimetal's handle.

Rohnert signaled to Jordan to stay behind him before he nudged the door open. They found a heap of ashes on the floor.

Not good.

He wielded his Kalimetal, and Jordan followed suit. Aiming the weapon, he expected to be jumped anytime, so he proceeded with caution. They walked slowly to avoid creating noise in case the perpetrator was still around. At last, they reached the bedroom, where the stench of blood assaulted their senses. Marania's body lay on the floor in a bed of blood.

"Marania!" Rohnert sprang forward and rushed to her side.

Slowly, he turned her body and cradled her. Her pallid features signaled that she was close to death. Marania's eyes quivered, then opened. Recognition flashed in her face. "Rohnert." Her voice was barely audible.

"Who did this to you?" he hissed through gritted teeth.

"Dr–drink . . ."

"No!" Rohnert felt an immense rush of anger sweep through him. "Who did this to you?" he repeated.

"Goran. Drink now . . . there's no time. Please. The black book . . . inside my drawer." She reached out to touch his face. "Drink . . ."

A tingle shot through his system, and he knew what his body wanted. With tenderness, he lowered his face and latched his fangs onto her neck. Hunger made him take everything she had to offer, and guilt washed over him while he sucked the remaining life out of her. He sensed her light dimming, until her inner illumination shut down for good.

Rohnert felt wretched, yet revitalized. What a deadly combination for anyone stupid enough to provoke him.

Death—humans feared it, but Rohnert's kind longed for it. After several centuries of living, you'd seen it all. Eventually, you'd find yourself invoking the higher powers to take you and set your spirit free.

But not like this. No one deserved to go this way, brutally murdered and robbed of dignity.

Rohnert had no idea how long he'd been staring at Marania's corpse. She had been a confidante, almost like family. They'd grown up together, were inducted into the Council at almost the same time, and had fed each other through the centuries since both had been without mates.

Of course he was pissed.

"Rohnert," Jordan whispered. "I think it's time."

He heard her, but her voice seemed so distant. Sounds were muffled, and faces were distorted. He glanced at her when she placed the Kalimetal on his lap.

"Give her peace."

He nodded and pushed himself up on legs that felt like lead. Death had never bothered him, but senseless murder did. His stomach roared in contentment, but his heart ached to avenge his friend. Jordan reached out and placed her arm around his waist.

"Lean on me. It's okay."

Rohnert pulled back and waved her away. "I'm good." He took a deep breath and cleared his thoughts. After a few moments, he picked up his Kalimetal and gestured for Jordan to step back.

He gazed upward as if begging for mercy, incanted the ancient rites, and thrust the blunt tip of his weapon straight into Marania's belly. Instead of the usual pop and sizzle that resulted from any Dangeran contact, a searing sound filled the room. Smoke rose from her body before it disappeared altogether.

Jordan stood very still, too stunned to speak. Rohnert concluded his chants by placing a palm to his heart. "She was a good woman, a friend," he murmured.

"I'm so sorry." There was nothing else to say.

Sheathing his Kalimetal, he turned for the door. "Let's go."

"What about the book?" Jordan asked, moving toward the Marania's dresser. She opened the drawer and rummaged inside until she found an unremarkable-looking, black bound book. She held it up. "Is this it?"

Rohnert backtracked and stared at the tome. He wondered if this was what Goran had been looking for. What information could Marania possess that would so enrage the leader? With trembling hands, he took the book and stuffed it in his waistband. If it were so important to Goran, then it had to disappear.

"Let's not hang around. I'm sure this place will be littered with humans and vampires in no time." He gestured for Jordan to walk in front him. When they passed the ashes of the fallen butler, he recited another chant—a call for peace.

Rohnert closed the door behind him with a heavy heart.

Once outside, they took to the dark streets. They walked in silence, too dazed to make small talk. Closer to midcity, they passed a bar known to be frequented by Council guards. Trying their best to act inconspicuous, they walked faster, avoiding any eye contact, but as luck would have it, a few guards trailed them.

Doing what Rohnert figured was safest, they headed toward the back alley, away from the general public.

"If you don't stop, we'll shoot," an authoritative voice commanded.

Rohnert shot a quick glance at Jordan and nodded. Slowly, they turned around, their hands behind their backs, gripping their Kalimetals and ready for action.

"We don't want any trouble. For your safety, turn around and pretend that we've never seen each other," Rohnert said, feeling the burst of energy made possible by Marania's generous blood offering. He eyed each one, gauging their frames of mind and knowing their threats were real. Three of them against him and Jordan.

"No one orders us around. If you're smart, which I think you are, you'll hold your girl's hand and come with us without resistance. Our leader might consider sparing your lives." The speaker eyed the bulky weapons behind them. Two vampires with Kalimetals was something that would make Goran extremely happy.

Rohnert smirked and shook his head. "First of all, I'm sick of you people telling everyone what to do. Second, she's not my girl. Do you need a third? Or can you follow simple instructions and mosey on back to your warm beds and stay alive?"

In the blink of an eye, gunshots rang out, and bullets rained on them. Anticipation and quick reaction enabled Rohnert and Jordan to pull out their Kalimetals in time to block the hail of bullets coming their way.

Separating, they jumped and somersaulted out of harm's away while crisscrossing their weapons to deflect the slugs. Jordan handled herself well. She was a magnificent creature, poised and in total control, but Rohnert still worried about her. Harrow had graciously allowed her to accompany him as a favor. He would make sure she went back to Harrow in one piece. With an innate sense of evasion, Rohnert used mental tricks against their opponents, scrambling their minds with confusing thoughts while he made his move. Turning around, he jumped against the wall, slamming his feet against the concrete and bouncing off, back to the group. He smiled with pure pleasure when he dove toward the surprised enemy, his Kalimetal aimed to do a clean sweep. In one quick slashing motion, he struck the trio with precision.

Three for the price of one! Their bodies crumpled to the ground, minus their heads, which rolled about ten feet away.

"Looks like you cleaned house," Jordan said, looking at what was left of the Council rats. She shielded her eyes from the specks of ashes when the three vampires disintegrated.

"All in a day's work," Rohnert muttered. He straightened his trench coat and picked up the badge each guard had had with him. Pocketing the seals, he watched Jordan, who was staring at him with gratitude.

"Thanks. That was intense." She laughed, but the trace of nervousness was hard to miss. "Shall we go?"

"Yes."

"Melissa, Goran wants to see you." Hamilton's voice echoed inside the training room, interrupting the lecture about evasion and escape.

Bretania, their instructor, threw a "what-the-fuck" glare at the second-in-command, but it failed to impress the offender. Hamilton filled the doorway, his massive body blocking the exit and his manner quite threatening.

Melissa straightened in her seat while twenty-five pairs of eyes turned to look at her. For a brief moment, she wondered what Goran wanted. She was certain it had nothing to do with his sexual needs. Over the past week or so, the mighty leader had been bedding each vampire in the harem. His rapacious appetite had to be sated by now.

Hamilton zeroed in on Melissa with inquiring eyes, one eyebrow raised at an annoying angle that made her blood boil. When she hesitated, he inched forward, and two guards sealed off the doorway.

"You wouldn't want to make Goran wait," Hamilton reminded her, his stance threatening. He took a quick moment to scan the room, like he was making a mental note of every person present.

Shrugging off the anxiety that blanketed her, Melissa got up and squared her shoulders. As if she were a fugitive facing a death sentence, Hamilton escorted her to Goran's door, with the two Council guards following them. It did not escape her notice that a group of guards was standing outside the training area, blocking the exit. Far be it from her to question their leader and his whims. She entered Goran's sanctuary, ready to face whatever awaited her.

"Hey, wait up!" Cyrus called out, his voice echoing in the deserted parking garage.

Tor, Allison, and Deuce stopped to watch him run toward them. He was wearing his dreaded duds—"the crisp, gray suit from hell," as he called it. They were on their way to the office.

"Hey, my man, where's the funeral?" Tor chuckled, fist bumping with the human.

Cyrus tugged on his jacket self-consciously. "Leo called and set up a demonstration meeting with some of his men. It's sort of last minute. Mind if I hitch a ride?" He looked unhappy.

"Sure." Tor looked at him with mischief in his eyes. Cyrus had been like a disgruntled big brother to them. The man was loyal and hardworking. "Why can't you go in your regular getup?"

Cyrus threw a glance at Allison, who rolled her eyes. "She made me do it. 'Cyrus, you want to look your best all the time. If Daddy were still alive, he'd be so proud of you'," he said, mimicking Allison's favorite comeback whenever he bellyached about her choice of work clothes for him.

Laughter boomed in the enclosed space, and Cyrus huffed in annoyance. The click-click of the car alarm sounded, and Tor opened the back door for Allison. Deuce took the driver's seat as usual, and Cyrus rode shotgun.

In the bulletproof and sunproof vehicle, the late afternoon drive was uneventful. Tor got out and surveyed the surroundings in the underground parking garage before letting Allison out of the vehicle. After all, it was still office hours, and he had no control over the people around them. Although Harrow had implemented a strict guest and employee policy,. No after-hours clients and employees must be off the premise after ten in the evening. There was no guarantee that it was foolproof. As a precaution, they took the service elevator closest to the back entrance. Cyrus went straight to his office one floor below Allison's, while the rest headed to hers.

Allison's secretary, as a habit, brought in the mail and a cup of tea for her boss, and gave Tor a smile. And as usual, Deuce snickered. Tor held up his hand as a warning, which always shut the other vampire up.

While Allison perused her mail, worked on her computer, and conducted via satellite meetings, Tor and Deuce alternated doing rounds and taking turns watching her. It was Tor's idea to switch her schedule around. He didn't like routine, especially when Allison was involved. No one expected her at any set time except when her schedule demanded she attend board meetings, meet with important clients, or conduct product presentations. This enabled Harrow to focus on the facility and its inhabitants, while overseeing the business side from his desk in the facility.

"Let me do the first sweep," Deuce said, putting on sunglasses to hide his whitish irises. He was part of the group that had benefited from the cure. The progression of the disease had halted following the switch in his diet.

Tor moved to stand by the door. It wasn't a boring job at all. He liked being needed. The money from the business funded a the effort to provide cure for diseased vampires. For once in his life, he was a part of a noble cause.

He watched as a stray hair fell over Allison's face, and he was struck with an urge to dash across the room and brush it back.

Dude, you're at work, in a place of business. Cut the romantic crap and concentrate! Just as he snapped out of his trance, the metal shutters began retracting. The sun was just a little dot of pink in the horizon, nothing that could harm them. By the time Deuce came back, most of the employees had gone home. There were just a few left who seemed intent on pulling all-nighters.

The secretary knocked and peeked through the door. "Mr. Takahashi is here."

Allison looked up. "I'll see him in the conference room. Do you have the contracts ready?"

"They're all ready, and the attorney is here, too."

"Very good. I'll be there in ten minutes." Allison waved her away and returned her attention to the paperwork in front of her.

Tor shifted his position by the door and began to count the minutes. Allison was a stickler for punctuality, and just as he'd predicted, she wrapped things up and stood after exactly 10 minutes.

Then there was a blast just outside her door. He heard the secretary scream, followed by silence. Tor jumped, covering the space between him and Allison in a single leap.

"Deuce, check it out!" he ordered and pushed Allison to the floor behind her desk, shielding her with his body.

The other vampire moved fast, drawing two semi-automatics before opening the door. He hadn't even completely made it out when gunfire erupted from several sources. Deuce exchanged fire with the shooters. Tor pulled out his rarely used cell phone to make an SOS call he never thought he'd make.

Where the hell are Drisco and his band of night watchdogs?

"Harrow, we're under attack!" Tor screamed over the phone amid the sound of gunfire. He hung up while Harrow was still talking. He didn't have time for chitchat at the moment. Easing his body a bit off Allison, he told her, "Here's my gun. Stay here, and do not come out until I call you."

He kissed her forehead, drew his axe and another gun, and shot his way out of their hiding place just in time to see Deuce drop to the ground, bullets striking multiple areas of his body. Tor cursed and took cover behind the door, pulling Deuce's body inside the office.

Unfortunately, he was too late. A Dangeran bullet had nailed his friend.

"Rest easy, buddy," he whispered in his comrade's ear.

Anger rode through his veins when Deuce's body fizzled into ash. This was it. Tor was next. He'd fight and most likely die before helped arrived. His one fervent wish was for Allison to be spared.

"Tor, no!" Allison screamed from her spot behind the desk.

Tor wanted to tell her he loved her, but there was no time. He had to lead their attackers away from her. Dropping to all fours, he crawled out the door to get the best chance of pegging them. With the cubicles blocking his view, he had to use the sound of their loud, thudding heartbeats to pinpoint their locations. Multiple partitions separated him from the four shooters.

Humans! What the hell? Who knew about Dangeran other than vampires?

Tor cleared the hallway, wormed his way to another cubicle, and rose to his knees. Taking a chance with his half-assed plan, he fired a shot through the flimsy wall just to get a feel for the situation.

A grunt sounded, followed by a dull thump. *And then there were three.* Tor smiled. This could work. Changing his tactics, he started speaking.

"Assholes, what the hell?" he shouted, bolting out of the cubicle when gunfire exploded again. A bullet zoomed by, just missing him.

"You're going down tonight, as well as that boss of yours."

The voice was familiar. Drisco.

"Drisco, you sonofabitch! Who are you working for?" Rage engulfed him.

"The almighty dollar. If you think for one moment you're getting out this alive, you're mistaken. Our orders are to kill everyone in this office."

One thing was certain—Drisco had a mouth on hiwas going to end up dead.

"Who ordered you to kill us?" Tor inched his way toward the voice. Without making the slightest noise, he stayed low, cleared several stalls, and found himself eye-to-eye with Drisco. Another round of gunfire rang out somewhere below them, and he thought of Cyrus. The human probably had his hands full, too.

Guns pointed at each other, Tor and Drisco straightened up, anticipating the other's next move. From the corner of his eye, Tor saw movement. Without a moment's hesitation, he launched the axe toward the attacker to his left and aimed the gun at Drisco's head.

"You first," Drisco said in a mocking tone and pulled the trigger.

A searing pain sent Tor staggering backward, clutching his left arm, which had been hit. The burning sting began, and time couldn't be wasted. Drisco shouldn't have missed, he was too close. His aim should have been dead-on.

And fatal.

Then, Tor realized that Drisco had been hit. Blood spurted from his chest, yet he turned and aimed his gun at Allison.

"No!"

Tor lurched forward in an attempt to stop him, but his knees buckled. The poison of the Dangeran was traveling fast. Another barrage of gunfire rang out, and he saw a familiar throwing star fly across the room. A loud thud echoed in the dead silence. Drisco fell to the ground and blood gushed from his mouth.

"Tor! Cut it off! Do it now!" It was a plea. Jordan was begging him to save himself.

Harrow burst from his bedroom with his Kalimetal strapped to his back. "Rayce, call Jordan and Rohnert. Mobilize every available hand over to the office building," he fired into his cell phone while he went through the first emergency exit and the alarm blared throughout the facility.

"Yes, sir," Rayce answered right away.

"And make sure you gather all information you can," he commanded before hanging up.

Harrow broke into a sprint, clearing the tunnel in a heartbeat. He tore through the city like a ferocious animal. Tor wouldn't call unless he needed backup.

This meant one thing—Tor was in way over his head. That idea alone was frightening. A chill ran down Harrow's spine, an unsettling reminder of how it felt to be hunted. He ran harder, willing his body to go as fast as it could.

Harrow was several blocks away from the facility when his phone went off. He pulled out the cell phone and glared at the blurry display. Good thing Rayce had suggested different ringtones to identify each caller, or he'd be stuck guessing on the run.

"Lambert." He breathed hard, feeling the burn in his calf muscles.

"Gates, we need backup. We're surrounded by vampires. They're like nothing I've seen before." Lambert sounded frantic, which was rare. The man was all about chill. Nothing ever fazed him.

"What do you mean?" Harrow screeched to a stop, not sure he'd heard Lambert correctly.

"They have Annie with them."

Fuck! This sounded like a setup. What the hell?

"Dammit. I'm on my way to the office. There was an attack there, and Tor called for help. Hang in there. Stay inside, and I'll get some people there."

"Hurry!"

The line went dead before he had the chance to reassure Lambert. Harrow punched Rohnert's speed dial code. "Change course—head to the mountains. Lambert needs help. Make sure Jordan doesn't do anything stupid."

He heard the other vampire mutter a curse, which was a rarity also. This night seemed to be drawing atypical reactions from everyone. "Keep us posted" was all Rohnert said before he hung up.

When Harrow rounded the corner, he saw Firman, one of his best vampire fighter, running at an unbelievable speed and Mark still a ways behind. The human looked like he was running on fumes; nonetheless, he appeared determined. Harrow hid behind a car in front of the office building until Firman joined him. After a few more beats, Mark arrived, followed by other vampires and humans.

"Hey, boss, what's going?" Firman asked, glancing around, his fangs bared.

"What the hell is happening?" Mark could barely get the words out, trying to catch his breath.

"We're going to move in. I don't know who's in there or what's going on. Tor asked for backup, so be ready and prepare to kill if necessary." Everyone looked determined while they voiced their agreement. "Use Dangeran weapons only."

With no details to work with, Harrow had to operate on instinct. He led the group to the back entrance. "Use the service elevator," he instructed the handful of humans. Then he turned to Firman. "You and I will scale the building. There are entrances on both sides. One is the fifth floor; take that with Jesse and Dirk. I'll go in through the thirty-fourth."

Firman and two other vampires nodded, looking twitchy and ready for action.

"On my signal." Harrow raised his hand and locked eyes with every single one of his men. "Good luck." And he gave the sign.

Each one moved into position. With Mark in the lead, the humans entered the parking garage and disappeared from view. Harrow and Firman moved to the other side of the building, separating to begin their climbs.

Harrow's decision to take the higher floor had been intentional. It left Firman and the others on the lower level. He bounded to the side of the building and began his steady ascent. It was sheer luck that he'd had the secret entrances installed in case an attack like this happened.

And shit, it had. Once he reached the thirty-fourth floor, Harrow opened the unlocked window, and the vacuum it created nearly pulled his grasp off the metal handle.

Slow and deliberate, he slipped through the little opening and pulled out his weapon. The building was eerie, quiet, and dark. With his Kalimetal ready to strike, Harrow moved forward, eyes closed and letting his senses guide him.

He took the stairwell to Allison's office, which was a good place to start scoping the situation. Once he got to the thirty-eighth floor, he sensed life and movement. He opened the door and moved stealthily into the long hallway that led to the offices.

A slight noise came from his left just before a gun began firing. With lightning-fast reflexes, Harrow counted out loud as he deflected every bullet.

"That's twelve, amigo." He sneered. "My turn."

Closing his eyes, Harrow relied on his hearing this time, zeroing in on the character who was loading another round in his Sig Pro. This was a human. Harrow kicked his heels on the floor while strapping his Kalimetal and pulling a knife from its sheath. He heard the gun cock and released the knife straight into the human's chest. Bull's-eye. The gun fired but the bullet strayed, hitting the ceiling. Then the human dropped on the ground.

Harrow looked down at the human and knew he'd seen that face before. Doing a quick mental inventory, he remembered the name of the guy they'd discovered scouting their building, the same guy Tor had reported a few months back. If Harrow wasn't mistaken, the man was Gralnik Lilic, the infamous bounty hunter.

"What are you doing here?" Harrow asked, pressing the sole of his boot on the man's neck to keep him from fleeing. He did a quick search for weapons and was surprised by the amount of ammunition the guy was packing.

"You don't sound surprised to see me," Lilic ground out.

"No, but I should've gotten rid of you the first time I heard you were scouting the building."

Lilic snickered, then coughed. Harrow smelled blood and knew the human's time was running out.

"Fuck . . . you . . ."

Those were the man's last words. Funny, Harrow had expected something more profound. *Well, different folks, different strokes, as they said.*

He surveyed his surroundings. Nothing greeted him but silence until he heard Allison's scream, followed by gunshots—lots of them. Then someone howled, a cry so loud and filled with pain it sounded feral. And it was a familiar voice.

Tor!

"Do it now!" Allison cried, reaching for another throwing star and flinging it in the direction of the man pointing his gun at Tor.

The human shot another round, and Jordan screamed in terror. "No!"

Without thinking of herself or Tor's warning to remain in her hiding place, Allison drew her gun and fired at the man, nonstop.

She knew from hearsay that Dangeran in any form allowed only a small window in which to react and do what needed to be done. Tor had wasted enough time already. He had a few seconds left before the unbearable pain would travel across his body, paralyzing and weakening him before the inevitable happened.

She saw him struggle with the knife—they all carried a blade with them for times like this. With whatever energy he had left, Tor sliced off his arm with the sharp blade, crying out in agony while she watched in horror. Blood squirted and gushed from the wound.

Allison crossed the room to his side. "Tor. Don't move. I'm going to take you home," she cried, dropping to her knees. Looking at his face, she could see the same fear that she felt. With quick, desperate movements, she removed her jacket and tied it into a tourniquet around what was left of his arm.

Tor looked at her, his face marred by a guilt she couldn't understand. "I love you, baby."

Tears rolled down her face while she attempted to lift him. Her knees buckled under his weight, but she was determined to take him home and get help. "I'm going to take you home," she said again.

"I'm heavy—" His words ended when he passed out.

"Tor! Tor! Stay with me!"

"Allison!" Harrow shouted from what seemed to be miles away.

She turned, her eyes blurring with tears. "Help me. I want to take him home." Her voice held a massive dose of hysteria, and she knew she was going to lose it soon. "Oh, God. Tor!"

Harrow was next to her in a flash, taking Tor from her. The strain of Tor's weight showed in his face, but Harrow moved quickly to the elevator. "Tor, buddy, I got you. You're going to be okay," he whispered.

Just then, the elevator opened, and Mark and the rest of the group spilled out, guns and weapons drawn. Allison aimed at Mark before recognition flashed in her eyes.

"Ms. Tack," Mark said, raising his hands and then glancing at Tor.

"We're taking him home. I want you to scout the entire building, secure it, and then call me. Block all exits and entrances, and I don't want anyone leaving alive!" Harrow barked the orders as they hustled into the elevator.

Allison punched the button for the parking garage with impatience. Tor's blood was everywhere—on her clothes, on Harrow's, pooling on the floor. "Hurry up! Hurry up!" Her tone was one of desperation.

The moment the doors opened, she ran to the car and realized that neither she nor Harrow had the key. Without hesitation, she bent her arm and smashed in the front driver's window with her elbow, sending shards of glass flying everywhere. She flinched at the pain, but she had no time to worry about it.

Then another realization hit her: She still needed the key to get the car to start. Allison wailed, feeling despair tighten around her chest like a vice. She turned to Harrow. "No keys!"

"Take the back," Harrow said. He laid Tor across the back seat, resting his head on her lap. He moved quickly, and before Allison grasped what was happening, Harrow had hotwired the car and the engine roared to life. "Am I glad I paid attention to Jordan," he said, more to himself than to her.

Allison had never been a religious woman, but she found herself praying to every saint she knew and invoking their help to save Tor. She kept glancing at his face while stroking his forehead. His heartbeat was growing faint.

"Go faster!" she cried as soon as Harrow exited the parking garage.

"Allison, you need calm down." Harrow glanced at her, and when they locked eyes, she knew her brother understood her grief. She couldn't even *think* of the possibility she could lose Tor. It wasn't going to happen; she wouldn't allow it. Harrow pressed a button on the steering wheel, and the car autodialed the facility. Rayce's voice filled the car. "Rayce, alert Shelly. We have Tor coming in, lots of blood loss. ETA is five minutes."

"Yes sir." There was a pause while Rayce hesitated. "Rohnert called. Said he spoke with Lambert and more men are needed. I utilized whoever we had left in the field to help them."

Allison didn't hear the rest. She was too focused on what had to be the longest, most painful five minutes of her life.

"God, let him live. I'll give anything, I'll do anything. Just let him live," she begged out loud.

When they were two blocks away from the facility, the dark sky broke open, and rain pelted the windshield. Harrow glanced in the rearview mirror at Allison. Her expression made his heart ache, not just for her, but for Tor.

Allison looked like she was on the verge of falling apart. Harrow knew firsthand how it felt to lose someone dear, and if there were anything he could do so his sister wouldn't go through that ordeal again, he'd do it.

He drove straight to the tunnel, ignoring his own protocol and not stopping to identify himself at the tunnel entrance. Instead, he barreled through the underground entrance like a madman. The gate was open and waiting when their car went past the set of security cameras. Flashes popped in several places, taking pictures of the car from every angle—an added security measure he'd put in place. Rayce would be checking everything before the last gate was opened.

"Damn it," Harrow muttered while he waited for the second gate to unbolt. He was running on fumes as it was, and it didn't help that his mind was elsewhere. Finally, their path was clear, and he saw Shelly's two medical assistants waiting for them.

Not bothering to turn off the motor, he shifted the car into park and jumped out. Allison was whispering soothing words to his unconscious friend. Slipping his arm under Tor's body, Harrow carefully eased him from the car with Allison's help.

"Easy," he said as they lifted Tor onto the gurney.

Shelly's ubiquitous rock music was pumping loud when they exited the elevator. She looked up, ready for action. Her eyes dropped to Tor and began to survey the damage.

"What happened to him?" she asked, removing the bloodied jacket that covered Tor's arm.

Allison gasped at the sight of Tor's stump and began sobbing.

Shelly shot a glare at Harrow. "Get her out of here."

Harrow quickly guided Allison out the door. "He's in good hands."

In the stark, empty hallway, Allison's grief was unleashed. All Harrow could do was wrap his arms around her and hold on. The storm inside her raged, and he waited it out. Minutes later, her screams had been reduced to sobbing, her head still buried against his chest.

"You think he's going to be okay?" she asked, her voice hoarse.

"I'm sure of it. The bastard won't ever leave you. He's too in love." Harrow paused when a sudden thought struck him. He'd been so preoccupied with Tor that he hadn't even asked Rayce about Jordan or the group.

Allison looked up, sensing his preoccupation. "I'm going to be okay here. I think they need you out there."

"I can't leave you—"

"Harrow, go!" Allison's voice grew hard. She swiped her tears away and straightened her shoulders. "Shelly's here. We're going to be okay."

"Are you sure?" Harrow's mind was already running a mile a minute. There had to be a quicker way to reach them than on foot.

"Use Daddy's 'Vette. It's going to get you there faster than any other car we have," Allison said. The 1957 Corvette had been Pritchard's pride and joy. The black monster packed five hundred horses under its hood and was a devil on the road. Yeah, it would beat running.

Harrow wasn't too sure it was a good idea, but he had no other option except the helicopter, which was not possible without a pilot. He nodded.

"Only if you can manage here—"

"Just go!" Allison pushed him away. "Tor's going to be fine. You said so yourself. So just go!"

Without a moment to lose, Harrow gave her a quick kiss and ran for the garage. "Call me as soon as you hear from Shelly," he said over his shoulder.

Rohnert had no idea what awaited them at their mountain retreat. Lambert had mentioned something about Annie and vampires—many of them. Rohnert knew Lambert wouldn't ask for backup unless the situation was dire. They were at a disadvantage considering they were protecting a human girl. All he could think of was getting there as fast as they could. Running at top speed, Jordan had been awfully quiet. Judging by the look on her face and the set of her shoulders, he knew she was braced for the worst.

Trees and rocks passed by in flashes of color while they tore through the forest. Once they were just a few miles away, Rohnert pulled out his cell phone and pressed Lambert's code. The phone rang and rang, but there was no answer.

"Damn it," he muttered. Then it hit him all at once. Voices in his head—women, many women. Then there was Lambert, Knox, and Peyton. He searched for Gail's thoughts, but the child was silent. An unfamiliar nervousness shot through him.

"What?" Jordan shot him a frantic look. "Rohnert, tell me."

She knew him too well for him to be able to hide anything from her. "There's too many of them." Abruptly, he stopped running. They needed to regroup and come up with a plan of attack.

"What do you mean?" Jordan sounded dangerously calm.

"We have to think of how to go about this. There's just the two of us."

"Wasn't Harrow going to send backup?"

Speaking of backup, he picked up on a group running toward them at an unbelievable rate. Then screeching tires sounded not too far away, coming from the highway that ran parallel to their route. This was their other backup.

In a few minutes, Brock, a reliable, young vampire full of potential, came into view, flanked by five other vampires.

"Sir, we were instructed to meet you here." He flicked a quick glance at Jordan, who was pacing back and forth, then looked back to Rohnert.

"I'm glad you came." Rohnert nodded to the other men—newbies, but well trained by him.

"The others should be here any moment." Brock gestured to the forest.

A few minutes later, Drake and three other human fighters appeared.

Drake and Rohnert slapped a quick handshake.

"What are we looking at?" Drake asked, eyeing Jordan, who acted oblivious to their arrival.

"The house is surrounded. I can't tell how many there are, but I expect a good fight. I want you guys prepared. This might not end well. But we have Lambert, Gail, Knox, and Peyton trapped inside. Lambert's not answering his phone anymore, and I have no way of communicating with him."

Drake cursed.

Jordan stopped pacing and shot them a baleful look. "I'm going to make a move now." *I can't wait here and listen to all this damn planning.*

Rohnert knew what she had in mind and dashed to her side.

"You're doing it again. What have I told you in the past? Think! You moving in without backup is a bad idea."

"I'm done talking. I want Gail. She's probably scared."

Rohnert couldn't tell her what he feared. "You're going to stay here until I say it's time to go." His voice carried a tone he rarely used. Jordan flinched but said nothing. He couldn't hold her here long, so he had to think fast.

He turned to Drake. "Stay here and follow after ten minutes. Brock and the rest will join me."

Drake nodded with a little too much exuberance.

"Jordan, don't do anything stupid. Think before you react. I swear—"

Gunshots ricocheted throughout the forest. Everything Rohnert had said was forgotten when Jordan sprang to her feet. She was gone before he could stop her.

"Hell!"

Rohnert led the group after her. The sound of Jordan's footfalls was the only thing that mattered at the moment. Harrow would have his head on a platter if anything happened to her. Scanning their surroundings, Rohnert looked for any possible edge their group might have, but with the lack of information on whom or what they were dealing with, he was flying blind.

The moonlight barely penetrated the darkness, but it was enough. Several more shots rang out, shouts filled the air, and the scent of blood wafted around them. By this time, they'd reached the clearing, and the landscape had shifted from dense forest to well manicured lawn. With very little time to survey the situation, Rohnert did a quick mental calculation of what they faced.

Women clad in white jumped into their path, blocking their way. They were everywhere. There were twenty or so, and even in the darkness, their intrinsic similarity was hard to miss—red hair, Goran's obsession.

Rohnert had heard about them, yet he hadn't been inclined to believe wagging tongues. Now surrounded, feeling their emotions and hearing their thoughts, fury replaced his astonishment.

Damn Goran. The bastard really is a pervert.

The harem was in full force. They were agile, well-trained, and strikingly beautiful. In the middle of it all, one woman stood out—the beautiful leader he'd heard of, the quickest and the one with the loudest lamentation.

Melissa.

With her every movement, the reek of her hatred assaulted him. It was so putrid that it gave Rohnert pause. Her consolation was death. She'd bring death to anyone who stood in the way of her revenge. She wanted revenge for the demise of her son.

Demetrius! How could he have missed this? Now, the puzzle pieces began to fall into place. The master puppeteer was allowing his best weapon to self-destruct. Goran was done with her, with all of them.

These weren't Melissa's thoughts but those of a familiar figure standing atop the hill not too far away. Watching the slaughter about to happen and enjoying everything unfolding before his eyes, Goran knew everything. Marania had provided everything Groan needed, and Rohnert's group wasn't going to make it out alive. Goran would see to it. He pulled a woman from behind him.

"Annie!"

Despite Annie's protests, Goran held her face and twisted hard. Her silhouette turned limp before falling to ground. In an elaborate fashion, Goran saluted, mocking Rohnert even more by placing his palm over his heart.

Anger surged within Rohnert like poison, but as much as he wanted to give Goran the same treatment, he couldn't leave his friends when they were facing imminent death.

The clash swelled, and flashes of parting thoughts screamed inside his head as some of his men breathed their last. There were too many attackers coming at them, and as fierce as Brock and the rest of the newbies were, they were outnumbered. There were just too many.

Jordan continued to kick butt, wielding her Kalimetal left and right, striking the vampires in her path. She had no fear, but Rohnert was afraid for her, afraid that he wouldn't be able to keep her alive.

This has been set up to perfection. Goran had never cared for his son, or for anyone. Rohnert balked against the weight of the emotions that rained upon him. Vengeance, hate, desire, desperation. And the echoes of death.

While his group faced a possible end, Rohnert moved as fast as he could through the barrage of voices that continued to ravage him: Lambert's dying thoughts, Knox's regret, and Peyton's valiant effort to fight off the harem.

The clash of metal weapons and the deafening blasts of gunshots continued around him while he kicked each woman who stood in his way with force, a trick not even Bretania could master and therefore had failed to teach her students.

With extreme speed, Rohnert landed kicks straight to their chins, either breaking their jaws or crushing their larynxes enough to disable them before handing them sure death with his Kalimetal.

The harem was still too much for their numbers. As he finished another kill, two people caught his eye: Jordan and Melissa. Both women had something to fight for, and each believed in her cause. Revenge was a dark emotion, the driving force behind their aggression. Things were happening fast, and their group was almost gone when he heard Drake and his men rushing to the scene.

"No!" Rohnert cried. He ran to intercept them, but it was too late. The remaining vampires converged and ran at high speed toward them.

Then the unthinkable happened, an ultimate sacrifice he'd never thought possible.

"Kill all of them!" Drake instructed Rohnert before he and his men slashed their own bodies with their sharpest knives. The scent of their blood startled the harem. The women turned their heads, swaying under the pressure of feeding. Their lust for blood clouded their minds and weakened their resolve. Blood squirted in every direction when the manic vampires twisted necks, splitting the human's bodies with their bare hands. They dove for Drake and his human comrades like vultures, killing them not with their weapons but their fangs, draining them of blood.

As stunned as he was, Rohnert granted Drake's wish. He leapt as high as he could and made a clean sweep, striking each woman with his Kalimetal and sparing no one's life. Painful cries resonated around him. The scent of death drifted in the air as the remains of the slaughtered humans lay on the blood-soaked field. Groans of satisfaction came from the women before they fragmented to their welcome end.

Melissa had known the moment Goran explained the harem's special assignment that it would be their final one. If Goran believed she was only smart enough to keep his bed warm, he was mistaken.

Now, in the midst of the slaughter, she found the inner peace that had eluded her for so long. Her only regret was leaving Zane, but she had left him a gift. She'd done what she thought was right all along.

Insulating herself against the cries of pain and the scent of death, she searched for her next victim. The house was well guarded, and she could only guess what was inside. This was not her concern. Her main focus was to kill.

She stole a quick glance at the hill where Goran stood with Annie, expecting to feel a pang of jealousy. It should be her up there with him, not the younger vampire. Now it was clear as the night sky that her reign as Goran's favored mistress had come to an end. Melissa felt nothing except revulsion for allowing Goran to manipulate her to do his bidding. She knew of his mind tricks and his method of inserting ideas into their brains to carry out his plans. Maybe Goran had pegged her as an idiot, but she knew what the outcome would be; in fact, she'd dreamed of it.

Still glaring at the duo on the hill, she pulled two throwing stars from her chest holster and let out a shriek. Her piercing cry reverberated across the battlefield, overpowering all other noise around her. She saw Goran's quick movement when he twisted Annie's head until her body turned limp. With her heart pounding hard against her chest, Melissa felt a surge of fury rush through her veins.

She pivoted just in time to see a female vampire walk out of a haze of ashes about fifty feet away. The woman was clad in a dark leather jacket and jeans, and she had the same hair color as the members of the harem. This was the one who'd gotten away, the reason Goran had been distracted and angry for so long. This woman was his ultimate prize. Melissa felt nothing but the rage she had harbored since Demetrius's disappearance. She flicked her wrist and launched the first of her throwing stars in the woman's direction.

Melissa watched as the vampire dodged to the right to avoid the incoming threat. Even in the darkness, she saw the woman smirk before unleashing a dagger at her. The blade came close enough that Melissa could hear a swooshing sound as it passed. Baring her fangs, she threw another star in the female's direction and saw her weapon once more miss its target. Her frustration and anger fed off each other, and before she realized what she was doing, she burst into a sprint toward the enemy. Another dagger narrowly missed her, but she didn't pause.

Her opponent ran to meet her, and they came to an abrupt stop several feet away from each other. With their fangs bared, they circled, sizing each other up and calculating their next moves. Neither one pulled out their primary weapon. Although Melissa itched to unsheathe her sword, she wasn't going to shy away from hand-to-hand combat. She would love to shove that lovely face into the ground and let the renegade vampire experience agony.

"If you want to live, walk away," the woman hissed in a low voice.

Melissa laughed. "I advise you to leave now, before you meet your maker," she replied, eyeing the female's movements. She paid close attention to the long weapon strapped to her opponent's back.

The stranger's laughter was bitter and laced with a sorrow only a chosen few could understand. In Melissa's case, she knew exactly how the other woman felt.

"Our maker? Point me to him so I can kill him with my bare hands."

Hearing this made Melissa stagger backward before she regained her footing. This creature had a different mind-set than she'd expected. Without a doubt, the woman's hostility was directed only at Goran. For a brief moment, Melissa envied her detachment.

No matter the outcome of this particular fight, one woman's suffering would end. It didn't matter whose anymore. With a lunge forward, Melissa caught the woman by the neck, and they fell to the ground.

They rolled on the muddy earth, grappling for supremacy. Without a doubt, her opponent had been trained by the best. Not only was she quick, but she employed the same techniques Bretania had taught the harem. And who had taught Bretania what she knew? The person who was the acknowledged Kalimetal expert, the vampire who had left the Council: Rohnert.

Each fighting maneuver Melissa made was met with equal intensity. They could fight forever, and neither one would lose. The woman, whose name escaped her, that got away. Annie had mistakenly mentioned it before. The one intent on eradicating Goran, and that thought alone gave Melissa the utmost pleasure. It was a feat she could never have accomplished because she had believed for too long that Goran was capable of loving her. And she had fallen for him. Her foolish dream had been crushed by her present predicament, so she eased off a bit and let the determined vampire pin her by the neck. Struggling less, Melissa continued to fight only to give an impression that she was still a threat.

Demetrius' face flashed in her mind, beckoning her to join him. Melissa briefly closed her eyes and removed herself from the ugliness surrounding her: the stench of death and the deafening cries of anguish. The chokehold loosened, and the moment air slammed into her lungs, she flipped to her feet and cartwheeled away. The other female narrowed her gaze, as if sensing Melissa's withdrawal. She would need to display more aggression in order to provoke the vampire into attacking again.

A harsh cry tore from her lips, and she pulled her sword from the scabbard on her back. Going on the offensive, she struck at the woman, who jumped away to yank out her Kalimetal. Melissa's opponent moved like lightning—fancy footwork combined with precise strikes, almost catching her on the right shoulder blade. The clash of metal on metal sparked in the darkness. Impressive. The woman was just as skilled as she was.

Another strike, and Melissa found herself in a defensive stance. The ringing sound of their blades added to the intensity of the struggle. Their shrieks echoed while they parried, sidestepped, and blocked each hit. Pound per pound, they were an even match. However, Melissa was already resigned to her fate, whereas she sensed that her opponent had something still worth fighting for.

"Avenge me, sister. Avenge all of us," she cried and brandished her sword, aiming at the vampire's neck.

Confusion marred the woman's face, but her automatic response came swiftly, her Kalimetal slashing through Melissa's shoulder and down through her hip.

The vampire drew back when Melissa dropped to her knees. The pain was soon replaced by silent serenity, a promise of the end. Melissa looked up at the face of her adversary and smiled.

"Thank you," she whispered.

No light beckoned her. There was only the assurance that she was finally free.

From the cloud of ashes and the stench of human blood, Jordan emerged. Death had spared her. She was miserable and tired, but alive.

"Good." Rohnert turned away, wanting to clear his head. So much death . . .

"That's all you can say?" Jordan wiped the grime off her face with the back of her hand before sheathing her weapon.

Rohnert watched her standing amid the carnage. "I'm so happy to see you."

Jordan laughed a bitter sound. "Happy to see I'm alive?"

He nodded, too distraught for words. The blood and the death of their friends would be an irremovable stain, a burden he'd carry with him for a long, long time.

"You know why I'm alive?" Jordan's voice cracked. "It's not because the woman lacked the combat ability. On the contrary, we were an even match." There was no hint of confidence in her voice. She was merely stating a fact. "She wanted to die, and I wanted to live, as simple as that. I could see it in her eyes."

He closed his eyes, attempting to wipe the gruesome picture of the slaughter from his mind. The scent of blood lingered around him, a grim reminder of the lives lost.

"You're in possession of something more important. She only had revenge in mind."

"What is that?" Jordan asked while she looked around at the carnage.

"You have love in your heart," Rohnert said softly. This had been the difference between Melissa and Jordan. Jordan had people to live for, while Melissa's life had ended long ago.

Stupid! Stupid! I should have seen this coming. Rohnert chastised himself.

A wail forced Rohnert to open his eyes in time to witness Jordan crumbling to the ground. Her face was hidden by her matted red hair.

"Where could Gail be?"

His heart broke into pieces, and yet he had no comforting words to offer. He'd always known Goran's greed, but involving children was a new low, even for that bastard. Rohnert walked over to Jordan, reached out, and patted her head. His hand trembled, not from fear, but from fury. "We have enough time. We can look for her," he whispered.

Lambert was dead, and so were Knox and Peyton, the last people who would know where the girl could be. It was heartbreaking to even imagine that Gail had been subjected to this horrible war. Rohnert continued rubbing Jordan's hair until her sobs ebbed.

Headlights shot across the distance, and the loud screeching of tires against gravel disturbed the morbid silence. Within minutes, the roaring engine stopped, and Harrow stepped out.

Even in the darkness, Rohnert could see the tension in Harrow's shoulders when he scanned the bloodbath. His grave expression gave Rohnert everything he needed to know.

"What happened here?" Harrow dropped to his knees next to Jordan and wrapped an arm around her.

Rohnert straightened and moved away. Placing his hands on his hips to support his depleted spirit, his finger grazed the book Marania had entrusted to him, still lodged in his waistband.

"We ran into an ambush," Rohnert waved his hand toward the pile of mangled bodies and mounds of ashes being blown by the frigid wind."

Harrow wiped his eyes and asked the question that was on all their minds. "Has anyone seen Gail?" It was almost a whisper.

Jordan's head whipped up and she jumped to her feet like she'd gotten her second wind.

"I'm looking for her." She now sounded more like herself.

Before Harrow could protest, she was gone. He and Rohnert exchanged looks of concern and followed her to the front steps. Jordan's cry of anguish filled the bitter night when they laid eyes on their fallen friends.

Rohnert signaled to Harrow, who looked like he was about to fall apart. He stared at Rohnert for guidance.

"Go ahead."

Harrow hesitated before punching the combination on the keypad by the door and disappearing inside with Jordan. If Rohnert hardened his heart, he could ignore the prick of sorrow that gripped him at the sight of Lambert, lying in his own blood by the front door and gripping a throwing star. He'd died trying to protect his adopted family. With reverence, Rohnert cradled Lambert's body and brought him into the house. He laid his fallen friend's body on the leather sofa.

So many questions had been answered tonight. The weight of that information burned in him, a silent reminder that death, just like living, was either welcomed or shunned. The courage displayed by his human and vampire friends astounded him. Noble until the end, they'd fought and bled for what they believed in.

The question remained—was outcome worth the trouble? So many innocent lives were caught in the dragnet, all because he'd been bold enough to involve himself with humans. He took a seat next to Lambert's body and rested his head against the luxurious leather cushion.

Stunned into inaction, all Rohnert could do was stare out the window, rehashing the torment over again. Frantic footsteps echoed throughout the house with Jordan's hysterical voice occasionally calling Gail's name.

If the little one had been taken, it'd be a personal attack on them, and Rohnert would not take that lightly. The wind gusted outside, rustling dead leaves, and the scent of blood drifted in. He held his breath and calmed his screaming nerves. So much for the peace and tranquility he craved.

Then Jordan screamed.

Allison sat on the cold tile floor, not sure what to do with herself. The crippling guilt and second-guessing hit her like a mean whiplash. The beeping of the instruments, the clang of metal, and the drip-dripping sound of the IV made her want to scream.

If Tor . . . no he won't! she corrected herself.

She stood up and paced. The facility was a ghost town except for the few medical staff on hand, Rayce manning the control room, and Jones in the lab. The silence was going to drive her nuts. At this point, anything could set her off. Teetering on the edge of madness, she needed something to calm her down. A drink sounded good at the moment, but she didn't dare leave. She sank to the floor, cradled her head between her palms, and rocked herself into a stupor.

Allison knew how it felt to lose someone who meant the world to you, and the idea of experiencing it again sent her reeling. Tor was her life now. They were going to build a life together. Surely, fate wouldn't toss her another twist. She'd had too many. But did tragedy discriminate?

No, please not Tor. She couldn't live without him.

The door to the clinic swung open, and Shelly emerged. It was exactly two hours after she'd started working on Tor, and she looked like she'd been to hell and back. She removed her mask and stashed it in her pocket.

"Allison?"

She looked up at Shelly, beseeching the doctor for good news. Allison braced her hands against the wall, not trusting her knees for support, and stood up.

"How is he?" she asked, feeling numb and very, very frightened.

The doctor gazed at her with kind eyes. Her mouth pressed into a grim line, but a little smile twitched at the corners. Shelly took Allison's hand and coaxed her forward. Face to face, Allison searched Shelly's eyes for answers.

"Tor's going to be okay. I had to amputate his left arm above the elbow, just to make sure that every particle of the Dangeran was taken out. I did my best to leave him a longer stump—"

Allison bit her lip to keep it from quivering. "I don't care about his arm. He's alive. That's all I needed to hear."

"He lost a lot of blood, so damn much that I had to use our entire supply. He's not going to be happy, though." Shelly smiled and pulled Allison into her arms.

Thankful for the support, Allison rested her head against Shelly's chest, taking in Tor's scent. Her tears of happiness and relief flowed in a mad rush. After she managed to control her emotions, she took a step back and shot up an eyebrow.

"What do you mean by Tor not being happy?"

Shelly giggled—a first for her. The doctor had always been formal around them. "Well, I transfused animal blood, of course."

This was enough for them to break into a nervous fit of laughter. Tor had refused to change his diet, preferring to stay with his donated blood regimen.

Happiness swelled within Allison. Squeezing Shelly's hand, she said, "Thank you for saving his life."

Shelly shook her head. "I doubt he'll be thrilled to see me once he realizes what I've done to him." She laughed.

"When can I see him?"

"I put him on a heavy dose of sedatives right now. His blood pressure has stabilized, and he needs to rest. But I can let you in. Just make sure you don't stimulate him." Shelly gave Allison a wink and nudged her toward the door. "Go ahead. Call me when he comes around."

Allison pushed the door open, catching the scent of animal blood right away. Two medical staff members, Cheryl and another one whose name

Allison couldn't remember, smiled at her. On cue, they left the room to give her privacy.

Just the same, Allison pulled the privacy curtain into place before she walked to Tor's bedside. Hungrily, she devoured his rugged features with her eyes. The worried lines around his eyes were absent, and his mouth was relaxed for a change. Unable to help herself, she leaned closer and touched his lips with hers.

"I love you," she whispered.

She rested her forehead against his and inhaled his musky scent, unable to prevent the tears that escaped. This was a joyful moment. He had been given a new shot at life. Allison lifted the thin blanket that covered his body, letting her eyes travel from his broad chest down to his heavily bandaged left arm. The skin peeking from the bandage was bruised and swollen. Her heart ached for him and his loss. And yet, she celebrated the fact that he was alive. One sliver of doubt crept in, however. How would Tor accept the change?

Feeling a little disheartened, Allison took a stool and brought it close to the bed. She sat, took his right hand, and squeezed.

"You're going to be okay," she murmured. And for some reason, she believed he would.

Allison woke up the instant she felt the mattress shift. A rush of panic swept over her when Tor started thrashing. His legs kicked, and his arms flailed. It took her a few moments to focus.

Remembering what Shelly had said about keeping him calm, Allison jumped to her feet and took Tor's right hand. "Tor, it's okay. You're safe. I'm here," she whispered. The minute their hands connected, he relaxed and a single tear slid down the side of his cheek. He opened his mouth, forming words without sound. Although she feared it would agitate him further, Allison brushed her lips against his mouth. "Don't talk. Just rest for now. I won't leave this room until you're up on your feet."

Tor's eyes peeled open, and after a few seconds, he found her. With an effort that made his body quake, he mouthed the three words that she'd never get tired of hearing—the only words that mattered to her. His lips trembled, and more tears followed.

Allison reached out and brushed the tears away. "I love you, too. Sleep for now, and you can tell me more about it later."

Her words had the desired effect. Tor began to relax, and soon after, he sank into a deep sleep.

At Jordan's suggestion, Harrow agreed that should separate, doubling the chances of locating Gail. He was afraid to even think that she might have been taken or killed. No, he could sense the little girl in the house. Where was she?

He was turning the house inside out to find her. Even though the house hadn't been ransacked, Harrow knew that the safety of their secret refuge had been compromised. It would be wise to abandon the place. Such a pity. They had forged some good memories here.

Harrow had almost reached the top level. He was looking under furniture, in closets, and inside cabinets when Jordan's piercing cry came forth. Quick to get on his feet, he took the spiral staircase and found her in the training room, crouched over one of the cabinets and pulling something out.

Rohnert was right on his heels, and they entered the dark training room together. Harrow fumbled, running his fingers along the wall until he found the light switch. ,The room was bathed in light. Sensitive to the glare, Harrow took a moment to adjust his eyes. Rohnert ran to Jordan, and before he knew it, they were pulling Gail out of a little cubby.

Crying and laughing at the same time, Jordan hugged the girl fiercely. She kissed her all over her face, an act that would normally elicit complaints from Gail. Why wasn't she complaining? Harrow rushed over to Jordan and placed his palm on their little girl's forehead. She was warm, and even though her heartbeat was faint, she was alive.

He angled his head sideways to get a better look at Gail's face. What he saw was the same cherubic face he'd fallen in love with—long, curly lashes that made her eyes sparkle and the perfect mouth that pouted whenever she didn't get her way.

"Harrow, let's take her to Shelly right now," Jordan pleaded, and he understood her concern. There were many questions in his mind, but first things first—Gail needed medical attention.

Harrow turned to Rohnert, who nodded, knowing what he wanted to say. "Go on. I'll take care of the cleanup," he said.

"I'll send a car to get the bodies." Harrow studied his friend, feeling his anguish. It tore at him.

"Take care of Gail," Rohnert replied, his voice clipped.

"Are you going to be okay?" Harrow asked.

Jordan had already carried Gail to the door. Her demeanor exuded relief and worry at the same time. Rohnert waved his hand with impatience, and Harrow suspected that he wanted time alone.

"Damn straight. Just go."

There was nothing else to say. Harrow slapped Rohnert's back and turned to leave. "If there's anything you need, just call," he said over his shoulder.

"Damn it, Gates! Go!" Rohnert roared.

Instead of heading straight back to Council headquarters, Goran had a stop to make. He had accomplished much in a short time. Marania had been very helpful, even if she'd resisted Goran's intrusion. In her last desperate minutes, the female had lowered her guard, and he'd gathered everything he needed, and more, from her thoughts.

So many surprises had sprung from that one fateful meeting. Who would have thought Marania had been keeping all those secrets? Not only was she maintaining records, she'd been the confidante of many Council elders. Covert plans had been shared with her in confidence but were now at his disposal.

Welcoming the feel of the crisp winter air, he sprinted through the forest, away from the slaughter. It had been a pleasure to watch Rohnert scramble in the ambush, and all because he was too kind, too nurturing to think of his own self. He'd always been noble in Goran's book, but hey, noble deeds weren't worth anything these days. If Rohnert were to open his eyes, he'd be in for a rude awakening. Power trumped righteousness, so the do-gooder vampire was at a disadvantage.

Goran had acted swiftly to set his plans in motion. Utilizing the harem had proven easier than he would have thought. Thanks to Marania's information, he knew that Melissa had approached Bretania for help in exacting her revenge against the group of vampires she suspected. He chuckled at the memory of Melissa's shock when he'd approached her with the idea to attack the suspicious group. The subsequent slaughter also released him from the responsibilities of nurturing his harem any longer.

In his unstable position as the Council's leader, the pressure to produce a rightful heir had been increasing. It was no secret that most, if not all, of the Council elders held his creations in contempt. In their eyes, the harem was a poor decision on his part, an attempt to satisfy his physical needs instead of ensuring the continuation of their race.

He'd led Melissa to believe his intentions were pure and based on his responsibility to keep a tight rein on his people. She had walked right into his diabolical scheme, without knowing that he was sending her and the harem to their deaths.

Goran grinned as he crossed the city limits, slowing down to enjoy his evening stroll. Things were falling into their rightful places.

Now it was time for another surprise visit. He scaled the familiar walls without effort and ended up on Iden's floor after a few minutes. Goran turned around to glance at the view, wondering why he hadn't taken the time to enjoy the magnificent city lights as he should have.

The harem had kept him too busy. Goran had spent most of his time closeted in the bedroom. But now, all that had changed. He'd gotten rid of them without a hitch. Placing his palms on the concrete ledge, he soaked in the magnificence around him. Everywhere he gazed, power beckoned him. That was what it was all about: power.

He breathed in deep, filling his lungs with air and enjoying every bit of his triumphant mission. The book was in his possession. All he needed was to check the recorded information about their history. To the best of his knowledge, no one but Marania and her predecessors had ever taken possession of the book. Rumored to contain trial proceedings, births, deaths, the talents of every Council elder, council business, and scandals, this book would be vital to his reign.

Goran was most interested in finding information he could use against the Council members who vacillated between supporting and defying his authority. Well, maybe he was interested in getting a little information on the abilities of his "friends", as well. That information could come in handy in the future.

A faint noise from the inside made him whip his head around to investigate. When he'd dropped by earlier, the bastard Iden was gone. In all likelihood, Iden and his daughter had gone underground. Who could have known the bastard had been keeping a secret from him? No wonder Iden had been cautious around him, often guarding his thoughts from intrusion.

Goran spotted an older lady, perhaps a maid or a cleaning lady. Quite curious, he walked closer to the sliding door and peered through the curtain to watch the woman going about her business.

While he had no reservations about employing ruthless questioning tactics, this human wasn't likely to know Iden's whereabouts, much less his real identity. He was a patient man. Iden would resurface and he'd be back. Either way, he'd get what he wanted: the one thing guaranteed to cement his continued rule. Turning around, he jumped off the ledge, enjoying the sensation of the wind blasting on his face and the promise of a better future.

Rayce's voice came through the speaker of the Corvette just as they cleared the bottleneck. "Harrow, I have a call for you."

If Harrow had his way, he would take Gail to the nearest emergency room. But given all the questions that would surely come their way, they had no choice but to wait until they could get her to Shelly.

"Who is it?" he asked, flooring the gas.

"It's Firman," Rayce said.

"Put him through."

Within seconds, Firman was on the line. "Boss, the building is secure. We have backup. General Krever sent some of his men."

Harrow applauded the General's help; the assistance was welcome now that their numbers had been severely crippled.

"Good . . . good."

He was half-listening, half-urging the traffic to keep opening up. Jordan had Gail wrapped up in her arms, the little girl still dead to the world.

"Um, there's one problem." The hesitation in Firman's voice placed Harrow on alert. They didn't need any more surprises on top of what they'd already had. Someone should tell the guy upstairs to ease up a bit.

"What's the problem?" He gritted the words out.

"We scoured the entire building for Cyrus, and there's no trace of him. We checked the control room for the tapes, but they've been tampered with. I called his cell phone several times—"

"You mean Cyrus is missing?"

"Yes," Firman confirmed. "I called his cell several times before we found it in the parking garage. There are drops of blood in his office and signs of a struggle, but we can't find his body."

"Fuck! No! Cyrus isn't dead. Do you hear me? He's not dead!" Harrow shouted, directing his fury at the wrong guy. Lambert was gone, which in itself was a hard reality to accept. They wouldn't survive losing another friend.

"Harrow, calm down, please." Jordan's hand rested on his arm, trying to soothe him. It normally worked, but this was turning into a nightmare.

"Boss, I'm sorry. Tell me what else to do," Firman croaked.

Harrow spotted an opening in traffic and swerved to take it. Honking horns blared from behind, but he ignored the fingers flashing. Speeding up, he took advantage of every opportunity to inch ahead.

He snapped his attention back to his man. "Firman, buddy, I didn't mean to lay it on you. You did a good job. I want everyone back in the facility in two hours for a group briefing."

There was a sigh before Firman spoke. "Yes sir. Is there anything else you want me to do?"

"Bring me the tampered disc," he paused. "Hell, bring me the whole computer." He thought about what he was saying. "And call Rayce and ask him what he needs."

After the call was disconnected, Harrow shot a glance at Jordan. She was staring straight ahead into the darkness, her expression unreadable.

"Hey . . ." He tried to take the edge out of his tone. "Gail's going to be okay. Don't worry."

"She will be." By the sound of Jordan's answer, Harrow knew she believed it. "I'm just . . . Oh, Harrow. So much death around us. This has got to stop."

Harrow thought about her words. It had to stop, sure. But how? At this point, they were at war with a powerful foe. For some reason, Harrow believed the fight had only begun.

Tor lifted his heavy lids, his eyes adjusting to the soft glow of the overhead light. It took a moment for him to recognize where he was. He was in the facility, inside the clinic, and lying flat on his back.

What the fuck? How long had he been out?

When he tried to move his hands, he found that wanting and doing were two different things. The right one lifted a fraction, but it felt like three hundred pounds of lead rested on it, making it impossible to move without pain. The left arm was another story.

His circuits began firing, and it all came back to him—the gunfight, Drisco shooting his arm, and the inevitable decision to cut off his arm.

Closing his eyes, he did a quick inspection of his body, checking toes, legs, torso, and upper limbs. When he reached his left arm, his mind faltered. It was real. This was so fuckin' real.

"Oh, God," he cried, his voice hoarse. His throat was raw, as if someone had taken sandpaper to it.

A shuffling sound came from his left, and Allison came to view. Something pinched inside him when he gazed into her puffy eyes. He'd made her cry, like the bastard he was.

"Tor, baby? How do you feel?" Allison leaned into him, smoothing the frown lines around his mouth with her fingers. The mattress dipped slightly when she sat at the edge of the bed. She looked tired and gaunt.

Allison! She's alive! It was the single most important thing to him. He wanted to cry, and for some insane reason, tears came down in torrents the moment he acknowledged it.

"How long . . . was I out?" Getting out the words was difficult; his mouth felt uncoordinated and bone-dry.

Instead of answering him, Allison pressed the call button. Shelly answered right away.

"Tor is awake. You told me to call you."

"Give me two," Shelly replied.

Allison turned back to Tor. "Are you hurting anywhere?"

He shook his head. The denial was a lie, but she didn't have to know. Allison had been through so much. The last thing he wanted was to look like a weak, spineless ass who couldn't handle pain. Still, his arm ached like a bitch from the pinpricking sensation that came and went.

The door swung open, and Shelly walked in wearing her usual cheery expression. Tor had always liked the woman. He could remember how Harrow complained about her confidence and her insistence that Harrow sleep when he had been flat on his back, too.

"So, Mr. Burns, you're awake," Shelly said, taking the chart from the foot of his bed.

"That's what it seems like. Unless I'm stuck in a nightmare," he retorted, sounding more like himself already. The idea made him chuckle. It was amazing how the right people seemed to bring out the best in him.

Shelly shot him a glare. "You sound upbeat for someone who's been to hell and back."

"What's there to be sad about? Allison is here and alive. I can't think of anything better than that." *Great answer, Tor! You'll earn brownie points for that.*

Shelly rolled her eyes before scanning the paper in front of her. She gave Allison a knowing look. Tor would have crossed his arms if his goddamn limbs didn't feel like boulders. His left arm was throbbing, and hiding the flinch was becoming difficult.

"Good answer," Shelly replied, as if she'd read his mind. "So you won't be upset if I tell you that I had to cut your arm a bit shorter?" Shelly maintained her gaze, but her tone softened.

"Nope. I tried to make it pretty, but given the available time, I think I did a pretty good job," he shot back.

Allison remained quiet and held his right hand; her palms were cold and sweaty at the same time. Tor wondered how she felt about the whole thing.

"Not bad at all. I made it even prettier." Shelly put the chart down and moved to the left side of his bed. "Mind if I check your stubby?"

"Go right ahead. I want to see it, too."

With his right hand, he tried to hoist his body up, but Allison was quick to push him down. "Don't move," she said and pressed a button. With whirring sound, his bed began to shift, raising him into a sitting position.

Without a word, Shelly removed the thick bandage that covered what was left of his left arm. The area surrounding the bandage was bruised and swollen, and his eyes fixated on the stump. It stopped right before the elbow and was inflamed. He tried to lift it, but a jolt of pain kept him from doing so.

"I think you're ready for another sedative," Shelly commented. "Let me clean the wound and change the dressing. I don't foresee any problems. You just have to give it a chance to heal, so you're not going to do anything strenuous for the next week or so."

"I think I can handle the pain," Tor said. Another lie. He knew damn well that even thinking would be a task with the nonstop throbbing from his amputated arm.

"Stop being a macho man. I swear you guys are the worst patients there are. You're all 'I'm good, I'm tight, I can handle the pain,' but deep inside, you're big babies. So cut the bullshit and listen to me." Shelly looked smug.

She took a syringe from the bedside table and went to work. Tor sank against his pillow and said no more. The doctor was one tough cookie, and arguing with her would be a waste of time. He shot a quick glance at

Allison, who was still as a statue, staring at his severed arm. A different ache shot through his system, and the medication began to course through his veins.

The last thought he had before he fell into a drug-induced sleep was that he was going to lose her. The idea was like a knife to his heart, but if he were completely honest with himself, he hadn't had much to offer her in the first place.

Once Tor had slipped into an induced slumber, Allison stared at his exhausted face with longing and marveled at his courage. Her mind wandered back to the terrifying scene at the office building. Tor had fought with one thing in mind—keeping her alive. It was a sweet gesture but had been extremely stupid.

What would Tor do now? The loss of a limb would be a big hit to any male's ego, Allison knew. This was something she needed to address right away. Tor could be an arrogant ass sometimes, but he always made sure he pulled his weight around the facility. He worked as hard, if not harder than, the rest.

It would be a pity if he felt like there was no use for him anymore. God knew he could kick ass even with his hands tied behind his back.

Shelly waved a hand in front of her face to snap her out of her trance.

Allison blinked. "I'm sorry, I was just thinking—"

"Thinking of how he'll cope with his missing limb?"

Allison nodded.

"I have seen many patients in similar situations. Of course, they were human, but their reactions tended to be self-pity. 'What am I going to do now?' type of shit. They worried about what they couldn't do anymore, rather than focusing on what they *could* do. I don't see that in Tor, unless he's fooling me."

"I was worried about that part," Allison admitted. "He's too proud, and he finds purpose in protecting people. I don't want him to feel he's anything less." She glanced at his sleeping form and rubbed his good arm.

Shelly glanced at Tor sympathetically and back to Allison "I think he's more worried about how the others will react to him missing a limb.

Knowing how Dangeran works, I expected this to happen. I just didn't expect our mighty friend to be the first victim. Anyway, I think I can help him with some prosthetic ideas I developed when I had some down time."

Allison's hope swelled. "Will you be able to help him?" She reached out and gripped Shelly's arm.

"Yes. All he has to do is decide which one he wants." She formed her hand into a claw. "He could have claw, a hook, or a hand, just like what he had before," Shelly said with a mischievous smile on her face.

"Thank you. I think that would be good for him."

Shelly sobered. "You do love him."

Allison nodded, but felt the need to add, "With all my heart."

The doctor was quiet for a moment and sighed. "Any news on Rohnert?"

"No, but I'm sure Harrow does. Let me call him right now." She pulled out her cell phone.

"It's okay—"

Allison waved her hand to silence Shelly's protest and dialed. Before she could press "send," the door opened, and Harrow walked in. His eyes were sparkling with unshed tears, and he was followed by Jordan, who was carrying Gail.

"Shelly, I need you to check Gail," he briefly glanced at Tor's sleeping form before casting his eyes toward Allison.

"Put her in the other room," Shelly instructed, already moving to the adjoining room.

Allison jumped to her feet and gave Tor a kiss before heading to the next room to offer her support.

"Place her here," Shelly told Jordan, pressing the intercom. "All available medical personnel, please proceed to room two." Harrow lifted the thin sheet, and Jordan laid the girl on the bed. Shelly turned to Harrow and Jordan. "Tell me how you found her."

Harrow looked at Jordan before he spoke. "Jordan saw her inside a little cubby, the one where we put our gear and clothes in the training room. Her heartbeat is faint, and she didn't wake up during the entire ride back here."

Shelly digested the information while she took an IV bag from the nearby shelf. She was inserting the needle into Gail's arm when the door opened for the first nurse to respond. Cheryl took one look at Gail and began gathering all the medical instruments Shelly might need. Then she flicked on the music that accompanied Shelly whenever she worked on a patient.

"This is where I say you guys are going to have to step outside and wait," Shelly said, waving Jordan and Harrow away. Once the room was clear and Mick Jagger started belting "She's So Cold," she began prodding the little girl.

"I need a blood sample," she ordered. "Tell Jones I need an answer right away."

Cheryl produced a vial, worked fast, and left once the sample had been taken.

Gail's skin was warm to touch, and her heart rate seemed normal. Lowering the stethoscope to the child's chest, Shelly listened to her breathing for any unusual lung activity. Physically, the girl seemed fine. She checked her head and entire body for any trauma. There was no blunt trauma injury anywhere.

The phone rang after fifteen minutes.

"Jones, talk to me."

"Blood test showed nothing abnormal, no irregularities, except there is a trace of anxiolytic."

Shelly immediately hung up. She'd prescribed sleeping aids to several humans in the facility. Now, she had to figure out how the child had gotten hold of a prescription medication. Running into the hallway, she found Harrow, Jordan, and Allison pacing. She understood their worry and was quite relieved there wasn't any immediate danger to the child.

She was also hopeful that she'd get a reasonable explanation soon.

"What happened up there?" she asked, leading the three to her nearby office.

Harrow and Jordan took turns describing what they'd seen. Whenever Rohnert's name was mentioned, Shelly's heart skipped a beat, and she felt all warm inside. However, she pushed away the fuzzy feeling, recalling the last time they'd been together. Rohnert had made it painfully clear that he wanted nothing to do with her.

"So Lambert was with her until he died?"

Jordan nodded. The idea was too sad to even imagine, but Shelly had to focus on the task at hand. There was a mystery to unravel.

"And she was inside the cubby?"

Jordan nodded again.

"What are you getting at, Shelly?" Impatience laced Harrow's tone.

"Wait." Shelly was beginning to piece together the puzzle. She had prescribed Ambien to Lambert not too long ago to treat his insomnia. It made perfect sense. "I think I have an idea about what happened."

They looked at her, their eyes full of questions.

"Lambert gave her a pill to put her to sleep and most likely placed her in that cubby to avoid detection."

Exclamations of comprehension slipped out of the trio's mouth in unison.

"Is she going to be okay?" Allison asked.

"Yes. She'll be fine. I'm going to flush the drug out of her system. I can let you see her in a bit. Don't worry." Shelly placed a reassuring hand on Jordan's shoulder.

Shelly went back to work on Gail, and after she'd finished, retreated to her office. She'd been on her feet for close to twenty-four hours now. Her back was killing her, and she was hungry. But the moment she thought of Rohnert, her hunger was forgotten.

She still ached for him, but she'd be damned if she would throw herself at him again. A person could take only so much rejection. Rohnert had made himself clear. Still, she agonized about him and his absent sense of self-preservation. The damn vampire should take care of himself instead of trying to read her mind all the time.

Well, well, it seemed like Dr. Shelly Anderson needed a doctor herself. She definitely sick. Lovesick, anyway. She had fallen for the quiet and elusive vampire, and there was no medication in her entire arsenal that would help that type of emotional affliction.

Tor woke up from what felt like a long-ass sleep. He yawned and tried to stretch, but then remembered. Squirming under the thin hospital blanket, he lifted it to survey the damage. It was there: his left arm in its heavy bandage, stopping short at the elbow.

He clenched his jaw and reminded himself that this would be his life now. Instead of fieldwork, he'd be downgraded to a desk job. What else could the group do with a fighter like him? Well, he'd have to show them there was still a lot of fight left in him.

What a quick turn of events. He should be depressed—pissed maybe—but somehow, those emotions eluded him.

When Shelly had put him to sleep, he'd been thinking his life had ended like his limb did, stunted. Somewhere in his deep sleep, he'd come to terms with it.

Looking back at what had happened at the office, he knew he'd done everything he could to save someone he loved. He'd sacrificed himself to allow Allison a chance to live and to spread her father's legacy. She needed to give more people a chance to live a new life. Tor's actions had been instrumental in making her future possible, and he'd given himself freely without any expectation beyond the hope of forgiveness and redemption.

In his tormented hour, he'd seen Jessie, the vibrant young woman filled with life and love, just the way she was when he'd fallen in love with her. No matter his crime, she had forgiven him, and nothing he believed mattered anymore. This new lease on life was a gift he'd earned by risking his life for another's. There was only one person left to forgive him, and that was himself.

With a sigh, Tor heaved himself into a sitting position, anxious to get his new life started. Allison's sleeping form caught his attention. She was curled up on a small cot, still wearing the suit she'd worn at the office.

How long had he been out this time? The woman needed a rest. She needed to feed. Tor felt a tug of tenderness he hadn't felt before. With difficulty, he turned his body and started to climb out of bed. One of the machines he was connected to let out a shrill beep, and Allison jumped to her feet. She was a sight to behold, pulling a throwing star from her chest holster. Her stance was predatory and protective, her eyes wild.

Tor stared at her in amazement, disregarding the screaming alarm.

It took a few moments for Allison to recognize that there wasn't any immediate danger. She rushed to Tor after she replaced her weapon.

"Tor, what are you doing? You shouldn't be up on your feet yet."

The door burst open, and Shelly walked in. Her hair blonde hair was tidy for a change, and her blue eyes were sharp as ever. She looked better than the last time he'd seen her, like maybe she'd gotten a little sleep. Tor swung his gaze back to Allison, who was shoving him back in bed. He tried to resist, but at this point, he was at a disadvantage. Blood loss had screwed with his strength.

"What are you trying to pull this time, macho man?" Shelly asked and pressed a button to stop the noise.

"I don't want to be in bed. I feel fine," he answered. Even his voice sounded stronger.

"Okay, and where were you planning to go? Going full monty on us?" Shelly's gaze slid down briefly, and she snickered.

"I want to take my woman back to her room. She needs to rest. And I mean on a bed, not some makeshift cot. She hasn't fed, either. I want to feed her myself." He sounded pouty—childish, even—but he didn't care.

His gaze went back to Allison, who was still trying to wrestle him back to bed.

"Tor, don't be stubborn. I'm fine. I can feed from our stash here."

Tor shook his head in adamant denial. "You need a long, hot bath. I want to pamper you."

"You want to give her your vein, Simba?" Shelly ragged.

He heard what Shelly said, but he didn't understand the reference. "What did you call me?"

"Tor, why don't you be a good boy and settle down," Allison said, and then turned to have a silent conversation with Shelly.

The doctor seemed undeterred. She crossed her arms and laughed. "I called you Simba. You know, the king of the jungle."

"I know what you said. What does it mean?" Tor gritted his teeth. He liked the doctor, but honestly, she was getting on his nerves. No wonder Harrow, Cyrus, and Rohnert swore she was the devil incarnate sometimes.

"Well, you needed a blood transfusion, and I thought it would be a wild idea to transfuse you with animal blood. So whatever you have in there should be safe for Allison."

He'd sworn he wouldn't ever hurt a woman again, but at that very moment, the idea of clobbering the smug-looking doctor was very appealing.

"You did *what?*" Tor felt strange. It might have been psychological, but payback was in order. He glared at Shelly.

"You heard me, Bambi. Go on and let the woman take as much as she wants. I'm going to give you lovebirds some privacy." Shelly headed for the door while Tor seethed.

"Wait!" Allison called out. "Isn't he supposed to be off his feet?"

"He should be. Remember, no strenuous activity yet." With that, Shelly winked and left.

Too stunned for words, it took a moment for Tor to speak. When he did, his voice came out husky. Feeding Allison would be too erotic to even imagine.

"Would you feed from me?" Tor patted the mattress in invitation. Allison shook her head as she sat next to him.

"We can have sex because you wear protection. If I latched onto your vein, you would get infected. No. I won't do it."

Shot down, Tor couldn't refute her argument. There must be something he could do for her. "I can take you hunting."

Allison stiffened, and she cupped his face. "You're in no position to do anything right now. You just had your—" She couldn't finish the sentence.

"You can say it, baby, I don't mind. Say it." He gazed into her eyes and smiled.

"Your arm amputated," she finished. Allison couldn't hold his gaze for long before she looked down and started crying.

"Hey, look at me." Tilting up her chin, he waited until she was looking straight into his eyes. "Don't worry, honey. I still have a one good arm to hug you with." To prove his point, he wrapped it around her.

She sobbed and buried her face in his chest.

"If you'll still have me, I would like to keep holding you for the rest of our time together."

"Oh, love, of course I'll have you. Why would you think otherwise?" Allison kissed his cheek, then his mouth.

Tor shrugged. "I guess I'm suffering from a blow to my ego?" He laughed shakily against her mouth.

Allison looked up, and despite her tears, she bristled. "Why do you think I didn't listen to you when you asked me to stay put and hide?"

"Because you're stubborn?"

"Well, yeah. That, and because I love you. I don't think I can live without you. It's us, Tor, together, in whatever form. I love you and that cute stump of yours."

That was possibly the sweetest thing anyone had ever said to him. Tor's grin got wider. "Next time you pull a stunt like that, you're in for a nasty spanking." He smacked her on the butt, and they sank against the mattress, laughing.

After a few minutes, Allison sat up. "Tor, you know I'm capable of fighting, too." She sounded hesitant, and he felt like a heel for making her feel inadequate.

He threaded his fingers through her hair, smoothing it away from her face. How he could ever hope to deserve a woman like her was still the big question, but as long as she wanted him, there was no way he'd let her go.

"I know. And for what it's worth, I owe you an apology for keeping you from doing what you're good at."

Allison's face lit up. "No apologies necessary. You think so?"

Tor laughed, loving the excitement radiating from her. "Woman, you kicked some butt back there. I'm lucky you were around. If you hadn't been, I wouldn't be able to hold you like this now." He pulled her closer. "I owe you my life," he whispered.

"You don't owe me anything."

Luck had knocked at his door one more time, and he'd be a fool not to seize the opportunity to land the biggest catch of his life. He kissed her, tender at first, but the moment she pressed her body against his, he knew that all the important cylinders were still firing. Allison kissed him with deep passion that sent searing heat through his veins. This one-handed thing was going to be a challenge, but he would make it work.

"Ahem." Harrow cleared his throat.

Tor groaned and tried to wave the vampire away with his bandaged stump. He continued kissing Allison, while trailing his hand along her back, but Harrow didn't leave.

With a frustrated growl, Tor broke away from the kiss. "Go away."

"I see that you're doing much, much better, my friend." Harrow walked over to his bedside. "You gave us a scare back there."

Allison gave Tor another kiss before hopping off the bed to sit on the chair.

Tor looked at Harrow. "Thanks, my man. I'm glad to be here." He offered his right hand for a handshake.

Harrow grasped his hand and pulled him into a bear hug. "I knew it would be impossible to get rid of you." He pulled back, his face grim.

"Say it, Harrow."

They had been through too much together for Tor not to notice the subtle change in Harrow's demeanor.

"We lost a lot of men," Harrow said in a solemn voice.

Tor felt it, although he hadn't heard the worst of the news. Harrow filled him in for the next hour on all the details. Every gruesome fact was a jagged pill, impossible to swallow. Allison sat very still, looking ill over the carnage they'd both missed.

"And Rohnert?" Tor finally asked.

"He just came back. I'm holding a meeting with whoever is left . . ." Harrow choked out the rest of the words, sounding distraught. "Tor, this is a hard blow for all of us."

"My man, we're in this together. We'll figure something out, hear me?"

Harrow nodded, and then glanced at Allison. "You think you can make it to the meeting?"

"We'll be there," Tor answered.

"But Tor . . ." Allison's voice trailed off.

"C'mon, don't make me miss an important meeting. I promise, as soon as it's over, I'm back in bed."

Allison seemed to consider his bargain.

"And please, help me out of this damn johnny. I don't want everyone to see my butt."

Harrow laughed, and Allison joined in.

"Fine, but you better be good to your word." Allison walked over to the bed.

"You have my promise," Tor said, silently adding, *and everything I have left to offer.*

Tor swore under his breath while he tugged up his jeans. What he'd thought was a simple task had proven to be a major pain in the ass, sapping his energy and his last remaining threads of patience.

"Baby, can I help?" Allison asked, standing by the door of the bathroom.

Tor was about to fire back a snappy remark, but he checked himself. Allison was just trying to help.

"Yes." He gritted his teeth, and added, "Please."

Allison moved closer and started to help yank up his pants. Tor hated feeling helpless. The mere thought of being at anyone's mercy was unacceptable. Then again, he didn't mind having her touch him. Especially if she were *undressing* him.

"I know these things take time, but I'm sure with a little practice and maybe a little ingenuity on Shelly's part, you won't even know you lost part of your arm." Allison successfully fastened the button fly on his pants.

Next was the cotton T-shirt, which would be impossible, considering the swelling of his bandaged arm.

"Not that witch again. I swear she is out to make everyone miserable."

Allison bit her lip to keep from laughing. "You make her sound like an ogre."

"What does the woman have in store for me?" He eyed her, suspicious. "If I didn't know any better, I think you're scheming with her already."

Allison gave him an impish smile, which made him want to tear her clothes off. However, there were things that needed to be settled first. The terrible attack on two fronts had left their numbers dwindling and the remaining forces emotional drained.

They'd lost their comrades, people they called family. Pritchard had instilled loyalty and friendship in them, and Harrow had done a successful job of keeping their group as tight-knit as possible.

"Tor?" Allison nudged him. "Is everything okay? Are you hurting?"

Tor snapped out of his trance and shook his head. "I'm fine." What was the point in crying about the pain anyway? Shelly would just dope him up like she would a wild animal.

"We have to put on your shirt," Allison said, angling his black T-shirt while she figured out the best way to get it on him.

Tor stared at the small sleeve openings and groaned. "This is going to be a problem."

"We can cut the sleeves," Allison offered.

"I'll run out of shirts," he complained.

"Why don't you use the johnny shirt instead?"

Tor stared at the hospital gown with disdain. "That thing again?"

"You have no choice. But don't fret, I'll get you a freshly-laundered one," Allison said, trying to hide a smile.

She was right. Either he showed up at the meeting without a shirt, or he'd have to use the poor excuse for a shirt until his arm was not as thick as a log. This amputation business was cramping his style.

"Fine, let's do it."

After donning the johnny, Tor and Allison went to the I-room. Tor's mood became solemn the minute they entered the conference room. The scent of misery hung thick in the air. Everyone looked up. Only a handful of the team was left, and their gloomy expressions left a bitter taste in his mouth.

Tor did a quick inventory of everyone present while he walked the length of the big room, and his spirits sagged. Harrow had filled him in on the details, but the damning reality was difficult to bear. Most of the people he'd fought with and shared long hours on patrol with were not there anymore. Jordan, in obvious distress, was sitting next to Harrow. Then there was Holt, who had been blinded by the earlier attack by Goran; he was sitting next to Firman, who seemed unusually subdued. About five humans and newly inducted vampires who had yet to see action were on hand.

Harrow watched Tor take his place behind Allison's chair.

"Man, I think you deserve to sit for a change." Harrow pointed at Lambert's vacated chair.

Tor's heart ached. He shook his head. "Thanks, but I'm good here."

Harrow laughed all of a sudden, and everyone stared at him with questioning looks. Tor scowled, sensing the laughter was directed at him.

"What the hell is wrong with you?" he demanded.

"I wanted you to sit because I don't want to be staring at your man boobs. Those things are on high beam and fucking distracting, even underneath that hospital johnny."

Tor growled. "You know, Gates, this hand," he lifted his bandaged stump, "is flicking a middle finger at you right now."

Their comic exchange was a good excuse for everyone to laugh, despite the gravity of their present situation. The moment of levity ended when Rohnert walked into the room. His usual calm bearing had been replaced by a withdrawn air, alerting everyone that the vampire was not in a good mood.

Silence followed Rohnert after he parked his rear against the wall behind Harrow. He gave each person present a brooding stare, and then looked down.

Harrow swiveled and cleared his throat. "Rohn, is everything all right?"

Rohnert shrugged. "As good as hell can be."

Harrow frowned but did not pursue it any further. At this point, Rohnert was best left alone. Meeting everyone's eyes, Harrow placed his palms on the edge of the table and stood up. He took a deep breath before he spoke. "We are faced with deaths of people we loved. Among them were Lambert, Knox, Peyton, Drake, Dave, Deuce . . ."

Tor tuned the rest of the names out. The sheer number of losses they'd suffered was a shock to the system. It was a pity that they hadn't seen this one coming. But what could they have done to prevent this? His musings led him to look around, and he met Rohnert's eyes. They were hard and devoid of emotion.

Willing himself to focus on what he wanted to say to Rohnert, Tor hoped the vampire was listening. *I know what you're thinking. None of this could have been prevented, with or without your abilities. This was fate running us over, plain and simple. Stop being hard on yourself.*

If Rohnert heard what Tor was thinking, he gave no indication. He continued to focus on the floor. Tor tried to reach him again, but he seemed to have lost interested in listening.

Tor tuned back in to Harrow's speech. "One of our guys turned against us."

There was a collective cursing at this news. Tor braced himself for the announcement.

"Who in the hell was it?" a human fighter asked.

"Drisco." Harrow blew out a sad breath.

Tor's fury multiplied. He should've said something about the twitchy guy when he'd had the chance. He should've listened to his instincts and scared the man off. Too fucking late now.

Another round of curses swept the room. Tor just hung back and stayed silent.

"If any of you have intel on this pre-meditated attack, I want the details right now."

Just about everyone in the room shook their heads, except Rohnert. Tor watched the vampire walk to Harrow. He whispered something that was hard to hear, especially with everyone talking at the same time.

Harrow nodded and stepped back. Rohnert's behavior was out of the ordinary. The calm he exuded was alarming. Tor sensed the shifting in the other man's emotions, and he got the impression that the vampire's mind was all made up.

Rohnert smoothed away the frown between his eyes before he spoke, his voice steady. "I didn't see this coming because I lost what could have been our best defense." He pointed to his eyes, referencing his gift of discernment.

Harrow started to protest, but Rohnert raised his hand to silence their leader.

"This is my responsibility, and therefore, my fault. I saw the massacre of our dear friends at the hands of Goran's vampires. Drake and five of our human comrades sacrificed themselves in hopes of saving us, and I will forever be indebted to them." Rohnert placed his palm over his heart, while the rest of the group fell into a tormented silence.

"Gail lost her mother in that massacre. Goran took Annie's life after leading her to believe that her daughter would be spared."

Jordan buried her face in her hands and sobbed at the announcement. Rohnert's eyes slid in her direction for a moment before he continued.

"Lambert stood guard at the door of our house, protecting Gail until his last breath." Rohnert paused, as if the next words he was going to utter were too difficult to verbalize. "His last thought before he died was feeling proud of what he had accomplished with all of us.

"Knox wished he'd told Peyton how he felt about her."

This was too much sorrow for one man to bear. Tor wanted to reassure Rohnert but remained glued to his spot. Men didn't want sympathy; they wanted to avenge their loved ones' deaths.

After a long stretch of silence in which no one said anything, Rohnert continued. "This was the result of the machinations of a sick vampire. He will stop at nothing to get what he wants and will commit any atrocity if anyone so much as offends him.

"He knows about our operation. He manipulated several people to disclose our location, and he even gathered a little information about me. We are all hunted now. Fair game, and targeted for eradication. I'm advising all of you to keep your associations with the outside world to a minimum. You can never tell who would turn against you next.

"I'm saddened over the loss of innocent lives, and I wish I could've done more. But I'm going to make sure that this doesn't happen again." Rohnert tipped his head slightly and returned to his spot.

It took Harrow a few minutes to take over. The entire group, what was left, fell into a deafening silence.

"I'm saddened to inform you that Cyrus is nowhere to be found. I won't speculate at this point. I can't—" Harrow closed his eyes and took another deep breath before he continued. "Cyrus has been like a father to me. I won't give up looking for him."

After a long moment, he spoke again. "This is a tough call on my part." He glanced at Tor and Allison as if pleading for their blessing. "I'm calling off our mission for now. Let us allow ourselves to mourn and mend first. I will continue to confer with General Krever about the approach we should take with regard to our business dealings. In the meantime, we're on lockdown until further notice. I expect you all to follow this."

Silence bounced off the walls in response, and each of them nodded their heads in agreement.

Tor realized that it would take some time before he could function at the level he was used to. For now, it was going to be all about healing and rebuilding. Deep down, he knew that with every strike that drove them down, they would rise, stronger and better.

Rohnert hadn't stopped pacing inside his room, wearing marks into the carpet. Feeling like a caged lion, he longed to get out. The time had come for him to separate himself from his friends and allies.

From what he had witnessed, it was certain that Goran would stop at nothing to rid the city of all the vampires who stood in his way, diseased or not. This also meant that Rohnert had to disappear in order to protect his friends from Goran's iniquity. He'd always wanted peace, but so far, only death and destruction had befallen the ones closest to him.

It wouldn't be fair to Harrow and the rest if they were further subjected to the curse that followed him. It was time for him to go. With a heavy heart, Rohnert took his weapon and the book that Marania had entrusted to him.

He strode out of his room, intent on leaving without a word, but his feet led him to the last place he wanted to be. Standing outside Shelly's office, he hated himself for not being able to resist. He wasn't intending to prolong his misery, yet he wanted to have one last look at her.

Rohnert quietly slipped in and found Shelly asleep on the little leather chair, her head resting on her palm. She looked peaceful and very, very beautiful. His heart ached at what could have been. If he weren't who he was, he would never have led her to believe that she meant nothing to him. On the contrary, Shelly had been a mainstay in his thoughts, in his every waking hour.

He moved closer and stood over her, watching her chest rise and fall, inhaling her scent to keep with him. He traced the lines of her face with his eyes and committed each one to memory. Unable to resist the urge to touch her, he reached out and ran his fingers along her cheek.

"Goodbye, Shelly," he whispered and planted a soft kiss on her lips.

Without looking back, Rohnert left the woman who had captured his heart with her outspoken nature and her guileless approach to the world. There was no doubt that he'd miss her immensely.

Several months later . . .

"Don't tell me you're tired already."

Tor playfully poked Allison with his new prosthetic hand, a state-of-the-art bionic arm made of lightweight metal. The hand had been designed with strength and maneuverability in mind. It enabled Tor to grasp small objects, and it was tough enough to keep up with the demands of firing a gun, flinging weapons, and even hand-to-hand combat exercises.

The prosthesis was designed by Shelly specifically for him. With his help, they'd crafted a masterpiece that could make him forget that he was missing part of a limb.

"Am not," Allison responded with an axe kick to his face that sent him staggering backward. She grinned and jumped repeatedly, taunting him to come back for more.

"You're dangerous woman, Tack." Tor gripped his jaw and cracked it back into place. "Don't you know you're just asking for trouble?"

"Well, see if you can catch me," Allison chirped and danced away like a ballerina.

Tor felt his body heating up, but not from sparring. He had to move fast if he didn't want to let this woman get away with her brazen mouth. She deserved to be chastised. In one swift move, he sprang forward, catching her off guard with a leg swipe that brought her down to the mat.

He pinned her down with his right arm and locked his prosthetic hand around her neck.

"You're dead," he whispered in her ear.

"You're sneaky." She squirmed beneath him and tried to wrestle her way out of his firm hold, but he planted his body on top of hers, trapping her.

"No, I'm horny," he corrected.

Without giving her a chance to protest, he seized her mouth. Tor kissed her, unleashing the fury of his lust. With one powerful maneuver, he switched the position of their bodies so he was underneath her. Allison straddled his waist and pushed him down.

"I want you naked," she whispered.

"Thought you'd never ask." Tor was already unbuttoning his jeans. He was jazzed about being able to do the task with his new prosthesis, and he grinned like an idiot.

The door swung open, and Harrow walked in.

"What the hell?" Harrow's voice echoed in the room. "Isn't that supposed to be done in the privacy of your own room?"

Tor groaned at Harrow's impeccable timing. He flipped a birdie in Harrow's direction with his brand-spanking-new metal finger.

"Go fly a kite, Gates!" he hollered.

"Must I remind you that we have an impressionable young girl living with us?" Harrow pivoted and walked out the door.

Allison collapsed against Tor, giggling. "I love you, Tor," she murmured as soon as the door closed.

He pressed his hard length against her thigh to show his appreciation. "Woman, you have no idea how I feel for you."

"Show me?" Allison batted her lashes, and Tor knew he was a goner.

He jumped to his feet and swiftly buttoned his pants. "Let's get this show on the road before I kill that bastard brother of yours for interrupting." He took Allison's hand and led her to their bedroom, where he planned to keep her holed up for a long, long time.

Sneak Peek from
Ascension,
the third book in
The Gates Legacy series
by Lorenz Font

Staring through the cracked ceiling at the wooden beams, Rohnert adjusted his body on the makeshift cot. He'd been hiding for what seemed like forever, lurking in the shadows, away from the vigilant eyes of the Council guards. In reality, not even three full months had passed since he left the underground facility he'd once called home.

Not a day had gone by that he hadn't thought of the place and its inhabitants, especially the bold and passionate human doctor who ran the in-house clinic. Dr. Shelly Anderson's image flashed before his eyes, and Rohnert sat up with a growl of frustration. He focused instead on the sounds of the storm outside, which had picked up momentum. The lashing winds rattled the shaky foundation of his hideaway, and the steady patter of rain continued to pelt the roof.

Rohnert picked up his favorite weapon from its resting place on the floor. The Kalimetal's familiar weight steadied him somewhat while he walked to the grimy window and stared outside. He'd been cooped up longer than he intended. Trouble was, if he set foot outside the confines of the house, he'd likely bump into a Vampire Council soldier. They had been in abundance of late.

As head of the Vampire Council, Goran had decreed that any vampire in possession of a Kalimetal was to be eradicated—no questions asked. Rohnert's big dilemma was his unwillingness to kill Council soldiers for following that order. So he remained hidden to spare the lives of the innocent.

Restless, he paced the empty room, which was an extension of a boarded-up apartment complex in a shady part of the Brooklyn. The abandoned dwelling served its purpose, providing cover until the need to venture out arose again.

He didn't know how long he could withstand the boredom that accompanied such inactivity. His sole mental exercise was trying to come to terms with the events that had taken place at the Tack Enterprises' stronghold upstate. The slaughter of his friends, human and vampire alike, might have been ordered by Goran, but Rohnert felt responsible all the same.

His mind rewound to the night Goran's Harem had attacked. The Council leader had ordered his redheaded mistresses to kill and had been willing to sacrifice them for a chance to cripple Tack Enterprises' operation. Rohnert couldn't shake the memories of his comrades' faces or of the shrieks of the female vampires as they perished one by one. Although his friends won that battle, the cost was high. Too much blood had been shed that day, and it had all been for nothing.

Rohnert ran his fingers through his hair and pulled at the roots. The damn stuff had sprouted into obstinate, snarled tangles. Before joining Pritchard Tack's band of vampires, Rohnert had been living with limited means—it had been his way of life ever since he left his position on the Vampire Council. Anything he'd acquired during his stay at Tack Enterprises was gone, too, since he had walked out of the facility with nothing but the clothes on his back apart from his weapons and Marania's black book. Without even the most basic possessions, the simple task of trimming his hair was impossible, but that was the least of his worries.

Pritchard had been a legitimate manufacturer of Grade A weapons for both the military and private sectors. Under the banner of his billion-dollar business, Tack Enterprises, he had been seeking a cure for the disease that afflicted his daughter Allison. She had been stricken by *Incomis Sippanus* when she'd been changed into a vampire, and Pritchard had vowed to help all those in need by finding the cure. His business had allowed him to create several strongholds for diseased vampires who were hunted without mercy. In the end, they had also become sanctuaries for misfits in both the human and vampire worlds, and he had given his life for them. Pritchard had left the operation in the capable hands of Harrow Gates, the vampire who had unknowingly spread *Incomis Sippanus* and had joined the fight to protect the afflicted.

Once Rohnert had joined the underground operation, he'd been a recipient of Tack Enterprises' generosity for a whole year. He'd found a place for himself there as a teacher and friend to vampire and human alike. For awhile, it had seemed possible that he had found a new home for himself.

He hadn't planned on Dr. Shelly Anderson, however. The clinic's doctor and resident ball-buster had found a way into his heart and left behind a massive void. If he'd stuck to his resolve to never tangle with a female, he could have avoided losing his newfound sanctuary. Despite knowing that Goran would go after anyone close to him, Rohnert had taken what she freely offered, her body and affection. When he came to his senses and realized the danger his actions posed to her, he'd left without saying goodbye. Not quite the exit he'd had in mind, but staying in the facility would have complicated matters further. She would never understand his rejection now that she'd felt his passion for her.

Although he had vowed to stay away from her and the underground compound, the task had proven difficult. There hadn't been a day when the human female was absent from his conscious thoughts. Every goddamn, waking hour passed at an excruciating pace because he couldn't manage to keep his mind off her.

As embarrassing as it was, he had succumbed to his weakness and dared take control of Shelly's unconscious thoughts in her deepest slumber.

Rohnert's power was not limited to the manipulation and mind reading that his fellow pureblood vampires all shared. Unknown to many, he could also mentally interact with any human or vampire when they were asleep. It was a special ability not many pureblooded vampires possessed. Each of them had specific gifts, and that was his—a power he hesitated to use due to its invasive nature. Desperate times called for desperate measures, however, so he had done the unthinkable and raided Shelly's dreams. The only excuse he could offer was his overwhelming need for her.

His last trip into her mind two nights ago had revealed that Shelly regretted the brief time they'd spent together. She couldn't have known that when he'd told her that he didn't want her, her pained expression had crushed him. Despite her attempt to mask the hurt, he'd seen what he'd done to her. There had been a sudden shift in her thought pattern that had startled him. Her thoughts had become clear and concise and were directed at him.

I might have fallen for you Rohnert, but I'll be damned if I let you walk all over me. Mark my words—you and I will never be together. Even if you beg me to love you, this woman has learned her lesson.

Rohnert had staggered against the weight of her rejection, but felt he deserved it after violating her privacy like that. He was fucked. The thought of Shelly ate at him, making his existence even more intolerable. This noble shit had to stop—she didn't need his protection. She was her own person, an independent woman who could take care of herself. He couldn't save the world, and she'd never asked him to save her. Rohnert needed to forget her before his need for her crushed him into dust.

"Damn it." If he had stuck to his plan to not get involved with Shelly, he wouldn't be in this crappy predicament. Too bad his heart had chosen to ignore his head.

"Talking to yourself again, sir?" Alonzo asked, slipping through the battered wooden door.

Rohnert pivoted and scowled at the vampire he'd allowed to squat with him for the past week. Alonzo had been one of his best students, a member of the elite guards Rohnert had helped create. Of Spanish descent, he sported a mass of thick brown curls, eyes the color of wine, and a witty personality that bordered on annoying. Zo, as he preferred to be addressed, was smart and had excelled in every weapons class Rohnert taught.

"Ditch the 'sir' if you want to keep breathing."

"Qué es el problema? Despertó en el lado incorrecto de la cama otra vez?" Alonzo said, rapid fire, in his native tongue.

Rohnert walked forward, releasing the Kalimetal from its sheath. "If you don't cut that Spanish BS, I swear in Buddha's name, I'll cut you up in little pieces."

Zo backpedaled and raised his hands in surrender. Every existing vampire knew the devastating effect of a weapon infused with the Dangeran metal, in particular when used by a master like Rohnert. His Kalimetal, which was a cross between a sword and baton, was a weapon that could tear anyone to bits. To the untrained eye, the pair of three-foot metal rods appeared benign, but their slim profile and light weight made the weapon easier to wield, providing a broader range of motion that gave the fighter an edge during an attack.

"Madre—sorry—sir, you're making me nervous."

"Translate!" Rohnert pointed his weapon at Zo's neck.

The vampire, though a head shorter than Rohnert, met his gaze with steady eyes. "You know I'd never say anything disrespectful." He pushed the tip of Rohnert's Kalimetal away with care.

"Translate!" Rohnert repeated.

"I said, 'What's the problem? Wake up on the wrong side of the bed again?' See? It's harmless." He broke into an irritating grin.

Rohnert blew an aggravated breath and lowered his weapon. "Where have you been? Don't you know that defection is a serious offense?"

"I was hanging out at the salsa club." Zo flopped onto the floor, still watching Rohnert with vigilant eyes.

His patience dipped to an all-time low. "If you want to keep on hanging out with me, lose the salsa outings and take this seriously. The minute you left the Council, your life ceased to be safe." Rohnert returned to the window and gazed out again.

"I was killing time. With you always moping around here, I needed to get some fresh air. Besides, I was armed."

Rohnert shot a quick glance over his shoulder to see Zo lift his tattered denim jacket to reveal a holster filled with every imaginable weapon, including several throwing stars, a Glock, and push daggers.

"Haven't I taught you to always stay away from those types of establishments?" When Zo nodded, Rohnert glared at him. "And yet you went?"

"I was following a couple of vampires."

"To at salsa club?" What had this world come to?

"I overheard them talking about a bunch of Kalimetal-carrying vampires, so I followed to get more information."

The mention of Kalimetal got his attention. He strode to where Alonzo was sitting and looked down. "And?"

"Some Council soldiers walked in, so I had to scram. All I know is there were six vampires." Although Zo had shed his accent, there were still moments when, if rattled, he reverted.

"Jesus," Rohnert whispered. He hadn't heard from Harrow and the rest, not that he'd given them a 411 on his location.

"Boss, what is *Buddha*?" As good as Zo was in combat, the idiotic things he spewed from his mouth were guaranteed to irritate Rohnert.

He sat on his heels and gritted his teeth, trying to keep his temper in check. "I told you I went to Asia a long time ago. To get in the monks' good graces, I had to spend hours upon hours in quiet reflection. Something I find you're not capable of." Rohnert closed his eyes and breathed deep, unsure if he should be thankful for Zo's company, or curse the day he stumbled upon him in an alley.

"You still haven't made the connection to Buddha."

Rohnert's eyes shot open. "Buddha was their savior. He grew on me."

Alonzo grinned, compounding his annoyance. "Sounds like you did a lot of traveling, boss."

"It soothes the soul." He sounded more wistful than he'd intended.

"I plan to visit my roots someday."

"You can do it now." Rohnert rose to his feet.

As exasperating as Alonzo could be, the vampire was loyal and a great soldier to have watching his back. Rohnert had instilled loyalty in every student he taught, and even combat instruction came second to that. He believed they needed their allegiance established before learning anything else. Little did he know that their sworn commitment had been directed to him, and not the Council, or its leader, Goran, for that matter.

"And leave you talking to yourself? No sir! I'm Robin to your Batman."

Rohnert couldn't help but chuckle. Wherever Zo had been hanging out, the bastard sure had learned a lot of dumb things. Pop culture had a way of streaming into one's psyche, no matter the nature of being.

"Thanks, but please keep your stupid ideas to yourself."

The winds continued to howl outside, and rain hammered against the roof. Hard. Rohnert sat down on the cot, listening to the calming sound. Funny, it seemed like his mood was the direct opposite of the weather. Go figure.

"What do we do now? It's a good day to stay caged in here. I bet we can find more people to join our little party." Alonzo stood next to him.

And add to the list of lives I'd be responsible for? He shook his head.

"I think two is already a crowd," Rohnert said. "We're staying in tonight."

Shelly entered her bedroom, feeling drained. In her years of practicing medicine, most of the patients she'd lost on the operating table had been gone even before they reached her, and there was nothing she could have done about it.

She dropped onto her sofa, not bothering to fix herself anything to eat first. Folded into a fetal position, she allowed herself to feel the weight of another life lost. Saving people had been her constant burden, and also her happiness. Having grown up in a stern household with parents who were both doctors, Shelly had felt the pressure to follow in their footsteps. She loved the profession, and the constant emergence of exciting diseases and innovative treatments had kept her on her toes. Her parents hadn't lived to see the day of her graduation, perishing in a house fire while she was away at med school. Still, Shelly could feel their presence in her life, urging her to continue their mission.

Tonight was a rough one. One of their new human fighters had accidentally fired a gun while cleaning it. She'd heard the sound and ran to the bedroom a few doors down from hers where she found the man gasping his last breaths, blood oozing from a chest wound. She called for help while performing CPR, but the man had checked out before additional assistance could arrive.

The scent of blood lingered on her clothes, but the stench of death was even more difficult to bear. In her chosen profession, she and her colleagues had to give themselves constant reminders to keep their emotions under wraps for the sake of their mental well-being. Shelly had been lucky enough to stay detached, but tonight, her inherent self-preservation took a nosedive.

She had no idea why she'd broken down and bawled like a child in front of the nurses, her determination to keep it together thrown out the window. Depleted, she had retreated to her office as soon as she had pronounced the time of death.

She was turning soft. The moment she'd allowed Rohnert into her life, everything had changed, shifting into unknown territory. Before him, she had managed to maintain her distance from emotional entanglements with men. Falling for a vampire of all things had messed her up real good. Rohnert had given her a mind-blowing orgasm, but then had immediately professed his indifference toward her. All it had been to him was sex.

That one night with Rohnert had proven to be a disaster. A big one. She had offered herself to a reluctant vampire, even though she'd known he wanted nothing to do with her. Pathetic. Had she not acted like a lovesick teenager, her pride would still be intact and her heart untouched. Maybe if she'd admitted to herself how deep her feelings for Rohnert went, she wouldn't have made herself so vulnerable. But fuck it, she'd made a mistake. She just hadn't realized how big a mistake it was until he left the facility without a word, disappearing like a ghost and abandoning everyone, not just her.

She had pulled herself together like she always did. Normally, it wasn't a problem, and yet, tonight, all she wanted was to cry her silly heart out. Shelly gave in to the misery and loneliness, letting out the tears and hoping that at the end of it all, she'd be able to forget.

The deaths she'd witnessed and the friends she'd lost at the hands of Goran's forces haunted her on nights like this. It was even worse to lose someone for nothing—a stupid accident and a waste of a life.

She succumbed to the ache she'd been trying to ignore, but after this day, she vowed, she would never shed a single tear for Rohnert ever again.

Goran paced around his chamber, seething at the most recent news from his second-in-command. Hamilton had ventured out several times in the past two months in hopes of locating Iden, a Council elder who had gone missing. So far, his efforts had been fruitless.

"Leave me." His voice boomed across the room, rattling the windows and the menagerie of fine artwork adorning the wall.

Hamilton bowed low and exited the room like his ass was on fire. Goran returned to his desk and deposited his shaking body on the chair. He wanted Iden found. There was no doubt that the vampire was in possession of something he needed.

He gave the drawer a hard pull, shaking the entire desk until the bust sitting on the edge fell on the floor with a resounding crash. No love lost there. He'd been trying to find an excuse to get rid of Grandpa's hideous sculpture once and for all. Instead of feeling a sense of loss, Goran laughed in contempt.

After he'd yanked the black book out of the drawer, he opened it to the marked page he'd read over and over. There, Marania had chronicled the popular prophecy of Gastarius—the oldest living vampire and a god-like figure to them all, both untouchable and unreachable.

Due to her position in the Council as the keeper of records, Marania had been able to secure an audience with the relic himself and found that Gastarius did possess the power to see the future, including their eventual emergence as a powerful race.

In the old manuscript, Marania had written Gastarius' prophecy:

> On the first sign of the moon's illumination, a vampire will rise into power, his heart filled with avarice. Among his peers, he will raise havoc, and death will augment the despair within. Mortals and vampires alike shall have no power to prevent the destruction he will leave in his wake. A disinclined soul shall be called, and a child borne to the rightful guide shall come to fulfill this divination.

"What the hell is the blustering idiot talking about?" He shoved the tattered tome away from him, and the black book landed on the floor with a thud. "No one speaks in riddles anymore." Goran huffed and rose from his seat.

A tumult of emotions blanketed him. With the fall of his Harem, he had no one to vent his anger on, no one to boost his flagging ego, and no one to bed and fuck. When was the last time he'd had a good lay?

His frustration mounted, increasing with every passing minute while he walked back and forth across the carpet. He made his way over to where the book lay and picked it up in haste. It had opened to the pages on which Marania had recorded the birth of vampire children belonging to Council members.

> Iden, son of Admar, and mate, Chandra welcomed their daughter, Isidora, on a bleak October morning, year 1938. Blessed with red hair and sable eyes, the babe was sequestered in the family's estate—reason not stated.

The crux of this whole damn thing was that the woman's identity was well concealed. Why? Goran had a nagging suspicion, but the answer could be supplied by none other than Iden himself. And the bastard was nowhere to be found.

He glanced at the other pages. Most entries were illegible. It appeared as if someone had made every effort to disguise the truth. Some pages were torn, others removed or tampered with. The blasted vampire, Marania, had eliminated the damning evidence because she had known of his intention. The indications of her interference were crystal clear.

His rage building, Goran armed himself with his sword and stalked out of his chamber. He walked with deliberate ease, every step filled with purpose. He entered the wing where he expected to find Hamilton. The blistering sound of wailing scaled the Council walls, anguished and terrified.

Inside the Blanch room, he found his trusted soldier sitting on the frayed Bergere chair that had been his dead son's favorite. He smirked at the thought of Demetrius. One less soul he had to worry about. He and his mother could carry on with their incestuous affair in hell.

Hamilton scampered to his feet while Goran walked toward the front of the massive room amid the weeping of petrified humans about to receive their lasting legacy. He glanced at the innumerable unknown faces before summoning Hamilton to him.

The vampire moved fast and bowed before him. "Yes, sire."

"You're coming with me tonight. There is someone I want to visit after I get something to eat." Goran was anxious to get going. His fangs throbbed with hunger. He'd held out long enough. The night was still in full bloom, and they had sufficient time before sunrise—enough to do some damage.

"How many men should I gather?" Hamilton straightened but kept his eyes averted in respect. The vampire hid none of his thoughts from him. His evil heart knew nothing except to please Goran and carry out his every wish.

"Just the two of us tonight. Prep the elite guards before you leave. I want them ready when I summon them." Goran turned and headed for the side exit.

Hamilton was quick to do his bidding, barking orders to his trusted men. Within a few seconds, shrieks filled the room and the process of creating new vampires commenced. Goran summoned the portal that would allow them to exit the Council's stronghold, and Hamilton walked alongside him through the hazy gate that appeared.

The evening breeze was welcome after the stifling confines of the Council walls. Goran inhaled deep, feeling his immediate surroundings and gathering the thoughts of those around him. The New York City plaza was, as usual, besieged with humans. The meal he'd been putting off wasn't necessary, but he was in the mood tonight.

Glancing around, he did a quick inventory for anyone close to palatable and spotted a woman looking lost in the crowd. Concealing his sword underneath his long trench coat, he walked over to the unsuspecting human, with Hamilton close behind, and struck up a conversation.

"Miss, are you looking for someone in particular?" He offered his most alluring smile, willing his fangs to retract until they were nothing more than prominent canines.

The months following the back-to-back attacks on the Tack Enterprises strongholds had been as difficult as the day they lost their leader, Pritchard Tack. His honorary son, Harrow, sat inside the I-room alone, still devastated by their losses to Goran's forces. The battles had left them depleted and in a state of mourning. Burying the remains of their human friends had been heartbreaking. As much as he'd tried to put the past behind him, the haunting images of the people they'd lost, both vampire and human, continued to remind him that he had failed them.

Pushing back his chair, Harrow got up and headed to the well-stocked bar. The revolving door opened, and he pulled out the first bottle he touched. He poured the liquid to the brim and chugged a quick one. Then he poured another.

The door swung open, and his adopted sister Allison walked in with Tor. Harrow glanced at them through his dark sunglasses, sensing their emotional grid. As distraught as they were over the death around them, one could not deny that Tor and Allison had something to celebrate. In the midst of the casualties they had sustained, and the loss of Tor's arm in the process, they'd found each other, and their happiness radiated in spite their efforts to hide their feelings. Harrow was as elated as a brother could be.

He opened his arms, and Allison ran into his waiting embrace.

"Glad you came right away," he whispered into her hair.

Tor snorted. "Of course we did. You left us without a choice. You have this entire place on lockdown. There's nowhere for us to go." He flopped on the chair, resting his prosthetic arm on the table.

Harrow kissed Allison on the cheek before letting her go. Holding his drink, he marched to the head of the table and settled. Tor's reddish-purple eyes watched him with intensity. The vampire hadn't vacated his duties as Harrow's bodyguard, even after he'd been given the task to serve as Allison's guardian instead. As much as Harrow wanted to curse Tor for being overly watchful, he could never thank the vampire enough for sacrificing himself for Allison's sake. Losing a limb could do a number on one's ego, but Tor seemed to have adapted to his condition. He continued to perform his responsibilities without skipping a beat. He might have lost his arm in that fight, but he'd retained his grit and perseverance. Tor was a winner in Harrow's book.

While the room started filling in with what was left of their team, Harrow did a mental count of those who'd survived. The skeleton crew consisted of newly recruited vampire fighters, the diseased vampires who needed homes, and the very few humans who had been lucky enough to miss the slaughter.

Following Rohnert's departure, Allison, Jordan, and Tor had stepped up to the plate to teach the martial arts and weaponry classes that were just too much for Harrow to handle.

It had been a huge undertaking to respond to the negative comments stemming from the closure of the Tack Enterprises production line. Harrow had been in nonstop discussions with General Leo Krever, their go-to guy for damage control. Krever was in charge of maintaining contact with Tack's clients and assuring them that shipments would resume soon.

Harrow waited until the last of the remaining personnel walked in before he got up to address the group. A wave of melancholy descended upon him when he glanced at the vacant seats that had belonged to his good friends, Lambert and Cyrus. It was a silent reminder of how their operation had been crippled by losing two such integral members of their squad. He took a deep breath, suppressing the sadness in his voice.

"Listen up. I've decided to lift the lockdown. I will—"

Hoots and hollers halted his announcement as the room erupted in a jovial celebration. Despite Harrow's somber mood, he couldn't help but smile at everyone's enthusiasm. He lifted his hand to quiet them down.

"I urge everyone to be vigilant. Watch each other's backs. Our first and foremost goal is to continue finding infected vampires and offer them help. Aside from that, I'm not going to account for your time while you're out. Stay tight and don't give our location away. Whatever you do, make sure you're never followed." Harrow eyeballed every single one of this team.

"If you are in any way threatened, it's never cowardice to back down. No heroic shit here. I can't pat your back if you're dead. Rotations are still in effect. Same arrangement, two per group, and report to Tor or Firman if anything's up. Are there any questions?"

Gunner, another new recruit, raised his hand, his gray-white eyes brimming with excitement. He was a young diseased vampire, and one of Harrow's most promising students. "If we are approached by a Council guard, what do we do?"

Harrow had expected this question. "If they say they're going to take you in, you're as good as dead. They have a way of knowing which ones are infected. I will let you decide at that point which way you want to go. All I ask is that you never divulge our location."

"You've got nothing to worry about, boss," Gunner said, looking eager.

"Well, then we're good to go. I'll see everyone here same time tomorrow."

Jordan barged into the room, hauling ass. "Sorry I'm late. What did I miss?" She looked around apologetically and strode to where Tor was standing.

Harrow smiled at her before continuing. "As I was saying, we'll meet again tomorrow. Everyone must check in with Tor or Firman as soon as they arrive."

When the room emptied, he walked over to Jordan, his mate for over a year. "I'll fill you in about my little announcement," he whispered, "in the bedroom."

Acknowledgements

To my beta readers and friends—L. Morales, W. Depperschmidt, K. Giles, J. Somera, C. Trapp, E. Banaag, C. Yu, and T. Lundin. I call myself lucky to have such a supportive group. Thanks for your friendship, which has bridged years and distance. I appreciate your encouragement while I navigated the murky waters of The Gates Legacy.

My family rocks—Bunny, Mama Rosy, Mama Cari, Sidney, and Belen.

To my sensei, Mavvy Vasquez—This has been another terrific journey under your tutelage. Keep the funny commentaries coming.

About the Author

A professional daydreamer, Lorenz Font discovered her love of writing after reading a celebrated novel that inspired one idea after another. Since being published in 2013, she has been conspiring, butting heads, and enjoying her spare time with vampires, angels, samurais, and other creatures she has created in her head.

Her perfect day consists of writing and lounging on her garage couch (a.k.a. the office) with a glass of her favorite cabernet while listening to her ever-growing music collection. She finds writing urban fantasy exhilarating and places an intense focus on angst and the redemption of flawed characters. Her fascination with romantic twists is a mainstay in all her stories.

Lorenz lives in Southern California with her supportive family and three demanding dogs.

www.ingramcontent.com/pod-product-compliance
Lightning Source LLC
Chambersburg PA
CBHW060138260626
47160CB00001B/21